By ERIC ARVIN

Another Enchanted April
Azrael and the Light Bringer
Galley Proof
Grand Adventures (Dreamspinner Anthology)
Kid Christmas Rides Again
The Mingled Destinies of Crocodiles and Men
The Rascal
The Rest Is Illusion
Simple Men
Slight Details & Random Events (Author Anthology)
Terms We Have for Dreaming
Wave Goodbye to Charlie
Woke Up in a Strange Place

SUBSURDITY SERIES
SubSurdity
Suburbilicious
SuburbaNights

Published by DREAMSPINNER PRESS
www.dreamspinnerpress.com

ERIC ARVIN

The
MINGLED
DESTINIES
of CROCODILES
and MEN

DREAMSPINNER
PRESS

Published by
DREAMSPINNER PRESS

5032 Capital Circle SW, Suite 2, PMB# 279, Tallahassee, FL 32305-7886 USA
www.dreamspinnerpress.com

The Mingled Destinies of Crocodiles and Men
© 2017 Eric Arvin.

Cover Art
© 2013 Adrian Nicholas.
Cover Photography
© 2013 Amy Morrison.
All rights to the original cover photography and associated photographs reserved by Amy Morrison.
Cover content is for illustrative purposes only and any person depicted on the cover is a model.

ISBN: 978-1-63533-816-4
Digital ISBN: 978-1-63533-817-1
Library of Congress Control Number: 2017904062
Published April 2017
v. 2.0
First Edition published by Wilde City Press, April 2013.

Printed in the United States of America
∞
This paper meets the requirements of
ANSI/NISO Z39.48-1992 (Permanence of Paper).

"How doth the little crocodile
Improve his shining tail,
And pour the waters of the Nile
On every golden scale!
How cheerfully he seems to grin,
How neatly spreads his claws,
And welcomes little fishes in
With gently smiling jaws!"
                              – *Lewis Carroll*

PART I—PRELUDE: A BIT ABOUT A GIRL

OF LIMINAL PLACES

WHO CAN truly say what the river valley looked like? Its appearance changed depending on one's perspective, for every soul sees the world differently. A patch of tree moss so apparent to one person might go completely unnoticed by another. The agreed-upons lay few and far between. The essential topography of the valley could be seen from a few specific locations: high on the barren rock of Beggar's Hill, or from the heights of the Lone Tower, at the foot of which rested an ancient orchard. These and a few other strategic plateaus looked out over the vast waterway to the first rising hills of the Other Side—that land across the great river where very few ventured—where the land fell ever-steeped in a thick, heavy fog.

Alongside the river, sometimes too close to its edge, homes of the valley folk clustered beneath the calm twin siblings of blue water and sky. Past these houses, when the hills did not rise immediately from the beach as they were prone to do, the hinterland spread in long acres of field and fancy—fancy having more than a little power in the valley— stretching out like yawning earth. A couple of lapzine fields had been left to struggle, having survived a swelling of the river; few people remained to tend their blue-tinged flowers or harvest their gel-like resin for lamplight.

Beyond the initial hills and inclines rose greater cliffs, at points almost completely hiding the river valley from the view or acknowledgment of the outside world, such was their height. And finally, before anything "modern" could be reckoned, there spread the Farlands. Still considered of the valley proper by most aside from the college, those of the outside world ignored them as wilderness. Things were changing, though. A new organism called 'Industry' was starting to take notice of certain regions of the Farlands. And Industry began to wander about this seemingly unused land, wondering how it might be used for its own industrious progress. This new attention made a few of the valley's unseen inhabitants very uneasy.

The valley's liminal quality, linking here to forever or never, did not dawn on Calpurnia Covington. The word 'liminal' itself sounded like a redundancy or mistake to her child ears, a stuttering of vowels and syllables. In all likelihood, the word had no meaning for any adult either, merely something they said to make themselves seem smarter, like 'Corinthian' or 'haberdashery.' She had never heard anyone who lived above the valley—in what she saw as the real world—use the word. And in this, she was correct. Only those who truly understood the valley and its purpose, or the pompous word-lovers of the nearby college, knew the meaning of that particular word.

Neither Calpurnia nor the "real worlders" understood that to *be* liminal was to slice through reality like a thin stream and then embrace every possibility that ever flowed from consciousness, to offer hidden hope against hidden horror. And that's what the valley did. Of course, it was only seen in its truest, most naked form to those who would see it. To all others it appeared but a river banked by giant, forested earth. Calpurnia—though a child and certainly able to see the things which adults refused to—took on the mentality of a conditioned adult and forced upon herself the most obvious sight and reasoning of the valley as well. Still, there were times when the truth peeked out at her. She couldn't walk along the river and not feel its stare. There was a place for her there in the valley, if only she would wake to it. She wanted to scream at the river. She wanted to tell it to stop pestering her, but to do that would be to recognize it. *Tricky river!*

Calpurnia was an outsider to the valley, orphaned when both parents had died under the hand of tragedy. So it was that she came to live with her aging aunt at the old Walterhouse estate that crowned Black Hill. She was dazzled by the mansion when she first saw it, as was everyone. Indeed, before Calpurnia's aunt Winifred Walterhouse became too ill to host, elegant parties streamed from the house and out onto the expansive fields of goldenrods and tiger lilies surrounding it, down through the tall, thick forest of Black Hill and onto the beach. Winifred's was a party invitation not to be turned down. The home shone proud and immaculate, neither a chip of paint missing from its pristine white sides nor a misplaced flower in front of its large front porch.

Calpurnia found the grand rooms easy to hide in; so many corners to enjoy solitude away from Aunt Winifred, whose eyesight was failing anyway. At times Calpurnia felt quite like a queen in her new home, but at others she missed the real world. The people of the valley struck her as strange just as her father had once said, and though she had lived there but a couple of months, she did not think she would ever truly take to them. They reveled too much in their mystery. One in particular, a woman named Minerva True, made her the most uneasy. When Minerva visited, Calpurnia would go outside—not retreat, never retreat—and play among the flowers in the fields. She avoided most of the grownups of the valley this way. The grownups, she thought, were as superstitious as children. The children were as dumb as animals. The animals were bearable because they did not speak.

Then, one day, she met a fox.

The old woman and the valley's unelected leader, Hamlin Marsh, were in the big house talking nonsense, so her father would say. Calpurnia preferred being out among the flowers. She had torn a red ribbon from her hair, which Winifred had tied there, and was dragging it among the goldenrods and tiger lilies. Each flower bowed as she passed it, brushing through the field. They were nearly as tall as she was and made a very good hiding place indeed.

Less intelligent children her age would run around the fields, claiming to see a fairy here and there, but not Calpurnia. She was a practical girl. As she strolled on, coming to the creek and the well-kept shack behind the house—a keeping-place for firewood and agricultural implements—she did not at first notice the little red fox following her through the flowers. He had been hidden even better than she, for he was three times as small, even when walking on his hind legs.

THE FOX had been watching Calpurnia for some time—from the day she arrived at Walterhouse Manor. He had been told the little girl was important, though he did not know why. Foxes, while cunning, do not think to ask such things. They nose it out for themselves.

Fox was a Passion. Passions were not animals as such. They were beings of nature, of the forest, and they took on whatever animal form they wished, including the instincts that accompanied each particular visage. They did this to look after the species and protect its interests. Passions, it was said, were all around the valley, many born of human emotion. One might come into being from a first kiss beneath a dogwood tree. Another could take form due to a quarrel by a stream. Like echoes, never seen, but always there, they could be the bringers of great delight or playful mischief, but never harm. They were the gleeful spirits of the world. A Passion would only become serious in the direst of circumstances, and Fox knew something dire when he felt it. Somehow the girl was related to the new sense of uneasiness that had begun to manifest in the valley.

The creek was flowing swiftly, too swiftly for Fox to venture across. Calpurnia was not content to remain on one side, however, and stepped into the precarious current, finding a half-submerged stone on which to begin her crossing. She wobbled and balanced. The stone knocked hollow under the stream. She found her footing.

From across the stream she heard: "Help me! Please help me!"

The small, rapid plea drew her attention quickly back to the flowers. She saw the little fox there, settling back down on all four feet. Calpurnia dropped her ribbon into the creek, and it was taken away like a red silk sidewinder. She stared suspiciously at the fox from where she stood on the stone.

"I cannot cross the stream," the fox continued in a hasty, almost frightened manner. "Might you carry me? It goes much too quickly for Fox. Yes, yes, much too fast."

"That's silly," Calpurnia replied. "Animals don't talk, and they certainly don't ask for help from humans."

"I do, or I can. I don't talk to people much. No, it's not a habit. What's to talk about?"

She watched how his mouth moved. An animal's mouth looked strange trying to form human words, as if it were chewing something gristly or tough. Its teeth were sharp and clearly needed a good brushing.

"Animals don't talk," she repeated, more in an attempt to assure herself of this than in response to the fox.

"I do! I do!" Fox insisted, standing on his hind legs again. "Will you please take me across the creek with you? I must go. I must."

"I won't," Calpurnia said resolutely. "Talking animals are rubbish. My father told me that the only talking animal was an evil snake in an ancient garden. Since then, no other animal has said a word, so you see, *you* cannot talk. It's impossible."

"But you hear me, you do," the shrill little thing answered.

"A trick." She shrugged. "A daydream. I just need a nap, and I should take one right now." Calpurnia pivoted on the stone, stepped broadly, and passed right by the fox, aiming toward the big house, marching once more through the brightly colored fields, her chin high.

"Wait! Wait!" Fox clambered after her, but she did not listen and soon was able to un-hear him completely as adults have the power to do. Fox chased her for a bit, still clamoring for her attention, but he soon saw that she would not be open to him, or any other Passion for that matter.

Fox watched the little girl disappear into the massive white timber structure built from Black Hill's ancient forest years and years before. He waited among the tiger lilies until he saw she was not going to appear again. He turned, defeated, back into the woods. Passions rarely revealed themselves to people, and when they did it was considered a wonderful thing…but not this time. Fox was saddened not to have brought delight to the girl. How strange it was that he could not reach her.

When Calpurnia had refused aid to the fox, she'd turned her back on the valley. She would never see a Passion again.

WINIFRED WALTERHOUSE EXPLAINS

WINIFRED WALTERHOUSE lay on her deathbed as Calpurnia played outside. The last of the great Walterhouse clan left in the valley. The family, like most of the once prominent lineages of the region, had either withered or fled. Even the Daventry-Blues and the Brennen-Blues had lost their once-powerful footing and were now but a handful of quarreling faux sophisticates. Her twelve brothers and sisters had one by one found grander estates elsewhere. "More socially relevant places," her sister Esther had once arrogantly expressed on a visit from somewhere up north. "*The uppity whore!*" Winifred was propped up by overstuffed pillows in her four-poster bed. Sunlight streamed through the long window that looked over the fields. Gold flooded the bedchamber. "She never could open her heart to the valley, but she opened her legs to every ferry boat boy and wanderer who ever walked through it."

Her good friend Hamlin Marsh grinned as he held the old woman's frail hand. Despite the age difference between them, theirs' had been a natural and immediate friendship. He loved her brash insubordination; she loved his subdued version of that same defiance. There had always been a Walterhouse in the valley, and Winifred was the Walterhouse everyone knew and loved the most. Thus her sudden illness and impending death were a tragedy, especially to those who knew her well. Winifred was an admirer of shock, though, so this final unexpectedness pleased her. Even before she fell ill, her once shocking red hair had been sheered to the scalp, a consequence of an unfortunate genetic abnormality that made her hair come out in ugly clumps. Only Hamlin Marsh knew this about her; she let those in the valley think what they wanted and would often laugh herself breathless on hearing the rumors and suppositions behind her sheering. "I'll not have my head become a relief map!" she'd pronounced, and so she'd shaved the rest of it. This had made her the favorite customer of the very best wig-makers in the area.

Winifred had never seemed too concerned with her lack of feminine appeal or suitors. Hamlin had many times commented on how fortunate it was that she possessed such an effectual personality, for she had the sagging face of a constipated bulldog. Were it not for her humor, she would have simply been regarded as The Crazy Old Woman with the Eccentric Wigs Who Lives in the Big Old House. "Well, sod-buggers! I have work to do, then. Toss the wigs!" she had growled in the moment.

"I still miss Esther, though," Winifred grumbled, coughing weakly. "I miss them all. Esther, Ashley, Beanie…" Her voice drifted off in a trail of regrets and whispered names. Her delicate, small, fleshen dome decorated with reddish-gray tufts sank into the pillows. She hadn't sheered much lately.

"The girl, Calpurnia," she said, coming to herself. "She's all set up? This old place goes to her when I drop off. I want Walterhouse Manor going to family, not squatters."

"It will." Hamlin nodded. "It's all taken care of. When she's old enough to live on her own she can move back here and care for the place."

Hamlin was a good-looking man of his age, Winifred noted, and not for the first time. He was by no means elderly, but he was not a young man anymore either. His gentle eyes and voice hid a powerful will that none would cross. The valley folk listened to and respected him. He was a leaning post.

"Good," the old woman gruffed. "It can't have been easy for the little thing, having lost her mother and daddy at so young an age. And then, sent to live here with me. Must have been terribly frightening for her. The first time she saw me without me head on"—she gestured to her patchwork skull—"she looked petrified as a deer in a hunter's sight. And too, look around this house. There are no toys, comforts, or knickknacks. Clearly, I'm not exactly maternal. What must have gone through her head? Downright selfish of parents to up and die on their child like that."

"Well, nonetheless, she had a good woman looking after her," Hamlin praised, patting her hand.

"Meh." Winifred fluttered her fingers, brushing the comment away. "She's only a girl. She's no lamb; she's got attitude. No disputing that. That's Walterhouse blood in her veins, after all. But anyone would have had pity for the little thing. Maybe someone else *should* have. I'm no good to her now laying up here. If I weren't about to die, I'd surely go mad as a jackal being in this room all day and night, not being able to walk in the woods or lounge naked at the river. I'm just thankful I pass out from the pain now and then. It separates my boredom into blocks of time. It's good to have variety." She coughed and shook her head. "S'not right I should have to be cooped up like an egg-layin' hen. My eggs are all dried up." She seemed on the verge of an angry fit, but calmed herself. "So, the girl will live with you then, after I'm gone?"

"Calpurnia will stay at my cabin until she's of age to live here," Hamlin answered.

"Assuming she stays around here," Winifred replied. "Everyone wants to move on, it seems. Leaving the magic of this valley. Why they leave, I'll never understand, Hamlin." She looked as if she were mourning for a dear friend.

"Nor I," Hamlin agreed. "But there'll always be the True family. Them and the remaining River Dwellers will do right by the valley and keep it safe."

It came as a puzzle and a relief to both Winifred and Hamlin that, like most of the small pockets of the world designated the Fringes, the valley was largely overlooked, even by those who lived near it. Deemed a place of little interest and even less worth, it was left alone by outsiders. Neither the college men in the school overlooking the valley, nor the farmers who grew their crops past the Farlands, gave the hillsides or their residents much attention. The river was beautiful, yes, and provided an excellent means of crop transportation from time to time... but it was only a river. Theirs was just another valley.

"The trouble with the world, Hamlin," Winifred continued, interrupted sporadically by coughing fits, "the problem is, people just don't look closer. Ain't nobody in the outside who sees, who really *sees*. They made their rules and laws, and they say that's all there is, like there's no such thing as growth beyond them."

"We're in a dark age. That's the truth."

"What people need is to be sat down and told things. Just have it hammered into 'em, I suppose."

"What would you tell them, Winny?" He stroked her hand tenderly. Her aggravation was disturbing her condition.

She looked at him a moment, chasing the words in her mind. "Why, I'd tell 'em for certain! I'd say, 'Now listen, y'all learned folk. Things are different here in the valley; things are how they should be. This here is a place where reality still runs circular. There isn't a beginning or an end. Things just *are*, see?'"

Hamlin gave her his attention as if he were a pupil listening to a stoic and strict philosopher.

She continued, "People from the outside just don't understand the Fringes, Hamlin. Here, where by some grand mistake the lines between worlds have never been drawn. They can't fathom how a person can interact with the earth spirits here, or that bugbears might even exist, though I've never seen one. It's like a…a…" She searched for an apt description. She had tried to explain the ways of the valley folk to Calpurnia just a few weeks prior, but found herself unable to remember her words. "An appreciated chaos," she said, settling on a suitable explanation.

"I see," Hamlin nodded, acting as if he were a stranger, new to the valley.

"Don't you go placating me!" Winifred chided. His serious attention to her proclamation tickled her so that she hacked until she turned purple, and Hamlin quickly poured her a glass of water from the china pitcher at the bedside.

"Oh," she moaned, drained and defeated. "Here," she whispered with her eyes closed and head resting, finishing her speech for herself; one last pearl of wisdom dropped into a lifelong bucket's worth: "Here in the valley, we live balanced on only one law, don't we? The Law of Perception. Even the laws of nature bow to that."

She didn't say anything else. Her eyes became heavy, and the room began to drift. Her sermon had tired her. Hamlin kissed her gently on the forehead, then rose and walked to the bedchamber door, the old floorboards creaking deafeningly beneath his feet. The house lay silent and expecting. Before Hamlin reached the door, though, Winifred felt a horrendous coughing spell rise from her lungs. Hamlin rushed back to her side. Raucous and violent, the spasms took hold of her completely, and no amount of water seemed to help soothe their ire. She squeezed Hamlin's hand tightly. Her nails cut into his flesh. She coughed and kafflummed and shook the room. And quite suddenly, the jagged coughing subsided and with a monumental exhale Winifred sat up and exclaimed, as loud as she had ever spoken, *"I just barked up my soul!"* Then she fell limp to the pompous pillows anew, having at last finished what she was in the world to do.

THE ORPHAN GIRL

CALPURNIA COVINGTON was an unfortunate favored girl. And by this, it is merely meant that while her life's current had for the most part run well, she was recognizably unappreciative of it.

She had been born to a well-to-do family; Winifred's sister Katie had married one of the wealthy limestone lords of the region. Raised in a city north of the valley, Calpurnia had lounged in pretty frills, taking afternoon teas from unhappy servants ordered about by a freckle-faced seven-year-old tyrant. She had never once heard the word "no." It certainly wasn't in her father's vocabulary, at least not when it came to her. She received whatever she desired, whenever she wanted it. Things always went her way, or else they were etched new, just like her father's limestone. Yes, things were bent, carved, and structured for the pretty little cupcake with the chunky vomitous filling. She was motherless, after all. Katie Covington (née Walterhouse) had died choking on a shellfish delicacy soon after Calpurnia was born, and offering Calpurnia the wide world became her father's duty. Thus, at a very early age Calpurnia learned to love the art of manipulation, the pleasures of control.

When her father was killed—a limestone column collapsed on him as he was inspecting it— the little girl's perfectly governed world was sent into a scramble. Plucked up from her home in the city and transplanted to the house of one of her few living relatives—or at least, the only one who would take her—Winifred Walterhouse, Calpurnia felt suddenly lost. The decision fell to Winifred's other brothers and sisters. Winifred lived alone in the rambling house and had no other family to look after. They all had their own busy lives to manage. Winifred did not truly mind, though. To once again have a child in the old house was very much needed, she thought, even if it was a bit uncomfortable at first. It would do the old walls good to hear young laughter.

It took a while for Calpurnia and Winifred to adapt to one another. The young girl's selfish mannerisms were finally curtailed somewhat by the no-nonsense-but-her-own-nonsense old woman, and Calpurnia had learned to accept Winifred's role in her life, if not value it.

Still, it was Calpurnia's belligerence and tenacity that first caught Minerva True's attention, and Minerva True, like Winifred Walterhouse and Hamlin Marsh, was considered someone of great importance in the valley. All Calpurnia had known of her was that she lived somewhere deep in the woods of Black Hill, a hidden cottage or shack on the pixie-walks that no one had ever seen. She had been told this by her new friend Lara Kempt.

"She guards the valley from the old preacher," Lara continued in a cautious whisper. Despite continued attempts, Calpurnia couldn't draw any more out of her friend than that cryptic, dangling sentence. Lara smiled obliquely. Her fever had scarred her mentally when she was a babe.

Minerva True was interested in Calpurnia, though. That much was certain. The child would see Minerva walk up Black Hill Road toward Walterhouse Manor and quickly hide around corners—and doorways in the house if she could not get outside—lest she be seen. Minerva made her apprehensive. She was young and old looking at the same time. She did not fit with any of the few rules of biology Calpurnia understood. Minerva's face held a lineless and serene beauty, and her hair fell in a flowing cascade of silver that sparkled beneath the sun. When she walked, her draping dark clothes seemed to curl around her in a caressing manner, as if there were life in the delicate fabric. Observing Minerva, Calpurnia could not deny the existence of the valley's magic. And that disturbed her. The older woman became her immediate adversary.

Calpurnia listened at doorways to the lengthy conversations her aunt Winifred conducted with the quiet, wispy Minerva True. By their demeanor, their comfort in each other's company, Calpurnia ascertained that they were indeed good friends who had known each other for many years. She herself had not known a friendship like that, but she immediately recognized that Lara Kempt could be such a friend in time. The young orphan was also able to determine by various conversations that Minerva had some romantic relationship with old Hamlin Marsh.

The two women always held conference—for that was how Calpurnia saw Minerva's visits—in the Great Hall, an enormous room with thick oak beams, a cold wood floor, and a hungry, massive hearth, nearly a room unto itself. The furniture in the Great Hall was spare and practical. Only a few more ornate pieces sat here and there, gifts from

Winifred's brothers and sisters who tried desperately to encourage her to live posher and flamboyantly "for the sake of the Walterhouse name."

"She's so aware of the world," Minerva observed one day in the Great Hall as Calpurnia listened from outside the room. They drank hot tea with fresh honey out of elegant china cups. Winifred had a beautiful collection of china. Aside from her wigs, it was one of her few indulgences. "I think she might be the one we're looking for." Minerva's voice was light and brittle, like a thin wafer.

"Are you certain, Minerva?" Winifred asked, her harsh voice a complete contrast. She wore her big red wig, a favorite, the hair piled high in rows like a log dam. No makeup embellished the attempted stylishness. She didn't want to look like her sister Esther, The Uppity Whore.

"No. Of course not. 'Tis a thing impossible to be certain of. If Mother True were alive, she would know. She could see much more than I ever will. But I hear whispers through the trees. And the Passions are stirring as well." She paused to look out the large window onto the fields of flowers. "But I do not know for sure."

"You will know. I'm sure. If our Calpurnia is of the Three, you will be the first to see it. You have your mother's power."

Of the Three? The phrase struck a certain stomach-churning dread in Calpurnia. It sounded like a great secret. Secrets terrified her. They made her feel out of control.

"Being aware, of course, doesn't mean a thing," Minerva whispered on. "But, there is something about her... some quality. She will be important. I can tell you that. Whether or not she is of the triad...." She shrugged, holding the cup and saucer to take a sip and not spill.

"*The Three shall vanquish Him,*" Winifred repeated an archaic line she had known since childhood as she stared at the large hearth in front of her.

"That's how The One Prophecy was told," Minerva agreed. "I once thought it referred to Mother True, myself, and my sweet sister Ingrid, but that was before both of them made the journey across the river. I know for certain that the Three will be needed soon. I was walking with Branwenn two evenings past—on one of their dusklit mother/daughter walks along the beach—and we caught sight of an abstraction, a mist hovering above the old chapel grounds at the base of Black Hill."

Calpurnia did not understand this enigmatic talk, but she didn't like the sound of any of it and so decided from that day forward to dislike Minerva True. She would not be designated for a life mission she knew nothing of by a woman who looked so very abnormal. She set her chin firmly against any of it. Winifred tried over time to curb the girl's distrust of Minerva, but it was of no use. Calpurnia's perception had fixed like feet in foot-high mud.

Calpurnia did make friends, though few they were, and it was slow-going. In time, Lara Kempt became the closest of these. From the first sight of her, Calpurnia was charmed by the cheerful, sweet young girl, initially unaware of her mental disabilities. Calpurnia appreciated Lara's eagerness to please people, her especially. The two became even better friends after Winifred died and Calpurnia moved into Hamlin's cabin nearer the river.

Lara lived with her two middle-aged aunts, Kayla and Brit Brennen-Blue, who, at first sight, Calpurnia imagined to be but another pair of eccentric women living in a Gothic house, far out in the hinterland. The birth of the two aunts—twins, of course—had caused the death of their mother, further proof, so the Daventry-Blues argued, of which branch of the Blue family was the strongest. The Births and resultant Death, referred to just so, weighed into the larger family quarrel alongside duels and supposed hexes.

The two aunties strolled through the valley, ever the picture of sisterly love, always clinging to one another's hands. Indeed, Calpurnia noticed, one could hardly tell where the sleeve of Kayla's fine gown ended and Brit's began. Their bond seemed unbreakable. They would sit holding hands in their rocking chairs on the porch of their grand house, the sisters often watching Calpurnia and Lara play in the barren yard.

Lara would follow Calpurnia's lead in most everything. She always did as she was instructed with nary a qualm. This made Calpurnia feel at home. They grew inseparable after a very short time, carefree as the day, chasing butterflies through the woods and laughing at silly boys. They made garlands of clover and mint and paraded around the fields. Calpurnia would create songs and insist that Lara learn them, and then they would prance off singing boisterously by the river.

Lara would often speak of seeing Passions, but Calpurnia knew not what these were, nor even that she had once spoken to one. She would simply explain to Lara that such talk was ridiculous and unbecoming, and thus, things would be set right in their day's play. The Passions would not be spoken of again. She struck away at every silly idea Lara ever presented to her. If they were to be best friends, neither of them would believe in nonsense. Neither would grow up to be like the crazy folk of the valley.

Still, Calpurnia was unable to forget the words of Minerva True that day in the Great Hall of Walterhouse Manor: the introduction of a nondescript number—*of the Three*.

THE WAKING DARKNESS

THE CHANGING of the seasons in the valley from summer to fall was a time for much celebration; Autumnday had ever been the most anticipated of the festivals. This attention to the natural world and its processes all seemed very confusing for Calpurnia Covington. The strange spiritual practices of those in the valley distressed her. Not that there were any of the sacrifice and bloody, perverted deeds she had been told were the mark of such nature worshipers. The spiritual practices of the river folk were undeniably graceful and beautiful. Small rafts piled with bouquets of highly scented flowers were set alight and floated upriver to some unseen place beyond the bends of the waterway; lovely music filled the air, sung by strange women adorned in flowing white robes. Even more ethereal music echoed from somewhere deep within the woods of the hillsides, a haunting melody of melancholy whose history Calpurnia never cared to know. Even the Othersiders, the hidden people who lived across the river, would come out of their hiding and sing enchantingly over the water. Some songs celebrated frivolity while others carried such deep tone they were surely prayers. But to whom these prayers of song and gifts of flowers were for, Calpurnia could only guess, and her guesses took the shape of gruesome things with fangs and red-eyes, giving the rituals an eldritch aura. Minerva had told her once on a visit to Hamlin's cabin, "We sing for the river, for the preservation of the truth it holds," but that meant nothing at all to young Miss Covington. Minerva's own daughter Branwenn seemed to understand everything that was said though, and that irritated Calpurnia to no end. Branwenn seemed a simple little girl. Why was she entrusted to know such secrets?

The valley boasted no churches. This Calpurnia had noticed immediately. She had even dressed up that first Sunday morning at Walterhouse Manor readying for her new house of worship, but upon heading downstairs to leave she found Winifred in the Great Hall, wigless and still in her nightgown, reading some obscure book.

Without her "head," Aunt Winifred looked like a witch ready to eat her up or at the very least pitch her into the hearth. A single small chapel lay at the foot of Black Hill, but none ever used it that Calpurnia could see. Ramshackle and falling in, soon it would be consumed by the vegetation of the hillside. Winifred explained to her that the spirituality of the valley was noninvasive, and they did not need structures to retain it.

"The celebration of one's own spiritual nature should be a personal thing. Why should every soul's spirituality be the same?" Winifred explained. "You and I are different; we have different life experiences. Our spirits guide us through these experiences. We each have a distinct vision of the world, and we should honor that how we best see fit, with your own chosen rituals and songs. Your ways may match perfectly those of another in one manner, like the River Dwellers, but then they may also be very different in others."

Calpurnia rolled her eyes. It all seemed pretentious, mythological nonsense to her, unlike the Bible she had been taught from birth.

Of what she knew of the valley's celebrations, the only thing that mattered that first year, the only thing that impacted her in any way, was the fun she would have down by the river during the late-night festivities of Autumnday. There were costumes and contests and dancing and lantern lighting. The lapzine fields were set ablaze to burn off the excess for the winter, and this was always a sight to see. The blue light was a favorite for lovers and families alike. The fun lasted well into the morning, the only time the children were allowed to be out so late. Any other time, the children were assured some stalking bogeyman would snatch their souls away.

Calpurnia dallied along the banks whooping and hollering, though to her the celebrations were nothing more than play. Lara Kempt tried explaining the importance of Autumnday once as she herself had understood from Kayla and Brit, but Calpurnia's attention never held for long. She and Lara would soon find excitement in games of hiding and seeking, or chasing about young Darcy Crocker and his best friend, Garet Cather. The two boys annoyed Calpurnia, but Lara found them extremely entertaining. Especially Darcy.

It was on a cool, celebratory Autumnday night during Calpurnia's first year in the valley, well past the midnight hour, when she became acquainted with a waking darkness. Something that had been quite dormant for a long time.

Though Calpurnia had been warned to stay clear of the chapel grounds by Hamlin and Minerva, she had so far not been known to follow the wishes of those she did not regard as "real worlders." She soon found herself distracted from her night play with Lara and the boys by a slight yet pressing call, a thin voice carried on the wind, which only she could hear. This gave her a certain pride, as if she were chosen especially. A secret finally just for her.

Cal-pur-ni-a, the wind seemed to sing. *Callie, Callie, come play.*

She giggled at the alliteration, and then at the sound of her own name having been shortened to such silly-sounding syllables. She followed the sound—for it was a sound, not a voice, an internal hum in her own head—carefully separating herself from those around her, completely unaware of the difference between a calling and a call.

Callie, Callie, come play.

She walked barefoot across the smooth stones of the beach to the coolness of the soft grass in front of the chapel grounds. Dew squished between her toes. She watched to make certain no one witnessed her venture there, wondering what type of frog Minerva would turn her into if she were caught. The fireflies glittered around her, some settling in her long red hair. The sounds of the celebratory crowds now fell far behind her, muffled by the river tide and the night. On the beach, the river folk danced and sang around the bonfire so expertly set by the metalworker, Prichard Parma.

"I'm here," Calpurnia whispered to the call in her head as she trod through the chapel gate. She crept over the marshy ground, studying her surroundings with interest, but no concern. Black Hill shot up like a towering behemoth above her. It eyed her with disappointment. The start of Black Hill Road could be seen from the chapel grounds, its ascent eventually rising to Walterhouse Manor.

Callie, Callie, come play, the wind whispered more urgently.

She followed the words as if she could see them, vowels and all, leading her to the rickety, paint-scuffed steps of the chapel's remains. Ever-shrouded by an oft-blanketing mist since she had arrived in the valley, this night she could see the chapel as clear as day. The moon hung like a faded star, lighting the valley and thinning the mist.

Above the steps, curling like a flirting cat, sat a single patch of queer-shaped fog, resembling the outline of a man, but with his insides missing. His center was a void. She watched in amazement as from this outlined form grew a wobbly, shaking stick figure assembled from twigs and refuse with snaps and crunches. Though not constructed of bone, the growing figure looked skeletal. Each arm and leg held a zigzagging, jagged configuration, each twig and broken splinter looking as if it were tied tightly to the next by bands and tendon, except there were no bands to be seen. The featureless torso and head was formed from large splinters, chaotic explosions of rotted wood. As the being descended the steps in crooked, twitching strides, the fog continued to wrap around it in thin streams. The moon shone clear, too bright to be anything but a warning. Calpurnia knew she was witnessing more of the ridiculous hallucinations of the valley, but she could not turn away. This was not like the fox; that had been a silly, childish daydream. This was something altogether more interesting, more complicated.

A gift, the inner voice whispered. *A loan. Keep it safe*. The splinter-skeleton man pointed down with a convulsive, uncontrolled gesture to something on the bottom step beside him. Calpurnia had not noticed it there before. She approached carefully and saw a large leather-bound book, a bible of some kind, but one much bigger than she had ever seen before.

"For me?" She grinned, taking the Bible in her hands. It was heavy, but the weight was good; it felt powerful. A surge of excitement rushed through Calpurnia's veins.

The Night Hammer, came a whispered reply.

Calpurnia examined the Bible. It was the most beautiful book she had ever seen: a strong leather cover, gold leaf pages, beautifully written words she did not understand, meticulous illustrations that almost seemed alive under the moonlight. Autumnday was forgotten. She smiled in delight at her new prize. "The Night Hammer?" she responded finally, her delicate hands caressing the leather. "No. This is the Bible. I know it." And then, at once, the words in the book took on the recognizable forms of stanza and scripture.

But as she looked up in query, she saw the skeleton man had disappeared completely. She stood on the bottom step alone. A pile of twigs and splinters lay in front of her, and the mist was closing in again around her. She hugged the book to her chest and leapt from the chapel steps, forgetting all about the celebration by the river, and instead running back to Hamlin Marsh's cabin so she could pore through her new possession. To have beautiful things was so wonderful!

As Calpurnia hurried past the crowd, the light from the bonfire casting large and bewildering shadows from insignificants, she noticed one small figure standing apart from the rest. At first she thought it Lara and was going to show her the treasure, but nearing the lone child, she recognized Branwenn True. Branwenn was younger than she or Lara, and very petite, to the point of being a dwarf. Calpurnia held the heavy book even tighter to her chest. Branwenn's face registered shock.

"You shouldn't have gone in there, Calpurnia," the smaller girl said in her small voice. "There're bad things in there."

"Who says?" Calpurnia responded obstinately. "I didn't see anything bad. I got a gift."

"A gift?" Branwenn inquired. She looked at the book, eyes wide. "What is it?"

"It's mine." She walked nearer to Branwenn, not wanting to be seen by any adult. "Who told you there are bad things in there, Branwenn?"

"Everybody says so. My mother told me so." Her tiny face was made tinier by Calpurnia's feeling of greatness.

"Well, that's just silly. It's a church. Churches aren't bad, Branwenn. Maybe your mother just doesn't want you to have a gift such as this. Maybe she goes there all the time, and gets lots of gifts, and wants to keep the gifts for herself. Have you ever thought of that?"

"No," Branwenn answered. The thought of her mother ever deceiving her was beyond her. Like another language.

"You should. You should think about things like that." Calpurnia looked about her for any sign of Minerva. "Maybe you should go there sometime and get yourself a gift."

"Oh, I couldn't!" Branwenn said. Her voice squeaked, and Calpurnia wished she could squash her like a bug. "Mother would never let me."

"You shouldn't tell her. You should go alone. I would think that because Minerva is your mother and such an important person in the valley you'd get a big present too, even bigger than this." She hugged the book.

Branwenn's name was called from near the bonfire. Calpurnia backed off.

"I must go read now. Goodnight, Branwenn," Calpurnia said, hastily stealing away into the dark again. She looked over her shoulder as she fled the beach to make certain Branwenn was not following her. But the girl simply stood where Calpurnia had left her, a tiny silhouette against the backlight of the bonfire.

THE RIVER DWELLER'S DAUGHTER

TWO LITTLE boys stood on a cliff in the morning light, overlooking the wide river and the ongoing festivities below. The final day of Autumnday had arrived, a more somber affair, when the summer is bid farewell. The boys watched their friends and family milling about far below them, readying for the final fires at sunset. The figures were so small and indistinguishable from the cliff that their game of naming proved much less enjoyable than the boys had first thought it would be. Their eyes were tired from the night before; they had stayed up through sunrise to watch the last of the lapzine burn off the fields.

Across the placid waters of the river lay the world of the rarely seen Othersiders, their equally impressive hills shrouded by morning vapors. Flocks of birds had been flying across the river all morning, perching on the limbs and branches there, but the boys gave them little notice. Who knew why birds did what they did? They could not see that the birds stared back out across the river with agitation, as if something had frightened them.

Garet Cather loved the fall festivities that welcomed the change of seasons. He loved the stories of the nature spirits told at the Parma's bonfires; he loved that he was allowed to stay up all night with his best friend, Darcy Crocker. Garet's father had instilled in him a strong respect for the river and valley at an early age. Nature was something to be feared, but also fiercely revered.

"How can anyone not love Autumnday?" Garet asked his friend as they sat on the grassy cliff. He picked at the fine greenery, twirling it in his palm with his thumb and forefinger. He was a usually content lad, sandy-haired and freckled. "Look at the valley! It's filled with fun. The last fun before the winter begins."

"It's not the valley some people don't like, Garet," explained Darcy, the broodiest little boy who ever lived. "It's the worshiping of it. That's what my folks say, anyways." Darcy's lips hardly parted. He could, at times, be a terrible mumbler, but when he was angry his tantrums could spark fires.

"Your folks didn't used to say that. They never used to talk like that at all."

"Well, they do now," Darcy mumbled reproachfully.

Darcy was not a big fan of the festivities. He loved staying up late as much as Garet, but the celebration of the changing seasons fell outside the mold of what his parents were now training him to believe. Garet simply assumed this was Darcy's way; he had always been a rather harsh little boy, never smiling and hardly speaking unless to Garet.

"Be careful," Garet replied. "You're starting to sound like Calpurnia." He smiled, his sweetness letting Darcy know he was teasing.

Darcy grumbled and picked a dandelion apart.

Garet stood and walked to the edge of the cliff in his ragged pants and bare feet to get a better view of things below. A sweet breeze played around him, and he grinned at its flirtation.

"Be careful there," Darcy hollered from the grass, looking over his shoulder at his friend.

The cliff plunged straight away, exposed rock the only catch. The sun glinted and shone off various stones, some of such exceptional beauty they looked like diamonds and emeralds, sapphires and rubies. Garet loved to come to this spot on the cliff and lay on his stomach with his chin in his palm peering down at the precious gems. They could keep him mesmerized in happiness for hours, their glittering displays more dazzling than any traveling show. He had promised himself when he first saw the gems that one day he would climb down the rockface and snatch a few of those jewels, one for every person he knew, fetching the largest for Darcy Crocker. Garet's father was a ranger after all, and such daring was in the blood. One day Garet would be a ranger too.

As he stood at the cliff's edge, Garet noticed a green stone that shone too lovely to leave sitting beneath the sun. Definitely a stone that needed a setting. It wasn't too far down either. He could get to it this very day if he were careful. He turned to Darcy. "I'll be right back," he called, standing with his back facing the valley, lowering one foot carefully down the cliff.

Darcy stood up immediately. "What are you doing?"

"I'll just be a moment. There's a pretty rock." He found what he thought was safe footing on the rockface and now only his head and arms were above the cliff.

"Garet! Get back here. It's just a stupid rock."

Yet as Darcy said this the air filled with the terrifying crumbling sound of rock. Garet screamed. Darcy ran to the edge of the cliff. His friend dangled there, his fingers red and white with exertion, clinging to the cliff's edge. Garet was skin, bones, and not much else. He couldn't hang on too long.

Darcy grabbed Garet's forearms, anchoring his own toes into the earth, and began pulling with all his might. Garet's eyes linked to Darcy's and between them passed silent messages of strength and fear. Neither truly thought Darcy would be able to do it. Garet imagined falling to the grounds below, ruining the festivities for everyone. This would become a legend: The Autumnday That Silly Boy Fell from the Cliff Looking for Pretty Rocks.

But to both their amazement, Darcy was indeed strong enough and pulled Garet back up to safety. He managed, with very little effort.

Once both boys were back on the cliff, having then scooted a good distance away from the edge, they hugged, with Garet pledging a parade of gratitudes, and Darcy countering with one of insults.

"That was real dumb!" Darcy admonished. "You're a big dummy, Garet Cather!"

"I know," Garet apologized breathlessly. "But you did it. I must have been real heavy, huh? I don't weigh as much as you, but still…"

"No," Darcy answered. "That's true. You're as light as a dandelion, my friend. A big, dumb dandelion."

MINERVA TRUE was one of the very last of the River Dwellers, and the only one left of any real power. She descended from a long line of watchers of the river valley, those so assigned by some focused power to keep guard against the fomenting imbalance of the world. Sometimes she won her battles. Others, her lone voice was not enough, and the iniquity would grow a little further, stretching its miasmatic fingers through marsh weeds and woodlands. The valley folk assumed there were many of her kind, keeping things settled, preserving their safety, but Minerva knew the truth. Far too many had shrugged off their purpose, confined in their growing complacency. The life of a River Dweller was a thankless pursuit, and the darkness was once again rising from the filth.

Mother True had passed on her knowledge to Minerva. She had been instructed from girlhood in the same earthen abode in which she lived now, on the side of Black Hill. From there she could watch over the valley and the green river that swam through it.

"This is the only spot we can be," Mother True had said, her voice like a whispering breeze, quick and lisping. "Any higher and our watch would be useless. The trees would block our view, and how would we ever get to the chapel grounds in time? Any lower and the chapel mist would threaten to suffocate us. We must know our place in the bedlam, my child."

Mother True taught both her daughters, Ingrid and Minerva, from the old stories, making certain they understood The One Prophecy regarding the Three.

That was ages ago, but even then Minerva understood the world needed certain beings, be they spirit or flesh, to help in the fight against a faceless élan with too many names: Religion, Disparity, Power. Yet strive as she might to continue her mother's lifelong battle, the chapel's influence had continued to grow. Minerva felt at times she had let Mother True down, but then, every so often, she would hear the ghostly curl of a crackling *S* and know Mother True was near and proud. She had faded from the valley into noncorporeal form long ago, now merely a phantom, a will o' the wisp, but always watching and aiding when she could. Mother True, like Minerva's sister Ingrid, was among the trees now, having returned to the elements of the world once again.

Minerva's last good friend, Winifred Walterhouse, was dead, buried in the nearly forgotten and abandoned barrows of Black Hill, as per her desire. Minerva now watched from the bluff of College Hill, beneath the hill's solitary tree, its branches curled in elegant lines. Mother True had always espoused a fondness for that tree. Behind Minerva lay the promising new school, Greenbriar, a college that had been founded in Mother True's time by an obscenely wealthy old coot named Castor Verona. The students of the college eyed Minerva as an oddity when they saw her daily vigil at the tree, but thought little else of her. Black Hill lay to the west of College Hill, at the foot of which sat the chapel grounds, a place to be guarded against at all cost, lest it fracture the world.

"Mama!" cried a tiny voice from a strong tree branch above Minerva. "*Look! The birds!*"

"Yes, Branwenn," Minerva lovingly replied to her daughter. "Autumn is here. The birds are making their passage south."

The last day of Autumnday was beginning along the river below. High above the river, guided by it as if it were a glassy highway, flocks of birds flew in great multitudes upstream or across to the other side. Birds of many species mingled, yet always led by a rain crow, their destinies having merged into a single truth leading them on. But this year Minerva noticed there was something amiss. Surely the valley folk who gathered as they did every year to watch the birds' flight on the beach below also noticed what was so evident to her. The foreboding augury of silence hung like guilt in the air. Not a whistle, call, or chirp rose from the winged creatures. Only the mass cacophony of flapping wings could be heard as the birds began to blanket the sky. The college students seemed not to notice.

Minerva pinched her brow in concern and pushed back her long silver hair. "Come down, Branwenn," she called. "We've things to do, young one."

Branwenn scampered down the bark of the tree, her dress torn and stained. She looked the spitting image of Mother True. Her black hair shone in the sunlight. Two braids twined with wheat grass framed the sides of her beaming face. "Are we going to perform the first rites of the fall?" the little one asked, taking hold of Minerva's hand. Minerva was proud her daughter understood the importance of what she did. Branwenn would be a River Dweller one day and lead the valley folk after Minerva was gone.

"That we are." Minerva smiled. "And you shall do even more than you did at the summer rites. You have more of a role, and that role will continue to grow as you do."

This made Branwenn very happy. She skipped alongside her mother, still holding her hand as they began to take the winding path down College Hill, through the woods to the beach. The sunlight faded beneath the trees, and a sweet river breeze blew up toward them.

"I'm gonna be just like you, Momma. The old preacher won't stand a chance against me!" she assured her mother. "Are we very close to winning?" Branwenn asked.

Minerva puzzled at the question. "It's not a matter of winning, my girl. This is not a game of catch. We only need to keep harmful things at bay. Darkness and light need to exist in balance. The world… She will take care of what ails Her in due course. We are simply nurses, I suppose: bandaging wounds that can be healed perfectly well by the body, that's all."

"But we shouldn't get too near the old chapel, right?" Branwenn hadn't told Minerva about her conversation the night before with Calpurnia Covington. She wasn't sure exactly what to make of it. She had never known someone with the demeanor of Calpurnia. Why should she not trust what she was told by her mother?

"Right you are, precious one. It lies waiting like a crocodile, and can sneak up on you when least expected." She made a snapper from her fingers and playfully poked at her daughter. Branwenn giggled.

"It won't never get me, Momma," Branwenn stoutly said. "But why do we perform the rites, Momma?"

"I've told you why, silly girl," Minerva replied, lifting Branwenn over a tree that had fallen across the path. "We do it because poetry, truth, and beauty are valuable tools against the darkness."

"And one day will I be a priestess, like you?"

Minerva laughed. "Who told you I am a priestess?"

"Darcy Crocker. He says you're a witch too. He didn't sound too nice when he said it."

"Did he now? Well, some might say I am. But in the end, I'm a person who is only trying to do what's best for me and mine." She looked down smiling at the girl. "So he can call me a witch if he wants."

"Well, a witch sounds a lot better than what he calls *his* mother."

"And what's that, darling?"

"A righteous Cathy-licker," she whispered, as if it were a curse word. "I don't know what that is, but it doesn't sound very nice at all…."

Branwenn kept talking as they walked the long path to the beach. She spoke of everything she could think of or had questions about, and everything in between those questions too. Her questions never ceased, and her observations were endless when it came to butterflies and blue jays. She talked even more as they ventured up into the woods again, climbing the steep, winding road of Black Hill. There had once been talk of connecting the paths on the hills of the valley somehow—a line from Black Hill to College Hill so one wouldn't have to make a descent to the beach before climbing the other—but the idea was always put on hold for later.

Midway they came to a forked trail. One path led farther up the hill whereon lay Minerva's home in the circle wood hidden along the elf-paths and pixie-walks. Farther still upon this part of the road was an abandoned shack, and then, of course, at the very top of Black Hill, stood Walterhouse Manor. Black Hill Road wasn't used heavily anymore, not since Winifred had passed. Now only Minerva and Branwenn were seen coming out from it to the beach with any regularity.

The other path at the fork was even more rarely taken. Only Minerva trod it, and then only to perform certain rituals. It was the closest she dared venture to the old chapel grounds at the foot of the hill. No one went there, or at least no one from the valley wise to its history. If they did, it was the deathly nightcalls that beckoned them. But those terrible incidents had stopped, it seemed, and had become nearly faerie stories.

But then the awakening….

In the past year, there had been the occasional vagrant or curious traveler who foolishly followed the moans and hum that issued from the place, and once they crossed the path onto the grounds they were never seen again. Only Minerva could hear their anguished ghost cries at night. Such was the curse of a River Dweller.

HAMLIN MARSH watched the sky with concern. The birds flew eerily silent, as if they carried a secret they were too frightened to divulge. Afraid that, in doing so, they would be weighed down, unable to ever fly again. This was a warning, but of what?

Hamlin had lived all his life in the valley. From young stag to bright buck, he had grown accustomed to the strange turns of season and stubborn ticks of time on the Fringes. He had known no other way. He had played by the river as a boy, ushering the birds onward every autumn, asking them to return come the next spring. He had attended weddings amidst the noisy canopy of wings. He had waltzed naked around bonfires. He had even made love beneath the large shade trees, had conceived a child there. But never had he witnessed anything of this sort. The birds migrated in a sullen brigade, almost a funerary mass. Such a hush had never descended upon the valley before at the time of the festival. The celebration had stopped dead. Husbands held their wives, standing on the beach, peering upward in utter bewilderment. The river folk from the forested bank opposite them, the Othersiders, came out of the cover of their woods to mumble alarm as well. Their younger lads could be seen hanging like primitive but lithe humanoids from tree tops, staring in disbelief. Even the river boat boys—whose job it was to carry people from one bank to the other— simply stood barefoot and naked-chested on their rafts, watching the sky in confusion. The slightest breeze of the day didn't dare impede the desolate hush, and Hamlin felt the shiver of cold portent run down his spine.

As Hamlin eyed the omen in the sky, whispers rose around him on the beach. Soon they would be asking him what was happening. As undisputed yet unelected leader of their hamlet, he would be expected to know. His father's mantle of respect had passed to him like some physical trait, like blue eyes or wavy hair. There was no shirking the responsibility of an uninvited duty.

"What is it, Hamlin?" came the inevitable question. "What does this mean?"

The query came loaded with a clearly formed answer already in mind. Rupert Toots, a somewhat less than intelligent man, had laid the inquiry out, plain as day. His voice splashed through the still like an anvil dropped into serene water from an extraordinary height.

Hamlin's eyes darted quickly to the young man. Others stood near him, waiting for an answer as well. Hamlin wished Minerva were by him. She would know. She was of the hidden worlds, however archaic and trite that sounded, and knew the truth of things that were passed down as faerie stories and romances. But it being the first of autumn, she would be performing protective rites on the path over the chapel grounds, doing her best to quell the ancient danger that rapidly, vociferously sprang across the world like a deadly cancer. Hamlin often wondered if all her work were in vain, for whenever things seemed at last quiet and safe, the darkness would rise again like a tide.

"What does it mean?" Rupert Toots repeated, his large eyes begging for resolution.

"It means what the flight of the birds has always meant: fall is here," Hamlin replied calmly. He had always spoken the truth, and, until he knew differently, this was the truth.

"But it's deathly quiet, Hamlin. *Deathly* so." Rupert glanced up at the sky, peeking from under his bowler hat with such a look of worry that

Hamlin's fatherly instinct made him want to hold the young man and say everything would be fine, even if that weren't true.

"We'll have to see what the season holds. I can offer nothing more than that," Hamlin said. Rupert looked again at the elder man, and nodded as if he had been justly scolded for raising alarm amongst the others.

Minerva would know, Hamlin reassured himself. Once she had finished her protective spell and came for the evening's celebrations and rites, he knew she would explain the birds' silence without him having to even ask the question. Such had always been her way. Even before they first kissed tenderly under the willow tree in that season long past—the night they had conceived Branwenn—he did not need to ask if he might make love to her. She had simply *told* him they would with a loving gesture and an adoring glance, drawing him close to her.

He knew Minerva had taken Branwenn with her to the trails above the chapel grounds. Branwenn was of the age to begin learning the rites, to take on the burden of her family. To be the protectors, the knights, of a regal, mysterious, and obscure valley.

"Be careful, Minerva," Hamlin whispered, as he walked closer to the water's edge. "Keep the girl safe." The shadows of the birds cloaked the river.

The only breath of life, of carefree innocence, belonged to the children. Their parents had brought them to the river thinking quite appropriately it would be another pleasant gathering, another celebration of a season's passing even if it had lost some of its original spiritual tones. Instead, they were witness to this strange phenomenon. This, though, did not matter to the children. They were still thrilled by the migratory spectacle, more so by its muteness.

Hamlin watched as his daughter's contemporaries, Calpurnia Covington and Lara Kempt, splashed their bare feet in the chilled autumn water. Two others joined them, the young Cather lad, Garet, and Darcy Crocker, a troublesome boy full of "sour puss," as Winifred would have put it. The boys teased the girls with slimy river weeds and wriggling, diabolical fingers. The girls replied in disgusted delight, though by Calpurnia's expression, the disgust was aimed more truly at the boys themselves than any repugnant plant they could wield. Hamlin wished Branwenn was there to play with them. She could do with some friends. Such a small creature as Branwenn should not face the world friendless.

It was the children who first took notice of the figure walking in faltering, stuporous lurches down to the beach from Black Hill. Darcy Crocker stood erect and stared with unsympathetic disgust as he raised his arm and silently pointed. Hamlin followed the invisible line that strung from the boy's finger. At the end of it was Minerva True. A rush of cries and screams rose in pockets from the crowd as they caught sight of her. Hamlin gasped and ran to her, nearly knocking down many a friend.

Minerva was beaten and dazed. Her eyes were glassy, her hair had lost its luster; her soul seemed flown. The beach crowd gathered around, whispering something-awfuls. Minerva's clothing was torn, her breasts lay bare to the cold air, and her right arm was bloodied and bruised. The flesh looked eaten away, flayed. Yet she did not cry in pain.

"Minerva!" Hamlin cried, rushing to hold her in his arms. A blanket was brought by one of the older women from a picnic site and draped over her. Hamlin helped her sit on a boulder, wrapping a tourniquet to staunch the flow of blood that trickled like a valley stream from her arm.

"What happened?" he pleaded desperately. "Are you all right? Where's Branwenn?" He failed to notice how his voice, the fear in it, shook the valley folk around him.

Minerva studied him as if he were a stranger. He had never seen her so unaware. More than the silent flight of the birds above, Minerva's silence spoke of horror and troubled times to come.

"Where's Branwenn?" Hamlin repeated, trying to focus her. The crowd listened closely.

"Branwenn," she whispered, and began quaking uncontrollably as if she were soon to spontaneously burst into flames. "She did not go willingly. It has that power now. It has grown stronger than I thought. I have failed to stop it. She did not go willingly to the grounds."

Hamlin's heart dropped. An icy prickle spread like rapid fire up his spine. Though he did not know his daughter very well—in fact, she was unaware of who her father was at all—she was still his daughter, an unbreakable connection. Hamlin slumped to the ground beside Minerva.

"I tried to stop her," Minerva continued, regaining some of her vitality. The throng of valley folk surrounded her, trying to hear her soft, trembling words through the drumming of their own heartbeats. "But her mind was too delicate, and the will of the chapel grounds too strong. Even as I looked she seemed to leap through the air, galloping through the trees in bounds. In my five steps, she was already down the hillside. 'Stop!' I cried. 'Branwenn, it's a trick!' But she didn't hear me. She couldn't. I sought help from a rain crow nearby, but even he could do nothing…"

Hamlin closed his eyes in grief and horror.

"I tried to get her back," she exclaimed, "but as I reached into the mist a putrid black vine of large, sharp thorns took hold of my arm and skinned it like a fish." She peered into Hamlin's eyes. "I screamed for her still, determined to go in after her. But then I saw…the preacher. Hamlin, old Dark Eyes walks!"

The crowd erupted in exclamations of panic. Parents yelled for their children to come to them, and they held them tight. What Minerva had just spoken was the stuff of nightmares.

"It gets stronger, though I don't know how," Minerva said. "Something feeds it, and I don't have the strength to stop it alone. It took Branwenn…." She shuddered, unwilling to ponder certain nightmarish outcomes, just this once avoiding a possible truth.

"We'll get her back," Hamlin said, his voice cracking under sorrow. "We'll get her back, Minerva. I promise. We'll destroy it once and for all." His words had a calming effect on the valley folk, but did little to alleviate his own concerns. He wanted to head to the chapel at once, but such rashness had caused nothing but calamity in the past.

She looked at him, pitying his resolve. "It's no use, my friend," she spoke. "The valley is lost. Mother True always said our fate was already sealed. There's nothing more we can…"

But as she spoke she caught sight of the four children Hamlin had watched earlier. An inkling, a prick of promise, pierced her mourning soul. Something about the children offered light, a possible road to a future reckoning.

Branwenn, I'm sorry….

Yes, there was light amongst the children. But darkness lay in wait there as well. The Imbalance. Yet in her state, Minerva was unable to discern from where either energy emanated. She was sure, however, that a reckoning would come after all. The ruined chapel under Black Hill and its dark parson had not the strength to defeat her tenacity. Even as she sat utterly devastated, she knew she would rise to fight again. She had to or Branwenn might forever be lost to the vagary of the chapel. The little girl was dead, but her soul might be rescued still.

"*They're gone!*" Darcy Crocker suddenly cried, pointing to the drab, gray sky. "*The birds are gone!*"

And they were. And the silence in their wake made the valley quake.

THE MONTHS passed. A solitary figure, that of a tall, slender woman in black, could be seen at the break of day every morning standing on the beach, staring down the mist that enfolded the chapel. It was an initiation of sorts for the few students of Greenbriar College who would come down the hill at dawn to catch sight of Minerva True. They would hide behind a boulder or a tree, studying the woman who seemed more a wraith than a human being, a phantom of the valley. And it was so. She faded from the lives of the valley folk, replaced by scattershot sightings and ever-growing mythologies. A slight apathy toward them nestled its way into her heart. This fantastic perception of Minerva True was not only propelled by her personal appearance when seen at dawn, standing obdurate, but by that of her surroundings as well. Those watching on certain mornings witnessed the rising sun clear a path through the vale of the chapel grounds. The mist would shrink from its rays, leaving the relics of Minerva's enemy naked and vulnerable. Those watching would see Minerva focus all her intent on the sickly patch of land, her eyes more compelling than the morning light.

Once the mist had cleared, the chapel revealed its unpardonable disrepair. The entire front wall had crumbled and splintered, exposing the guts of the abandoned house of worship, its rotten pews slowly disintegrating. Still, the young students who watched her as one would watch a circus freak failed to see the truth of what *she* saw; their vision not as strong as her own. Every morning at the momentary breaking of the mist, Minerva peered deep into the pulpit, to the altar and crucifix balanced across it, which had fallen when half of the roof had collapsed. The chapel yard had become a swamp of decrepit, mournful willows and moss trees, and a fallen bell, cracked. Long black vines crawled from beneath the chapel in every direction. Minerva held her arm when she challenged the chapel every dawn, still nursing the pain of the vines' tearing menace.

The brightest sunrise in the valley seemed cheerless without the birds, their songs and their chatter banished. Not even spring would return them that first year after the awakening, nor would many out-of-valley birds venture through in the winter months. No, Minerva knew they would not return. At least, not anytime soon. They had known, as smaller beings always seem to know, that danger was imminent. Perhaps the birds had been giving the valley folk signs of the approaching terror all along, but no one recognized them. Minerva admonished herself for not seeing the signs, for becoming as complacent as the rest. They were a yellow army of fools.

Oftentimes, through whatever challenge of weather, the figure of Hamlin Marsh could also be seen standing stoically with Minerva, if a few feet behind. His was the only company she ever had. Words never passed between them, nor the slightest hint of touch, but they seemed to share an understanding. They needed one another. Aside from their mourning, they simply struggled to survive as if they were the twin souls of the valley, one unwilling to let the other disappear completely.

THE NIGHT HAMMER

CALPURNIA WAS so shaken by the sight of Minerva coming from the dark places of Black Hill she stayed well away from that side of the valley for some time. She did not make the connection between the chapel and what had happened to Minerva. Calpurnia thought that in some way the old woman had brought down evil—that thoroughly undefined yet exacting notion—upon herself. At night, she hugged desperately at her Bible, believing it would suffice to protect her from the practices of Minerva and the other river folk. She felt sure they were the cause of all the upheaval. After all, she was raised the right way by her father, and things like this never happened to those who walked the right way. The valley folk had been led astray somehow. Even poor Lara.

Calpurnia had lived with Hamlin Marsh for a while now. His tiny cabin was a mere dot among the hills. But it stood a strong dot, and had weathered whatever had been put upon it. Though Hamlin tried to explain that Minerva had nothing to do with what was happening in the valley, Calpurnia refused to believe it. She thought it strange, too, that he grieved so for the midget Branwenn. What did he have to do with her? She supposed older folk cried that way for anyone. Calpurnia often opened her Bible right in front of Hamlin while he was talking to her and began reading. She wouldn't stop until he had left her alone. It was something infinitely more interesting than his conversation anyway. He was not her father, the limestone lord. He hadn't her father's strength, so she thought.

She noticed particular verses had stronger effects than others when she wanted him away from her. "*Get thee behind me, Satan*," she always read when Hamlin tried to convince her of things she was not ready to hear. Her guardian would immediately leave. Though, being in a cabin split into only two rooms by a stone fireplace, there was hardly space for him to go anywhere but outside.

She felt in command of her situation when she read; a pleasant warmth overtook her. She imagined at times that the Book was like a wishing star. She seemed to get whatever she desired if she asked at the right passage. But which passage was the "right" one proved ever a mystery.

Her hopeful suspicions about the power she held were confirmed not long after, on a cool afternoon as Calpurnia played with Lara in the lightly wooded area behind Hamlin's small cabin. The two girls were playing a game of giddily swinging one another in circles when Lara stopped suddenly, stumbling a little due to dizziness. She stared in delight as a tiny fox peeked out at them from the underbrush. The girls went searching, but were unable to lure it from where it remained hidden, watching.

"Oh," Lara moaned in disappointment. "I just wanted to care for it. Do you think it's lost its mommy? It was asking for help. I heard it, Calpurnia."

Calpurnia's mind raced back to the time in the fields of Walterhouse Manor when she had daydreamed. But this was no daydream. This was just an ordinary fox. "Do you want it, Lara? Do you really want it?"

"I do," Lara said, tears forming in her precious eyes. Lara had big eyes, like the coins Calpurnia's father used to flip between his fingers.

"Follow me," Calpurnia said, grabbing Lara's arm and pulling her inside.

She pulled the Bible from beneath her bed, its heaviness sliding on the floor. Lara marveled at the beauty of the Book. "Where did you find it?" she asked.

Calpurnia was pleased by her friend's admiration. "It was a gift," she replied. She opened the Book carefully, lovingly, its mass supported by their small, crossed legs as they sat side by side. Lara was the only other person Calpurnia would ever let touch her Bible. "We just need to find the right words," she explained.

Lara stared at her for a more pronounced explanation, but there was none to be had. Calpurnia was too preoccupied in examining the passages for the "right" one. She had now become quite familiar with the Book (it served as bedtime reading for her, the language surprisingly understandable to her young mind), so several phrases immediately came to mind, but which to choose? Lara sat simply entranced by the beautifully rendered pictures. Gold-touched illustrations of awe and the things, Calpurnia had said, that "God wants us to see." When she moved to touch the lovely art, though, Calpurnia brushed her hand away.

Finally, Calpurnia settled on a passage and spoke it fiercely: "And let them have dominion over—" She paused, and then continued. "—everything living that creepeth upon the earth."

Lara once more looked at her friend, puzzled, but Calpurnia smiled knowingly in return and closed the Bible, sliding it again beneath the bed. Lara followed her friend's lead, and they ran back outside. There, waiting for them, was the little fox. It leapt to Calpurnia like a playful pup, and the girls spent the rest of the day coddling it.

"Oh, thank you! Thank you!" Lara exclaimed as she petted the creature gently.

"Anything for you," Calpurnia replied. "You're my best friend, Lara."

Though the day's happiness was complete, the fox did not seem to want to go home with Lara. It desired to stay with Calpurnia instead. To keep her new pet, Lara picked it up so as to carry it back with her to the hinterland and her aunts' large house. The fox did not like this. No, not at all. It growled and scratched the girl angrily. She screamed and dropped it to the ground, whereon it fled into the woods. Calpurnia rushed to her best friend's side, cradling her, but keeping her hands clear of the frightening red scratches on Lara's arms.

"Don't worry, Lara," Calpurnia comforted her sad playmate. "Don't cry. You still have me. Who needs a dirty old fox anyway?"

When Lara had returned home, her aunts had noticed her scratches at once. Lara explained to them that she and Calpurnia had found a fox and had tried to befriend it. Kayla and Brit were furious. They weren't so much angry at their own niece, for, after all, she possessed a damaged mind, but at Calpurnia, who they believed should have known better.

"They are not to see one another for a week," Brit said as she and Kayla stood hand-in-hand at Hamlin Marsh's cabin door. Calpurnia stood behind Hamlin, this once thankful for his blockading presence.

"You should not play with the wild things, girl," commanded the other aunt sternly, gazing down at Calpurnia. "Wild things have wild minds."

Calpurnia thought the aunts dreadful. Kayla and Brit were identical in every way, from their cumbersome, out-of-date gowns, their tiny, round spectacles, and tightly wound hair to their emotionless voices. When they spoke, whoever they spoke to had to be watchful to see who addressed them, for they seemed to possess the same larynx.

"Calpurnia will not go near the hinterland for a week," Hamlin assured the sisters.

His answer was good enough for the aunts, and they turned around, wide like a wheel, and made their way home where Lara was obediently waiting. Calpurnia wanted to object, but she was frightened of the women. She stared at Hamlin pleadingly, but seeing his disapproving glance and knowing not even the Book could sway him, she ran to her bed and cried.

The next morning Hamlin found a tiny dead fox outside his door.

The week passed torturously slow for Calpurnia. Lara was her only true friend. None of the other children in the valley wanted anything to do with her, but this was fine because most of them did not interest her. Garet Cather and Darcy Crocker had come over once, thinking Lara was there and wondering if she and Calpurnia would want to play with them by the river, but the angry little girl turned them away and went back to her Book. The Book kept her up. She could not stop appreciating it. She would sneak a read when Hamlin had drifted off to sleep, stopping only when the strain became too much for her eyes.

When at last she was allowed to see Lara again, Hamlin came with her and urged her to first offer an apology for causing the aunts such concern. Calpurnia obliged reluctantly. If she didn't do as Hamlin wished she knew she would not see Lara for an even longer period of time. Her anger at the valley folk, and especially Kayla and Brit, was growing.

Even the aunts' home looked foreboding and undesirable to Calpurnia. It stood alone and friendless in the barren fields of the hinterland. Everything about the house resembled the women who resided within. It was painted a dark color, not black, but some shade more morbid and aged. The windows and doors were tall and thin like the house itself; it looked constipated and long-faced to Calpurnia. A circular tower rose on one side and at its top a large, condescending window peered out onto the hinterland with the haughtiness of a dethroned steward. There were no flowers or trees around the house, only golden grass and brown earth.

Calpurnia sat in the front parlor on a plush blue chair of exquisite velvet. Hamlin stood behind her. They would not be staying long. Lara and her aunts sat across from them on an equally lovely sofa. Calpurnia would have been furious if Lara hadn't greeted her with such a warm smile when they entered. Kayla and Brit were stiff and unmoving in their seats, peering at Calpurnia through their spectacles, their chins raised.

Calpurnia noticed what fine things they had for being such unreasonable, horrid people. Their sofas boasted the plushest material, their fine porcelain vases held the freshest flowers, the walls were decorated with gold leaf and floral prints, and their mantelpiece was carved as ornately as any she could remember from the city. The house bore an air of contempt. Contempt aimed directly at her, and it was masked by the scent of lilacs and roses. The grandfather clock—the tallest and thinnest clock ever made—clicked its golden tongue at her.

Hamlin encouraged her to apologize with a gentle nudge from behind. "I'm so sorry," she said, sounding rather unconvincing and rehearsed. "I didn't mean to cause any trouble."

As she spoke she avoided looking either of the two older women in the eyes—who could do that?—but instead focused on the linked hands between them. But as she looked, there was a slight jostle of arms between the aunts. Nothing so big as to be seen by anyone if they weren't focusing on the exact area to which Calpurnia had fixed her stare. Still, in a fleeting moment, the lace and black satin of the aunts' gowns revealed a horrific deformity. There was no separation between Kayla and Brit; they were linked eternally not only by sisterhood, but by flesh as well. Where fingers and lovely, feminine knuckles should have been was nothing but a continuation of smooth flesh, one aunt's arm flowing into the other's like stretched toffee, as if they were one person.

Calpurnia stood at once, turning her gaze first to Lara, then to Hamlin, and ran from the house without waiting for the aunts' acceptance of her apology. The aunts watched her run with indifference, as if they had expected as much. They gave one another knowing glances. Hamlin found Calpurnia in front of the house where she had stopped to ponder the nightmare within. Her eyes were wide in fear and disgust.

"Did you see?" she asked. "Did you see their hands?"

Hamlin took hold of her own trembling hand. "Kayla and Brit are just a little different. They have different trials to endure than we have."

"But their hands! They're monstrous. This whole valley is monstrous!"

"They're good women, Calpurnia. You must learn to look past what you first see." They began to walk across the hinterland back to the cabin. Calpurnia looked back at the house where Lara waved from the doorway, the shadow of the aunts behind her. "They have given permission for Lara to spend the night with you. Isn't that kind of them?

They don't want to see you separated either. But when you do wrong, you have to make it right."

Calpurnia was certainly happy that she would be seeing her friend again, but paid little attention to what had been said after that. She was worried for Lara now. One night away from her aunts' wretchedness wouldn't save Lara from having to see them every other night of her life, or living in their haughty house in the hinterland. Not only were they mean, but they were deformed and unnatural as well.

"Poor Lara," Calpurnia whispered. And it was decided right then that the aunts must leave the valley and that Lara must come and stay with her. When they were both old enough they could move into Walterhouse Manor together. Yes. Her decision was made. She squeezed Hamlin's hand.

If Hamlin imagined this a sign that she had begun to warm to him, he would soon be disappointed. Calpurnia had no desire to be Branwenn, and he would never again have the chance to be a father. She envisioned his loss formed in him an echoing ache that would not be healed until he died, a chamber hollowed and drawn.

Calpurnia had plans. Lara came to the cabin, but this was not simply a little girl's sleepover. This was a matter of future happiness. Calpurnia would make certain that Aunt Kayla and Aunt Brit left the valley and Lara would never need to go near them again. She felt certain Lara would be appreciative. She searched the Book for the right passage, her mind still flooded by anger at being forced to apologize. Apologies, like any other words, didn't mean a thing if one didn't put her heart into them. She needed something that would make the aunts leave and never return. They could move away to a city or another small town if they wished. Somewhere up or down river where other undesirables ambled.

One trick to the Book that Calpurnia had not figured out threatened her peace of mind concerning her plans. The wishes did not seem to have great staying power. There was a slight regression to everything. She was concerned that wherever the aunts moved, after a brief period they would return for their niece. After all, everything Calpurnia had demanded of the Book so far had been short term: Hamlin always returned to bother her again, and the fox had run off into the woods. Nothing had really stuck. She desperately hoped the Book would hear her plea, pity her plight. All she wanted was to save her very best friend from a nightmarish existence.

The two girls sat by Calpurnia's bed with the Book opened wide between them. They munched on popcorn Hamlin had made for them. He sat out on his steps, admiring the night. "This story," Calpurnia began, quietly enough that her voice would not carry through the window, "is one of my favorite stories ever! It tells of how God destroys two evil cities for their inhospitality to his angels."

"Sounds scary," Lara said, hugging herself tightly. A valley draft chilled her from the open window. The candle beside them on the floor flickered.

"Don't worry, Lara. I'm here. It all turns out for the best in the end."

And she began to read, her words taking on a breathless, quickening cadence. As she turned the first heavy, gilded page of the story, the breeze created by its fall joined that from the porch, and the outside air carried the page's draft off into the valley night. It brushed past glow flies and owls alike, collecting strength as it went. The breeze passed unnoticed by other homes and valley folk who were readying for another day's end. It carried leaves and scents on its way, harmless and unimportant. But then it caught a spark from Prichard Parma's nighttime metal working. The anvil and the hammer clanged and little eyes of flame came into being. The spark carried farther inland into the hinterland, where at last it entered an open window in the front parlor of Kayla and Brit Brennen-Blue's large home, alighting on the plush sofa Calpurnia had so admired that very day. The spark nearly went out with a black wisp of smoke, but a brief gust of wind encouraged its hunger and the spark became a flame. The flame lounged backward onto the sofa with seductive ease, and soon the room was alight.

By the time the aunts realized what was happening, beginning to smell the smoke, it was nearly too late. Yet they still could have descended the stairs from the second floor where they were readying for bed and escaped in time. *Time can be slowed or hastened, depending on perception.* The aunts began to argue, however, over what to save from the burning house, what treasures should they bring with them. Each wanted to go in a different direction and neither was willing to give in first to the other's stubborn suggestion.

"Mother's quilt in the lookout!" Kayla argued.

"Mother's wedding dress in the sitting room!" Brit countered.

It went on like this for some time, much to the flame's hungry pleasure. They pulled back and forth on one another, an impossible tug-of-war. Neither of the ladies was to get what they wanted, however, as the fire quickly began to climb the stairway toward them.

"Sister!" Brit exclaimed. "Sister, we are doomed!"

There were a few folk from the valley who had seen the brightness of flame from the river and come as quickly as they could to see if the aunts were safe. Yet when they reached the house it was already engulfed, but for the lookout. Such an old place, its outer wood so damaged, the fire easily feasted on the timbers. The house soon looked as if it were one huge ball of flame. The last anyone in the valley ever saw of Kayla and Brit Brennen-Blue was a stoic silhouette of two linked figures in the lookout's large window, a fiery glow surrounding them as they acquiesced to their fate.

The burnt ruins of the place would stand for some time after, and Calpurnia Covington would be there to comfort her friend Lara Kempt in her time of mourning.

PART II—
THE BIRTH OF THE THREE

THE HUNTER: A BRIEF SUMMARY

HE COULD barely be heard, so stealthy and accomplished was Darcy Crocker as he trod over fallen leaves, hunting for that prized buck with his handmade bow and arrow. He delved deeper into the unending density and growing darkness of the woods of Black Hill. The brooding boy had matured into a brooding, deep-chested young man. The valley folk—those who hadn't left out of fear of omens or been tempted by tales of finery up north—admired him, both for his hunting prowess and his impressive physical strength. There was no man around who could best him in a May Day wrestling match or an Autumnday log pulling contest. It was said he had even once managed to single-handedly pull a small home from a cavernous sinkhole with a simple rope. Both men and women swooned at his approach. Darcy found the attention a bit overwhelming and altogether irritating.

Despite his legendary strength and intimidating eyes, Darcy Crocker's life had unfolded much like a timid flower afraid of the frost. He was careful of most everything and everyone in his path, passing with a suspicious once-over glance and sometimes a very slight nod. His eyebrows furrowed in constant distrusting examination, a young man who had rarely been seen to smile. A smile would invite conversation.

A twig snapped beneath his bare feet, which were callused and hardened by years of shoeless hunting and rock-beach running. He heard his prey bound in another direction, and he turned in pursuit beneath the birdless trees. Every so often an out-of-valley hawk or sparrow could be heard, but they soon moved on. Though Darcy missed the calls of birds in the morning, their absence over the years had made hunting easier. No quail or other grounded bird would suddenly take flight, scaring his prey at the sound of his approach.

As had been expected, Darcy had married Lara Kempt three years before. In truth, it was more out of necessity than for any romantic feelings between the two. Darcy's only true companion would be Garet

Cather, but as a teenager he had learnt his lesson from caving in to those beautiful desires. His parents had grown concerned about his deep friendship with Garet, and soon after Darcy and Lara were "groomed" to marry, even if she wasn't entirely of the mental capacity to understand what that meant. She was, though, one of the only girls of his age left in the valley, and certainly the only one who didn't tremble and ogle at the sight of him. He knew that Garet was heartbroken by the marriage, but he could do nothing about it.

"If only you followed your own nature instead of their rules," Garet had bemoaned.

"If only my heart were my own," Darcy replied. He did not look into Garet's eyes when he spoke.

Garet fled Darcy and Lara's wedding, his eyes wells of hurt and love. He had disappeared for a few days into the forests of the valley until his hurt was assuaged. Even when he reappeared he would not come near Darcy for a while, as if some invisible barrier had been constructed between them.

He means to kill me, Darcy thought. *He means to break my heart.*

Soon after Darcy and Lara's marriage, Lara gave birth to a boy named Elijah. Garet was there at Darcy's parents' house for the birth, trying to come to terms with their strained ties. Lara had missed Garet. She often inquired as to why Darcy did not talk to Garet as much as he once did. Darcy had invited Garet to the birth. They were surrounded by arrows of grief. Above this pain, the birth was easy.

"A good, strong name," Darcy said of his son, Elijah.

"It's not a river name," Garet reminded him. "He is of the valley. He should go through the ritual and have a river name like you and me."

"That would do him little good," Darcy growled. *The art of avoidance is all about the eyes.*

After Elijah's birth they moved from their temporary residence at his parents' home into the battered, vacant shack on the side of Black Hill. Darcy noticed that Calpurnia, angry that he had married Lara in the first place, grew furious when he took her to his very own home, and on top of that impertinence, a home just below Walterhouse Manor. Without the birds to quell them, insect infestation became a troubling problem Darcy first had to deal with, but aside from that, he and his wife and child were quite content being alone among the whispering woods.

Between the two of them, hardly a word was spoken, and Elijah was a strangely mute baby. He never cried or whimpered for attention. He stared with a wide-eyed amazement at everything, as if the world had left him speechless. Darcy tried to play with the child, but he was never very good at it. He couldn't make his voice go shrill in that baby talk way, and sounded like a grunting bear when he tried. Still, Lara was ever-attentive and loving. She was a good woman even if Darcy did not love her the way a husband was supposed to. He respected her, but never touched her affectionately unless she asked it of him.

Darcy's only reservation about living in the shack—a creation of mismatched wood, separated into rooms by walls from other places—was the knowledge that somewhere in the forest, behind overgrown vegetation, lived Minerva True, the witch. The trail to her cottage had long since been lost, taken by the will of the forest. The elf-paths could not be found. She was never seen anymore, but Darcy resented the thought that she still performed her fiendish rites and devilry so near him and his son. Perhaps it was she who had taken Elijah's voice.

Some time after Darcy and Lara were married, Garet Cather and Calpurnia Covington had been joined in a commitment ceremony presided over by Hamlin Marsh. Darcy didn't understand why Calpurnia had suddenly agreed to be with Garet. She had never expressed any feelings for him other than tolerance and vague friendship, and Garet certainly had no interest in her. Darcy wondered if it was an attempt at revenge against him. If so, it had worked. He knew he had no right, but he detested Calpurnia for joining herself to Garet. She could never appreciate the gentle soul inside the man.

"We're the only Godly folk here," Darcy once remarked to Lara. Theirs was a religion in its infancy.

Though the real world's God had made his way into the valley at last, his worshipers were still in the minority. They kept secret their rituals, whereas the other river folk were more open and free about theirs. Calpurnia had, in fact, once worshiped the same God as Darcy Crocker. She had come to the valley as a child worshiping that God, but he had seen a subtle change in her over the years. He wondered now if she believed in anything at all.

An adult and soon to be a mother, Calpurnia had finally moved into Walterhouse Manor atop Black Hill with Garet, high above Darcy and Lara's meager shack. Darcy saw this as but another attempt by Calpurnia to keep an eye on Lara. That was tolerable, as long as her eyes never fell upon Elijah.

Calpurnia gave birth to her son just a little after Elijah was born. It was then that Minerva True made a rare appearance to the few other residents of Black Hill. She was called to Walterhouse Manor by Garet, against Calpurnia's wishes. The birth was a hard one, the labor proving intense and taxing. Calpurnia felt nothing but anguish and resentment throughout. The midwife was a young thing from near the river, more fearful of Calpurnia than of any complications related to the birth. Slapped and clawed until she bled by the expectant mother, she fled weeping from the house. Garet had placed a whispering request on the wind, and Minerva came.

Calpurnia's rage was quelled by one good slap from Minerva, and once the tension was released, the baby came more freely. Calpurnia listened to Minerva. She did as she was told, reeling from the shock of the slap. Even when the older woman lit some herbs and made some tea, Calpurnia did not resist.

The child was named Leith soon after the birth, at a ceremony by the river attended by very few. For what did Calpurnia care about the child's name or how he received it?

"She gives your boy a river name," Darcy gasped, taking Garet aside as they stood by the calm water. "The congregation won't look kindly on this. They have rules. You know this. Even if you're not a man of our God, you will be shunned." Then he lowered his voice. "Do you not remember what happened to me?"

"I remember it too well," Garet replied, his words tinged with bitterness and grief. "Minerva is a good woman and says the name will bring him strength. The two of us were named in the same manner."

"But I shrugged off that name," Darcy replied. "You can as well. It's not too late." He was genuinely concerned. The new religion was growing. It would not be unheard of for Garet and the other nonbelievers to be run out of the valley.

Garet's expression registered his friend's concern, but confirmed his refusal to abandon his own convictions for those of another. Darcy knew then he would not win this battle. The boy would have a river name.

Darcy paused and listened to the quiet of the forest. His eyes scavenged the dark, taking note of the shades of light. Though it was but midday, the trees let little sunlight through their robust limbs. This allowed his memories to nearly overtake him, his mind prone to wander when he hunted in the woods of Black Hill.

Finally, he heard movement on the other side of the brush. The hunter sprinted after his prey, easily dodging the lower limbs of trees, leaping swiftly over fallen vegetation. He cleared everything in his path with admirable skill, his eyes intent on his purpose as he was led deeper into the dark. The chirps of bugs grew louder. As long as he ran, as long as there was some other goal, the memories and disappointments would not harass him.

His prey disappeared again into the undergrowth. Silence. Even the bugs hissed to an intermission. It was as though the young stag had come to a complete halt and was waiting on the other side of a wall of greenery. Darcy stopped abruptly, considering his surroundings, controlling his breathing. Black Hill could never be totally known. Darcy had lived all his life in and around it and still had not seen everything there was to see about the forest. It harbored countless tricks and secrets.

There was not a sound to be heard. Darcy approached the thick wall of rich, green ivy and fern leaves the stag had vanished into and, with the tip of his readied arrow, pushed the ever-changing forestry aside. Peeking through, he caught sight of a circular clearing, in the center of which stood the unmistakable lost earthen cottage of Minerva True. His pupils dilated and adjusted, shocked by the discovery as much as the new yet still dim light. Without meaning to, he had somehow run onto an elf-path, and it had led him here. It seemed something of an impossibility. One does not simply accidentally wander into magic.

He had only heard the cottage in the circle wood described once, as a boy, when Garet had stumbled upon it. Minerva had let the children venture freely on the paths in those days. They were playfully termed pixie-walks then. Darcy had never seen the cottage. His parents had warned him against even so much as thinking of Black Hill, as if it were host to demons that might vomit from its top any day, like a volcano. After all these years, the place still looked as Garet had described it. Quaint and simple, but fantastic as well. Round windows and a door blinked out from the large mound of earth, itself the shape of an opened eye. An herb garden crowned the top of the cottage mound, and other gardens surrounded Minerva's abode: some with plump vegetables, others with strange mounds of stone. A modest water well stood to the side of a walkway, a dark wooden pail sitting on its ledge.

Darcy recognized the figure of Minerva True emerging from behind the cottage, and there beside her stood the stag he had been chasing. He remembered now the friendly deer of the forest, the Breed that Minerva and the River Dwellers had been said to gather and raise. He had played with many of Minerva's deer on the rocky beach many times with the other children, but hadn't seen them since childhood. He had been hunting one of these gentle creatures, and that thought made him ashamed. The most brooding of men often have the biggest hearts.

Minerva glided over the fine grass and wild flowers like a faerie gracing the land with virtue. She still appeared unworldly after all these years, a sure sign of her practice of the dark arts, Darcy thought. Minerva only looked to be around middle age, though it was common knowledge she was much older. As old as she was, one would have expected to see wrinkled skin and other unmistakable signs of the passing years, yet only her silver hair gave any hint of her true age, and still this was discounted because she had *always* had silver hair. He could not reconcile what he had been told about her by his parents and others with what he knew in his heart.

Her arm remained ravaged-looking and scarred from that day years ago when she had come down to the beach. Darcy closed his eyes and winced at the thought of that day. The day Branwenn had disappeared. The day the birds had left.

He watched Minerva as she began speaking in low hushes to the stag, crouched to the ground as if eye contact might make it understand her words. Having seen enough, and having lost any desire for the hunt, Darcy slipped away from the wall of vines and crept off into the blackness of the dense forest. He would find his way back to Elijah and Lara without a prize. He would leave the stag be; he would leave Minerva alone.

ONCE CERTAIN she was no longer being watched, Minerva draped her black shawl over her head and walked into the woods. The stag remained behind like an observant friend. She was led along the elf-paths without needing to think of course or direction. The touch of Being was thick on the elf-paths; the connection to all, uncomplicated. Minerva glided along the forest floor, her long, dark mourning gown trailing behind her like peacock feathers on the moss-masked path. She rarely wore shoes, and the moss sent cool, velvet refreshment throughout her body. Above her, a familiar whisper and scratch floated through the limbs of the imposing arbors. Minerva felt it encircle her, wrapping around her like an infant's blanket. She smiled at the touch of the welcomed presence.

"Good day, Mother," she whispered to the breezy ambience.

The air gathered itself into loops and whirls, replying in syllables too secret for anyone but Minerva to understand. "Too many have been taken," it said. The voice was then carried away, flying like a bird higher into the foliage, looping around the trees once again in a wind-inspired echo.

"Yes," Minerva agreed, solemnly. "Too many of our Breed have been taken, but the young hunter Darcy is not the one taking them."

"No. You know what takes them."

Minerva missed her mother's voice, her *real* voice, and she missed the sight of the woman who spoke it. *Grief weighs the same as the heart. That is why one can so easily fill the other.*

"Yes. It's the same thing that has taken many a Passion, leaving their bones scattered about the fringes of the chapel grounds. Like Branwenn, it is my fault, my failing. Now I fear my heart is too weak to be of any use to the valley."

Mother True sighed her compassion along the forest path. "You have done your best, Minerva. More good than you know. You fight an ever-growing enemy. It grows by the blind will of the world. It claims the folk of other regions as well, but here in the valley you have saved many men from their demise. Do not doubt it."

Minerva's constant guilt at her failings was appeased a little by Mother True's reminder. In the fifteen years since Branwenn had vanished into the mist, Minerva had indeed been able to warn many travelers and vagrants from the chapel. There had been only a few lost, and so the power of the place was staved. Minerva wondered why the chapel grounds had not at once grown stronger at the taking of her daughter. Branwenn was of a powerful lineage after all. There was both appreciation and grief in this inquiry. She was thankful that the chapel had not suddenly grown more powerful, but she also realized that because this had not happened she had not been a very good teacher to Branwenn in the secrets of the valley. For if she had been, the valley would certainly be devastated by now, Dark Eyes having used that knowledge to his advantage.

Still, the influence of the chapel was growing. Minerva could feel the tug on the mind of the valley. This became evident when poor Rupert Toots rose from his bed one early summer morning and walked in slumber to the marshy grounds. Minerva was on her perpetual watch. Yet even as she tried to stop him, she knew the draw of the chapel was too strong. Poor Rupert pushed her to the ground, and by the time she had risen to her feet his waking screams were already fading behind the mist. Dark Eyes the preacher had minions now. Minerva could see their movement through the fog, crawlers that clawed along the earth like diseased men creeping about on their hands and knees. She knew who they were, of course. She had seen at least two of them fall into the darkness many years before; they were no longer human at all. Now, even entering the chapel grounds meant something far more terrifying than death.

But the living were not the only beings Minerva watched out for. The dead, too, those who did not cross the river, walked the world and needed a sentinel. She knew the truth about their wanderings. They did not seek to haunt the valley as many people thought. They were not the bogeymen of children's stories. In fact, the dead were mostly unaware of the living, just as the living could not see the dead. *Perhaps the dead tell stories of their own.* There were, of course, exceptions to every rule, and Minerva would have to warn those few exceptions about the chapel ground: "Those who enter there never leave." And most all of the spirits listened to her. She was a River Dweller.

"Oh, Mother. I'm so tired," Minerva sighed, feeling a ray of sun break through the leaves of the giant trees and warm her skin. "I am getting older, and things are getting harder. Much too hard for a lonely old woman."

"It is the burden our lineage bears," came the reverberating voice. Not chiding, but reminding.

Minerva nodded as she remembered Mother True bearing more than her share of burdens. Even as she bandaged lost souls and rescued folk from darker demons, even as she had lost Ingrid to someone else's foolish pride, she had cared for the ailing Widow Lone—her spark, her reason to be, her one love outside of Minerva and Ingrid.

"*Widow Lone.*"

The name lilted through the air like a melancholy sonnet. All the valley knew the tale of the Widow and her son Lucifer. The trees caught the words and cradled them. And that was how it had always been. The trees held the truths of the world. They were the keepers of secrets. That was one of the first lessons Mother True had ever taught Minerva: the Memory of Trees. In their branches and leaves and harsh, cracked bark lingered the essence of everyone who had ever gone before. The Being. Minerva hoped for the day it would be possible to release Branwenn and the others caught in the chapel grounds into the Memory of Trees. She couldn't cry anymore over this though. It would take too much from her, depleting her of the vigor she needed for the battle that was surely to come. A battle that felt more imminent than it had in years.

She reached the old tree on the bluff at the edge of Greenbriar College. The walk from Black Hill to College Hill was becoming more tiresome for her. Her knees had started to ache just recently, reminding her of the vindictiveness of time. Minerva rested her shoulder against the tree as she looked over the river valley, a river valley that would go on without her, one way or another. Did her efforts truly matter in the end? A hue of hopelessness set in, the nagging fear that she would not be able to continue alone.

In a hoarse whisper, from somewhere in the limbs of the tree, she heard: "Do not despair, my girl. Help is coming."

THE PURPOSE OF ANGELS

"IF WE say it together, we are married."

Those words he had spoken to Darcy came back to Garet, heartbreaking in their clarity. Garet was thinking too deeply on memories, traveling Black Hill Road, now a young man, a ranger as his father had been. It was his duty to keep watch on things on Black Hill. His sword, the sword of his father, hung fastened to his belt. Three years before, beneath these very trees, Garet Cather had promised a lifetime to Darcy Crocker. Now it was Darcy's twenty-first birthday. Three years down and nothing proven. They were to have a dinner tonight, Garet and Darcy, Lara and Calpurnia, but that sworn devotion of years past would not be acknowledged at the table.

"Just say it with me and no one but the two of us will know," Garet remembered whispering. It had become a plea, not the romantic gesture he had originally imagined. He hated the way that moment twisted in his mind, like a cracked mirror. Did his bottom lip twitch when he had said it? He had the faintest memory that it had.

Darcy had held Garet's hand to his chest. "God will know."

"No, he won't. These trees will protect us from your angry God."

Garet's eyes glistened thinking back on what occurred next. He forgot his duty as a ranger for once and leaned back against a thick tree, remembering, holding on to the hilt of his sword.

"I love you, and will forever," they had both whispered. The gentleness of the words coming from Darcy's unsmiling face were like the light at the Beginning.

Garet spoke the words aloud once more, now three years hence and alone in the forest. He turned around to feel the moss of the tree's bark on his forehead. The bugs were especially loud in the forest. More memories came to him. He cradled his hand, letting his thumb glide gently over his ring.

"Remember when we were kids?" Darcy had asked, having brought him back to the sheltering trees, the God-shielders, a week after their declaration. "Remember when you almost fell off the cliff trying to get that stone on Autumnday? The day Branwenn...."

Darcy pulled a dirty cloth from his pocket and unfolded it. Held within was the very stone Garet had tried to obtain and had almost died for. "I had forgotten exactly where it was," Darcy said. "It took me a while to find it."

He slid the stone into Garet's hand, but looked away. He could not see Garet cry, not even tears of joy. An avalanche can occur with the slightest drop of water. Garet knew this and so waited to speak until he was over the initial emotional hill. "It's the best gift I've ever gotten," he finally managed, unsuccessful in his attempt to stifle the strain in his voice.

Garet asked the metalworker Prichard Parma to shave the stone and make two rings from it, a simple design, emerald surrounded by a gold band. Darcy would not want anything more extravagant than that. Garet wondered, though, if Darcy would wear the ring at all. Would he worry about explaining it to others? Who would he need to explain it to? His parents never came to see him, nor he them now that he lived on Black Hill. Still, Darcy was stubborn in his ways. To Garet's surprise, however, after he had gifted the ring to Darcy, the brooding one had worn it every time they had seen one another privately. This in some way made up for their lack of intimacy.

Snap!

Garet heard a sound above him and returned his hand to the hilt of his sword, wiping the tear from his cheek with his shoulder. The treetops reached so high that some could not even be seen through their neighbor's wide-reaching limbs. Garet stepped farther from the road and into the forest, still staring skyward. The bugs quieted, and he listened intently for any more sounds of breakage. His first thought was that a squirrel or woodland creature was springing limb to limb, but the sound was too heavy for that. Then there was a splintering noise; something was breaking through the foliage as it fell. Leaves and branches tumbled to the ground in front of him, and then a great whooshing crash reverberated as a large mass nearly fell on top of him. The fallen leaves were lifted into the air again by the *whoosh* and through them Garet saw a figure lying flat on the forest floor, two enormous black-violet wings spread out around it. Garet's heart pounded as he approached, readying his sword for a fight. The forest of Black Hill had never shown him anything as strange as this before. The notion of the preacher crossed his mind, as well as any number of bogeymen and snovelfarks.

Garet had not gotten very close before the creature rose to its feet and cradled itself with the large wings, the effort making a great clap in the air. Loose, downy feathers floated about Garet. The two stared at one another anxiously for a moment. Garet saw before him the strangest of men, though undeniably beautiful in his nonconformity. His thick hair was the same shimmering black-violet as the wings that now peeked majestically from behind his bare shoulders; his skin had a faint tint of blue to it; his eyes were black, no whites visible. His stare proved one of curiosity, not of hate or harm, and this gave Garet some relief, for he considered himself a good judge of character. The individual who had fallen from the treetops cocked his head quite like a puppy and held his mouth agape as he examined Garet.

"Who are you?" Garet said forcefully. "Where do you come from?"

The strange man at first cooed like a dove, but then answered: "I am Azrael. I am not the chapel. No fear."

"Where do you come from?" Garet repeated, his hand still on the sword. He controlled his fear well; that was the first lesson for any who wished to become a ranger.

The man who called himself Azrael looked up to the treetops and cooed inquisitively. "I fell. You are not supposed to see me. I wanted to get a better look at you, but I lost my balance. I have never lost my balance before. It's very strange to fall. Do you fall often?"

"You were in the tree? All the way up there?"

"Yes. Not just me, though. There are others. Angels watch from the treetops. We watch from anywhere there is height. Others are watching now."

The forest was quiet around them. Even the bugs seemed wary to interrupt the conversation.

"Watching? What are you watching?" Garet was not yet convinced of the angel's intent.

Azrael cocked his head to the side again. "We are watching you. We are watching humans. We are always watching humans."

"Why?"

"We are curious about you. Again, we always have been. We learn, but we never learn it all. You are layered and so different. We know we are linked to you, but we do not understand how. We seek to understand."

"You've been watching us?" Garet asked.

"A very, very long time, you might say. Though time is a matter of opinion."

Garet carefully stepped closer to the angel. "So, you see everything? You witness it? If that's true, then you see what is happening to the valley from up there. Why do you not help?"

"We cannot interfere. It is not our purpose to do so, as far as we know. We watch. We wait. That is the purpose of angels, as far as we can see." He parted his wings a little, sensing that Garet was not as frightened or concerned anymore. "Only after you leave the flesh can we help you. Then you become something more comprehendible to us. I have led many across the river."

"Are you an angel of death? Darcy has mentioned an angel such as this."

"I am Azrael," the angel replied as if this were all the explanation Garet needed.

Garet smiled. "As curious as you find me, that is how I find you."

Azrael imitated his smile and made his bird sound again. "Maybe we could learn from each other someday. It would be an interesting conversation."

"When you lead me across the river?"

Azrael nodded. "It is not a sad thing to cross the river." He cooed excitedly. "It is a glorious thing. Though, some souls cannot know it because I have lost them."

"I don't understand. Why have you lost them?"

"They have vanished before I could get to them." This saddened and perplexed the angel. His eyes lost their curiosity and became grief-stricken. His great wings seemed to sag, losing some of their vitality. "My sight of them dims."

Garet knew at once what was behind the lost souls: the chapel.

"If you see my lost souls will you tell them to look to the trees?" Azrael asked hopefully.

Garet nodded his head in agreement and Azrael smiled again. A wind swept through the treetops, and the angel peered upward and cooed. "They are calling me back," he said. "They will be most intrigued by what I have experienced. Very few ever have contact with a human until after they have passed."

"You're leaving?" Garet was disappointed by this. He could have spent the whole day beneath the trees, picnicking with angels. He wanted to learn more. "You could stay a little while longer, couldn't you?" He let go of the hilt completely.

"I'll be watching. I'll be seeing you." He glanced to Garet's sword. "Keep good care of that. It will be most important one day."

The angel Azrael then spread his glimmering wings, exposing a nude but featureless body, and leapt into the air, causing a great storm of leaves and twigs. He was gone before Garet could look for him, vanished once more into the treetops with the other angels. Garet felt his sword with both excitement and concern. The Angel of Death was watching the valley.

Onto the Chapel Grounds

ELIJAH AND Leith lay together in the bed, just as they were an hour earlier when she had last checked on them. The little ones had neither tossed nor turned. Though there was no light in the small bedroom of Darcy Crocker's cabin—the lone bedroom window faced the immense black forest—aided by the candle flame in the adjoining room, Calpurnia could see the forms of the two small boys huddled against one another. The singular sound of their tiny breaths would make angels sigh in admiration. She oftentimes wondered if she were ever meant to be a mother. Her partnership with Garet was nothing more than a strategy. The truth was, she didn't feel maternal. Leith could be pleasant enough, but he was a nuisance at times. He, like his father, was a stranger who could easily wear out what diminutive welcome she gave him. And Elijah Crocker? Though he was but a baby, Calpurnia felt a nagging bitterness toward him. What mother would feel that way toward a child? But he was, after all, Darcy's son, and Calpurnia's contempt toward Darcy for marrying Lara was ever pressing and often overwhelming. She didn't believe any woman would react differently in her place. A handful of slights when given in the right measure lead everyone to the same place in the end.

The previous week, when Lara had journeyed up the hill to Walterhouse Manor to tell Garet and Calpurnia of the birthday dinner she was planning for Darcy, something had snapped. Calpurnia's jealousy—the fact that Lara, who still looked so lovely and fragile, would care enough to make Darcy Crocker a special dinner—why, the idea began to consume her. With Lara beaming before her and excitedly detailing what she would make for Darcy, how the evening would be perfect with his favorite dishes and ale, it was too much for Calpurnia. Three years of too much. Though Calpurnia smiled and nodded to the plans as they were explained to her in the Great Hall, she boiled inside. Lara left with a gentle kiss on the cheek and a concerned expression.

"Why, what's the matter, Calpurnia? You look frightened," Lara said. She still spoke slowly and almost childlike. Slow-wit, dimwit, dimly-lit rooms.

"Oh, no, Lara. Frightened is the one thing I am not," Calpurnia replied in a glib manner. When she, from the Great Hall's large window, had seen Lara coming up the road from the forest she had thought her friend was simply coming to visit. She had thought Lara was at last taking time just for *her.* Instead, Lara had spent the entire afternoon speaking of the dinner and her special little, voiceless Elijah. Calpurnia thought of the Book as she watched Lara leave. She thought of the strength she had felt when she first found it. Even as she waved good-bye to Lara from the porch of Walterhouse Manor she began to reassociate herself with passages. She hadn't turned its pages since the night years earlier when Kayla and Brit Brennen-Blue had perished in the fire. She had begun to fear the Book that night. She feared its skewed choices in granting her wishes. The temptation to use it again had been strong, but she had managed to suppress the urge.

"But she is mine," Calpurnia convinced herself. And in her head the golden leaf pages turned one by one.

She climbed the old stairs to her room, Winifred's room—she and Garet slept separately most of the time—and opened the beautiful Bible that lay imposingly, majestically on the bureau. All these years it had become like a museum piece to her: admired from afar but left untouched. To touch it felt wrong, like sin, but it felt so good as well. Like a long breath before a shattering scream. She opened it carefully and turned the pages for the passage the moment required. It was in her mind already, just waiting. *Imagine that.* Calpurnia was intent on Lara's release from Darcy. Let him lose interest in her. Let the forest swallow him whole. Let a plague upon an apocalypse drive him to his knees. She remembered a story from the Book about a wise king who settled a dispute between two women over a child. He did this by threatening to cut the boy in half, right down the middle, giving each of the quarreling women an equal portion of it.

It seemed at the time an appropriate scripture.

She walked away from past frustrations for the time being and back to the small front room of the shack where the candlelight trembled. At the rough and uneven wooden table—a throwaway piece, but not without use—sat the trio of Lara, Garet, and Darcy, merrily discussing the past and hoping for a more favorable future. It was always a fact that when they got together, the Now came up empty-handed and forgotten until the Now became the past. The three at the table seemed to lose some of their passion for conversation at Calpurnia's return.

"I suppose," Darcy spoke, the constant specter of reservation in his eyes, "as far as birthdays go, this is an important one." He ran his palm over the flickering flame of the candle at the table's center. A night moth drawn to the flame—some dead writer's metaphoric epiphany—cracked and fizzled, having flown too close.

"Twenty-one," Garet nodded. "I'm right behind you, my friend." Every word he spoke to Darcy might as well have been *love, love, love*. Garet clasped his ring hand.

"Listen to you two!" Lara teased, perhaps a little too loudly. "Talking like old men whose best years are behind them! What do you think of that, Calpurnia?"

Calpurnia sat stiffly beside Garet, leaning back into shadow. She said nothing, only stared across the table at her best friend. The dim light hid the resentment in her dark eyes. Garet touched her arm gently, sensing something was amiss, but she shrugged his touch away.

"There's a ring around the moon," Garet said quietly, reinforcing the mood Calpurnia had brought with her. "It speaks of bad omens," he said with a wink to lighten things.

"Meh!" Darcy groused. "Omens! That's superstitious nonsense. The sort kindled by ol' Minerva True. It's far from righteous, any of it. 'Do not suffer a witch to live.'" He took a drink of beer from his stoneware and set it down hard on the table. The empty china plates and used silverware Lara had borrowed from Calpurnia for the dinner rattled and jumped. Darcy's emerald ring winked in the candlelight.

"For once, I'm in agreement with you, friend," Calpurnia said, still with a hint of seated animosity.

"Calpurnia!" Garet objected. "You would both rally for the death of a River Dweller?"

"It says so," she defended. "It says exactly that in the scriptures. I remember the very verse." She had realized long ago that her interpretation of the scriptures was usually very different than that of others, so it was nice to have some corroboration over something every now and then.

"Leave poor Minerva alone," Lara pleaded with Darcy. "She's been through so much. Let's not speak of these matters. Not on this night. It's your birthday."

Don't cry for that woman, Calpurnia screamed in her head. *Don't you dare!*

Darcy, heavily intoxicated already, ignored her request and continued. "I came upon her today while I was out on the hunt."

"You found Minerva?" Calpurnia leaned into the light. "How did you find the cottage?"

"'Twas the stag that led me to her. Doubt if I could make it back there on my own being that the elf-paths don't open to just anyone. Don't see why I would want to. But it was just as I remember you telling me, Garet, 'cept more overgrown. The path has been wiped clean as if it were never there at all. I was moving through weeds and brush."

"So, the Breed, it still thrives?" Garet inquired, sliding forward in his eagerness to hear more. He swatted at a bug flying about his head. The infestation since the absence of birds was at times intolerable.

"I only saw the one, but, yes, I would wager the Breed is still strong in number. Not as strong as they were, though." He paused, taking another long drink. "She talks to those creatures as if they were snakes in the garden, you know what I mean?"

"Darcy is speaking of a story from his Bible," Lara explained, proud that she understood him. She curled up to his shoulder.

"I know of the garden story," Calpurnia nodded, watching Lara intently.

"And the woman doesn't age," Darcy grumbled. "There's mischief there."

Garet chuckled. "Now you do indeed sound like one of the old men from the valley, confused and complaining. Living lives of rumor."

"I have a very hard time believing Minerva is anything but a gentle soul," Lara countered her husband. "She's never harmed anyone. She only wants to help."

"Remember the other day," Garet spoke up on the subject, surprising even himself, "when Leith disappeared?"

Calpurnia was shaken from her angry trance. "Disappeared?" she remarked. "But I thought you had taken him for a walk."

Garet stared blankly at her momentarily, and then looked away. The candle became the light at the center of the world; they were all in the suffocating dark. "He wandered into the woods. Too far," Garet continued, trying to avoid making judgments or eye contact with Calpurnia. Instead, he stared at the candle flame. "Down by the chapel grounds."

Lara gasped and held to Darcy tightly. "That's where you found him?" Darcy asked.

"I didn't find him at all. Minerva did," Garet answered. He took a large gulp. Calpurnia simmered in the heat of embarrassment. "It was as if he had been called... like Rupert Toots. But he was rescued just in time."

"Oh, Calpurnia," Lara said, tears in her eyes. She reached across the table to her friend's hands.

Calpurnia appreciated the attention, her resentment assuaged for the time being. She smiled, taking Lara's hand. This was what Calpurnia longed for, to have Lara dote on her. If things were allowed to be just this way forever—*oh, what joy!* She knew, though, to hide her feelings for Lara. She had seen the example made of Darcy in his passions for Garet. She and Lara would not meet that same dishonor. Theirs was something more pure than that of their husbands, so she thought.

"Minerva said she had sensed a *walker*," Garet continued. "That's what she calls them, the ones drawn to the grounds: *walkers*. So she went to the chapel grounds and caught Leith just as he set foot to the earth of the place. She snatched him from it just in time. She said it took all her strength. The vines tore at his clothes."

Calpurnia sniffed in show. She did not believe there was anything truly evil about the chapel grounds. That was all just a story made up by the valley folk. But she would play along.

"He toddles with a limp now. Who knows if he'll recover? No greater infirmity." Garet sat stone still. "I suppose," he said to Calpurnia, the ale to his lips, "a toddle can look like a limp, and that's why you haven't noticed."

"Your son is strong," Darcy consoled.

"He will be a ranger," Garet replied.

Calpurnia watched Garet. "But I thought... I mean, I didn't realize," she said, letting her gaze fall to her hands, still clasped in Lara's.

"I came upon Minerva with him as soon as I realized he was gone. They were struggling up the road," Garet said, resuming the tale. "Minerva marveled at the fact that Leith wasn't more impaired. '*He's strong*,' she said. '*Stronger of will than many a grown man.* '" He stared into the blue light of the flame. "And she looked so knowing when she spoke. As if there were a purpose to what had occurred." After a moment Garet's eyes rose to meet Darcy's.

"Strange," Darcy replied, "that she should be the one to find him, don't you think? Maybe it is she who has a purpose for the boy. She could have lured him there herself."

"She saved our son," Garet answered. He folded his hands before him on the table.

Darcy spoke plainly, "She's a witch."

"Yet that which haunts this valley doesn't come from the ritual places of the River Dwellers, does it? It resides among the ruins of a church. Do you not find *that* odd? Is not the very idea of devilry an invention of your beliefs?"

Darcy snarled and returned his gaze to the candle. "There is evil, my friend," he mumbled. "Evil in the guise of harmless folk. Even respected folk. There is a devil among us."

"*Evil* is an overused and old-fashioned word," Garet said, ending the argument. "I miss the days when such talk did not enter our conversation."

The evening ebbed into a drowsy, drunken quiet. None but the candle flames danced. The dark turn of the conversation had bled the night of its levity.

Just before dawn broke, as the sky held its hopeless state of extreme darkness, Calpurnia retrieved Leith from where he slept beside the mute child Elijah. She felt something like accusation toward the child. As Leith slept tightly snuggled in Calpurnia's arms, she encouraged Garet to come along home. She held Lara's gaze once outside the shack, as if she might say something.

"Yes, Calpurnia?" Lara inquired from the doorway where she stood leaning against Darcy.

"Nothing," Calpurnia surrendered. She wanted to tell her to be careful. She wanted to tell her about the Book and what she had asked it for. But the cacophony of night bugs drowned her confidence. Besides, Lara had most likely forgotten all about the Book and wouldn't believe her. "Get some sleep," Calpurnia chose to say instead. She turned and, with Garet, headed up the winding gravel road to the old stead at the top of the hill.

Lara and Darcy watched their friends as far as the dark would permit. It seemed the night forest engulfed them almost instantly. The only light was that from the candle inside the shack. Lara giggled as Darcy's strong, callused hands tickled her sides. She felt the pressure of his sex as he grinded into her backside. His thoughts digressed to younger days, wet afternoons by the river with Garet. He recalled the glint of Garet's ring and remembered his own identical band. He was torn in two halves. Every night he had to live without Garet, every night he had to swallow his heart. How would he ever reconcile his opposing thoughts?

The call of the night forest was too strong to ignore. It pulsed with melancholy nostalgia. Under the ringed moon, Darcy and Lara danced in drunken gaiety, life seemingly slowed to the point of dreams. In each other they had found true friends if not romantic ideals. Darcy could envision himself with Garet instead of Lara in the woods without worry of punishment, the darkness cloaking any indiscretions. Darcy felt free this birthday night. Under the cover of the trees, the world was alight with the beetles of early morn and the pure, glowing white of morning's hope. Day's birth.

Darcy chased Lara about, catching up with her under behemoth oaks or twirling her on the great roots of a gnarled cypress. She laughed as he caught her beneath a drowsy willow, its leaves dripping with dew, and kissed her roughly. She stared into his dark eyes and, with a wink of mischief, pushed herself from him, laughing once again as she ran deeper into the forest. She was a slither of light vanishing into the woods.

"Catch me, Darcy!" He heard her voice giggling from the dark.

Yet as he ran after Lara, Darcy felt an uneasiness. Though dark enveloped the world around him, and the drink had impaired his sense of direction greatly, neither was the cause of this sudden disquiet. He felt as if something were pushing into his stomach, pressing the wind from him. With each step he felt more apprehensive. His balance, too, was affected, causing him to cease his pursuit altogether. He staggered and swayed as his vision became blurred. The small dose of light which the rising sun was casting into the forest only served to confuse Darcy's senses more.

"Lara!" he yelled. "Lara, come back!" His voice trailed off in whispered words as nausea took hold of him, and he belched stomach acid onto the forest floor.

Too much alcohol? Food poisoning?

He heard Lara's call once more, far off. Farther than she should have gone. Her voice echoed hollow through the woods of Black Hill. Darcy stumbled deeper into the forest after her, bracing himself against trees and tripping over roots. The bugs were silent. He had somehow lost the trail, lost track of where he was just as he had earlier in the day. He looked around, but could gain no recognition of place.

"Lara!" he called again, his booming voice waking spirits unseen to him. He was panicked; everything was unreal, unnatural. He felt as if the control of his own body had been stolen from him and he was now only viewing from some distance.

Darcy grabbed his stomach with a grimace of pain and fell backward onto the trunk of a tree, its roots stretching like armrests to the sides of him. He couldn't breathe and could barely keep his eyes open. His shouts for Lara were barely audible now as he clawed at his muscular chest.

Through his nearly closed eyelids, Darcy recognized a figure, very faint at first. His hopes that it was Lara were quickly routed, for it was clearly a man walking slowly, deliberately, toward him. On the man's face shone a strange fluorescence, making his skin appear too white, but with a startling crimson about the edges. His dark hair was combed back neatly, and a clean-cut moustache and beard encircled his thin lips. Where the man's eyes should have been there was nothing but emptiness; large dark caverns as if they had been hollowed out. The skin around them seemed to be constantly stretched and pulled into the eyeless fissures. His long arms were crossed over his body, and he wore a solid black suit, so black it was undistinguishable from the pitch around him. But it was the white collar that caught Darcy's attention and made him struggle with all his might to speak.

"Father!" he addressed the preacher in a scratchy shell of a voice. "Father, can you help me find my wife?"

But the parson did not respond. He only continued to approach the tree at a steady speed, staring unrelentingly at Darcy.

"Father? What is this? Can you help me…?"

Yet before Darcy could finish his plea, the preacher suddenly rushed at him. His speed seemed effortless, without use of arms or legs. Darcy guarded against an attack, drawing into a ball, knowing he was too weak and sick to defend himself. But upon opening his eyes again, the man was nowhere to be seen. Darcy studied his surroundings, his vision and breathing having returned as if never problematic at all. He rose to his feet, the morning beginning to take form in the forest. He felt his own body for comfort and assurance. It had been an alcohol-induced nightmare. That was all.

A shattering scream whipped his head around.

"Lara!" he cried and charged down the slope of Black Hill, swimming through the morning fog. The trees were a hindrance to him, their branches catching and clawing at him. Never before had they appeared so foreboding and unfriendly.

The world stopped spinning at once as he came breathless to the bottom of the hill. What he had subconsciously feared from the moment Lara had run off into the dark now came to light before him. He felt his heart shudder and spike, as if he were man being taken apart by God, particle by particle.

The heavy, poisonous fog of the chapel grounds stretched like a green sea in front of him, and shuffling through it, away from him, was Lara. He screamed her name, tears breaking the syllables, as she climbed the steps of the chapel's remains. Though he tried, he could not catch up with her. His limbs felt too heavy again, and there was a complacency settling into him, wrestling with his fear and winning. Thick black vines like cords tripped him at every exhausting push forward; their thorns tore at his clothes and flesh. There were other beings crawling along the grounds as well, though Darcy could see nothing of them but their shadows.

Suddenly, he noticed the walls of the mist closing like a curtain in front of him, a veil shrouding Lara from his heavy eyes as she entered the chapel. Quickly, Darcy jumped forward, lunging up the steps toward Lara. He felt as if his skin were burning, boiling, melting from him, yet nothing would deter him. She was his dear friend, and he would not abandon her. He broke through the complacent comfort. As he grabbed her shoulder, he heard a great ruckus of screams. Like agony bottled up and at last released, hundreds of voices. He covered his ears in excruciating pain, feeling himself lifted from the ground and thrown through the air.

So Came Aubrey Avonmore

"You need to come with me."

Calpurnia stood in her doorway, holding her blue satin robe together. If she were still in the city, if she hadn't been forced to live in the valley, she would have had servants to get the door for her. Such a big house should have servants. There should be constant bustling. Her eyes ached as they strained to take in the late morning light. When the initial shock of light wore off, she realized Minerva True stood in front of the sun's glow, her dark clothing equaling her dire expression.

"Calpurnia, you need to come with me," she repeated. "Make haste. Collect your husband and follow me. There's no time to waste."

Calpurnia stared for a second longer. She had never heard Minerva talk this way. Suddenly the urgency of Minerva's voice struck her. She thought of the Book and wondered if perhaps it had done its work. Wasting no more time, she collected her husband, and they were soon in the little-used wagon with Garet at the reins. Calpurnia sat between her husband and the ageless pagan who held Leith tightly. He played with Minerva's silver tresses. They exchanged no further words. The chilly spring air was too crowded with tension, and they raced toward Darcy and Lara's shack. Garet drove with such frenzy Calpurnia was afraid the wheels would break from the axle.

Arriving there, Garet helped the women down. Minerva handed Leith back to Calpurnia. Garet was then led swiftly inside by Minerva. Calpurnia inched slowly after them. The table from the night before had not been cleared. The bugs gathered in swarms. The candle was now a lump of wax, an ode to neglect.

"He's in the bedroom," Minerva said. "Prepare yourself," she warned, her eyes lit with terrible concern. "He is not as you knew him."

Garet stared at her with apprehension. The world grew small and insignificant for their fear. Calpurnia, hearing Minerva's warning, brushed past them and hurried to Darcy and Lara's room. A sharp cry rose in her throat and pierced the day. She clutched desperately at Leith, who began to cry as she focused on the bed. Garet raced toward her and took hold of her shoulders before he saw the wretched sight for himself.

Darcy lay in the bed, alive, but seizing with anguish and torment on the twisted, blood-stained blankets and sheets. No longer did he look the handsome and brooding strongman of the valley. Every inch of exposed skin—that which was not wrapped in gauze—was hairless, boiled and patched as if he had been dunked into a blistering cauldron and then hung out to fester. The room had the thick odor of burnt hair and flesh, of decomposition.

Garet gagged, holding his gut. Minerva waited as he composed himself. Calpurnia stood pale and silent at the door. Garet walked to his friend's bedside, tears streaming. He reached out and touched him, but then drew back in gut-wrenching incredulity. Darcy's eyes peered from beneath red and blistered eyelids. A brief moment of recollection seemed to pass between the two, and then Darcy's eyes glazed over again, and he seized in agony. Garet expelled an inhuman wail and fell to his knees beside the bed. Darcy resembled something inhuman, more a crocodile than a man, and the sight had reduced Garet to a blithering child.

"He ran onto the chapel grounds after Lara," Minerva explained as she came fully into the room, bearing the silent bundle of Elijah in her arms. Elijah peered curiously at Leith as he cried in Calpurnia's arms. "I tried to get to him in time, but I saw it from the beach. I sensed there were walkers. I thought, having lived near it for so long a time, the call would be no match for the four of you." Her eyes spoke volumes of regret; too much grief for too long. "But its power has grown."

"But he lives," Garet cried through his groans. "He still lives! He *is* stronger. It didn't kill him."

"It seems he does in fact live," Minerva agreed, though her tone withheld some dreadful secret.

"Lara?" Calpurnia asked in a terrified whisper. She had backed away from the bedroom door. Her voice shook like a barn in an approaching twister's gust. She barely clutched Leith. "Did she…?"

Minerva's face conveyed the answer. Calpurnia turned and found a chair near the table they had celebrated at the night before. Beetles and gnats scattered in a hurricane of angry whirls. She still held Leith, but so loosely he threatened to fall. He cried and clung to her still, his grip making up for her lack of one. The room grew quiet, as if a caul had been placed over it, halting the passage of time. Garet's writhing sobs and broken breaths punctuated the chilly air of the shack.

"He'll need constant care," Minerva finally spoke in a whisper.

"We'll do it," Garet said, immediately. "We'll look after him. He's my… he's our friend." Tiny pests swarmed about the blood and exposed skin, and Garet swatted them angrily away.

"I'll take the child," Minerva offered, regarding Elijah in her arms. "It's no good leaving him here with an infirm father. And you two will have too much on your hands already. The child will need just as much caring as his father."

Garet agreed through his silence that hers was the best solution. Darcy's parents and family would not even associate with him now. He had been touched by the chapel.

Minerva roused Calpurnia from her grief trance at the table. "We'll prepare a pyre for Lara," the old woman comforted. "Grab some of her things."

Calpurnia was too dumbstruck to say anything in return to the old pagan. She gazed past her. Her mind echoed with accusations which ricocheted around her skull, pointing the blame for Lara's death back at her. She put Leith on the floor and moved blindly to the bedroom. Leith toddled after her, a slight gait to his step. As she collected some of Lara's clothes, smelling them, she searched for explanations. She had asked for Darcy to be the one taken away, not Lara. The Book had betrayed her; it had manipulated her wishes again. In her muddled thought process, she came at last to the conclusion that she must never use the Book again. Why had she done it this time? Questions, accusations, storms of fury. But did any of it matter now that Lara was gone? Did anything matter?

AT SUNSET, a funeral pyre for Lara Kempt was set ablaze on the beach. Since there was no hope of recovering Lara's body, what clothes she had were set among the branches and brush to be consumed by the flames. A silent crowd gathered around, watching as the fire licked the evening air. Calpurnia leaned heavily on Hamlin Marsh, who kept her from keeling over. Theirs had never developed into the relationship he had hoped for, but he realized that had been an irrational dream anyway, something more akin to contrition than connection. He knew she needed him, yes, but only as far as something to lean on to avoid a fall. He finally resolved to look after her the best he could. That was the extent of things. That was what Winifred Walterhouse had asked of him after all.

Calpurnia had been lost and wandering in her mind all day. As he watched the pyre, it seemed no more real than a daydream.

Garet did not attend the burning, but instead stayed by Darcy's side in the small shack on Black Hill.

Hamlin occasionally glanced over his shoulder at Minerva, who stood well away from the valley folk. Many were surprised to see her at all. She had not been seen by a crowd in many years. There were whispers and excited glances.

Toddling beside her, Leith and Elijah each held an arm. Minerva's silver hair glowed, rising and whipping in the river breeze. She caught Hamlin's stare once, confirming that, yes, the worst was yet to come. He turned back to the pyre and did his best to comfort Calpurnia. He could only manage a sigh to comfort himself. His loss over the years had taught him to harden.

They had not taken the wagon from Black Hill to the funeral. Minerva decided it was better that they all walk. There were no complaints. Calpurnia seemed as though she were on a silent journey anyway, walking a long and lonely trail through some spiritual limbo. Respects were paid, and the crowd slowly began to dwindle. The pyre was set afloat upriver. As they made their return to Black Hill, struggling, but numb, it was Minerva who held fast to the children. Calpurnia was blind to them and walked on, unheeding of Leith's calls. Hamlin had offered to walk along with them so to see Calpurnia home, but Minerva convinced him she could manage, thanking him graciously. So he remained by the river with the other mourners, the last few residents of the valley.

When at last they reached a path it seemed only Minerva could see, one which led to her sheltered earth home, Calpurnia walked on, not quite oblivious, but unwilling to be bothered all the same.

"Take the boys," she said, absently. "Take them to your cottage. I have… things to do." She did not wait for a reply and turned for the shack.

"Calpurnia," Minerva called after her. She knew, however, that it was useless, and watched as the soul-staggered young woman made her journey farther up the hillside road, her long skirt muddied and dragging dead leaves and twigs. "Be careful," Minerva said anyway. "He's not himself, young Darcy's not. He'll not be the same again."

"Momma?" Leith inquired, glancing intently up at Minerva. He pointed at Calpurnia as she left him.

Minerva smiled kindly. "She's gone on ahead. She'll be back. In the meantime, how would you two like to play in my gardens?"

Leith smiled broadly, his eyes large and dark. Elijah, while silent, made his excitement known as well with a giddy jump, after which he nearly fell backward.

Minerva laughed and offered her hands again. She noticed that Elijah had a very strong grip, an inherited trait from Darcy no doubt. She led the boys through the growth, the vines draped with moss and the thick trees. If Leith and Elijah had been grown, they would have marveled at how the path seemed to appear before them even as they walked it. But they were children, and to children wonders exist everywhere and are quite commonplace. The elf-paths were no more astonishing than a bumblebee on a rose. *Astonishment is laid in spades for the very young. Eyes will stay wide if cynicism is denied.*

Coming into the circular clearing where winked the cottage from the earth, the boys bounded off into the grass and flowers, Leith giggling and Elijah grinning. Scattered torchlight dotted the garden paths. A lapzine lamp hung at the door to the cottage. A few of the Breed greeted the youngsters with playful nose nudges and head butts. The boys returned the greetings with petting smacks on the Breed's pelts.

Come twilight, the moon laid claim to the sky. There was no ring encircling it this night. Perhaps, Minerva thought, the danger had passed for the time being. Perhaps there would be no walkers for a while. But then, she had been fooled before. Too many times to count. How could she ever think she could have taught Branwenn well? She was such a poor student herself.

A rustle in the woods brought her back to the moment, causing her a momentary fright. Had the boys gone into the forest? But immediately she saw Leith and Elijah, sitting on the ground, petting a lounging stag. She knew they would be protected as long as they remained in the circle of the cottage woods. Cautiously, she glided into the dense patch of trees at the far side of the cottage mound near the cliff where it overlooked the chapel grounds. She walked, touching the trees, asking for information as she went. They were calm, unmoved. If there were something wrong, she would have sensed it from them. Yet even as the trees showed no alarm, there was something watching. She was certain.

Then to her surprise, she saw a small form: a slender, boyish silhouette standing against an ancient and massive oak that overhung the cliff and whose roots protruded and seemed to hold up the hillside. The small figure at first stood with his back to her, but upon perceiving her presence, he turned around. He was a boy around ten years of age, and Minerva noted his angular, pretty, yet dirty elfin face. His hair was dark, curled, and tussled. Leaves were caught in it as if he had slumbered in a large pile of them. He wore rags of brown and beige, and in his hand— Minerva gasped at the sight, her heart nearly burst from relief as she steadied herself against a tree—he held a bird, an injured rain crow. The first she had seen in many years.

And thus, when hope was dearly needed, Minerva True met Aubrey Avonmore.

WHO THEN IS AUBREY AVONMORE?

MINERVA TENDED to the rain crow as young Aubrey watched her keenly, curiously, asking question after question as if he had just awoken to the current of life. He left hardly space for a breath in between them. Minerva found it delightful.

"Why you doin' that fer?" "Why's it squawk so? Cain't it see yer tryin' to help it?" "How's come there are deers in your front yard?" "Why do you live way out here?" "Where's your family?" "Can I have som'n to eat?" "Ain't it hot in that black dress all the time?"

She tried to answer him as best she could. His lack of boundaries was refreshing. His honesty, charming. Every query was asked in earnestness with—as it has been said—the seriousness of a stroke. Yet when Minerva inquired of his own past, a mere nine or ten years at the most, he did not reply. He simply stared at her as if he did not understand the question, and then went skipping off into the forest, humming to the trees or chatting with a scampering chipmunk. He would be with her for a while, however. She would have time and opportunity to inquire further. He now considered her his friend, and told her so.

Most of the time Aubrey stayed near the circle wood, but he never ventured inside of the cottage mound, not even for rest. He chose instead to sleep beneath the hulking trees just outside the circle wood, curling up at their trunks, a skinny lump of audacity dreaming the night away. This worried Minerva, and she found herself checking on him every evening, searching for him under every oak, cedar, elm, or ash at the break of each new day until she found him.

She brought him food and water, and to her enchantment, he would always tell her whenever something was not so good. "This biscuit tastes weird," he would say aloud, crinkling his dirt-smudged nose as he ate it anyway. Minerva sat, usually on a nearby stump or stone, and watched him until he had cleaned the plate. She would bring Elijah with her, and Aubrey would entertain all of them by making faces as he munched.

If Elijah could have giggled, he would have been in fits. Aubrey liked making the toddler smile.

"Thanks!" he always hollered after eating.

"You're very welcome," she answered.

After his meals, Aubrey's adventuring in the forest would continue, heedless of the danger that lurked there. When the rain crow had recovered enough, it followed him on his journeys, flitting and squawking close behind like an exasperated guardian. Aubrey did not go too far from Minerva, though, and the closest he ever went to the chapel grounds was to gaze down on it from the cliff behind the cottage mound.

The first clear spring day, Minerva climbed College Hill for a lunch under Mother True's tree. Hamlin came along, grinning to have been asked, carrying the ever-silent Elijah in his strong but gentle arms. Aubrey followed behind, insisting on carrying the large basket of food and drink Minerva had packed. Trailing him, the old rain crow skipped and hopped along the ground frenetically, his wings still bandaged, but his attitude ever-contentious. Aubrey occasionally looked over his shoulder to shout words of encouragement at the struggling fowl, and the crow shouted back with a loud, irritated heckle. At last, the young orphan (for that is what Minerva and Hamlin thought Aubrey to be) took pity on the bird and carried it the rest of the way atop the basket.

Minerva and Hamlin sat quietly on the quilt, a handicraft of Mother True. They gazed out respectfully, admiringly, at the wide river valley, its reclining hillsides. The calm sky offered a light breeze, and the water shimmered with serene austerity. The limbs of Mother True's tree were beginning to bud. The trees of the True clan had always been the first to show. Not so much a matter of pride, rather a matter of necessity. Purity of purpose always caught the attention of the most bitter of winds.

The rain crow pecked at the scraps of bread Hamlin had thrown its way as Aubrey played gleefully with Elijah farther off, in the center of the small college grounds. Aubrey ran about the grassy quadrangle of buildings with Elijah on his back, both of them careless and happy.

"He's got a way with young Elijah," Hamlin said, regarding them over his shoulder.

"He does indeed," Minerva agreed. Her voice was smooth as glass. "Over the past week he has found good friends in both Elijah and Leith. That one seems to charm anything he comes to meet. The Breed let him ride upon them with nary a thought. Even the trees seem to give a sort of gentle sigh when he stretches out over their trunks and roots."

"And you," Hamlin added with a grin. "He has charmed you as well. I don't think I've seen you this cheerful since…." But he stopped before the words touched air.

"It's all right, dear Hamlin. We can say her name. We can even speak of what happened. Branwenn's memory, our daughter's soul, depends on our recollections of her." She smiled slightly. "And you are right about our strange little newcomer. It is very pleasing to have some youth so near me again."

He reached for her hand and felt it. The boys played rambunctiously in the distance, almost running into a group of academic-looking young men. Aubrey could be heard ejecting a long parade of meaningless apologies. The rain crow, not satisfied with thrown scraps, stole Hamlin's bread from his lap.

"It's good they're becoming so close," Minerva said. "They'll need each other. I fear we'll all need them before this is over. This pocket of wonder may very well be theirs to save."

"I figured as much." Hamlin sighed, his gruff façade cracking. "Things are in motion now. What happened to Lara and Darcy—that was not by blind chance, was it?"

"Chance doesn't come into play in this valley, Hamlin. You know that. We are surrounded by grace and darkness; we are those caught in that struggle." She watched the scholastic gentlemen of Greenbriar College wander to and fro about the quadrangle, Aubrey dodging between them in play. "These fine young men, they know nothing of what danger lies beneath them by the river."

"Perhaps it is their ignorance which keeps them safe."

"It won't be enough; it can't last. Someday, something will happen here. The darkness of the chapel grounds will want freedom from the river and the valley floor. It will climb the hill just as we did. If there isn't someone here to fight it…." Her distressed gaze passed over the river. "The tension is building, and there is bound to be some type of explosion."

"If only my father and your mother had managed to put a stop to the building of the chapel, none of this would matter." Hamlin did not try to hide his regret.

"You're mistaken," Minerva corrected. "Though the instrument is man-made, the source has always been here, waiting for its invitation to rise. And in some form or another, it will continue to be here after we are gone."

"And the chapel was the instrument."

"Religion," she corrected. "The reason for the chapel was the instrument. That power over others, that structuring and bending of will. And once it was started, there was no way to rid the world of it. We can now only hope to weaken its resolve." Her eyes regarded him like a teacher. "Do you see, my love? Do you see what we face?"

"So, the battle will never end?"

"I don't know," she whispered. "But it can get easier, the struggle more worthwhile, if we are steadfast."

Aubrey and Elijah, having tired of wrestling and running barefoot in the grass, joined their elders under the tree once more, nibbling at bread and jam and slurping iced tea.

"What do you s'pose is a'matter with *him*?" Aubrey asked with a mouthful of bread, nodding toward the old crow at the foot of the tree. It hopped and bobbled around the trunk looking as if it were set to climb the bark. Agitated, it twitched and flitted its bandaged wings.

"I believe he might be ready to fly," Minerva answered. "Why don't you bring him to me, Aubrey, and we can see how we might be of help?"

Aubrey jumped to his feet and went to the bird, gently cradling the rain crow in his arms. It squawked at this intrusion. "You mean he's healed?" he asked with a gleam in his dark eyes. "He's all better?" He stroked the crow's head as it pecked admonishingly at his fingers.

"We'll see," Minerva said, taking the bird from his arms. The boys watched in wide-eyed wonder as Minerva unwrapped the wings with care and set the crow on the quilt.

It endured a moment of fluttery disorientation. Then, with a jump and a skitter, it managed an uncertain but successful lift from the earth. Aubrey yelped, clapped, and stamped in approval, and little Elijah's smile spoke as loud as any cry of laughter. The bird flew up to the largest branch of the tree.

"Do you think he's happy, Miss Minerva?" Aubrey inquired, standing at the foot of the tree and staring up. The rain crow gave a call that echoed down the bluff.

"Oh, I think he's quite content." Minerva smiled, glancing at Hamlin.

"Well, he's still as cranky as he ever was!" Aubrey exclaimed.

"A bird in the valley," Hamlin commented. "A good sign, I think."

"Fly!" Aubrey shouted up the bark. "Fly, you ol' rain crow!" He danced about the tree trunk, flinging his arms wildly as he skipped. Elijah followed and mirrored Aubrey's actions, taking a few tumbles due to his fairly new introduction to bipedal mobility.

The old bird gave the group below one final cantankerous look and call, and then spread a more assured wingspan, taking flight over the valley. Higher and higher, the rain crow climbed over the curves, cliffs, and slopes of the river land. It sensed the joy, the love, the connection yet the danger and the shadow. Obstacles to pass through but never avoid as it flew, and the sweet breeze of newborn spring glided over shining black plumage. The rain crow, such a small thing in the grand scheme, was going to help return the valley to better days. And at that moment of epiphany, it was more albatross than rain crow.

The sun rounded the blue vaulting sky as Aubrey Avonmore led the way down the college trail to the rocky beach. Far from saddened by the farewell of his feathered friend, he was pleased it had recuperated and taken to the sky again. He whistled down the hillside free and easy. Minerva carried the picnic basket.

A young bare-chested ferry boat boy in tattered pants, bronzed from the stare of the sun, waited lazily at a raft station as the small group descended from the hill. He stirred briefly, but then resumed his daydreaming when he realized they weren't college students looking for a quick jaunt down the river. The ferry boat boys were known to be very accommodating to the college men, in ways both carnal and otherwise.

"Hiya!" Aubrey shouted gleefully at the boy. He received an unimpressed glance in return.

"Do you know him, Aubrey?" Hamlin asked, carrying Elijah, who had fallen asleep against his shoulder.

"Well, I sure *saw* him," Aubrey answered. "Don't know why he wouldn't recognize me. Don't make any sense. I passed him right by as I swam over here. Maybe he's just sore that his raft couldn't beat ol' Aubrey Avonmore."

"I wager that's it," said Hamlin. He looked to Minerva and winked, saying quietly, "It is doubtful that even a grown man would have the strength to swim across the river, the current being so strong. But a young boy of ten? Someone is telling tales."

"Aubrey," Minerva enjoined, "did you come from there?" She pointed across the water at the other side as they walked. She carried the basket in her other hand. "Just over there?"

He glanced at her strangely. She was seemingly certain he would prove evasive yet again about the whereabouts of his genesis. He picked up a small broken limb from among the rocks and began knocking about the stones in his path. "Not directly," he replied, much to Minerva and Hamlin's apparent surprise. "Over and up a bit after you cross the river. That's where I came from." He outlined an invisible trail in the air along the tree-lined hill opposite them. "There's all sorts of things over there that ain't here," he explained. "Things just are, without even thinking about it. Things just… things have always been, y' know."

"How do you mean?" Minerva urged him on.

But Aubrey ignored the question. In his mind, he had explained everything quite sufficiently. He swung mightily at a large rock, knocking it into the river with a splash. "I woke up under a big ol' willer tree on that ridge right over there. Its branches tickled me so, like someone was taking a feather to disturb my sleepin', y'know. 'Cept there was a lot more willer branches than feathers." He cackled like a newly set bush fire. "And there I was. Some nice folk helped me out, asked me things. Like you. But I cain't remember anything beyond wakin' at the willer tree. Honest. I'd tell you if I could. I didn't even know my name until I saw it written on some stone in this yard with a bunch o' other stones. The folk over there, they live in these big houses on long legs that stretch straight up to the treetops so as they don't get wet. Their homes look like they're gonna walk off. I bet if I had me a tree house like them, I'd ha' caught me the moon herself!

"Anyways, those river folk, they still called me Orphan even after I already told 'em my name. I thought Orphan was a peculiar type name. I liked much better Aubrey Avonmore. Cain't tell you why for certain. But there was this old woman who wasn't too happy that I was calling myself Aubrey Avonmore. She said that name belonged to someone else, someone who was sleeping under the stone it was written on. Can you figure that! How's it that a name can be someone else's when it's my very own!"

"So, you just decided to swim over here one day?" Hamlin asked. His boots knocked and toppled small rocks around his feet. Elijah stirred in his arms.

"Yep. Woke up in the arms of an oak tree; the willer was too prone to tickling. I climbed up there in that oak, you see, cause the moon was so big the night before that I wanted to see if I could grab it. Wouldn't it be some'n if I could have me a moon to play with whenever I wanted?" He glanced at them, sure that they would share his excitement at this prospect. "Well, as I woke up and looked out on the river, I said to myself, 'Aubrey boy, you ever swam the wideness of a river?' And I answered to myself, 'Nope. I don't reckon I ever swam the wideness of a muddy river before.' So there I swam it, and beat that raft boy with my own two arms. He's just sore, like I said. But I'd race him again if he's a-lookin' for another good beatin'.

"When I got over here... Just there"—he pointed—"I walked a ways up yonder, just below your cliff, Miss Minerva, and heared the most unpleasant ruckus that I ever heared, right in those ol' briar bushes, just outside that stinky old church below your own place...."

Minerva and Hamlin gaped at one another in disbelief at the mention of the chapel, their steps coming to an abrupt halt.

Aubrey sensed the quiet and turned to face them. "Well, you sure do have queer looks on your faces! What's a matter?"

"Aubrey," Minerva spoke. "Did you go onto the chapel grounds? The old white stinky church... you went onto the grounds?" She approached him. "Do not tell tales, Aubrey. Speak the truth."

"Surely, I did! I had to save the poor ol' crow, didn't I? Why's it got you all bothered so?"

"And you were able to leave the church without anything happening? Nothing tried to... harm you?"

"Well, the rain crow lurched at me, but after he saw I wasn't meaning to hurt him, we walked on just fine, Miss Minerva. Did I do some'n wrong? Some'n I weren't s'posed to?"

Minerva smiled broadly as she looked the young elfin child in the face. "Oh, far from it, dear boy," she whispered in hushed excitement.

Aubrey shrugged. "I gotta say," he admitted, turning around and walking on, "you two are great folk, but you sure is weird."

Hamlin Marsh Remembers the Events Which Led to the Chapel's First Restoration

HAMLIN WATCHED Minerva and the boys travel farther up the sloping trail of Black Hill, the swooping trees' limbs quickly concealing and hoarding them like prized things. Once they were out of his sight, Hamlin journeyed along the beach, his eyes to the multicolored stones at his feet, but his thoughts remained focused on the patch of sickly, white, and withered trees that surrounded the chapel. When he felt he could no longer avoid looking directly at them, he stood, his back to the great river, and stared the mist down. The sallow trees had long since given up hope of rescue from the choking mist and the preternatural vines. Beyond them the ruins of the chapel beckoned with a strengthening tone. Its call was indeed heard throughout the valley, taunting and tempting with lies. The soup of fog, once waded through, did not lead to any grand kingdom of God, but from what Hamlin had seen, only decay. Years earlier, he had been awestruck by that decay, having witnessed it firsthand. Mother True had told him when he was younger that the chapel had been foolishly constructed on troubled grounds, but until he'd seen the sight for himself when it was restored for the first time, he had not truly believed her. He had been energetic and daring then. He might have been able to do something at one time if he had listened to the Mother with more than passing intrigue. But now he saw himself like a trustworthy old fence post, strong and rooted deep, alas past its prime all the same.

As Hamlin Marsh glared at the chapel grounds, the flow of the river and rays of the sun warming him, the memory of the valley's past played before him as though awakened spirits had been called forth, real and tangible. Their actions were every bit as alive as the stones beneath his feet….

Hamlin's first reaction upon seeing Parson Wade standing uncertain but hopeful on the approaching raft had been one of confusion. The new preacher, the first church leader to come to the valley in quite a long time, seemed so very young. Indeed, he'd looked to be around the age of Hamlin himself. He'd proven nothing at all like the preacher Hamlin remembered—vaguely—from his youth. That figure was more of a sliding suggestion than a man.

As the raft nudged onto the rocks of the beach, and the river boat boy slipped the holding rope around a wooden pole, the young preacher jumped enthusiastically onto the land. His face shone at Hamlin with bright, innocent eyes, and a smile that could break hearts and capture souls.

"Are you Hamlin Marsh?" asked the handsome young man. His hair was brown, flecked with gold, his eyes large and green, and his smile broad and white. He wore a black-brimmed hat pushed back on the crown of his head. He was just happy to Be.

"I am," Hamlin answered. "You're the... Parson Wade?"

"Yes," he answered, shooting out his hand for a shake. Hamlin obliged. The grip was strong and excited. "You look at me like I'm the new kid at school," the parson joked, assuming Hamlin had ever attended school. "I guess that's not too far from the truth, though."

"It's just... you can't be much older than me."

Wade simply smiled. "I heard the calling when I was young. A child, I was, of three."

The particular phrasing the parson employed to explain his choice of vocation caught Hamlin off guard. In the valley, when someone was 'called' it had not been a good thing, especially of late. Hamlin was of the opinion that if someone was meant to be somewhere they shouldn't need to be 'called'; they should already be there.

"Is this all you brought, Parson?" Hamlin asked, nodding to the small, dark carpet bag in the preacher's hands. The river boat boy had already pushed off, uninterested in their conversation.

"I don't need much," the parson answered, almost apologetically.

"Well, lemme show you to your place," Hamlin offered, leading the way along the rocks. The wide-eyed parson excitedly strode beside him, looking around with the precocious nature of a child. "I don't suppose you drink, else I'd invite you back to my place for a round," Hamlin continued.

Parson Wade laughed uncomfortably. "I've never touched alcohol, though I don't judge those who do imbibe."

"That's good. The chapel's nice, I hear," Hamlin said, sparking a new point of conversation between them. "I've not ever been in it myself. They've gone and fixed it up real nice for you." 'They' being the few who would be attending, the few who were new to the valley and paid no attention to the rumors of yesteryear.

"You go to another church? I wasn't aware there were any others near these parts." A hint of concern crept into his voice.

Hamlin squinted over his shoulder at the young man who had fallen a bit behind, awestruck by the landscape. "I'm not of your ilk, Reverend, if you'll mind the term. You'll find that most here aren't."

"Yes. I had heard there was a more… earthly faith in this valley. I guess that's why I was so keen on coming here." The Parson quickly made up the ground between them.

"Plans to bring us all into the flock, Mr. Wade?" Hamlin asked without a hint of sarcasm.

Wade laughed lightly. "No such thing, Hamlin," he said. "There are many roads to the same end, I believe."

"That's good to hear you say," Hamlin responded. And he sincerely meant it. This new parson of the valley was different than those he had heard of. There was a gentler quality about him, more tolerant of other views. The preacher who held the position before Wade had not particularly endeared himself to the valley. After his disappearance, the chapel grounds brought a chill to the surrounding hills. It was enough to spark legends among the children.

Hamlin saw Pastor Wade occasionally around the valley after their initial meeting. They were always congenial, but nothing of importance ever passed between them. The only folk who seemed at all excited by his arrival had been the handful of converts who, up until then and until the chapel was completely renovated, had met in their own homes for Sunday services; their congregation, they called it. Hamlin thought it very strange to worship any god inside a building, hidden from view. What secrets would one be ashamed to show the sky?

Still, it wasn't uncommon in those days before the chapel's renovation for the two differing faiths to convene for a lovely late dinner on the beach. There was a mixture of Lord-be-with-yous and blessed-bes all around. It was how things had always been: respectful. And it was *during these dinners that Parson Wade made his attempts to convert more of the valley folk. Though at first not terribly effective, he did manage to lure over a few well-respected members of the valley, Angela Children, a barren and lonely midwife, being the first. Nothing seemed off kilter at all. The river was smooth.*

It wasn't until the chapel restoration neared completion that things became truly tense. A rigid crispness stifled the air of the valley and many eyed the structure suspiciously.

From the start, however, Mother True, who spent her days lovingly caring for the ailing Widow Lone, warned the young preacher to think of building a chapel elsewhere in the valley. She tried to tell him that even the hinterland would be a better place for his church. She offered a patch of ground not far from Lone Place, in a field crowded with sunflowers.

"Now, why would I do that?" he asked politely standing on the sprawling, columned porch of Widow Lone's manse with his hat in his hand. That day he had been going house to house in the valley, trying to stir interest in his services (his following was loyal, but remained small). He wiped a bead of sweat from his brow. "Why would I build a new house of worship when a perfectly good one stands ready? It creaks and groans aplenty, but it's sturdy. And we've just added a new coat of paint." This was years before the place lay yet again abandoned, before the façade fell into disrepair and the cross crashed onto the altar.

Hamlin stood on the porch alongside Minerva. The Widow sat in her wheeling chair, one of Mother True's quilts covering her legs. She stared blankly down at what was left of a dying orchard near the river. She always watched the orchard these days. Since her illness had returned she kept her eyes to the trees and the shine of a black box held there by roots and earth. Memories of another tale…

"The chapel stands on spoiled ground; rotten and festering," Mother True explained. "Your church will falter, I promise it. That is not a threat, but concern for you and your congregation. Why, it happened not ten years past."

Parson Wade gave her a look of compassionate condescension. "God would not allow evil to enter His house," he pronounced, taking his leave with a tip of his hat. Mother True could say nothing to convince him otherwise. She could not explain the battle she had had at the chapel years ago, of the many fluctuations of light and dark.

That was the last time Hamlin knew of that either Mother True or the Widow Lone ever saw the young preacher. The widow continued to get worse, and Mother True, bound to her with a covenant stronger than any man-ordained ritual, stayed at her side until the very end.

The parson soon after fell deeply in love with one of his flock, Naomi Hallenfeller, a young unwed woman who happened also to be pregnant. A larger girl with dark hair and ivory skin, she spoke rarely, but when she did it was with a soft lilt, so that people listening would need to crowd in to hear her. Though none in the valley would think to judge the parson or Naomi for their relationship, Parson Wade chose to hide, as best he could, his involvement with the girl. He was a poor actor when pretending not to notice her when their paths crossed outside the chapel. His humorous attempts at denial were mocked by some of the younger valley folk. It was widely known, however, even by his own church-goers, that Naomi came and went in the night, a visitor to the pastor's living quarters at the back of the chapel.

The chapel itself had been polished, wiped of its ill-use, it seemed. Fresh paint made it gleam white and proud beneath the sun, Angela Children and Naomi Hallenfeller planted flowers along the front, the windows were cleaned every day, and the pews were sanded and waxed until their dark wood felt smooth to the touch. Even the surrounding trees had revived from their strange sick slumber. Still, Parson Wade could not get the area out back, directly behind his residence, to grow much of anything. The soil there was putrid, and at first glance he imagined he saw faces in the mud. Faces, screaming with mouths agape. He refused to use the back entry after that, despite his conviction, convinced he possessed a fanciful mind that had created the ghastly image of its own accord.

Though only a handful ever attended the services held on the quiet Sunday mornings of the valley, passers-by could hear the youthful voice of Parson Wade echo through the grove of the now beautiful trees in the center of which the chapel stood. While the sermons were innocuous and at first quite in line with the tolerant views of the valley folk and the warmth Parson Wade had first espoused to Hamlin, the balance was gradually thrown off. Occasionally, when someone was out very late in the dark hours of night there could be seen a strange light coming from within the chapel. An angry orange light. And Pastor Wade could be seen through the windows, kneeling in penitence at the altar, his face aswim with a disassociated fervor that seemed not his own. The passerby would gather himself quickly and hustle homeward.

Slowly, Hamlin and others noticed a change in the demeanor of the preacher outside of the chapel. No longer the cheerful soul he had been upon his arrival, he became instead a fearful, stuttering and balding man, who clung to his Bible—an enormous book—as if it led his way. If Mother True had ever seen the book, she would have recognized it at once.

Word spread throughout the valley that Parson Wade had lawfully wed Naomi Hallenfeller, and taken as his responsibility the upbringing of her unborn child. They were joined in a small ceremony seen only by those faithful to the church and its God. The exclusion of the valley folk from this celebration was a sting the like of which had never been felt before, for all of the locals loved a good party. Hamlin had been shocked that Mother True was not at least asked to attend given her standing in the community. In fact, as Mother had been the midwife at Naomi's own birth, it seemed a direct attack on her.

Only Angela Children protested the wedding. She did not attend the affair, but instead visited Mother True at Lone Place, appearing at her doorway, fidgeting and frowning.

"Something is wrong there," Miss Children warned, her voice high and breathless with worry. Angela was a naturally nervous creature. Years of midwifery had done nothing to sort out this problem. "They speak in strange, hushed tones, worshiping with secrets." She was clearly concerned and frightened. "Parson says to shun the valley folk who are not of the church. I do not want to shun anyone. You are all my friends. His looks have changed along with his person. He was so lovely and handsome when he first came to the valley. He spoke with such a charming, elegant voice." She drifted off for a moment like a girl remembering the feeling of a first crush. "But now... he doesn't seem the same man at all. Dark rings circle below his eyes as though he hasn't slept in a month. He rips at his hair when he preaches, and there is a... smell...."

"You must encourage everyone to leave at once! They must escape the chapel," Mother True said. The forwardness of her blunt command caught Angela off guard, but Mother was on her feet and adamant. Though she was small in stature, her commandments were never broken. "It's beginning, and I feel it's stronger this time. I warned him about the

grounds. If you can't get them to listen to you, get yourself from there immediately."

Angela cradled herself in her arms as if chilled to the bone. She rose in fear. "What about Naomi and her unborn child? I must try to help them."

"It may already be too late for the child, my dear," Mother True solemnly countered. "But we shall see. I will watch. But you make certain you never go back to that place. Do you understand?"

"Yes, Mother," Angela said. "Thank you, Mother. Thank you."

She scurried away, leaving a chill in her wake.

Just before the chapel grounds' spoiled earth at last rose in fumes and venom, the valley folk noticed a most significant change about their chapel-going neighbors, a haughty resentment aimed at those not of the fold.

There was a plaque erected—nothing more than a slab of wood nailed to a tree and painted haphazardly—that warned the rest of the valley to stay off the chapel grounds. Someone had made a sloppy job of it, but the point was clear: in hasty black letters it read HEATHENS AND WITCHES NOT WELCOME. Mother True was barred from checking in on any of the parishioners at their individual homes, especially Naomi Hallenfeller. The shunning had begun.

The small band of the parson's followers disfellowshiped their families and friends. They took on the pallor of illness. Their eyes, though filled with a segregated anger and determination, were bled of any color. Their flesh became as pale and dry as rice cakes. They dredged rather than walked, and they coughed in long, hideous spells. It seemed the symptoms only worsened when the parishioners struggled home from their Sunday services. The services began to take many hours and Pastor Wade's lectures took on hushed, conspiratorial tones, his once-powerful voice now reduced to a scratched, hoarse reminder of what it had been.

One gray winter morning, the valley had been awakened to cries of horrible pain. It came as no real surprise to any that it was from the chapel grounds they resounded, yet the sight which greeted those who rushed to the chapel struck them all with terror. Tied in quarters by strange thick vines between two wilting trees was Angela Children. She had been stripped bare and was being beaten by Pastor Wade with a lash from the thorny vines that now choked the flowers in front of the chapel. The small congregation watched in stony silence.

The men of the valley charged the chapel grounds at once, but they met with the resistance not only of unyielding parishioners, but winding vines which whipped at them ferociously.

"What is this?" Hamlin's father cried. A vine had slashed him severely across his cheek. "Stop this!" he yelled at the pastor.

"She has sinned against God!" Pastor Wade rasped, his voice crawling from his lungs like vomitous debris. He lifted his whip to strike again, the vine curled around his wrist, drawing blood as thorns had fastened into his flesh.

"How?" Prichard Parma yelled. "How could a good woman sin?" He still fought violently to get onto the grounds, suffering with his sons the stings of the vines' wrath.

"She is an apostate," the preacher replied. "She tries to turn others against the true God." He paced behind her weeping form with the vine in his hand. "She tries to take my wife and child from me."

"She's a midwife!" Hamlin's father cried. "She's a good woman. Her sins are your imagination."

"She's a witch!" The parishioners behind the preacher seemed to cough and hiss in agreement, but they never said a word. There were five all told.

"I'm no witch," Angela mumbled breathlessly. "I know nothing of witchcraft."

Pastor Wade pressed himself to her back and spoke to her, "How do you know you are no witch, if you do not know what a witch is?"

The pastor continued to whip the woman as blood dripped from her wounds and she fell unconscious. The valley folk's attempt at rescue proved futile, and they finally retreated into gasps and cries on the beach and the surrounding hillside. Women and children who had known the loving if nervous hand of the midwife covered their eyes and ears at the spectacle. Their tears of pity fell into the river but did nothing for Angela's case. Pastor Wade remained unmoved. When all hope was lost, just as they had given up and settled into a funerary trance, Mother True finally appeared in front of the chapel grounds' entrance, Minerva at her side. Pastor Wade stopped his lashing and leered at the woman daringly. The crowd pleaded with Mother True to do something for poor Angela. Minerva began a soft hum that built to a low chant.

"The River Dwellers are on their way," Mother True admonished above her daughter's voice as they both approached the chapel grounds.

"We do not need them for a trifle such as you, but I would slink away if I were you."

The crowd stood hopeful. It was a rare thing to see a River Dweller casting a chant. Minerva's voice stilled them all.

The vines curled and whipped, but with one mighty swing of her hand Mother True fearlessly flung them aside. "Be Gone!" she shouted, her tiny voice booming with the ferocity of a cannon.

The parishioners, though subservient to the pastor, did not dare touch her or her daughter. They merely hissed in strange tones and cowered away. The creepers which bound Angela Children released her, slithering away to some place beneath the foundations of the chapel. Hamlin and the Parma sons caught the unconscious woman and carried her carefully from the grounds.

Mother True then turned her attention to the pastor who had disappeared momentarily into the chapel, returning with his Bible. It was then that Mother True recognized the book of her childhood nightmares, The Night Hammer.

"You have no power here, witch!" he cursed, racing at her with unnatural zeal. Minerva's song continued still. The pastor held the Book aloft as if to bash her head with it. But as he came upon her, she took hold of the Bible and flung it from his hands onto the chapel steps where the parishioners were now watching in confusion. Fear shot through the pastor's eyes. Past her, riding rafts up the river, was a small band of women, the River Dwellers.

"You are not the one he has chosen," Mother True intoned. "I know who has corrupted you, and you haven't the strength to do what he requires, Pastor Wade. If only you had listened to me."

Pastor Wade cringed as if she had hit him. He crept away to the steps of the chapel, joining the others. He then crawled up the steps backward, keeping his eyes upon her, burning with a hateful gaze. Mother True kept her eyes upon him as well, until he and his handful of crawling followers had closed the large doors to the outside world, locking themselves in for good.

"She's dead," young Hamlin had whispered, holding Angela Children in his arms as Mother True returned to the waiting crowd outside the chapel grounds.

"Do not pity her now," Mother True replied. "Her pain is over. But those who were dragged into the chapel…their pain has only just begun, I'm afraid. It is complacency that has caused it."

The old chapel had begun to fall into disrepair once more, paint chipping from it at such a rate that it seemed time had chosen to focus on it over all the other abandoned structures in the valley. One day's neglect gave the impression of a hundred. Around the grounds, even the novice could tell that the natural world was losing a battle with something more dogged and destructive. The chapel's foundations now seemed like roots snaking into a swampy ground. A mist began killing or maiming any vegetative life surrounding the vacant-looking structure, anything that grew, except for the twisting, dark creepers.

After many days had passed with no sign of the pastor or any of his flock, Mother True had decided a group of valley folk should enter the chapel and discern what had become of the parishioners. Hamlin and his father, as well as a few of the stronger people of the valley, accepted the mission. As they approached the chapel, they saw tiny skeletons and the remains of birds fallen to its marshy earth, littered among its dead-tree grove. Scattered, pointless death. The mist clung to them like a thick soup.

Almost immediately, they felt a sting to their skin and a burning in their throats. Being the men and women they were, however, they held fast to their purpose, though with a certain amount of natural fear. The fear would keep them alert.

The chapel doors were pushed open with ease, the lock having given, and a whining echo of the hinges filled the dark room before them. Hamlin entered first. There was no light, only that which the torches they carried gave off. The room reeked of human waste. The silhouettes of human forms could be seen in the pews. Four of them. The wood floor had creaked and groaned in such a way that Hamlin had thought the very building was alive and angry. No words were said between the small group of searchers. The torch flames whispered in their ears, and the shadowplay in the corners taunted them.

Slowly, Hamlin had made his way past the others to the pulpit. His breath heaving, his heart had thudded in his ears. As he'd neared the pulpit, a white terror ran through him. Standing motionless in front of him, face staring at the floor, had been Pastor Wade. Below him, lying most certainly dead, Naomi Hallenfeller, her stomach ripped open, her baby extricated. Just then he'd realized her absence from the crowd of parishioners at Angela Children's torture. There was no sign of a struggle. Hamlin hoped she had died long before her body's mutilation.

And where was the baby? There had been a baby.

Hamlin had whirled around in sickness as one of the other members of the search party, Aife Grayshall, screamed in shock. She stood against the back wall, shielding her face. Her torch had dropped to the floor. Hamlin's father had quickly picked it up and waved it toward the source of her terror. The gasp that had risen from the group reverberated as loudly as if someone had shouted profanities during prayer.

The faces, the faces of the lost parishioners in the pews…

None who saw those faces on that day, not even Hamlin, would be able to shake them from their minds. They were seared into their memories. Never again would they have dreams. Only nightmares. The sudden sound of retching echoed throughout the chapel.

As Hamlin collected himself, he turned again to Pastor Wade's form and cautiously raised the emaciated head. How had this man, who seemed so kind and good, fallen into such depravity? Hamlin's skin had crawled at the feel of the decaying flesh. He still hadn't ascertained how a dead man was yet able to stand at the pulpit. The dead don't stand. But then, Hamlin's eyes widened in realization, and he let go of the preacher's lifeless chin.

"Everybody out!" he'd yelled so loudly it shook the rafters.

Something in the church stirred; some vitriolic presence. The pews had trembled, exaggerated by the shadows cast by the torches.

The searchers had begun coughing uncontrollably, running clumsily, frantically from the chapel. Hamlin and his father had made certain all the others were safely out before they'd followed. Hissing and the sickly sound of slithering had surrounded them as they darted through the mist. The vines snagged and tore at their clothes and flesh. Once outside the chapel grounds, they had collapsed onto the rocks, their throats sore, their skin blistered and burnt. They had lain there silent and shocked for a moment.

"There's no hope for them," Hamlin had gasped in his youth. "They're gone. They're not who they were."

It was only after Hamlin had said this and belched out a spew of black gunk that he had realized his father was not with them. He had fallen, and through the mist Hamlin had seen the long figure of a man being pulled pliantly up the chapel steps.

ON THE PRECIPICE OF MADNESS

DARCY STRAYED deep in a dream state, covered by thick waves of conscious separation. He stood in the mist, and yet this time there was no sting, no burning of the skin. He was, in fact, completely unscarred, still the strong, indestructible man of the valley. Whispers gathered in the mist around him. Voices he had never known before. They spoke as if in benediction.

The mist became transparent, fading to the edges of the chapel grounds, so that he stood now in its hollowed center. Darcy recognized wanderers, walkers, passing aimlessly all about the grounds. They were numerous and naked, blindly bumping and falling into one another like toy boats set sail on a pond. In the crowd of whisperers, Darcy observed the form of his wife, Lara. He found his way to her through the mash of souls, his boots sticking unforgivingly to the thick gray mud. He opened his mouth to call her name, but no voice issued forth. Normally, he could make a mountain lion whimper in embarrassment, but not here. Instead, he whispered, like all the rest.

He grabbed Lara's arm, but as he did so, she and the crowd vanished completely as if they had never been there at all. The whispers suddenly ceased as well, drawn back into the edges of the mist. In front of him crouched the chapel, only it wasn't in ruins as he had remembered it, but gleaming, new and white. A proud, commanding structure. At the door, Garet, standing as naked as the others, watched Darcy lovingly. He seemed oblivious to any queerness around him, but Darcy at once sensed the horror of the situation. Garet was not supposed to be here. Garet's gentle soul would be crushed. As Darcy climbed the steps to persuade his friend to leave straight away, the chapel door swung wide, and the eyeless preacher he had seen in the forest, neatly groomed and clothed, approached in the same effortless manner as before. Darcy pulled pleadingly at Garet's arm, but Garet did not respond. Darcy's strength meant nothing here. Garet simply stood paralyzed, his expression of love now merging with unimaginable grief; the face of one at a dying lover's bedside. Darcy felt as if he had seen that face before, and the expression filled him with regret.

Darcy's feet gave out beneath him, and he tumbled to the bottom of the steps. Quickly, glancing up once more, he saw his friend reduced to ashes before his eyes. Darcy tried screaming, he tried to rise and seek vengeance on the preacher, but the vines and the mud pinned him to the earth. The preacher stepped through Garet's ashes as if they were fallen leaves, making his measured advance toward Darcy.

Garet sat at the bedside, his head resting in his arms. Little daylight filtered through Darcy's bedroom window. Garet didn't want to move Darcy to Walterhouse Manor though that would have certainly made caring for him easier. The big house was Calpurnia's domain, and anywhere she dwelled was steeped in resistance. It might hamper Darcy's recovery.

He watched the erratic breathing of his dear friend. Darcy had only awakened a few times, whispering half-coherent sentences. Mostly he slept and dreamed. Minerva said that was for the best, as the pain from his wounds would be too much for even a man as strong as he to bear. Her healing knowledge could only help allay his pain so much.

Whatever fantasies or nightmares Darcy's mind was dreamscaping, Garet could sense the intensity of them. Darcy hardly ever lay still in the bed. He kicked and flailed about as though he were a captive trying to free himself from a shroud of chains. His bandages constantly needed reapplication from being thrown off and bled through. Minerva had tried to see into his visions, but his mind was too dark, too clouded. She confessed she did not understand what was happening. "I have never encountered such darkness before," she said.

Garet wondered if he should seek out Minerva again. Something new was happening, something very peculiar, and frightening as well. As Darcy dreamed, whispering his way through what Garet was now sure were nightmares, there emerged a second voice, rasping alongside the first. An altogether different tone and carriage competed and seemed to argue and berate Darcy's own voice, yet it rose from the same larynx. At times, Darcy's face would contort in such ways that his appearance became even more terrifying than his boiled, pocked countenance already was. The alien voice would sometimes take over the dreams wholly, hissing unrecognizable curses. The strange whispers from Darcy felt like a thousand tiny spiders crawling on the skin. Darcy's true voice would only return hours later. It was those moments that Garet cherished, for it was then that Darcy would occasionally open his eyes and look upon him with a slight twinge of recognition and love.

And sorrow.

CALPURNIA STUMBLED wearily into the dark room, every step a struggle. Darcy twitched and spasmed under the sweat-soaked sheets. Garet had gone in search of Minerva, though if he could come upon the cottage in the woods was hard to say. Certainly, he wouldn't find it on his own. But Calpurnia knew there were other forces at work in the forest of Black Hill. This was something she had become keenly aware of from her dallying in the hidden arts.

She shuffled cautiously to the window, her eyes never straying from Darcy, and pulled back the curtains to let some light into the room. Garet kept it dark. She supposed the shadows were a comfort to his mourning. But what did he have to mourn? His friend was alive. It was her dear Lara who had vanished. The light, however, seemed only to make Darcy seize and groan, that mysterious second voice clearly overtaking his. Calpurnia had never heard such a vicious-sounding tongue. Quickly, she drew the curtains anew, and the rabble of the menacing tongue quieted to some extent. Calpurnia stood with her back against the wall, terrified.

"What have I done?" she mumbled. "Where did I go wrong?"

The Book had never before delivered such a disastrous outcome. It had only ever brought her what she'd asked. She had long ago convinced herself that even the deaths of Lara's aunts were for the best. But why had it now taken Lara and left behind the grotesque body of Darcy Crocker?

"I'll never understand it," she cried.

Calpurnia hated being in the dark room with Darcy. It reminded her too much of Lara. She hated seeing the bed they had slept in together, the bed in which they had conceived young Elijah. She could not think of her friend too much or she might break down in uncontrollable sobs and wake the Devil. *Without Darcy's influence*, she convinced herself, *Lara would never have ventured near the chapel grounds.*

Calpurnia noticed Darcy was no longer shaking and tussling about. The sudden lack of commotion was startling. The white of his eyes could be seen, and he was staring at her. She wondered how long he had been watching her stand there. She wondered if he saw her thoughts. Shaking, she approached him, trying to emit some warmth and love, unsure if her resentment was sufficiently masked.

"Darcy," she whispered, her voice rattling like windows in a storm. "Are you all right? Can I get you anything?" Venom laced every word. The pillows were nice and thick. He wouldn't be able to fight her off....

He gaped at her, his eyes searching her face. His cheek muscles spasmed in the waking pain. She could only stare at him for so long before she had to turn away from the blood-darkened bandages that covered the exposed muscles of his face, his skin having been eaten away while he trespassed on the chapel grounds.

Then, to her astonishment and terror, he gripped her wrist tightly, nearly breaking it before she wrested it away and jumped backward.

"*Leave!*" he choked out at her.

Hearing him speak coherently struck terror in Calpurnia, something out of an old horror story where the dead return to seek vengeance on the living who have wronged them.

"*Leave now!* You... have to... Garet. Tell Garet...."

"Darcy, what's wrong?" She stood once more against the wall, absently massaging her bruised wrist. Her breath came in rapid bursts.

"Danger," he spit. "It's not me... I'm not here. Run... leave... now...." The veracity with which he spoke caused Calpurnia to shrink into the corner of the room. She couldn't scream. She was frozen and powerless.

Darcy's eyes rolled back in his head. He began to convulse much worse than before, gripping the bed in anguish. The bandages began to shake loose, and the room's gnats and flies scattered in frantic storms. His head flailed from side to side, his limbs those of a man without control of his own muscular movement.

Quite like a doll, she thought.

"Darcy!" Calpurnia cried his name, but there was no response. Then, like a creeping trickle before a dam break, the darker voice emerged. A solitary note that stretched beyond breathing and rose from the very center of Darcy's being. The humming of the note grew like a monstrous awakening, shaking the room. Then, just as suddenly, there was no noise at all, and Darcy lay completely still. Calpurnia could hear her own breathing again. She took her chance. With all possible haste, she raced to the doorway. Yet before she got there, Darcy sat up limber as you please, as if the bed were spring-loaded, and he leered at her. She froze again and managed a weak cry of terror. The large misshapen mass of a man mirrored her pose.

"Callie, Callie, come play," he said lowly.

"Darcy?" she inflected quietly. But she knew Darcy was no longer in the room. Only his shell remained, and what lived inside it was no more a man than a corpse.

"Where's my Book, Calpurnia Covington?" the voice calmly answered. As he spoke, he rose from the bed, a being adjusting to its new form. The limbs cracked and popped, the head swung limply on the thick neck momentarily. Then, the body of Darcy Crocker suddenly stood erect, bloodied bandages tumbling to the wood floor. "You have chosen the broad path leading to misery and torment. Only the narrow path, my path, will lead you to the Everlasting."

He held out a deformed hand. She stared at it, trying to devise some way of escape. She stood near the door, but felt uncertain as to whether she could make it. He seemed so strong again. Her mind raced, but offered no other alternative; the decision to act was soon made for her. Without a hint of warning, he lunged at her, as if he had somehow melded into shadow, and then reappeared right before her face. Too late, she moved toward the door. Darcy caught her, pulling her to the floor.

"Where's my Book?" the voice asked again.

Though she fought harder than she ever had, it was useless. Darcy's body was so much stronger than her own. His sickly, scalded flesh covered her as she finally managed a respectable scream. This carcass should be nothing but food for the bugs now. How was it he moved so briskly?

"Come with me," he whispered ferociously in her ear, licking it with his hot tongue.

"No!" she screamed, her mind beginning to loosen around the edges. She still retained her grip on the moment, but just barely. She heaved and sobbed as he tore at her gown, and her screams deflated to whimpers. The gnats swarmed his head.

Suddenly, as she began to retreat into herself, Darcy's body went limp on top of her, his strength snuffed like a lapzine lamp. Calpurnia gazed up, weakened and enfeebled. Garet stood over them, breathing heavily, a large shovel in his hand.

GARET TRUDGED the dirt and gravel road back to Darcy's shack, each step a miracle of persistence. His legs felt so frail and weak, he wasn't sure he would make it to the front door. He had carried Calpurnia back to Walterhouse Manor, her sobs and gasps the most frightening noises he had ever heard, for they were for the first time something real, not a ploy. Not a grab for attention.

Before Garet left Walterhouse Manor, having laid Calpurnia to rest in her bedchamber, he grabbed his sword from the Great Hall above the stone fireplace. He trembled at the thought of what he now felt forced to do. He struggled to convince himself that Darcy's hulking frame no longer contained the spirit of his one true friend. He kissed his ring, hoping for forgiveness.

"He is not himself. That which squats inside of him cares nothing of you," Minerva said. He had at last found her—or rather, she had let herself be found—so that she might care for Calpurnia and Leith while he did what needed to be done. "He will try again if he is not stopped," Minerva assured him.

"But we can't kill whatever it is that eats him from the inside," Garet protested. "And I do not want to…."

"No, we cannot." She was gentle, but resolute. "But we can keep it at bay. We can be ever watchful once we have sent it back into the mist. One day, perhaps it will give up." The likelihood was scant, but it was something for the moment to cling to.

So Garet trudged down the hillside road, his guts pulled tight, wishing for rescue by the angels in the treetops. On occasion, he doubled over and threw up his pain. The thought of destroying Darcy, the physical form of the man, as deformed and twisted as he was, shook him to the core. Darcy had been more his life's partner than Calpurnia or any woman would ever be. The being he had to slay was once his own strong, vibrant friend and lover and would have remained thus if not for other people's rules seeping like poison into the valley. He clenched the hilt of his sword, his father's sword, tightly in his hand as he deflected bitter tears and anger.

Nearing Darcy's shack, the surrounding trees began taking on transformative qualities; that caliber of existing which only the forests of the valley knew. Their limbs became ushering appendages, pointing him toward his nightmare. The road itself rose and folded, clay bursting and cracking, bringing him closer in earthen waves. Sap wept in sticky gobs from conifers; oak trees whistled mirthless, sepulchral songs from gasping, hollowed holes. The world around him took on the ephemerality of whispered fairy tales with grim, unexpected endings.

Garet faced the shack, gathering strength, tiptoeing on the precipice of madness. Then, before his mind could snap, through the trees behind him he heard a soft rustling of twigs and leaves.

"I wouldn't go in there if I was you, Mister Garet, sir." Young Aubrey Avonmore had followed Garet from Walterhouse Manor, where he had traveled with Minerva and Elijah. He had left them there to tend to Calpurnia, much more interested in what Garet was up to.

Garet took no heed and strode through the door, his every step seeming louder on the wood floor in the darkened shack. He stumbled through his state of queer comprehension, making his way to the bedroom where he had bound Darcy with rope and chord to the ragged mattress. The room swam in odd shapes and shades of blue. Garet stepped back. The bonds lay shredded on the floor. Darcy was gone.

Sword still in hand, Garet looked about him, frightened and unsteady. The whispered winds from the trees were slowly subjugated by another noise; a sliding, slithering, gnawing chorus that rose throughout the shack. Something black and wet fell from the ceiling onto his face, causing him to lose balance and crash to the floor. All around him, crawling over him and wiggling under him, worms and spiders and beetles congregated and converged. The furniture, walls, and ceiling suddenly swam with them.

Garet fumbled for light, any light, his feet smashing the many-legged crawlers along the way. Other winged things flew in his face, making him pitch from wall to wall, disturbing even more insects.

At last outside, his surreal disorientation vanished. The woods were as stoic as any normal day. Garet shook and swatted the remaining bugs from his body, letting his sword fall to the ground with a loud *thlump*.

"That's somethin', huh?" Aubrey exclaimed, pointing at the house. He hadn't moved from where Garet had last seen him.

Garet turned around to reassess what was happening to Darcy's shack. The entire place had come alive with earth worms, beetles, and mites, and every tiny thing that ever made its nondescript mark upon the earth. They dropped from the rain gutters and feasted on the wood and on one another. The earth burrowers and small thousand-legged things, having no cause for concern from birds, were ravenous, rising in salacious hunger. The cacophony of squishing and slithering, the buzzing and chirping, drowned out the forest. In very short order, these things of the earth did what would have taken Time decades to accomplish. Before Garet's eyes, the sorry old structure folded in on itself and fell apart, devoured in orgiastic fervor.

HUNTING THE WORLD
FOR DARCY CROCKER

THE WIND, murmurous over the deep snow and trees, echoed the sound of lost souls wandering. Calpurnia had always thought so. It was an idea borne into her while still very young. When she had first come to the valley, her winters were spent playing along the riverside with Lara. Valley children all knew the dangers of horseplay on the fringes, and so treated the river with the respect it warranted. One night, as Calpurnia and a number of the other children had huddled around Prichard Parma and his sons' magnificent bonfire, telling midnight stories and enjoying hot cocoa, several white, elegant forms glided past them quite quickly just beyond the bonfire's light. These phantoms seemed to levitate above the snow, right past the boisterous group of young people, ignored by all but Calpurnia. She had been the lone soul to be beckoned by the stick man at the chapel ruins, and apparently the only one to see these figures as well. Intrigued by the thought of a mystery uncovered, she carefully traced the path of the apparitions. Her last nighttime adventure had left her with a gift, the Book. What delight would she come upon now?

After following the forms a good distance, having left the bonfire behind in exchange for the moonlit cold, she found herself alone and vulnerable. Calpurnia wondered how long it would be before the others at the bonfire would notice she had snuck away. She heard nothing but her own feet crunching on the snow, her shivered breaths, and the susurrous swish that, to her thinking, came from the white-robed spirits. She hid behind a boulder and watched until the spirits faded from view, climbing elegantly up College Hill. Dejectedly, she returned to the bonfire where she was greeted with a smile by Lara.

It wasn't until years later that she learned the spirits she had seen were no phantoms at all. They were simply the last of the River Dwellers, like Minerva True, who soon vanished altogether from the valley. The images and sounds of that night committed themselves to her memory like ghosts from a childhood campfire tale.

Now from her front yard, she watched over the vacant field next to her inherited home, at the far end of which edged the dark forest of Black Hill. Dawn had just broken, and the sun touched the virgin snow like a painter creating gentle lines of shadow and light. An icy wind blew past her face, playing with ringlets of red hair. She thought herself far from the image of a River Dweller in their gowns of splendid white. Not even Minerva wore the white gowns anymore. Calpurnia stood gaunt and dark in her long black coat, clutching it tightly at the throat.

It had been a bitter year. The tracks of its foul touch stretched aching and cumbersome into the past days and months. Hamlin Marsh had organized search parties in the spring to find the deranged Darcy Crocker, and they had continued all summer and into the fall. The ever-changing forest of Black Hill was scoured, as were the surrounding valley and— quietly and with the trustees' permission—even the college on the bluff. In truth, the valley folk knew their efforts were making them showmen without purpose. Darcy would not be found in any cave or fissure, for he wasn't hiding at all, nor had he run off elsewhere. Everyone recognized exactly where he was. But because the chapel grounds were so poisoned, the air so acerbic, no one could expect to enter and come out as they had been, if they came out at all. Every attempt to destroy the place had been unsuccessful, and the Parma's declaration that they could stoke a fire that would flush any vermin or villain into the open was thought too dangerous to the surrounding hillside and the oblivious inhabitants of the Greenbriar College to even attempt.

Calpurnia plodded through the snow to the wood pile near the old paint-chipped shed at the back of the house. She collected the firewood in her arms, each block making a neat, sturdy knock against the other. The frigid morning air was refreshing. She felt much happier, much more at ease, when Garet was gone, and gone he was. Every morn, before the sky began to color, Garet would rise and leave the house, hunting the world for Darcy Crocker. His eyes had dimmed at Darcy's downfall, just as hers had when told of Lara's disappearance. Calpurnia wondered if Garet felt responsible for Darcy's madness in the manner she felt responsible for Lara. Perhaps they were a perfect match after all, locked as they were in their bitterness and grief.

She realized a while after the incident with Darcy that Garet was feeling just as crushed by her presence as she by his. Almost in silent agreement, a secret understanding developed, and they went about their days with barely a word between them. When words were spoken, they rang like gunshots through the silent old house. Whatever force had changed Darcy, whatever had gestated in the chapel, was tearing the valley folk asunder, and those with the weakest ties were the first to suffer. The house echoed with quiet every hour of every day. It contained all the vacancy of a canyon.

Calpurnia spent her days taking care of Leith, playing with him and nurturing his inquisitive mind, at last trying to play the part of his mother. Why not? Aside from Lara, Leith was the only one she felt she might ever have truly loved, and that was because he was part of her. *Of her*. With Leith, she began to think, she could set things right, correct past erroneous miscalculations. Her uncertainty lay in how that might come about.

As Calpurnia opened the door, stepping back into the house with the firewood, she felt a prickling in the air. A dreaded peculiarity, as though the valley had sucked in its breath, pretentious in its withheld foresight. She hastily shut the door behind her.

MINERVA WATCHED the boys playing with the Breed in the deep snow from her small kitchen's window in the compact earthen home. She swirled the creamy hot chocolate in the tin pot, a treat she made on the coldest of winter days, serving the warm beverage with fresh-made butter cookies. Her home was warm and cuddlesome on the inside, like an embrace. Comprised of one circular room, her bed and a strongback chair sat to one side, a fireplace and a kitchen to the other. Dried herbs and flowers hung en masse from the low ceiling. She could certainly never have held any parties in the cottage, but she had lived there quite comfortably as a child with her mother and her sister, and she had continued, on her own, now with Elijah.

The cottage had been more or less covered by the snowfall, and yet still looked perfectly snug, adapting to and embracing the ever-shifting moods of the valley. Smoke curled from the chimney, lifting into the air and vanishing above the trees. Aubrey Avonmore laughed buoyantly as he pulled Elijah through the billowy white powder on a small beechwood sled. A pair of young stags of the special Breed pranced around, kicking their legs in the air in merriment, scattering snow over the boys.

Minerva laughed when she saw Aubrey take a fall, face-first, into the deep snow. He jumped to his feet quickly, his resplendent smile beaming at Elijah whose adoration of his older "brother" proved ever-apparent. Aubrey brushed the thick snow from his wool coat, and commenced pulling the younger boy about, the stags following in parade. Aubrey had accepted Minerva's invitation to stay in the cottage with her and Elijah on the colder nights of winter. "If it'll make you happy, Miss Minerva," he said. "I don't want you frettin' none." He claimed he never got cold. Ever, ever, ever!

Minerva was about to call them in for the hot chocolate when it happened. Even before Aubrey stopped in a sudden startled stance and gazed into the trees, even before the stags bolted toward the back of the cottage, Minerva was out the door. She had abruptly sensed something burning the air, like cinders eating kerosene fumes. Wrapping her black shawl about her, she ran through the snow to the boys.

"Back inside," she said to Aubrey in an excited whisper. "Take Elijah, and the two of you get in the cottage!"

Aubrey pulled his stare from the woods and locked eyes with her searchingly. But he did as he was told, and took Elijah by the hand to lead him back to the cottage. Still, he walked reluctantly, keeping an eye over his shoulder in tense protectiveness. The snow was piled nearly as high as he in some spots, but he would have taken on the world if charged.

A smoking gash cut through the brush and foliage of the circle wood. Minerva approached it cautiously. Roots and dark brown earth lay exposed to the winter air as if some great hand had hollowed out a fresh pathway. Everything around, from sycamore tree to mulberry bush, was roiled and shriveled. At the end of the new pathway stood a mountainous silhouette.

Surely, Minerva thought, *surely it is not he.*

Minerva strained to see through the gusts of drifting snow and the shadow that clung to the creature until at last a familiar face appeared.

Darcy Crocker stood opposite her, but not as she had last known him, not beaten and burned. He stood instead once again proud and erect, wearing a strange, thick coat of dark brown fur which made him seem all the larger. Gone were any disfiguring burns or signs of struggle and battle. In fact, Minerva noted, Darcy was more striking than ever. His brooding eyes fixed on her as a menacing smile slid across his face. Darcy Crocker never smiled.

Stand your ground, Mother True whispered to her daughter. *He is not indestructible.*

Minerva gained strength from her mother's phantom words, returning the challenging stare. Snow fell in great clumps from the branches above. A transmutation began beneath the canopy of dark trees. The eyes of Darcy Crocker sunk inward so that he resembled the old preacher Mother True had first encountered years before. The very one she had kept at bay, and then defeated again even as he sought new flesh in the body of Parson Wade. With Darcy, though, the preacher had found a body with enough strength to match his will. And with Mother gone and her curse lifted, the danger was palpable.

"He returns," Minerva spoke softly. She knew then that there would need to be a resolution between the two of them. She and the preacher would need to meet in a battle for the valley. This day, however, he had not come seeking that fight. This was only the warning, the invitation, as it were, to a day of blood. He was letting her know by the familiar guise of another that he meant to stake his claim.

She knew he could not pass into the circle of trees. Presently, Mother True's wisdom held too strong, even for him. The boys, at least, were safe. But what of Garet and Calpurnia? If the preacher walked Black Hill, how safe were they? She needed to get word to them, perhaps bring them to the cottage. Journeying to warn them, she would need to be watchful and keep her faith in the forest. It would be potent enough to lead her through. She wasn't certain exactly how strong the preacher had grown. But she still had the wisp of the River Dwellers and the trees of Black Hill.

Having accepted the challenge the preacher extolled, Minerva exercised her own strength. The exposed roots and burnt brush were quickly covered and taken over by neighboring vegetation, like skin healing a cut. With astonishing speed and grace, leaf and vine vanquished the scar. Just as rapidly, the figure of the dark priest melted into the undergrowth. The wind howled around the circle wood.

Minerva rushed back to the cottage. The stags peered nervously around the corner, perceiving the danger had been abated. Closing the door gently behind her and descending the few steps into the cottage, Minerva's thoughts focused on what she must do. Darcy had returned, but not the man Garet and Calpurnia had known. If he got to them before her, there would be no telling…. No telling at all.

"Don't worry, Miss Minerva," Aubrey said, standing on a footstool peering out the kitchen window to where she had stood. He had been watching all along. "We're stronger, we are." He turned to her with unparalleled assuredness for such a small boy. "And when it comes time, good ol' Aubrey Avonmore'll earn his keep!"

The valley echoed with wintersound, a hush spread out in layers by which every living thing sighed, transfixed and reflective. Garet climbed a steep wall of rock, the sun before midday streaming upon him and melting the snow from the rockface. He climbed alone—*his* feet, *his* breathing, and the lilting impressions in the air about him. He was the only man in the world, scaling the steeper side of Black Hill, distancing himself from everyone who had ever been, from anything that tore at his heart. It was only in these solitary moments that he managed peace, defeating the cliffsides that overhung the valley, these same bluffs which had nearly defeated him years earlier. Had Darcy not been there, he would never have become a ranger. He would never have been anything.

He scaled along Painters Pass—the cliffside called thusly because of its colored stones and earth—trying to not think. He wanted to be like the cold winter air that swooshed over the river. If only he could be that cold, that formless, that quick and decisive. Without regrets. He would feel none of the weight of humanity but still witness the beauty of the world. If not the wind, perhaps he could be like Azrael and become an angel. *Can humans become angels?*

Garet wouldn't waste his time watching folk; he would watch the river turn across acres, or spend ages watching the rocks of Beggar's Hill being eroded by the elements. Not a thought. Not a single distraction.

He came to a narrow shelf and rested there before his final ascent to the top of the bluff. He had not given up the hunt for Darcy. He knew it was probable Hamlin and the valley folk were right. Darcy was gone, taken to the chapel grounds. Garet's heart still stopped every time he thought of never again seeing those suspicious, loving eyes or feeling those callused, tender hands. But Garet wasn't searching for Darcy in the same way the others had been. Not by mere physical manifestation. Instead, he sought his friend's signature on lost and broken paths, scattered among the ruins of childhood campsites, or etched into cave walls and tree stumps. He was listening, very mindfully, for a memory in the trees.

Perhaps Calpurnia believed Garet still hunted for Darcy in order to kill him. Perhaps not. Perhaps she never had. His connection to her, their strange partnership, had been severed the night Lara had foolishly run off into the woods and Darcy had just as foolishly chased her. For his own sense of duty, for a grasp at honesty, Garet rose every morning before the house stirred, grabbed his revolver from the closet, the sword from the wall in the Great Hall, kissed Leith on the forehead, and headed into the pitch-black forest before the sunrise. He stayed away from Walterhouse Manor most of the day, returning at nightfall with some game, mostly deer—never the Breed—or cougar or wild hog. Being a ranger, he was an excellent hunter… when he wanted to be. He imagined if he ever did find Darcy, he would need to leave the valley with him. He would care for him. To kill him seemed an impossible thing. He would expel whatever had control of his friend using Minerva's lore and set off with him up the river. Eventually, things would be wonderful again. Just the two of them, like it was when they were children. They would find some place even more remote than Black Hill. These were his most yearned-for dreams, the thoughts he had to possess to keep moving through life sometimes.

Warmed by these thoughts—*Why do you keep thinking? Just stop thinking*—Garet watched his frozen breath rise into ether and leaned against the rockside. A biting wind off the river touched him with snowflakes. It felt numbing and peaceful. His fingers ached from the cold and the climb. Above him, he heard the gentle displacement of small stones. He glanced up in the realization that he was not alone. Some animal most likely stumbling about. But what he saw nearly made him stumble over the narrow ledge he was situated upon.

Darcy Crocker stared down at him from the precipice like a risen hero god from some ancient half-remembered religion. His arms were crossed inside of a long, thick fur coat. Snow collected in his dark hair and the coat's pelt. Garet could do nothing but smile, tears breaking free.

"*Darcy!*" he whisper-shouted. "You're back!"

For the moment, Garet completely forgot Darcy had ever been horribly disfigured at the chapel grounds. He assigned the incident to a bad dream after a night of heavy drinking. No, Darcy had never been hurt, and things would continue just as they always had. Maybe things would even be better. Hope kindled by illusion surged in him.

Though not a word left his lips, Garet heard Darcy gently urging him upward: "Come to me, Garet. It's been too long. I have something to show you. Be with me."

It was his voice, but more gentle. The hint of suspicion was gone.

Garet absently dropped his revolver to the rockshelf and untied the burdensome belt that held the sword to his hips. As he climbed, as his hands were torn and ripped by the merciless, jagged stones. He sobbed joyously. Happiness was lifting him now, pushing him on, pulling him through the pain. The closer he came to Darcy, the more beautiful Darcy grew, and the safer Garet felt. Darcy uncrossed his arms and held them out, ready to take Garet into them.

THE OLD Walterhouse place looked ever-lonesome in its snow-covered surroundings. A glorified farmhouse, Winifred Walterhouse had once called it. Only the shell of an old pine stood crookedly in the front yard, its brown needles vaguely resembling the aged, paint-chipped house. The sun was setting, colors slowly creeping westward. Silent fields rimmed the house in the winter, the distant forest cascading like a vast waterfall down to the valley.

Young Leith Cather observed the changing landscape from the long window in his mother's room as the sunlight took its final bow. Calpurnia's bedchamber had not changed much from when Winifred slept there. The same four-poster bed stretched to the ceiling, the same washbasin sat on the same table. Only the clothes in the closet and drawers were different.

"What's over there?" Leith asked of the retreating sun, his face and fingers pressed against the glass. "What do you see?" He wanted desperately to know the answer, to adventure on with heavenly bodies. "Fine. But I'll know someday!" he shouted defiantly when he received no answer.

His attention was soon drawn elsewhere. A shadow void of form lingered for a moment by the old pine in front of the house. It rolled in waves, transforming, *becoming*. At last, standing in the thick white snow, was the silhouette of a man, a giant of sorts with massive shoulders and arms. The kind Leith had been told of in tales as he, Elijah, and Aubrey lay huddled around Minerva by a hearth fire at the cottage. He stared in curiosity, questioning the makings of such a being, unable to discern the specifics of the giant due to the arrival of night but still dazzled by its inimitable presence. He pressed closer into the glass trying to get a better look.

Unexpectedly, the giant strode across the snow, heading to the back of the house. The long dark train of his coat crawled after him. Leith's small hands smudged the window as his eyes followed the figure, spellbound. The giant paused momentarily, as if perceiving the boy's stare, but then moved on, disappearing from sight.

KNOCK KNOCK KNOCK

They came so soon after the giant had vanished around the house, and so very loudly, Leith found himself jumping back from the glass. He raced from the bedchamber and down the stairs barefoot in his little white pajamas. He hurried as fast as he could, though his combination toddler's stride and limp somewhat impaired his speed. Still, a giant was something he would not miss. Suddenly it seemed the sun had missed a great opportunity by not sticking around.

Leith immediately forgot about the giant, however, for his mother—however hesitantly—was welcoming Minerva True, Elijah Crocker, and Aubrey Avonmore through the front door. Though it was odd they would visit so late at night, never mind the bitter cold, Leith was only too happy to see them. They were bundled in thick covers, Elijah carried by Aubrey, the latter boy leaning back a bit now due to the former's increasing size and weight. Leith ran to his friends, delighted, as they knocked loose the snow from their shoes and shook free the dusting that had fallen from the trees onto their clothes. The three boys toddled off in pursuit of some quality adventuring. Leith thought he might even tell them of the giant. The next day they could go hunting for it. They could find where it slept and wait for it to return there.

Minerva stood stoically, barely moving from her stance at the door.

"Is there something the matter?" Calpurnia asked as she padded away to prepare a pot of hot tea. She could tolerate the old woman's strange behavior only so much.

Minerva's gaze rose to the younger woman, and she followed her to the kitchen. The children were off making a racket, abusing dust-laden furniture in the Great Hall. "Where's your husband, my dear?" she asked softly. "Where's Garet?"

"Hunting, as usual. He hunts for Darcy even in his sleep. He's been gone since before I woke."

"And that is not odd?"

Calpurnia turned and studied her. "It's not unusual for us; not for the times, anyway. Most of the time he returns before it gets too dark, but occasionally he will stay in the forest. How is that your concern?"

"I do not think Garet would be so foolish as to stay in the forest on such a bitter cold night." Minerva stood near the kitchen doorway.

"Well," Calpurnia responded coldly, "you would know him better than I. Everyone does. It was he and Darcy who should have seen sunsets together, not he and I."

"Perhaps you are right. You had Lara."

Calpurnia's heart paused a beat at the mention of her friend's name. The implication of that truth—that Minerva had known of her feelings all along—troubled her. "Yes… I did have her," she said, drifting off into memory. "Garet's perfectly fine." She collected herself, turning her attention back to the tea. "He's a hunter, remember? He knows Black Hill better than anyone, except maybe you."

"The forest is dark this night…."

"He knows the spells; he knows the words to say, Minerva. He went through the rites as has any boy in this nonsensical valley." Calpurnia found two china cups from Winifred's prized collection and washed them out indifferently.

"My child, the forest is dark this night," Minerva repeated.

The reiteration sent a chill up Calpurnia's spine. She dried a cup in her apron, slowly turning to face the old River Dweller. She could see now that Minerva was trembling; her black shawl had fallen to the floor at her feet. Her hand held a long, gleaming piece of metal that caught the light from the candles.

"That's his father's sword. Garet's sword," Calpurnia said in shock. She laid the cup on the sink. The air filled with artless connotations, and Calpurnia understood Garet was gone. While she did not love the man as a husband, she certainly saw him as someone—some*thing*—connected to her life.

"I found it upright in the middle of Black Hill Road, its blade sunken deep into the earth. It was intentionally placed there, there's no doubt. Do you know what this means, child?" Minerva drew closer to

Calpurnia. The quiet of the kitchen felt displaced next to the rumpus in the Great Hall.

"I am alone again," Calpurnia replied, her eyes wide in confusion and fear. "Garet has gone, and I am alone." Realization upon realization poured over her, and she looked accusingly at Minerva. "I thought you… I thought the River Dwellers were supposed to stop all of this. Why does the chapel continue to plague us? What have we done, Minerva? What have *you* done?"

"We have done absolutely nothing. We have only respected the world and its inhabitants without imposing on them our will. Alas, the chapel requires nothing but the blindest of faith."

"But I don't believe…. So… there's nothing can be done." Calpurnia let loose her desperation at last as she wandered, stumbling into the Great Hall. The walls of her mind thinned. Minerva followed her closely. The boys had moved their playing upstairs.

"We should go for help," Calpurnia stated suddenly, standing before the roaring fire of the massive hearth. "Hamlin or the Parmas… someone will look for him! Perhaps he's still alive. Perhaps he simply lost the sword. The forest takes things at will. It's a strange place. When I was a child I saw a fox and…." But Calpurnia didn't want to share that story with Minerva, so she stopped herself.

"Sweet Calpurnia," Minerva said, handing the sword to her. "He is gone."

The difference in their tears was abundantly clear to both. Minerva shed hers for the loss of Garet as a human being; Calpurnia's tears were for what Garet meant to her.

"But how do you know?" Calpurnia protested.

"He is gone. You are not, and I have a feeling there is a reason for that."

Calpurnia gripped the sword tightly and hung the heavy thing again above the hearth. A mindless action; something to fill the moment. She remained frozen in the position, an arm on either end of the sword. She spoke with venom in her voice. "If you were any sort of witch at all, you could have stopped this. You could bring him back now. *I cannot be alone!*"

MINERVA IGNORED the assault and moved to sit on the long emerald-green sofa, a place she had rested on many occasions while speaking with Winifred Walterhouse. It was torn in a few places now, and the color had faded somewhat. Minerva decided she would not tell Calpurnia of all she knew, of all she had seen and heard that day, starting with the preacher resurrected. She would not speak of the uneasiness she felt in her stomach as she readied Aubrey and Elijah to make their journey to Walterhouse Manor, or how she had stumbled out of the cottage, drawn to the backwoods and the cliff. How, as she peered down onto the chapel grounds, she leaned against the large oak tree and went to her knees. She would not tell Calpurnia she had heard Garet's last breath, and been unable to do anything. She would not say any of this; for she feared Calpurnia was very near her own breaking point.

Minerva remained in the Great Hall through the night, as did the others, though neither she nor Calpurnia slept. The grandfather clock dolefully marked the hours. Occasionally, Minerva would stoke the fire, but there were few words exchanged. Only the boys had any exuberance in them, but soon they fell silent and drifted off to sleep, unaware that something was not right.

The house responded to the winter wind with creaks and groans. The candles spread throughout the Great Hall had one by one extinguished themselves. A tasteful lapzine chandelier hung gloriously overhead and would have provided ample light, but Minerva could see that it had not been used in years. They waited in darkness.

During the night Minerva noticed a change come over the young mother. Her countenance, even the aura around her, lessened in its resonance. Calpurnia never had a playful yellow or violet aura around her, but at least what color she did have had been strong. Now, it had begun to change; a change Minerva knew could never be redressed. She had seen that loss of color before in the witless and insane. Calpurnia's eyes glazed over. She stared into the logs on the fire and smoothed Leith's hair as he slept on her lap.

As first light gave color to the room, telling lies of hope, Minerva rose and walked to the kitchen. Aubrey and Elijah still slept in a huddle on the massive brown rug that stretched the width of the hearth furnishings. Calpurnia rose as well, attempting not to disturb Leith's sleep. But Leith was always a boy easily awakened. He sat up quickly, rubbing his eyes and watching Calpurnia join Minerva in the kitchen. He stretched and crawled off the sofa and curled up with Aubrey and Elijah on the rug.

"I was going to make some tea. You should get some sleep, dear," Minerva suggested. Calpurnia wore the same gown she had worn the night before. "I can get the boys ready, and Aubrey can hitch the horses. We'll head to Hamlin for aid. It's safer now."

Calpurnia appeared not to hear. Instead, she donned her black coat with clumsy, inattentive pulls and tugs. "I need to get the wood… for the hearth…," she mumbled and headed toward the back door.

Opening the door with considerable effort, as though all her strength had left her in the night, she looked silently out onto the snow. The cold draft of winter swept quickly through the first floor of the house, but Calpurnia did not move. She barely breathed.

"Calpurnia?" Minerva queried, approaching from behind.

"I can't go," Calpurnia muttered, fear and pain crowding her heart. She stared blankly before her. "I can't go out. I shall never be able go out again, I think."

"I'll get it. I will get the wood. You stay here with the boys." Minerva pulled her back into the kitchen. She tightened her shawl about her and marched out into the snow. Immediately she began to tremble from the chill air.

It was a quiet winter morning, the kind of morning that suffocates sound. The kind that anesthetizes sound with a glacial stare. Approaching the shed, Minerva caught sight of a dark blue bag wrapped and sitting on an old tree stump like a gift. She paused for a moment, and then cautiously drew near the stump.

Leaning over with one hand still clutching her shawl, she pulled on the white cord tied around the bag's neck. So full was the cloth that its contents came tumbling out onto the ground as if in search of air and breathing room. A large human skull first, and then bones, many bones, stripped clean of flesh, the skin and muscle having been cooked right off, boiled like chicken. Along with the bones that lay scattered on the ground around the stump Minerva saw the glint of emerald and gold. She gasped at the truth she had already known.

"Is that Garet's ring?" Calpurnia screamed from the doorway. Her eyesight had always been acute. She held herself up by clinging to the doorframe.

"Is that Garet's ring?" Her words fell away like fading drops of rain, and she slid to the floor, bellowing her pain into the world, a wounded animal initiating its lonesome new life.

Part III—
Minerva & the Boys

Collecting Bones

MINERVA WALKED steadily along the cliffside, Hamlin always a few steps in front of her. It was a day for bone collecting, and he would more forcefully grab at the bones than she, ripping them from the grip of the black briars as though tearing a stubborn weed from a garden. It had become a recent chore, the collecting of the bones, and it required some effort now that they had aged. She carried with her an old scythe for the task.

"Let's rest," Minerva said. Hamlin's breathing had become labored. "It will do us both good."

He knew she was right. The years were creeping up on him. He saw it every time he looked in a mirror, his eyes wrinkled at the edges, his skin tanned and leathered, and his hair still dark but graying now.

The sky was pleasant, cloaking the threatening weather soon to come. Minerva and Hamlin leaned their backs against the wide gnarled oak tree that dared to extend its ancient roots over the cliff. Hamlin set the gunnysack of bones beside him and lit his pipe. The smoke carried out over the black vines that had climbed up the walls of the bluff from the chapel grounds. He imagined the smoke drifting over the river, making its passage through strange air to the mysterious river folk on the opposite bank.

"Strange," he whispered to himself as he took a puff.

"What is, my love?" Minerva queried. All these years she had loved him, and not once had he ever doubted that.

"I have lived here by the river all my life, but have never adventured across it," he mused. "I never once asked a ferry boat boy to take me. What are they like, do you suppose? The Othersiders, I mean."

"They keep to themselves. But they find us just as curious as we find them, I'm certain."

"Have you been there?" Hamlin asked, his attention drawn to her serene face. He was always discovering new things about Minerva, even now as they both entered their twilight years.

"A couple of times when I was a young girl I was supposed to go with Mother True," she answered. "They're an ancient people. They have much to teach if one can get them to come from their hiding places. As a River Dweller I was to be instructed in some of the rites on the other bank, but it never came to pass. Mother True thought Ingrid more prepared than I, and she was right. I was not ready."

"Minerva True, not ready? That doesn't sound like the gal I know."

"Were you thinking you might go someday soon? There's still time left to adventure, darling." She touched his face with her soft palm.

He kissed her open palm tenderly. "There's still much to be done here. Even if our side of the river is nearly empty, there are still some who look to you and me. But one day I'll get there, I suspect. It'll be my last great adventure. What do you say to that?"

She took his hand and returned the kiss.

The river valley had become vacant. Miserably so. Most of the homes were abandoned and falling apart, and no one from the outside had moved in for a very long time. The people had become frightened of the rumors, and instead of searching for the truth, relied on scattered hearsay. They blamed the old ways of the valley for its misfortune; they began to forget the good and grabbed for a trendier, more easily explainable faith. Minerva and the memory of the River Dwellers had become synonymous with a character from another ancient text, a character known as the Great Opposer.

"Oh, these old black briars distract our view," Hamlin grunted, leering at the sickened plants as they peeked up over the cliff's edge at them. "We need to be careful. They'll be at your cottage door before too long. They're a dangerous weed." He remembered with grief the torture and death of Angela Children.

"We have time still," Minerva replied. "But an eye will be kept on them all the same. At present, however, they would not dare enter my circle. And the big oak here growls down on them. He is my guard."

"I suppose the vines do serve an ominous purpose. They remind us that the chapel is still a threat, as if we could forget."

"Yes," Minerva said, sounding suddenly sad and distant. "The chapel sleeps for some reason. I have found shades of complacency coming over me every now and then. For fifteen years there has been not a whisper of darkness, neither a trace of Darcy Crocker. Not since that winter morning when he left the bag of Garet Cather's bones on the stump outside Walterhouse Manor."

"And Old Dark Eyes? Has he not been haunting your dreams these years?"

"Not once," she answered. "And that worries me. He has a victory planned. He means to take me down with the valley in one swoop. I'm the field mouse to his hawk. He's setting things in motion, I fear, but I cannot see what is going to happen. He waits."

"He isn't strong enough," Hamlin stated squarely, though he was becoming less certain of the valley's survival. "And then there's Aubrey. You and I both know that boy—born across the river as he was—well, there's something special about him. There's a familiarity to his look as well. Like I've seen him before. A face from a long time ago. And, you know, I'm beginning to believe he *did* swim the river after all. Maybe that ferry boat boy had something to be embarrassed about." He paused, searching for answers in his smoke. "Are you sure the black briars are an indication of the coming battle?"

Minerva nodded. "Even if the briars hadn't grown so quickly in the past few years, there are other signs. The Breed, those few that are left, refuse to leave my circle as of late. They sense the scald of things. And, while the trees have not been restless, there is an energy here. It stalks the night like a hunter, scanning the fold."

"I blame myself for some of it," Hamlin said, puffing, puffing, puffing away.

"You couldn't have known what would have happened. You did what you thought was best for the valley."

"I should have listened to you, just as the Parson Wade should have listened to your mother," he insisted. "But I was desperate, thinking there might be an easy solution; hoping for it anyway. I never asked to be anyone's leader, dammit!"

"The way I remember it, my love, Prichard Parma gave you very little choice in the matter. He and his sons were intent on setting the chapel alight, and they had the valley folk behind them. You would have been outnumbered if you had tried to stop them. What happened would have happened no matter."

"Chapel-goers out to destroy their own chapel, and in the process they end up damaging the beauty around it as well." Hamlin huffed in puzzlement. "It's something to think about."

"They believed what they were told. A lie had been cast out onto the river that the chapel had been taken by the Opposer. It was a successful lie from the unseen lips of a missing villain."

"And I helped it flourish. As sure as spit, I did." His voice was broken as he puffed on his pipe without pleasure.

Minerva took hold of his hand, and the two sat in combat against the worst of memories. When was the last drop of happiness washed from the valley and carried down river? When had that occurred? Hamlin remembered every moment of the day the chapel was set ablaze. It had been over seven years past, but the fire that burned useless then licked at his keen mind as if it were in front of him now.

"Prichard believes he can do it," Hamlin said to Minerva as they sat on the steps of his small, lonely cabin, squat at the bowl of two knolls and in front of a small band of trees. His years of housing Calpurnia and Lara were long over, and while they'd given him a great deal of purpose, he was glad to have his home to himself again. "His boys say they can strike up such a fire that the Devil would run from its heat." The bright day encouraged him as only bright days can.

"Their devil is not whom we need fear," Minerva replied. "We will regret it, Hamlin. The valley could fall for this."

"Can't we have faith that they might succeed?" he said, somewhat irritated at her dreadful doomsdaying, her sad soothsaying.

"Faith... Yes." She nodded with a pacifying smile. "We do need faith."

The night of the fire, those who were still left in the valley amassed outside the chapel grounds, holding out for some courage or sense of religious righteousness. They were of the new faith now, and their God would triumph. He would reclaim His house. They stood stoic and silent, yet anxious as Prichard Parma and his nine sons marched into the chapel grounds with their torches. The reserved nature of those gathered was strange to see on the beach. Where once there had been nothing but the most raucous convocations and celebrations of an older faith, now hardly a syllable sounded.

The crowd roared at the Parmas' safe passage through the chapel grounds. Their new God was with them. Mumblings of religious fervor and pride rose like cinders from amongst them. Hamlin looked at Minerva with surprised hope. She stood a ways back by the river with those few others who refused to give up the older ways. Aubrey Avonmore stood with her, holding the hand of young Elijah. Through Hamlin's optimism, Minerva's face remained dread-set.

The new chapel-goers—though none had ever actually been inside the chapel—began to sing a hymn they had acquired from a more important congregation of the upper lands. There was a sense of togetherness and unity against the likes of the Devil and Minerva. They applauded with zeal as the youngest Parma boy, Aiden, kicked open the chapel doors and threw his torch dripping with oil and flame into the guts of the structure. At once, the inner core of the chapel seemed to burn bright. The windows shone orange with flame. A great hoopla rose from the converted. Aiden pranced around like a hero having tamed a beast; like Heracles after having slain the Nemean lion. His father and brothers worked around him, casting fire this way and that, all to the delight of the singing, ardent crowd. Stoking both the crowd and the fire, the Parmas were careful not to light the marshy ground surrounding the structure so it would not burn out of control.

Minerva felt the winds change.

A subtle creeping rose from the ground around the Parmas, something only she and those of older faiths could see. Roots of a far more powerful kind were anchoring themselves to the unwitting family of heroes. Suddenly, the fire that had blazed in and upon the chapel whooshed out as quick and simple as a candle being blown on a birthday cake, the chapel hardly burnt at all, its windows dark once again. Not even a whiff of smoke ascended into the night air.

The devotees stared in frightened anticipation, their breaths not daring to interrupt the paused air. Hamlin shot a terrified glance to Minerva.

"It's too late," she seemed to convey through the distance.

He returned his attention to the chapel just in time to see the Parma clan disappear into the structure to investigate, their pride unwilling to admit defeat.

"Get out!" Hamlin yelled, running toward the chapel. "Get out of there, you fools!"

The assemblage did not know what to think, their confusion compounded as Hamlin ran forward.

He managed only a few yards before a horrible suctioning sound echoed through the valley, as if a giant had yawned. In a blast of mythical *proportions, the flames consumed the structure once again. Fire bellowed from its doors like a great furnace, and the conflagration reached high into the night, climbing the ruined outer walls of the chapel, scaling the very air around it—a new and altogether mightier church made of flame.*

Cinder and ash flew mercilessly toward the beach. Hamlin was knocked to the ground as the crowd dissolved in panic. Minerva and the boys came to him, helping him to his feet. They stared in incredulity as the fire reached for the forest of Black Hill. It ripped through the trees like a lava blade. Minerva heard the wailing memory of the trees, the escape of souls, and she gasped.

"I'm a fool," Hamlin whispered to the night.

In no time, the fire decimated the hillside, preparing the way for the dark briars to creep in its wake. And grow they did over the years, with greater strength, like dark rays emanating from a deconstructed star. Upward they crawled, an army of vengeful death toward Minerva's precipice, where she held her constant vigil over the chapel grounds.

Minerva squeezed Hamlin's hand, rescuing him from his scolding memories. He breathed deeply, resurfacing from his thoughts. He cleared his throat and took another puff from his pipe.

Soon it was time for him to leave; there were things to do. Hamlin rose with effort. Minerva, ever the independent, did not wait to be offered a gentlemanly hand and took to her feet with somewhat more ease. Together, holding the gunny sac between them, they walked into the woods and entered the cottage circle.

"I ought to be gettin' back to the valley," Hamlin said, handing her the sack. "There are still a few who foolishly look to me for answers. They worry when I come to Black Hill."

"Aubrey and Leith should be coming back soon. Are you sure you won't stay for lunch?"

He leaned in and kissed Minerva gently on the lips. "Still my beautiful lady with the silver hair." He smiled. "I should git."

"Well, then you git," she returned with good humor. "The boys will be upset to have missed you."

Once alone in the circle wood with only the Breed and the trees and the blossoming flowers to converse with, Minerva kneeled on the patch of ground in the rock garden she had designated as a temporary resting place for the Parmas. She began gently planting each of the day's bones in the soil alongside those that she or the boys had subsequently discovered. She had no idea which bones belonged to which of the Parmas. They had risen stripped and clean, the black briars bragging of their work as they brought each individually to her attention. Another warning from their master, she was sure. In lining the bones together in the ground, she hoped there would be some kind of peace for the Parmas, but knew that their spirits were most likely bound below in the confines of the chapel.

It was Elijah clothed in his simple drawstring trousers and nothing else who came barreling through the earthen cottage door that autumn day when first the hint of bone was seen creeping up the cliff wall. He nearly tore the door off its hinges, a thing he had done many times due to his unnatural strength; strength that had only grown as he became a young man. Minerva had become adept at reading his eyes, the emotion of his movements, and he was frantic, pulling at her with frenzied excitement. He led her by the hand through the circle wood to the cliff where Aubrey was kneeling, looking down into the chapel grounds.

"What do you suppose?" Aubrey asked, nodding down the cliffside.

Minerva knew exactly what she was seeing. She knew the eerie gleam of stripped bones; she had seen it before. "We must watch the briars," she answered. "When they come level to the precipice, the bones must be taken from them and cared for."

"But what are they? Whose are they?" Aubrey reiterated. He still preferred the forest to a man-made home. Sometimes Elijah would join him under the trees for days at a time. Only when Minerva grew concerned did Aubrey agree to spend an evening in the cottage. "I'll climb down and get 'em now. Who needs to wait?"

"No, Aubrey." Minerva put her hand on his shoulder. "That would not be wise. We will wait."

And so they did. Aubrey refused to leave his vigil, waiting day in, day out, as the bones made their way ever upward. He was impatient for them. Finally, one morning as the winds turned a bitter chill, the hollowed eyes of a man's skull peered at Aubrey as he woke up under the shelter of the oak. It had crept up over the night. He jumped to his feet and ran to the cottage, waking the forest with his cries.

"It's time!" he cried. "The bones have started to rise."

At last, the time came to free what was left of the Parma's physical bodies. Minerva held an ancient, beaten-up scythe she had used for gardening. It had leaned against the cottage since she was a child. Only once did she see Mother True use it, and that had nothing to do with gardening. She stood majestic and battle-ready at the cliff, a queen the likes of Boadicea. She stared down at the skull, tangled in the mass of deformed vegetation, which clung to it violently. The strength of the vines could have turned the bones to dust. Aubrey and Elijah stood to either side of Minerva, their faces just as determined as hers. With one vigorous and well-placed swipe from the scythe the skull somersaulted into the air and Aubrey caught it with ease. Minerva swung her weapon twice more, freeing a shoulder bone and a broken femur. The separated ends of the offending vines withered into dust, and the entire mass of dark briars cowered back down the rockface.

She tenderly took the skull from Aubrey, peering into it so as to answer her questions. "Prichard," she whispered. "You proud fool."

So the important task of cleansing the bones began. Every day Aubrey would keep watch at the cliff, and always new bones were brought up. And always, the vines would shrink at the sight of Minerva and her scythe. The bones were collected and buried one by one in the strange garden of rock—brought from the creeks of the forest—amongst the bluebells, begonias, and gladiolas.

Only one of Prichard's nine sons was ever buried whole. Young Aiden ascended the cliff wall slowly. His death stench warned of his slow coming. When he arrived high enough to be freed, to Minerva's horror she saw he was still flesh and muscle, though burnt and scarred. His face had grown hair and he looked starved, with eyes colorless and wide in horror. She realized he had lived until very recently, bound by the briars, hearing the suffering of his father and brothers as they died one by one and were digested by worms. She cried for him then gave him a proper burial in the garden. Hamlin and the boys were in attendance. They were all who would come.

After covering the new bones she and Hamlin had just retrieved, Minerva waved off her own disturbing memories and entered the cottage. Leith and Aubrey would be back from their school lessons soon, and tonight Elijah was at last choosing a river name. His new name would give him strength. He would need that strength if he were—as Minerva suspected—of the Three.

THE ALL-BUT-FORGOTTEN
CEREMONY OF RIVER NAMING

ALBERT HIGGINS, one of Greenbriar College's most promising students, had been sought out by Leith and Aubrey to educate them on the workings of the outer world. They believed knowledge thereof might, in some way, help them with the restoration of balance to the valley. Albert Higgins embraced the opportunity. As a tutor to these two young men from the valley below, he would be able to hone his skills as a professor of the liberal arts. It intrigued him how innocent and uninformed they were, as if they had been hidden away behind walls all their lives and had just recently emerged. Their sheer excitement to learn was inspiring. Some of his fellow students should be as thrilled, he thought. They were hungry for everything he told them; sometimes their sessions together stretched well past what he had originally set down, inching into his own study time. It was an enjoyable challenge to try and find things to satiate their voracious mental appetites.

Albert himself understood their hunger; he felt the same. His father was a preeminent doctor of history at a highly respected university to the east. He'd encouraged his son to learn, to seek out explanations, to study the course of mythology and society. Reason was of the utmost importance; it would save humanity.

It was up to Albert, though, to make his name in the widening halls of academia. To do this, he would have to distance himself from his father's own suffocating reputation. He opted to travel west and attend the burgeoning humanities college of Greenbriar founded by an eccentric family friend, Castor Verona; a man his aunt, Esther Walterhouse, had known in her younger years. She had lived around the college at one point, but was never too forthcoming about any more than that. Though his friends and fiancée remained east, Albert had no problem creating a distinct identity for himself in this new place. Soon, he had ingratiated himself with the student body as well as the faculty with his good nature and determination.

Albert enjoyed the lessons with Leith and Aubrey. "They're such charming young men," he wrote to his fiancée. "It's a shame about their upbringing. In the right setting they could have been gallant citizens. I fear it might be too late for their restructuring now. But I shall give it a good go."

The boys took to mythology sometimes too fervently, as if the stories he taught of Poseidon, Gaea, Odin, and Baal were not myths at all but recounted histories. He reminded them constantly of the differences between truth and fabrication, but they never seemed to hear him. Still, he could see his two pupils in ancient heroes' roles: Achilles and Patroklus, David and Jonathan, Gilgamesh and Enkidu. The thoughts excited him somewhat, and made him envious of the boys' freedom.

"They are not real," Albert assured them as they sat under one of the large trees in the quadrangle. They preferred this area to the Point on the bluff where there was no shade from the sun. "They are only inventions, made up by those afraid of losing power. It was a way to control the populace with the threat of divine retribution; sociology in its simplest form."

"But then, what about this God of the Bible? Your God?" Aubrey inquired. "Is he a means to power as well?"

"Absolutely not!" Albert laughed. "We're learned men. We understand there is but one creator. He gives us science and philosophy so that we may know him better."

"But how do you know?" Aubrey challenged. He sat with his arms wrapped around his knees. Leith leaned on his shoulder. They were both barefoot, and, while Albert frowned upon this as socially unacceptable, he said nothing.

"Because it is undeniable."

"*How* is it undeniable?" Aubrey's searching, honest eyes held neither contempt nor stubbornness. He just wanted an answer he could believe in.

Albert thought for a moment, and, unable to come up with an answer that satisfied himself, simply said: "That which cannot be proven with sufficient evidence is most likely rubbish. The Good Book gives the world plenty of insight into the workings of God. Perhaps we should not question that."

"But this is a school, ain't it?" Aubrey complained. "It is a place for questions, right? Besides, it was you who told us that Homer's writings were thought to be just as real to people of ancient times as people think the ol' Bible to be today. And now no one believes that Homer is true. Couldn't it be the same with your book?"

Albert was becoming less comfortable with his control of the situation. He played with his thin moustache absently.

"Seems a lil' hypocritical, s'all I'm saying," Aubrey finished. Leith nodded in agreement.

"All right then, Mr. Avonmore," the young professor said, "you believe what you will despite the evidence. Believe in a battalion of gods or your River Dwellers and snov... snov—What were they again?"

"Snovelfarks," Leith said, trying to be of assistance. He was well-versed in the old stories of the valley and surprised to learn that snovelfarks did not exist anywhere else in the world.

"Yes, thank you. Believe in your snovelfarks. But try and keep an open mind to what I'm trying to teach you as well, hmm?" He said it so sympathetically that Aubrey resisted the urge to retort. He merely smiled, as if to appease his tutor.

"That one," Albert would later write to his fiancée, referring, of course, to Aubrey Avonmore, "is a piece of work."

But he couldn't help smiling at the boys' tall tales of life in the valley. He began to wonder how such uneducated boys had obtained such fantastic imaginations. What was so special about the abandoned valley where they resided?

"Yes," he agreed with a previous thought. "Very much Achilles and Patroklus."

Their lessons at Greenbriar College finished for the day, Leith and Aubrey walked lazily through the gray and blackened remains of the lower forest of Black Hill. It had been many years, but the scarred landscape at the base of the hill persisted as a desolate memento of an angry day. Winds whipped over ash, lifting it in whirls; trees and stumps stood petrified from a onetime heat rarely imagined. The boys traveled through a graveyard of misery. The chapel remains could be viewed without obstruction through the cold stone limbs of a once thriving wood. Only the mist obscured the swampy grounds.

"Do you think it'll ever be green again?" Leith asked, kicking at the soot of Black Hill Road.

"You know I do," Aubrey answered. As always, he held both of their books in his hands. "You ask me all the time, and I always tell you the same dang thing."

"I know. But I don't see how. It's all become stone. There's no soil for any life to grow." The limp from his childhood trauma at the chapel grounds became more pronounced as they made their way uphill. Aubrey always stayed with him; Leith never had to ask him to slow down so he could catch up. On level surfaces, though, Leith could run if he needed to.

"Nothing is set. Not even stone. Nothing is impenetrable, Leithy."

They had grown into strong young men and would have made proud scholars. Albert Higgins had told them as much. Their only real chance for education came by way of the college and its hopeful young students. Five days a week Leith and Aubrey happily trekked up and over the valley hills to enter the Greenbriar College grounds. Elijah chose not to attend. He was quite satisfied with the more natural education Minerva and the forest and river provided.

"Looky here!" Aubrey playfully exclaimed as they approached a petrified oak. Leith smiled generously in the presence of memory. A few days after the Parma's great fire had been defeated and the smoke was yet curling, Aubrey had come down to see the devastation against Minerva's pleas for him to stay away from the chapel. After all, he couldn't be asked to do *everything* he was told. Angered by what he saw, and as a show of defiance to the preacher, he'd etched his name into the hard, mineralizing wood of the tree:

AuBrey AvonMore was right here!

As the boys grew, it became a favorite spot to plan and plot the downfall of the chapel, which could easily be seen from the tree's cold branches. Leith was sure he couldn't have been more than seven or eight at the time the inscription was carved, and he remembered Aubrey as being around the age of ten.

But then, curiously, it seemed Aubrey had been ten for a long, long time before he started to age at all. The adults in his life, at seeing his invariant characteristics, thought him to be cursed with some disease that stunted growth. However, as Elijah and Leith grew to be about a decade old, so also Aubrey began to age along with them, like he was just waiting for them to catch up. They entered puberty together, and grew into young men together. Many remarked in wonder at this, most assuming that whatever deficiency he possessed had cleared of its own accord. Some chapel-goers thought it a miracle of their God. Others imagined it a spell of Minerva's devil.

Now Aubrey was one of the handsomest young men most had ever known. His elfin looks gave him a beautiful, almost feminine quality, yet his voice still echoed from one river bank to the other, dancing a jig with itself on its way back. Leith had grown a little more ordinary-looking, not leaning too handsome, but fine just the same. Near Aubrey, however, he seemed just as beautiful. He felt as much too. The two were, despite the begrudging horror of the chapel-goers in the valley, an exceedingly attractive couple.

"This is my mark," Aubrey stated, tracing the letters of the carving with his fingers. "Everyone who sees this… they'll know fer sure I was here. I wager that's why we haven't heard tale of Dark Eyes for so long. He's scared of my name." He then leaned against the tree as though he owned the wide world.

"Ah, Aubrey," Leith countered. "You're not likely ever to be forgotten, even without that inscription."

"You neither," Aubrey insisted. "When people think of me, they sure as toads in mud'll think of you! Count on that."

"I don't need to be remembered. Not really. You can go do your great things. I'll be happy to say I know you." He danced around Aubrey in a shy waltz, both of their feet dusty and gray. Leith had developed a healthy streak of reserve and caution, attributed to his upbringing by Calpurnia.

"You possum! Come here." Aubrey pulled on Leith's shirt collar, kissing him at length under brachia frozen in time.

"We'd better get going," Leith said, pulling away with an embarrassed grin. "Elijah gets a river name tonight, remember? We gotta get ready."

"'Course I remember!" Aubrey assured him. "He's my brother, ain't he?"

Aubrey flung his arm around Leith's shoulders, still holding their books in his other hand, and they continued their walk uphill. Soon, the dismal ashland gave way to the life and dark green vegetation of Higher

Black Hill Road, as it was referred to now. No one ever used it, though, Lower Black Hill Road having been annexed by the chapel.

Never the types to stick to the paths assigned them, the two wandered off the lonely road and investigated the hidden parts of the forest. This was a daily thing. They flirted in mischievous games of tag in caves and wrestled atop the old burial mounds in the deeper woods.

As they neared the road once more, breathless from their afternoon games, Aubrey ducked quickly and pulled Leith down with him, nearly ripping his good shirt in two.

"What is it?" Leith asked as they crouched behind a pile of forgotten firewood. There must have been a home nearby at one time.

"There's our boy," Aubrey explained. He was giddy as he nodded his head in the direction of the road. Elijah stood in the center of the old road, staring blankly at the empty space where once stood the shack he had lived in as a baby. He was, as always, in naught but his drawstring pants, his skin golden from the sun, his back displaying the musculature of a climber and forager. "He's out for a walk. Let's surprise him. We could scare his name out of him right now. We wouldn't even have to go to a ceremony."

"We'll never do it!" Leith chuckled. "He's got a sixth sense. He can always tell when he's being watched. He'll turn around any minute and call us out. You wait and see!"

"Hush now!" Aubrey chided.

They observed as Elijah walked into the foundation of his former home, now overgrown with weeds and fledgling trees. Minerva had told him a few things so he would know where he was from. Not a scrap of wood remained from furniture or floorboard. Only questions that could never be asked or answered.

Suddenly, as if hit by a pebble from behind, he straightened stiff and upright. His trapezius rose, mountains of muscle tensing for combat and action.

"See?" Leith said. "He senses us."

But Elijah did not look their way. Instead, his attention was drawn in the opposite direction. He began to fumble backward apprehensively toward them, as though pushed by a stare from the forest.

Aubrey and Leith glanced at one another, and came out of hiding just as Elijah turned around and began breaking in their direction.

"Whoa!" Aubrey exclaimed as Elijah ran into him, nearly knocking him to the ground. "What's wrong, brother?"

Elijah's panic melted into relief, and he wrapped his arms around his friends, both of them. Like his father Darcy, Elijah had grown into a strapping young man, with large arms and a grand embrace.

"Let's get you home," Aubrey said. "We need to get ready for tonight."

Elijah nodded and then glanced quickly over his shoulder at the old foundations. His attention to the spot made Aubrey nervous. Aubrey remembered the last he had seen of the shack. That had been a dark omen. He had told Leith about seeing Garet enter, and then come running out flanked by creepy-crawlies on all sides. The bugs were plentiful in the valley, but that had been the worst he'd ever seen them.

"I'll see you tonight," Leith said. His look changed from happiness at being with his friends to a troubled expression of duty. "I have to check on Calpurnia. She'll want her dinner."

"See you there. Don't be too long." Aubrey gave him a quick kiss, handed him his books, and they parted. Aubrey and Elijah walked off to find the elf-paths, Aubrey trying his best to wrestle Elijah to the ground, very unsuccessfully. Leith limped leisurely uphill to his mother, a voluntary captive of Walterhouse Manor.

THE LONELY Walterhouse place looked indifferent to its own decline, the dead conifer in the front lawn its sole companion. The pristine white paint had all but disappeared from the husky wood. Shingles fell like autumn leaves from the roof, letting rainwater inside to begin the process of wood rot. Leith walked reluctantly toward his ramshackle home, his schoolbooks carelessly at his side. He glanced by habit at the long, narrow window on the second floor where Calpurnia peered out onto the fields of goldenrods and tiger lilies, hanging on to a dusty curtain of burgundy velvet, watching her son come home. Her face shone pale and lifeless from the lack of sunlight it had seen in the years since Garet's taking. Minerva and Hamlin had helped look after Calpurnia until Leith could manage on his own, and Hamlin still came around to check on her at least once a week, but for the most part, they were alone.

In the kitchen, Leith prepared his mother a bowl of stew, sided with bread and water. Her meals were her sole comfort, and she looked forward to them immensely. She worried when they were not brought to her at the same time every day. Leith would try and find something special to serve her if he could—an apple, crisp and red, or something sweet from the campus. She had reacted with petrified fury when he'd told her he would be going to the school a few times each week. That would mean less time with her. To say she had gotten over it would be liberal; Calpurnia never truly got over anything. She coped.

Leith had managed to obtain a couple of oatmeal cookies that morning, a treat from Mr. Higgins for work well done. He was sure Mr. Higgins hadn't made them; more likely they were sent for him to enjoy by his fiancée. They were brittle, but still edible. Leith placed everything neatly on an old finger-smudged tin platter, a remnant from more prosperous times. Most of the good dishware had been lost or broken by now.

"*Leith!*" Calpurnia called from a crack in the door of her room. "Is my meal ready, darling?" Her voice had the edge of concern and sorrow, as if she were afraid he would not answer.

"I'm coming!" he assured her, climbing the stairs carefully. The steps creaked and popped underfoot.

With each passing year since the morning of the bones on the stump, Calpurnia had retreated further and further into her solitude. The outside air was venom to her, laced with fear. Her upright, sure-footedness became a shuffle; her posture became compliant, as though she were being pulled to the earth by some unseen force stronger than gravity. She regarded everything and everyone with suspicion and consternation, and in that way had become somewhat similar to her sworn enemy Darcy Crocker. As her solitude became her sole companion, she receded farther into the house, room by room, like a deep lake drying up over decades, until at last her bedchamber—Winifred's bedchamber—became her entire world. She knew every splinter and dust bunny therein.

Leith pushed open the cracked door with the edge of the platter. He noted the hinges needed to be oiled. "I brought you some cookies," he said, trying to add some excitement to his voice as he stood in the doorway. He always paused before entering.

She stood grasping her bedpost with one hand. Her other hand's fingers played with the collar of her tattered black coat. The same coat she had worn every day for fifteen years. Underneath she wore a white sleeping gown.

"What did you bring me?" she asked. Her mouth trembled with a frail smile. Her hair was wild and unkempt, half-fallen from a careless ponytail.

Leith set the platter on her writing desk over stick figure sketches supposed to represent her younger life and friendships. "Oatmeal cookies," he answered. "They're from the college."

Calpurnia covered her mouth in excitement. "Oh! I adore oatmeal cookies!"

Her enthusiasm was at times too childish for him.

She scurried over to the desk as Leith pulled the chair out for her. Winifred had written invitations to grand parties at this desk; Calpurnia drew stick figures and collected cookie crumbs on its scratched surface. She reached for a cookie, holding it protectively with both hands as she nibbled on it.

"How was your day?" Leith inquired, seating himself on the bed.

"I did some wonderful drawings!" she said. "Did you see them?"

"I did, Calpurnia. They're lovely."

"Yes. I think so as well. When I was a girl, I was always drawing…." Her voice broke off in a whisper, and she stared vacantly at the cookie, reading the oatmeal like tea leaves. Had she always drawn as a girl? "How was school?" she inquired absently.

"School was fine," he answered, detecting his mother's disinterest. Something else was crowding her thoughts.

"Do you still talk to Elijah Crocker?" she asked suddenly. Her demeanor had changed into that of a suspicious mother. These alterations of mood happened so quickly, they always took Leith by surprise. If he had to choose, he much preferred the Obnoxious Little Girl to the Suspicious Mother.

"Of course. I just saw him in fact, near where he lived as a baby." He realized too late that he had said too much. His mother had never cared for either of his friends, but she seemed to dislike Elijah the most.

Calpurnia rose, stumbling over her frayed coat. "*Oh no!*" she exclaimed, stretching out her hand to her son, her eyes wide with panic. "You must stay away from him! Promise me! Stay away from that boy. Stay away from that place."

"Calpurnia, what's wrong?" He stood abruptly as she nearly fell on top of him, landing instead on her knees in front of him.

"He'll take you! He's just like his father. They take everything from me. Lara, Garet, and now they want you! I see it in my dreams." She squeezed his hands till hers lost their color, and his began to ache. She peered up at him pleadingly.

"I'll be fine. Elijah is nothing like Darcy...."

"You don't know anything!" she screamed, gripping harder and shaking his hands to get her point across. "Stay away from him! Do you hear me? Do your mother's heart good, won't you?"

"He's my friend."

"Stay away from him, you stupid boy!" she cried, rising to her feet, grabbing his shoulders and shaking him violently. He could tell she wanted to slap him. She had done it many times before, and it always stung. "That ignorant Crocker boy should be run out of the valley!"

Leith loosened himself from her grip and backed to the door. She slouched to the large four-poster bed in what some might call a dramatic pause.

"Why... are you... looking at me like that?" she managed in broken syllables. "I'm trying to... to protect you. I've only ever done things with you in mind. When you are in this room with me, why, it's my entire world. I need nothing else."

Leith stared at her for a moment, at a loss. She had mentioned Elijah before this with slight resentment, but never anything comparable to what he had just heard. He supposed nightmares did that to people if they were as constant as hers. The bitterness of fear could enter the everyday world through nightmares. He swiftly turned and walked out of the room, closing the door behind him. She was too much for him today. He needed space from her.

Calpurnia called after him pitifully. "Leith! Come back! Are you leaving me? Leith!"

Her voice echoed through the empty house, a raving banshee.

LEITH HAD tried his best to close his ears to his mother's pounding on the long window of her bedroom as he walked away from Walterhouse Manor. Yet her pleading echoes always reached him. He hated her for making him care. Going down Black Hill was always easier for him than coming up because of his injury. There was a glee to it. But this day she had ruined even that satisfaction.

His face was cast to the dirt when he recognized Hamlin's boots ahead of him. "Is there something the matter?" Hamlin asked, pausing on the road and leaning on his walking stick.

"No, sir," he answered. "Nothing's wrong."

"That was a pretty poor response," Hamlin teased. "On your way to Elijah's river naming, are you?"

"Yes, sir. It should be a big night for him. I wonder what he'll choose—and how, since he's never spoken a word."

"We know ourselves best in silence," Hamlin replied. He paused for a moment, seemingly refelecting on what he had just said. "Well, off with you, then. I'm aiming to spend some time in the circle wood, so we both have big nights ahead of us."

"Yes, sir," Leith repeated, resuming his march, his head bowed.

Hamlin watched him for a bit, thinking himself a similar soul, more comfortable in the lonesome call of the forest and a few hard-won friendships than a city of casual acquaintances. He noted that Leith's limp was hardly noticeable any longer and counted that as a victory against the preacher. But the boy still had his troubles. Calpurnia was a handful, Hamlin knew that. Hopefully, she would not drain the life from her son. Thankfully Leith had Aubrey and Elijah to keep him going. If Minerva was correct, the valley would need Leith in the ensuing years.

Minerva hadn't asked Hamlin to watch over the circle wood while she officiated the river naming ceremony, but he felt a personal need to do so. The woods had not been threatened, nor was there any premonition that something would happen to Minerva's home during her absence. A rustle in the trees had drawn him; a nostalgic convocation with times past. His second trip up Black Hill in one day, he quickly found the right elf-path—the Trues had taught him a few tricks—and very soon the charm of the earthen cottage at dusk came into view. The last of the special Breed lazed beside the memorial garden under which lay the bones of the Parmas.

Flowers were closing for the night, and the tall grass collected the first of the evening's dew. Fireflies bejeweled the earthen cottage roof, spurring the surrounding gardens and forest in celebration of the moonrise. Hamlin rested from the climb on a large block of wood positioned against the side of the cottage mound. Minerva's powerful scythe leaned in repose against the quaint structure alongside him.

Emulating the scythe, Hamlin leaned his head against the wall and soon the perfume of dusk-dusted spring air lulled him to sleep.

When he awoke, night had fallen over Black Hill. A blink if it had been hour. A strange feeling greeted his awakening, a giddy euphoria he had not experienced since he was a young man. It took him by surprise and enlivened him. He heard laughter, like drops of water in a shallow pail, and stood, squinting in search of its source. There was no fear in him. The laughter seemed only natural, a familiar laugh. In some life or other he had known it. He felt as if he were a young man at the height of the Autumnday festival.

He had not lit the torches when he arrived in the circle wood, and the moon was blocked by the trees overhead. The only light was that which the fireflies provided by means of their tiny bottoms.

A fleeting visage flashed beneath the trees, hanging alongside the lightning bugs like a full-fleshed ornament. Hamlin gasped as a broken part of his heart mended in an instant. He nearly fell to the ground before he managed to collect himself.

It was his little girl. Branwenn had smiled at him in the night, dancing among the trees. Whirls and twirls. Hers was a face he had seen in neither dream nor vision since the day she was taken. Seeing her now and thusly filled his old heart with joy and relief. Her spirit somehow roamed free of the chapel, and he did not care to know by what means. He only wanted to hold his daughter, to tell her his secret: that he was her father. And then he wanted to find Minerva.

Heaving himself against his walking stick, Hamlin followed the laughter, catching her countenance every now and then in the dark. He chased her whispers about the trees in a playful game of tag, something he wished to have done when she was alive. The forest glowed with a quality like the manifestation of hope riding the moonlight: a lazy, grounded, sweet-smelling haze. He found himself laughing at the game along with his daughter, surprised to hear such a pleasant sound rise from his own self after laying silent for so very long.

Finally, he found Branwenn by the cliff, under the giant oak he and Minerva had rested beneath earlier in the day. He halted, wanting at first to look on her more: his lovely little girl, the delight of fireflies. As he approached slowly, she smiled brightly. Free of the forest, the moonlight embraced her.

"There's always hope, Daddy," she breathed, fading into the night glimmer.

At once, Hamlin was both a grief-stricken father and joyful parent. She had known after all. He stumbled for ground and sat beneath the oak once more, letting stubborn tears at last fall. Their release became an explosion of life, his many regrets lessened by the words of a phantom child. All his wishes and could-have-beens concerning Minerva and Branwenn no longer mattered. His closeted resentment of Minerva's solitude, which had in turn condemned him to solitude, vanished. In that moment, he was finally able to love fully and freely, without condition. He saw the perfect smiles and beautiful eyes of those he had cared for: his father, Minerva, Branwenn. It was the most beautiful moment of his life.

The dark sky rumbled above. Clouds had moved over the moon. Downriver, Hamlin's dazed eyes saw a light show dancing above the clouds. How appropriate, he thought, that a spring storm should be the last thing he would ever see in this life. Peaceful and quite content, he closed his eyes. And so ended the troubled days of Hamlin Marsh.

"Hello, Hamlin. My name is Azrael. I'm here to take you across the river."

AT SUNSET, a single small raft drifted up the river carrying three silent occupants: Elijah Crocker, standing center and wrapped in naught but a gold thread coat made especially by Minerva for this day; Minerva True herself, standing proud and enduring beside him in her black gown; and the last of the ragtag ferry boat boys to remain on the river.

The advance of roads and bridges and the declining population of the valley had caused the use of rafts to be nearly obsolete. The river kicked up a song of chimes and colors every time the oar pushed into the water.

Elijah conveyed no sense of anxiety at the thought of his initiation. An approaching future of new truths to learn, a natural progression; his past did not concern him. He did his best, in fact, to distance himself from much of it. Aside from his parents' nightmarish disappearances, he had other problems to deal with as a young man. Elijah was his father's son, and his strength had long made him an outcast in the valley, especially to the other children who mocked him as a big dumb and dangerous ox of a boy. Never did the other boys allow him to play games with them, harboring the very real fear he would playfully knock one of them down and they might never get back up. The girls ran from him squealing in fright, their parents having warned them about Darcy Crocker's son. But Elijah was wise to his limits. He had learned to curtail his strength at a very young age. While playing with one of the Breed, he'd given it a loving hug and broken the poor thing's spine. Though Minerva tried to comfort him, he had never really gotten over the accident. His strength was his great failing.

The raft was guided handily by its helmsman to a bend in the river bearing special significance. A place camouflaged by hills and trees, most passed it by without even noticing the small stone platform between two large boulders. Elijah and Minerva stepped onto the platform, then past it, onto the overgrown stone path that led inland through lichen, cattails, and weeping willows. It was a timeworn place, once full of ritual. The river naming ceremony had always taken place at the third bend of the river under Lone Tower. Yet it had become a neglected sacred spot. The coming of the new faith into the valley had turned many from the rites of the older beliefs. Best not to acknowledge the old ways, they thought, and so forgot everything associated with them.

As they passed the languid willow trees, moving up a slight incline, misty apparitions danced beneath the fading light among waking crickets and night bugs. These were the River Dwellers of the past, and were among those spirits who could interact with the living. Ahead, the path ceased at a large circular stone clearing, two large limestone pillars to each side, their ancient carvings nearly covered completely by honeysuckle and morning glories. Trees branched overhead here, like hands enfolding something unique and precious. In a man-made grotto, only an impression really in the cliff wall, Aubrey and Leith waited. A stately fire burned behind them, and shadows outlined and caressed their fine features.

"This is where I leave you, love," Minerva whispered in Elijah's ear. "This is a young man's journey. You find your own faith from here. You will no longer be led by anyone else's after tonight." She kissed him gently on the cheek, then turned and walked back along the path to the waiting raft and its owner.

Elijah stood between the two pillars in the center of the stone circle. Aubrey and Leith approached him, smiling lovingly. Formality in ceremony never interested them. Their eyes were painted and lined—

their own personal addition to the rites. Neither of them wore anything at all, and soon Elijah was nude as well. His gold coat slipped from his broad shoulders and fell to the ground. The night air on his bare skin refreshed him. He was led by hand to the fire. Smoke curled around the three of them, and the flames made the stone walls come alive behind them, scrawled with figures and symbols, some of which Elijah had seen Minerva transcribe when teaching him the valley's history and secrets. The apparitions of the ancient River Dwellers mingled with the smoke and the flames and the lightning bugs so that the air became a glittering mist. The scent of honeysuckle and wood wafted about them.

Leith retrieved a wooden vessel, which rested on a small stone stool at his side; it was a traditional and well-used thing containing a symbolic amount of river water. He lifted it high and slowly poured the river water over Elijah's head. The water ran in small streams down Elijah's body, the sensation giving him a pleasurable shiver. His skin glistened, reflecting the growing firelight. Aubrey and Leith took hold of his hands again, and they all three sat down in front of the fire. Leith began washing Elijah with damp moss as Aubrey fanned the intoxicating scent of honeysuckle and wood toward him. Amidst the pleasure, the sky moaned above with the ruckus of the thunder gods.

Elijah began to see things differently around him. The world was deconstructed of form, recreated in bright, fluorescent thoughts, and deep, penetrating colors. It was as if an illusion had finally been seen through, and the truth was made apparent. The arrogance of the world lay bare. Elijah swam through the mingled ghosts and smoke, exuberant in his epiphany.

A flash of lightning lit up the ritual place, and across from him, across the blaze, the smoke billowed like white satin curtains caught by the wind. It was an introduction. Sitting on the other side of the fire now, against the stone wall, sat a small but beautiful woman, olive-skinned, her hair long and dark. She appeared translucent, but wore a dark blue gown, a silver tree stitched into the bosom. The roots and limbs of the embroidered tree resembled one another to the point that it was indistinguishable which was which, top from bottom. The woman rose and held her small hand out to Elijah over the flames. He took hold of her hand without pause, certain that not even his awesome strength could harm this woman, and they walked from the fire between the two pillars, down the willow path to the river. Elijah peered over his shoulder, not at all surprised to see himself somehow still seated in the grotto and being cleansed by his two friends.

The river was lit by dazzling flashes from the sky as Elijah and the woman, a woman he knew to be Mother True—for who else would it be?—stood on the shore hand-in-hand. Down the beach, on either side, were an army of souls, some waiting, and others being led by a beautiful, black-winged man across the river to the far shore. Those led by the winged man were the souls of the dead. The others were merely ambulatory souls of nighttime slumber. Mother True ushered Elijah on and they too crossed the waters, joining a spiritual parade into the electric night. The river felt cool and glassy beneath Elijah's feet, and though he was never in any danger of sinking, his footfalls caused gentle ripples on the water. The river erupted in a chorus of ripples.

As they reached the other side, Elijah recognized one of the many travelers who crossed the water alongside him. Hamlin Marsh passed, unimpaired by age, following the winged man toward the dense forest and hills. He turned once to glance backward at the riverside from whence he came, before vanishing forever into the trees.

Mother True led Elijah to a small waterfall hidden by low-hanging trees. The falls spilled into a stream, which contributed to the mighty river. A beautiful creature, neither man nor woman but with attributes of both, lounged nude on the moss of a flat stone nearby. The being's hair fell long, flowing and silver, and adorned with lilies and butterflies. This was the River, holding all the sensuality of the world, all the orientations, because in variety is strength. The River was the masculine and the feminine; gentility and rage.

Elijah stood still before the figure on the stone, and the figure rose and separated as if two souls had occupied the same space at once. A woman and man stood before Elijah now, the woman of transcendent beauty, and the man so handsome that when it began to rain, Elijah thought the sky had begun to cry. They were both nude, their skin like flawless china. The woman's breasts were succulent and pointed. The man's penis was erect and unsheathed. The music of chimes lingered in the air as the two looked upon Elijah from indulgent eyes. They moved between one another with a grace and sensuality he had never seen. Like the masterstrokes of a classical piano piece.

He realized Mother True was no longer with him. But he did not bother to look for her. He knew she was in the trees.

The silver-haired man beckoned him forward with a fluid gesture from his hand. At the same moment, the woman advanced and clasped Elijah's hand, her touch as refreshing as a stream on a summer day, leading him to the man's side. The man kissed him on the mouth, and a feeling of newness blossomed within him, almost a deliverance from darkness. Through the man's delicious and invigorating kiss Elijah felt his first true breath of life, honest and undiluted, passed onto him. This man and this woman formed the current and stream of the world, deities that could envelope him in euphoria before releasing him to their blessed creation, or alternately, keeping him beneath the tides forever. It was their choice to make.

The River began to caress him, washing over him with tender waves. He made love to the masculine and the feminine, each in their turn, becoming the giver and the receiver, penetrating the feminine and letting the masculine enter into him. These paths of erotic touch were undefined, the great force of which was explosive and dangerous. *Who can survive such harmony?* As waves of ecstasy surged over him, and the River gave him its gift of euphoria, he let out a cry, a name that parted the waters in which they made love, exposing the white-pearl bottoms of the river bed and every truth they knew.

When Elijah opened his eyes from the blinding rapture, he stared at the thundering sky, a light rain kissing his face. He recognized he was again in front of the fire in the grotto, Aubrey and Leith to either side of him. Leith no longer cleansed him, but the faces of both of his friend shone with pride. Things had changed.

"You did it, my brother," Aubrey said. "Elijah is no more. Your name is Deverell."

The newly acquired name was spoken through the smoke like a ceaseless echo. When Elijah became Deverell in the embrace of the River, he had shouted the only word he would ever speak in his life. His transformation, after all, warranted such a commemoration, a shout that challenged the mighty thunderstorm and which the clouds kept as their own, so impressed were they by the strength of the word.

THE IRON KINGS

THE THUNDERCLOUDS were only the beginning. The valley soon plunged into a long season of sullen skies. At first the rains sprinkled intermittently for days, like mist spraying the rocks near a waterfall. Then the sprinkling became more focused and fierce until the days and nights were peppered with fitful downpours the likes of which the valley had rarely witnessed. Minerva could see the omen in the clouds, war chariots led by frothing horses. The Battle was approaching.

But Minerva found the ensuing battle no longer mattered to her. On her return to the circle wood the night of Elijah's river naming, she had come upon Hamlin strolling disoriented and seemingly awestruck down Black Hill Road. He passed her as if he hadn't seen her at all, even as she called his name. At first glance, Minerva thought her eyes were finally failing her, for he looked so miraculously young and healthy. Gradually, the inevitable truth began to slice into her gut. She accepted it only after she had called to him three times and still he had not responded. Instead, he continued down the road as though following someone. He was now of the wandering souls. A chill stretched over her skin. She watched him leave her forever, and her heart broke with the lightning flickering over the forest.

After a brief and struggling search, Minerva found Hamlin's worldly form leaning against the old oak tree by the bluff, a final and long-earned grin across his face. He had been taken peacefully across the river, and that was all she could have hoped for. She lay beside his beautiful shell for the rest of the night under the thundering sky, and held him as it rained. Beneath her controlled sobs she sang psalms of safe journeys and thanks. She sometimes wished she were like her mother. Mother True could weather all grief without a tear or show of emotion. Even Ingrid's death had been unable to pull Mother to maudlin insobriety. But Minerva had to cry. And she did, for those who meant the most to her. She had shed tears for Mother True and Branwenn, and she cried for Hamlin Marsh this night.

His body was prepared as if he were a king, with fine scents and white robes. A funeral was arranged; a sendoff fit for a true patriarch, every soul left in the valley in attendance. The sky mirrored Minerva's mood, though her rumbles were kept quiet, deep in her heart.

Hamlin was laid on an abandoned river raft—the last of the ferry boat boys left at word of his death—lilacs, rose petals, and honeysuckles scattered about him, an ancient tradition he had always admired in life. Minerva spent one last mournful day alone with his body at the beach. She did not move from the raft's side. Her form took on that of Death's own mistress, her black veil catching in the slight winds. As the sun set, the others paid their respects. Aubrey, Deverell, and Leith stood in file, side by side, their heads downcast. Calpurnia remained in Walterhouse Manor, mourning in her own way the only father figure she had known. The only family left in the valley had come as well, though the Daventry-Blues would be leaving forever once Hamlin had been set off on his new journey.

"The valley as we knew it will never be again," Alice Daventry-Blue explained to Minerva. "You are the last of the River Dwellers. After you, there are no more. What will happen then? It's better to embrace their God than battle the will of the chapel. You should leave too. You are too tired to fight alone."

But she never would leave and they knew it. She would give herself to the waters first.

As the daystar set, Aubrey lit the raft and loosened the rope from the anchor. Hamlin's pyre drifted away as if into a painting, such were the colors in the sky—orange, yellow, blue, and red. He was carried upriver, a floating torch of light inextinguishable by wind or rain.

When sufficient deference had been paid, the Daventry-Blues departed. They said their farewells, though Minerva could not hear them. Her grief remained too great. The large gathering of adults and children made a somber trek by wagon and foot along the beach and then up a distant hill to a distant town, defeated and heartbroken but alive.

As the moon rose high in the sky, Minerva kept still, watching motionless from the shore even as the pyre disappeared behind Lone Tower. The boys seated themselves on an aged log and waited for her.

The valley grew desolate. There would be no other celebrations by the river, no more Autumnday, no more children's laughter. Only silence.

Gracefully, Minerva turned and walked to them, the farthest she had moved since adorning Hamlin's body on the raft. The boys stood as she approached. She kissed them individually on the foreheads and then turned and walked quiescently toward Black Hill.

"Miss Minerva," Aubrey called, confusion etching his features. "What'll we do?"

"Go somewhere, boys," she said, her whisper floating to them even as she departed. "Leave the valley. Find some place to be happy. This place is lost." The words stung the wind like arrows.

As Minerva walked the trail to her small earthen cottage, the elf-path—which had once again been worn from years of the boys coming and going—was at once overgrown with vines and weeds, lost to any who had at one time traveled it. No sooner had her foot left ground then the path behind her ceased to exist any longer. At last, as she entered the circle wood, turning her back on the valley, the coppice closed after her like a heavy gate.

Deverell started to run after her, but Aubrey held his arm. Minerva ascended the hill road, detached and disconsolate, her black gown fading into the night forest.

"I think it's broken her, Aubrey," Leith pronounced solemnly. The hairs on the back of his neck stood. "What a thing to see."

The three of them stood staring about at the abandonment around them, more terrified of this sudden displacement than they had ever been at the notion of the chapel.

"She will come around," Aubrey hoped aloud. "She bends; Minerva True don't break."

Deverell and Aubrey took up residence in one of the many abandoned homes scattered throughout the valley. Aubrey could have stayed in the forest, a scavenger and nomad, but he knew Deverell could not, at least not at the moment. Deverell was his brother, and he would stand by him and care for him. Aubrey struggled to sleep surrounded by walls and ceilings, though, so he compromised, choosing to welcome his dreams every night in the yard or on the porch.

In the days following Hamlin's cremation, the boys stayed on Black Hill, searching for, and failing to find, Minerva's cottage and the circle wood. Aubrey knew Minerva could only be found if she wished to, but he kept quiet, allowing Deverell his hope. At last, they squatted at the empty residence that once housed Clara and Prichard Parma and their nine sons. It was too big, and the air of the place reeked with tragedy, but it was one of the nearest homes to the forest of Black Hill and by far the least ramshackle. Hamlin's cabin was closer, but they could not bring themselves to settle there.

Clara Parma, the boys' doting mother and Prichard's devoted wife, had surrendered herself a week after Prichard and her sons were consumed by the chapel grounds. Having remained shut in for seven days, she had woken one morning and walked among the many large metal pieces of art that littered the front lawn—gifts her metalworker husband had lovingly crafted for her—touching each one as though it were another child. She strode clad in black as a quiet mourner joining her family willingly in the chapel grounds. The last anyone ever saw of Clara Parma was a slow fade into the darkness of the chapel.

Now, years later, the house was a wreck of rotted wood and collapsing carpentry. The rooms howled in the night. Deverell only ever slept in the front gallery, leaving the ghosts alone to wander the rest of the place. The front lawn was overgrown with weeds, and the ironworks and copper figures sat shrouded in english ivy and morning glories. A wild and unkempt mimosa grew from the center of a ringed sculpture Prichard had made to represent the rising moon. The soft pink flowers of the tree crowned the phases of a silver moon.

Aubrey was adjusting to the change of not being near the earthen cottage or in the dense forest, but Deverell felt sick with worry. He stared up to Black Hill most of the day from the porch, naked and absentminded, and would only eat when reminded to do so.

At night, after he had taken Calpurnia her dinner, Leith always visited the boys, taking the dangerous road down to the valley. He felt an eye on him, but refused to let his mind wander. Wandering minds were easily lost. He and Aubrey drank strong homemade brew—brew-making being an essential valley skill—among the waltzing lawn ornaments and orchestral katydids. The two lounged on Prichard's works of art like kings on thrones. Aubrey took the same position every night, ever the blessed prince under the mimosa on the moon.

Their lessons with Albert Higgins were sporadic now. They still hungered for knowledge, but the same sense of futility that clung to Minerva began to reach its long, dirty nails into the boys as well. The valley seemed so very vast, and they were but three young men, left without direction.

"Deverell," Aubrey called from his spot on the ironworks one evening, the fragrance of the feathered pink blossoms of the tree fanning about him. "Why not come and join us? We miss you, brother."

Deverell remained on the rotten steps of the Parma's porch, staring up at Black Hill.

"It's been over a week, and still he stares like a dog waiting for its master to return home," Leith said. "What should we do?"

"What can we do? He wants to be with her. She was his momma, Leithy. The only one he ever knew. She says she wants to teach him the ways of the River Dwellers before the end, or she wanted to. He's gotta wake up from this. He'll be no good if we have to fight. We'll be ruined without him."

Leith glanced to the sky, searching for a sign. A light mist blanketed the valley. He knew there were no longer any birds living in the valley, but he had hoped to see at least an out-of-valley sparrow fly over the river on its journey elsewhere. "Maybe everyone else was right," he said quietly.

"Whatchya mean by that?"

"Everyone who left. Maybe they were right. It's over. The valley will disappear and be replaced by machines and thoughtless civilization. It never was ours, really; not mine, yours, or Deverell's. It was ruined long before us. The beliefs it was settled on are all fading away and have been losing their power since before me and you ever came to be. No River Dweller can bring it back." He took a contemplative swig from his cup.

Aubrey leaned forward from the arms of the ironwork in which he sat. It moaned at his flexibility. "What are you trying to say, Leith?" He was almost combative, and it threw Leith.

"I'm saying we should leave, Aubrey, just like Minerva told us to. We can't be of any help."

Aubrey stood up, throwing his libation to the ground. "Don't you never say that! Take it back! Take it back, or I'll knock you from where you sit."

Leith was startled by Aubrey's sudden change of demeanor. His gentle elfin looks had become fierce and challenging. Deverell remained rooted where he sat, not taking his glance away from the hill. If he knew Aubrey and Leith were there at all, he didn't let it be known.

"Aubrey," Leith said, standing as well. "It's not our world. It's not for us, and we can do nothing to protect it, certainly not against the chapel; not against Dark Eyes and his hounds."

"You ain't gonna leave, Leith!" Aubrey exclaimed. He seemed as animated as a puppet on strings. "We've all got a part to play. You can't leave before you played it, understand!"

"I got to get Calpurnia away from here. She's a ghost in her room." But that was an excuse, and he knew it.

"You hear this, Dev?" Aubrey shouted with disgust, keeping his eyes set on Leith. "He wants to leave. Wants to give up. Well, I'm sickened by it! You done made me ill!" His voice was on the crest of collapse. "I thought we was a clan. Why do you want to break my heart?"

Leith was speechless. "Break your heart?" he said. "Aubrey, I would never…. You're the most…."

But he found he couldn't articulate anything through such raw emotion. He could only watch as Aubrey ran off over the rocks toward the beach, stripping clothing as he went. Aubrey hastened into the black-as-night water and, at an acceptable depth, dove in. The river took him with a near soundless splash. He didn't come up for some time, and Leith ran toward the shore in panic. Clouds let through slivers of moonlight. At last, and quite unbelievably, Leith saw a bobbing head above the current nearly midriver, strong arms pulling at the water. He stood watching, eyes straining in the dark. As the light mist became rain, Aubrey crossed to the other side and Leith lost sight of him.

"Aubrey, come back!" Leith cried desperately. But his request was only met by the alternating pitches of the night river and its echoes.

LEITH'S WALK home was a long, lonely one. Abandoned homes moaned as he passed them, loose window shutters smacked against rotten wood, and forgotten wind chimes begged for attention. The valley had *never* been alive, not as long as he had known it. Everyone talked of a time when life went skipping through the valley like a little girl with a basket full of kisses and chocolates. It was a ridiculous fairy tale. Leith had seen no proof of any skipping… ever. The sense of decay had been present from the very first scene of his very first memory. He imagined the old homes—houses known by the names of their owners: Lone, Parma, Toots, Cambermoore, Ambrose, Cordelia, Daventry, and so many others—stretching along the bends, being alive once upon a time when birds settled on their windowsills in the morning and whistled greetings. He was told laughter was once carried on the wings of those birds over the valley. But that had all ended. The valley lay forgotten. Shamefully, Leith admitted he wished he could forget it as well. He couldn't understand why Aubrey didn't feel the same.

The rain had soaked Leith to the bone by the time he reached the bottom of Black Hill. He was still too engrossed by what had happened at the Parmas to pay heed to most of his surroundings. Yet when one passed the chapel grounds, his attention was ever fretfully drawn to the structure, even if all he had known of the place was rumors. Leith noticed a figure shuffling through the rain toward the chapel grounds. At once startled and confused as to whether he was witnessing phantom or fantasy, he nearly took to running the other way. Peering with more intensity, he saw it was no trickster or even the Dark Preacher himself. Nor was it one of the roving phantoms of the valley. It was a simple man, a stranger dressed in ragged clothes seeking shelter from the rain. Leith hadn't seen a traveler or vagabond by the river for quite some time. Even the college students stayed out of the valley now. The trail down College Hill had become overgrown and treacherous. Thus it took a few moments for the correct course of action to occur to him.

He raced through the rain, hollering to the man over the gentle storm. The man stood still, seemingly at a loss as he saw Leith running toward him.

"Sir!" Leith exclaimed under labored breaths as he came to a dead stop between the man and the chapel grounds. "The chapel is old and abandoned. It might collapse any day. It might not be wise to go in there." He saw no reason to scare the traveler unnecessarily. He could hear the creeping of the hounds and the crawlers behind him in the mist, readying themselves, he felt sure, to claim another victim.

"But there's light in the window," the man answered. He was a darker-skinned man, older, but his eyes shone bright with promise, like a man who had found something in the middle of his life he hadn't known he was looking for.

Leith turned around, and indeed, an eerie dim orange glow flickered from within the chapel; a menacing welcome.

"Come to my home instead," Leith offered, turning his attention back to the stranger. "It's farther off, at the top of the hill, but you'll have a good meal, I can promise you that. You can't get that at the chapel."

The man seemed to weigh his options, and then nodded. "All right. Something to eat would be quite welcome." His voice had a strange accent, one Leith had not heard before in the valley. "My name is Tristan," the man said, offering his hand.

"I'm Leith," he replied. "Follow me, sir. We'll get you some dry clothes too. You look like my father's size." He wasn't sure who the man was or where he came from, but a sudden sense of accomplishment overcame Leith. As if his distracting of the stranger from the hounds of the chapel was somehow in line with what was required of him from the valley. How strange, this change of feeling!

They journeyed upward, getting acquainted, even laughing on their steep sojourn through the forest. The trees shielded them from the rain, though their feet grew caked with mud and clay. Leith ascertained that Tristan was a learned man, a philosopher in rags. And wasn't that the best kind?

Leith remembered a knight named Tristan from one of the older romances Mr. Higgins had Aubrey and him read. That Tristan was a hero, a brave soul in love with a beautiful girl. A fleeting comparison, and a heavy-handed one, but Leith appreciated it, for the valley's new visitor had rescued him that night from his own worries for the time being.

DAYS PASSED and words were sparse in the valley and atop Black Hill. With all the families truly gone, desolation claimed every sound. Tristan noticed this at once on his first day there. "Where are the birds?" he asked. "This is most unnatural."

Minerva True had not been seen or heard of since Hamlin's pyre floated past the bends. There was an anxious vigil for her return among the woodland spirits. The Passions remained hidden due to their fear of the chapel, but occasionally they would peek from their thickets, inquiring of the wind and the forest for news of her return. The same answer always came back to them. The elf-paths were closed.

Aubrey Avonmore lived in silence alone with Deverell; he had grown used to it. Recently, however, in the midst of Deverell's mournful state, even recognizable glances or gestures became sparse between the two of them. Aubrey now spent most of his time diving into the river or sitting on the other bank with his arms wrapped around his knees. The Othersiders never noticed him. Or if they did, they never let him know.

Aubrey and Leith were both too proud and stubborn to admit defeat, even as their deep need for one another caused their stomachs to hurt and their heads to throb. Leith, of course, would have deferred the contention but, never finding Aubrey at Parma Place, assumed he was being purposely avoided. He went to the river every day as well, but was unable to see Aubrey sitting on the rocks of the opposite shore. He returned to Walterhouse Manor each day, as sullen as the sky.

THE ONLY words spoken in the valley proper passed from the lips of Calpurnia Covington to the vagabond—"the adventurer," as she referred to him—Tristan. She had taken a strong liking to him when Leith had brought him home, though at first, she had been reticent about letting him stay even a night. A stranger he was, and from "out there." There were no longer any barriers in her mind between the valley folk and the real worlders. It was she against everything that wasn't she. Her first inclination was to distrust anything that came from the valley through the dark forest. She had watched Leith and Tristan trudging up the road from the woods and had raced to her chamber door when they entered the house. Leith had been forced to introduce Tristan as Calpurnia peeked out of a crack in the door.

"Who… who is that?" Her voice shook with recrimination. "Why is he in my house?"

Flushing with embarrassment, Leith braced for a cacophony of rants and screaming.

Yet Tristan easily charmed Calpurnia, telling her of the lands he had seen and the adventures he had known, all as he stood outside her chamber. Slowly, her anxiety lessened.

"Why, you're not of the Northern Country Covingtons, are you?"

Yes, she was!

"Wonderful! I know of them. I've had dealings with a few."

Truly?

Leith grinned as Tristan won his way into Calpurnia's heart. She allowed him entrance to her bedchamber. She still held her tattered coat to her throat, but she drew herself a bit taller hearing Tristan mention the Northern Country Covingtons. She had never before even mentioned them to her own son. In fact, she had never spoken much of anything concerning her past, aside from the city where she had been born—its towers and great spires reaching up and unending. Tristan's aging beauty was intoxicating and exotic, and he spoke with such ease that every word dropped like sugar, making his stories and compliments all the sweeter. Before the sun rose the next morning, Calpurnia asked if he might agree to stay a few days more.

"If only to give us some respite from the insufferable quiet," she pleaded, batting her eyes, a remnant of girlhood flirtation, something she had never been very adept at. She had fixed her hair for the first time in years and persuaded herself through much late-night self-bartering to remove the tattered coat and throw on instead a sun-dyed white summer dress, all lace and ice cream. He was, after all, the first man near her own age she had seen in some time. And though her thoughts of Lara never left her mind, his company was appreciated.

He agreed to stay, offering a handsome grin and a wink, and Calpurnia cackled with glee. "Aside from the pleasant company," he told her, "this will be a wonderful chance for me to observe. I *am* a man of science, after all." This was spoken with pride as though 'science' were an honor or special designation.

"Science? Is that a religion?" she asked cautiously. Her rambling mind had begun to fragment from its earliest scholarly lessons.

"Certainly not," Tristan tsk-tsked. "Science, my beautiful lady"—she loved how he said *lady* with a rolling *L*—"will one day explain everything. Science will save the world, save us from ourselves and the monsters we have created. It will cast away all this superstition and religious fraud. In science we find that there is no need for God."

"Oh, it sounds wonderful! Science sounds absolutely fascinating!" she exclaimed. "We do create monsters, don't we!" *And we refuse to kill them.*

Tristan then spent the rest of the day telling her about his experiments with water and fire, and the use of electricity on the corpses of rats. Calpurnia struggled to follow the scientific jargon, but that was unimportant. He knew of secret things, weapons against monsters that would save the world. He spoke with such assuredness, how could he not be right? Maybe... maybe... possibly he might even be the one to save her from the valley. And, she thought, she definitely needed saving.

THE SILENCE encouraged by the few other inhabitants of the valley was soon also put to an end. Aubrey, having lasted as long as he could without the company of Leith, lost the battle with his will just this once and found himself, on a dreary, rain-soaked morn, sloshing up Black Hill Road. His stubborn streak ever-etched on his stern face, he could not deny the truth of the matter any longer: without Leith he found himself incapable of even a modicum of concentration. From the Other Side, he had simply sat on the rocks trying to track Leith's comings and goings over the distance. Such were the drawbacks, he told himself, of love in the time of war.

Leith was out back doing his chores, chopping blocks of wood by the shed, when Aubrey came to Walterhouse Manor. A brief look of joy lit Leith's face. Though his heart leapt at seeing Aubrey, Leith set the axe down carefully and folded his arms, clearly expecting an apology. "What have you to say for yourself, Aubrey Avonmore?" he inquired shortly.

Aubrey said nothing. He walked swiftly toward Leith, taking his hands from his pockets where they had been tightly balled throughout his walk, and grabbed Leith's face greedily. He gave him a kiss of such passion, Leith had to do everything in his power to keep to his feet. Still, after a lingering moment, Leith withdrew, having none of it.

"You'll get no sugar from me, Aubrey Avonmore! I want words. Everything's best said in words." He violently shirked Aubrey off, throwing him to the mud and wood chips. Aubrey had barely touched ground before he was up again. Undeterred, he charged at Leith once more, tackling him with a loud grunt, and they both tumbled, landing in one large puddled, gunked mess. Leith punched and kicked as Aubrey held tight to him. They rolled about in the muck until Leith's anger gave way to giddiness, and the fight that had begun in annoyance had turned somehow, quite delightedly, into a lover's roughhousing. As they rolled down knolls and through dirty water, they disrobed one another. Their clothing scattered in a trail behind them, and they lay laughing and naked, covered in mud, beside one another behind the shed.

"So, we're made up now?" Aubrey asked petting Leith's soaked hair.

Leith kissed him in reply and then rose, pulling Aubrey with him to wash off the mud in the small stream near the edge of the homestead. The stream lay in the opposite direction of the river, and it was the farthest from the valley Leith had ever been. He had never even managed a crossing, though he had dared himself on occasion. They washed each other lovingly, splashing and giggling aplenty. The rain at last let up, and light broke through the clouds.

Aubrey touched his friend's chest, placing his hand flat to feel his heartbeat. "About the other night… you should do what you think is right for you," he said. "I do want you to be happy, Leithy. I was just moanin', I guess, 'cause I can't see being without you. Besides, if there's gonna be a battle, the valley will need every man it can get. "

"Aw, Aubrey. I could never leave without you," Leith assured him. "If you think it's important we stay, then we'll stay. Me and you and Deverell… we'll get through it. We'll die taking care of the valley if we have to. You're right. We've got important stuff to do. I'll die fighting right beside you, I promise; just like those Thebans that we learned about from Mr. Higgins."

"You ain't gonna need to do that, Leith," Aubrey promised, holding his palm to the side of Leith's face. "You ain't gotta die. I just know we have a part yet to play, is all. Minerva too. She'll come out of hiding eventually, and Deverell will wake from his sadness. There's gonna be a whole lot of wakin'. Then we gotta be strong. 'Cause then… that's when the fighting begins. We have a valley to save."

"To hear you say it, we're like knights from an old story. It's a nice idea, huh? Imagine us, defending some treasure against a great dragon."

"Naw. We're not knights. Just three boys with the world on our shoulders and no one to heed our warnings."

"You're no boy," Leith winked with a sly look of knowing. "You're a river sprite, Aubrey Avonmore. You can't fool me. You're about as human as the river itself. You don't think I know, but I know. No human could swim across that river unbothered by the current. And how I feel about you is stronger than I think anybody ever felt for anyone. There's something special about you."

Aubrey grabbed him in a suffocating embrace.

"There's even better hope for the valley now," Leith continued. "We're not alone in our fight. The stranger that's staying with us, Tristan, well there's something special about him too. He talks about science. About how it's going to save the world." Leith's face brightened as he spoke. "I think he's going to save us, Aubrey. I think science will save us, just like he says. The chapel will be put to shame by its power. There will be a struggle, but I truly think science will win in the end."

Though Aubrey was less than convinced by the assertions of the philosophizing vagabond, he smiled with acceptance and hope as Leith spoke. Religion and science to Aubrey formed a strange sort of either/or proposition. It seemed from what he knew of both, one extreme was no better than the other.

"We'll see," Aubrey said. "Might be something to it."

They raced each other back to the shed, gathering their strewn clothes along the way in competition. Aubrey had often let Leith win when they were younger and Leith's leg was still affecting him, but now he no longer needed to do that. Leith kept up with him just fine. That is, as long as Aubrey didn't really try.

They kissed one last time at the porch before Aubrey made his way back down the hill road. "You're the pick o' the litter, Leith Cather," he flirted with a wink. "Come see me tonight, eh!" he called before he disappeared into the trees.

Deverell sat bewildered and resigned beneath the wet leaves of a large fern on Black Hill. Through the trees he spotted Aubrey, muddied and half-naked, walking downhill, back to Parma Place, but he chose to remain hidden from him. He knew his solitude was worrying his brother, but there was nothing for it. He needed desperately to sort things out in his mind before he could be around anyone. He had to find the circle wood. He had to be of the River again.

He had been meandering about the woods off the safe path of Upper Black Hill Road, desperate to find Minerva. She was a member of his family, the family he now realized he had chosen long before he was given the physical attributes of Elijah Crocker. He knew the danger of roaming alone on Black Hill, that something resembling his father was said to walk about. But he had not seen this being, and as of that moment, it failed to concern him. Locating Minerva was his sole aim. Too many days had passed. He had at last found purpose in the valley, in becoming joined to it by ceremony. The terrifying thought of that being taken away from him so soon afterward propelled him to search for the woman he knew as his mother with unmitigated determination. Perhaps the pixie-walks would never open to him again, but he would search nonetheless. He would hunt until his mind went mad with maps that continuously redrew themselves.

After a final search for the circle wood, Deverell decided to return to Parma Place for the night. It was getting dark, and Aubrey was sure to be out looking for him. As always, he would return the next day. He had found something pure to believe in; he had found faith at last. A faith not built on someone else's philosophies, but on his own experiences.

As he stepped onto Black Hill Road from the great fence of trees, he was greeted by Leith, who was speedily, happily descending toward him with a look of supreme relief.

"Deverell!" Leith exclaimed as he jumped on him, putting his arm around Deverell's neck. "What on earth are you doing on Black Hill at dusk? Not that I'm complaining, you understand. Frankly, it's good to see you out and about again, and it's nice to have someone else to walk with at this hour of night. I know if we stay on the road we're safe, but still…."

OUT OF SHADOWS

THE DAY the so-called Battle for the Valley truly began, Leith woke with a headache. A nervous restlessness set about him. He pitched and moaned through Walterhouse Manor and its fields, like a dandelion seed in the wind. Chores could not keep him busy enough. *Keep busy, keep moving, Do! Do! Do!* cried his inner voice. He felt dizzy with some sourceless excitement.

Leith's mind was preoccupied with the faceless anxiety as he prepared his mother's breakfast. It irritated him to have an unknown worry, as if he were forgetting an important date. He knew the day would only grow more perplexing as it went. And it did.

He had expected to climb the stairs as always with the silver platter of food and find his mother still asleep. He always had to wake her. But before he reached the bedroom door, he heard the sound of feet on the hardwood floor and a gentle, deep humming intermittent with Calpurnia's breathy giggles. Leith pushed the thick door open to a new optical experience. Calpurnia and Tristan waltzed around the room. She, still in her nightgown and bare feet, and he, already dressed in his most dapper rag suit and strong brown shoes. He was humming something quick and lively in his tenor voice. Tristan had been staying in a never-used guest room downstairs, but Leith realized he had at least stayed with Calpurnia that night, if no other.

"You can take that back to the kitchen, darling," Calpurnia said, not taking her attention from the waltzing vagabond. "Tristan made me something this morning. It was quite lovely. He learned to cook on one of his adventures."

An empty white china plate—one of few not smashed by Calpurnia in her rages—lay on the bed with small crumbs from some bread or cake. Two glasses of milk sat half-finished on the bureau.

"Sorry, Leith, old boy," Tristan crooned as though the words were lyrics to his tune. "Didn't mean to step on your feet."

"Oh, he's fine," Calpurnia replied for her son as she was swung around the room. There was a nightmarish elegance to the sight. "He's happy not to have to wait on me." She gave Leith a sideways, condescending look. "You may go, Leith."

Leith backed out of the room slowly, leaving the waltzing pair to their strange romance. Giggles and humming followed him. Descending the stairs, he felt the oddest sensation of jealousy. Not toward Tristan, but toward his mother. How could she possibly understand Tristan? How could Tristan not see through the insanity of his mother? He was a man of science; they were supposed to be able to see things more clearly. Or was it a case of out of mind, out of sight?

No matter. This was also the day Tristan the vagabond chose to leave, much to Calpurnia's dismay.

Midday found Leith beneath the sun, by the shed. He had decided it was time to remove the stump. It proved a useful surface for splitting wood at times, but other than that it was naught but the ghost of a tree. He started with a splintering swing from the axe and never let up. The stump itself came easily; the roots would be the hardest thing. Though not one of the more ancient trees in the valley proper, it had still grown to a good size before it was felled. The roots had grown thick and burrowed deep.

It hadn't rained all day, and the clouds in the sky only occasionally hid the sunlight. Looking over the fields of goldenrods that surrounded the house, things didn't seem quite as foreboding to Leith as they had in the morning. A nice breeze tickled the sweat on his back.

"I'm off, young man," Tristan said, catching Leith off guard. He approached with a dandy gait from the back of the house. "I wanted to thank you for the hospitality before I left." He held his straw hat by the brim, his eyes orbs of generosity and knowledge.

"I'm sorry to see you go," Leith replied. "I haven't seen Calpurnia this happy in many years. In fact, I don't remember ever seeing her happy. It's a strange thing for a son to see his mother smile and mean it for the first time only after he has already grown."

"She is making her way the best she knows," Tristan replied.

"But it's what she knows that's the problem," Leith countered. "Or, what she thinks she knows." He swung the axe so that it stuck in what remained of the stump.

Tristan did not try to decipher the meaning of the cryptic statement. "I'd like to return if you'd have me."

"I thought you might," Leith said with a grin. He imagined Calpurnia lying against the wall in her chamber, wishing she could see to the back side of the house. "I was hoping you would. I think this place would benefit from you, you know, being a man of science and all. I think it may help matters a good deal. The students from the college don't come down here anymore." Leith wondered how he would explain to Tristan about Dark Eyes and the chapel. Surely, he would think they were mad with superstition.

"That's it, then," Tristan finalized the agreement. "I'll be back. First, though, I'm heading up river to satisfy my own curiosity. There's a little jetty just under the water, I hear, shallow-like, that I would like to see. After that, there're some books I have. I think you might like to see them. I hid them away in an old encampment, but I can get to them easily enough."

"Science books?" Leith inquired excitedly.

"Just like those the college professors teach from," Tristan stated firmly. "My lessons are on a much grander scale than any of those professors or books will teach, though. I use only the best animals for experimentation."

"And you're sure science will save us? It will make things better?"

"How can it not? Everything can be explained, Leith. Soon there will be no mysteries at all, and we'll have science to thank for that. Think of the possibilities! Think of how many people can be helped when all the diseases in the world can be treated and there's enough food to feed every living thing. It would be ridiculous for the world not to fall into peace when everything could be solved so easily."

"But maybe," Leith said cautiously, "you could teach me your lessons without harming any animals?"

"Dear boy! That's what they are there for. We are their masters. They do their part in making the world more civilized by acting as my living textbooks." He paused and drew closer. "Take care of your mom. She's a splendid woman, a fragile woman."

Leith nodded, the stab of jealousy returning. Did this man know Calpurnia at all?

Tristan took a bow, put the hat atop his head, and turned and walked toward the gravel road, his small sack of belongings slung carefully over his shoulder. He whistled the same jaunty tune to which he had waltzed earlier with Calpurnia.

"Have a wonderful day, Leith! The valley awaits my learned presence."

CALPURNIA WATCHED Tristan leave, having said his farewell to Leith. She was, as Leith had expected, wishing the walls were windows to the back fields. She had run from the walls to the long window, anxiously waiting for Tristan to come about and make his journey down the gravel road. She saw him at last and sighed most contentedly. He walked with his head held high. He often turned and waved at her as she stood in the long window. He knew she would be there waiting for him; she had told him as much.

With each of his steps, she felt the pressing weight of normalcy returning to her bleak existence. The last couple of days had been the most marvelous she could remember in all her adulthood. She had pleaded with Tristan to stay just a while longer, but the man's mind was set. How strange it felt, even now, to be denied what she desired. If she had the Book in hand, she could have forced him to stay that very minute. She wondered what scripture she would have used. She still knew them all by heart, though it had been many years since she had last turned the golden pages to any real purpose. Where was the Book anyway? It no longer lay like a museum piece on her bureau.

"Come back soon, my adventurer," she whispered to the glass in the theatrical fashion she had adopted over the years. Unbeknownst to her, she had only become more histrionic with age and internment. "My rescuer." She traced his dwindling image with her ring finger. *Tears now, Calpurnia.*

Before Tristan entered the forest of Black Hill, he plucked a tiger lily from the edge of the field. Turning to Calpurnia, he gave her one final, vigorous farewell with a kiss on the orange flower, tossing it into the breeze to be carried back to her. She smiled grandly at the gesture, humming their song.

Her eyes, however, changed from sweet, melancholy joy to inexorable horror in a blink. Tristan had wandered off the road when he picked the flower and was now standing amongst the trees. A prickling sensation cascaded down Calpurnia's body, and her hair stood on end. At once she began screaming his name, pounding the glass with her fists.

The sudden change in her demeanor startled the man.

"Turn around, Tristan! Run! The road. Stay on the road!" Her voice pierced the glass with ease, but it was of little use. Her warning came too late.

The expression on the vagabond's face was one of supreme confusion as he slowly lowered his waving hand in puzzlement. He did not move, but still seemed to fall deeper into the shadows, the forest belching the dark into the light.

Calpurnia continued to rant and scream, hoping her voice and the pounding the window was taking would somehow be enough to drive back the dark figure slipping around the curves of the forest toward Tristan. It appeared as a black fog at first, and she could not tell if he noticed the semblance of a large man forming before him as he turned his face to the woods. But she saw it. Her voice cut the air as Tristan was snatched like a rag doll into the tentacles of the black fog. It happened so quickly that if she had but fluttered an eyelash, she would have missed it. And then the blackness was gone, taking the man of science with it.

Calpurnia pushed herself from the glass. Barely able to breathe, she fell to the floor in a convulsive fit.

LEITH RACED up the stairs and into the room. He found her nearly paralyzed, lying on the floor, her body bent in a U formation, one hand outstretched and pointing at the long window.

"Calpurnia?" He tried to revive her, but his light smacks did nothing against the quagmire her mind had fallen into. Her eyes twitched and she drooled and grunted. Bewildered, Leith left her side and followed the line of her extended hand and pointing finger.

He saw nothing but a sunny day at first. Nothing but thousands of goldenrods, tiger lilies, butterflies, and large healthy trees. Fields and trees and—

Just as he was about to return his attention to his mother, he recognized a small lump laying in the road, almost blending with the mud and dirt as if it had been thrown there. Tristan's bag. All he possessed in the world—a few items of extra clothing and some food from Walterhouse Manor—lay spilled, seemingly discarded on the ground.

MINERVA'S SOFT bed had not been used in days. Inside and outside the earthen cottage, all was quiet, like a moment encased in a glass bubble. Everything was paused like statuary, perfectly formed yet ill-equipped for any use and purpose. Even the Breed had vanished. If one were to search for the old woman, they would not find her in the kitchen baking or outside tending her gardens and keeping the dark vines at bay. For days Minerva had been seated in the very same position on the floor, leaning distractedly against the rounded wall of the cottage. She rested limp, eyes open but vacant, her face nearly as white as dogwood blossoms. She held conversations with vindictive, condemning ghosts in her mind. Each conversation became a battle lost. She concluded she was a woman without purpose, whose most cherished friends had all, in some form or other, been taken by the darkness, and that blame was all hers.

Mother True, aware of the battle to come, had searched for Minerva throughout the forest, but could locate her nowhere. The vines peered boldly up and over the cliff at the circle wood. She had seen the creeping darkness drifting out of the chapel grounds and presumptuously into the forest. She called to Minerva from the trees, from the highest branches where angels clung, but received no response. She waded across the waters and down among the barrows. Still, nothing. It came as a surprise to the wise spirit, finding her daughter, Minerva, shut up and nearly dead from despair in the little cottage that had never known the Imbalance.

Minerva did not move as Mother True settled into the air around her, brushing past the hanging herbs. She seemed not to be alert to the change in current. Mother True saw Minerva's thoughts as if they were her own memories. Minerva's regrets had formed an obsidian anchor wreathed around her neck. On the anchor shone images of Hamlin Marsh and their brave, tiny daughter Branwenn. Countless other faces and incidents glimmered in reflection as well, things that could have been if Minerva had taken other paths. They flashed in quick, rebuking glints, followed by the stone-like darkened faces of all who had passed into the chapel grounds: Rupert Toots, the Parmas…. One by one, in a carefully orchestrated caravan of denunciation. Even the valley itself appeared reflected in the weighted anchor, an obscure and lost land, smothered by a wretchedly thick yellow-brown dust that overhung a dirty river like waiting Death.

"Enough of this!" The whispering crackle of Mother True struck the air. "*You have not lost!* You have only begun to win. Wake up now, girl!"

The obsidian anchor at once shattered from around Minerva's neck, the pieces vanishing into a gaseous void even before they hit the floor. Color crept back into Minerva's face and eyes, like paint meeting canvas. Her head stirred as if whipped from a dream. She breathed in deeply and expelled the poisonous thoughts. She sat dazed for a spell, sensing that Mother True had been to see her but was now gone. Slowly, she came back to herself, like a helianthus drawn to the sun.

Without warning, a piercing cry vanquished the silence of the cottage. Minerva jumped, her heart pounding in distress. A portent.

"*Deverell!*" she cried.

LEITH HELPED Calpurnia to her bed. She sat against the headboard, staring ahead, her mouth atremble. The light from the long window was fading, the sun once again hidden by dark clouds. Still, the room hung thick with humidity and a musky smell, made worse because Calpurnia would not allow the windows to ever be opened. Leith dabbed at her forehead using an old handkerchief. Her breathing was erratic, and the muscles above her right eye twitched wildly.

"Oh, Leith," she finally whispered, grabbing his wrist none too gently. "Where do you think he's gone?" She gazed at her son pleadingly. "Who was that who came upon him? What type of man can fold out of the air?"

Leith swallowed and shook his head in uncertainty. He didn't yet know if he believed his mother's tale, even more befuddled and confused in the telling. Yet Tristan's belongings lay abandoned near the forest edge. He would not have just left them there. He had things to collect and he would need his bag for that. Black Hill hid glories and horrors alike with relative ease. Sweat dripped from the tip of his nose to the bedspread. His shirt clung to him, soaked clear through.

"Do you think he'll return?" she asked.

"Maybe," he found himself lying, the words a scarce echo of his voice. "He said he would after he had researched more of the valley. He told me just that."

"You're a comfort, my dear." Calpurnia brought his hand up to her lips and held it there. She kissed his ring; the one that had belonged to Garet. Possessions of the Lost. The chapel was forever coughing up undigested bits of the past.

"I remember your father had a ring similar to this once," Calpurnia murmured. "It was given to him by Darcy Crock—" She didn't finish his name, her mind resting instead on the ghostly remembrance of Lara.

She forced her lips to the green stone of the ring for a long, uncomfortable moment. Leith felt a strange fear and eyed her suspiciously, as if the woman in front of him was one of those slide shows he had heard tale of, flipping from one scene to the next without warning. By now, he knew the prelude to a change in her mood.

He watched her face change from an expression of complete disorientation to one of revelation. "I have something I want to give you," she said. Her face became calm and resolute. "You need to have it. Garet would want you to have it. It's there." She pointed with her long, crooked nails. She never cut them, and only bit them off when they snagged at her skin. "In the bureau."

Leith thought it odd that his mother had held on to anything that belonged to his father. It was Minerva who had packed Garet's belongings away for safekeeping in the attic. Calpurnia had wanted them all destroyed.

Following his mother's gesture, he removed the quilts from the ornately carved bureau top. It squealed reluctantly as he opened it. Inside was a plethora of pictures, old china dolls, and more quilts. It smelled of age like an empty crypt.

"It's beneath everything," she said. "Throw everything else out! Those things don't matter."

Leith removed the items carefully as Calpurnia urged him to move faster.

"They don't matter!" she shouted. "Throw them about, foolish boy. The only thing that matters is under them."

He went faster, but refused to throw anything. The broken face of a smiling china doll was not the image he needed at the moment. Finally, he uncovered the hilt of a sword, the blade of which was wrapped not in a decadent sheath, but in a man's tattered work shirt. There was a comforting smell to the old shirt as he lifted it from its long repose; Leith imagined it was his father's scent. He unclothed the blade and decided he would keep the shirt. The metal gleamed even without the light of the sun, casting silver flashes throughout the room.

"Bring it to me," Calpurnia instructed tersely.

He walked to her and put the sword in her hands. She took a quick breath. "This was your father's," she explained. "This is what's left of him; what Minerva brought back of him. He was a ranger. And a fool. He was many things. It's yours now to do what he could not."

"What's that, Calpurnia?" Leith inquired, quite certain he did not like the tone of her voice. It matched too perfectly the growing impetuousness of her expression. "What would you have me do with it?"

She put the sword on the bed beside her and leaned forward ominously. The bed creaked. "You need to find and kill Darcy Crocker before he kills you. Before he takes all of us. Do you understand?"

"But Darcy is dead. He died when I was a baby."

"No, no, no. He lives," she assured her son. "He lives because your father wasn't man enough to kill him. He let his lust distract him from those he should have looked after."

Leith flinched at this, stepping back. "Father was a good man," he defended. "Everyone said so. Minerva said he was one of the kindest in the valley."

"Kindness counts for nothing against the likes of Darcy Crocker! Not against the will of the chapel!" She reached for Leith, pulling him closer with a violent tug. "He's taken too much from me already," she whispered beneath gritted teeth. "Not only my rescuer Tristan, but your father as well… and Lara." She fell back against the headboard. "Oh, my love! Oh, my Lara!" She raised her hand to her mouth, putting her index finger between her teeth in a sign of unbearable heartbreak.

"You think he will come for you and me?"

"I'm certain of it, darling. Darcy was a selfish man. He wanted everything I ever had. Do not make me live in fear! I can't have you taken from me as well. When he shows himself to you, and he will, defend yourself. Defend me and mine. Kill him! Strike him down with your father's sword."

"Minerva says it's not Darcy, but the one the River Dwellers called Dark Eyes; the Dark Preacher from long ago."

"River Dwellers," she spat out. "I was to be a River Dweller once. Did you know that? But I saw through them. I never took a river name. And now, you've gone and made yourself one of their frivolous group."

"You chose not to become a River Dweller?"

"I rightfully denounced it! There are no gods, Leith. There's nothing divine, no great plan to any of… *this*. There are only different forms of misery. How can you not see that?" She appeared ready to strike him. "But now, I've upset you. I'm sorry, my love, but I only say these things out of love. You understand, don't you?"

"Love?" he said. "Yes. I suppose I can understand you saying such things out of love."

"Promise me you'll use the sword," she pleaded, clasping his hand tightly, her nails digging into his tender flesh.

"I promise," he answered. "If needs be, I'll use the sword." But it was a lie. He didn't see a way to defeat the chapel. The one hope he had, Tristan, the vagabond, adventurer or scientist, had been dealt with just as easily as everyone else. His talk of grand experiments that would change the world had resulted in nothing but more grief.

"Good," Calpurnia said, a mournful, half-crazed smile crossing her face. "Very good."

As Leith left the room, sword in hand, his head downcast in dejection, Calpurnia was perfecting a plan. Something she had come upon quite miraculously as she kissed Garet's ring and was reminded of Garet and Darcy's kinship. The connection of father and son was a strong one, a connection that might make a wandering soul do anything to be reunited with its family, so she thought. Darcy was quite simply waiting for Elijah, or Deverell as he was now called. Once he had him, once they were brought together again, maybe he would leave. Maybe he would even give Lara back to her as a token of appreciation.

She smiled at her own cunning. She would be free after all. She would have Lara again. She *would* get what she wanted.

The vertigo set in quickly.

Deverell was searching Black Hill and had been all morning. He was in a patch of forest he recognized from previous explorations. A peculiar-shaped tree trunk here, a jagged pile of rock there, and so on. But then, something shifted, and the sky grew deadly dark, like a lid being slid over a coffin. The forest seemed to crowd suddenly around him in fear; he heard the wood of the trees crack and moan. He leaned against a small tree to steady himself against the dizziness, and closed his eyes momentarily to the world. When he opened them, he no longer recognized where he was. The entire landscape had grown as dark and colorless as coal and ash, his hands covered in black soot. Death lay heavy on the wind, and the trees were silent.

Fighting the instability, Deverell walked between the trees with the queer sense of tiptoeing about the edges of a waking dream. The smell of burnt wood permeated the too-silent air, and not even his feet made noise as he stepped on leaves and twigs. He turned round and round, trying to make sense of his environment. Then a sound, like wind through a tunnel, swept around him. Quite suddenly, without the warning of approaching footfalls, a large man in a thick fur coat stood just a few feet away. It was as if he had appeared from the ash of the trees, formed from it in a cryptic metamorphosis. He smiled queerly at Deverell. The smile was not returned. Ferocity met ferocity, and began the brooding. The man before Deverell fit every description Minerva had given him of Dark Eyes/Darcy Crocker.

The sound of the tunneling wind changed to that of a thin stream of air blown through a whistle until a hissing *S* was audible, gradually forming into a single whispering word, "*S-s-s-s-son.*"

Darcy had not moved his mouth. His face kept the same unwavering grin, handsome and charming, but distant. He offered his large hand for Deverell to take.

Though weak and lightheaded, Deverell found the strength to retreat a few steps, while still keeping watch on the coated man. This took a great amount of effort, and he found himself tiring almost at once. Yet even as he backed away, Darcy seemed to come with him as if they were tied together by thread or chicken wire. Deverell crumbled to the blackened ground, becoming increasingly dizzy. He felt nauseous, as though perhaps he might vomit. Glancing up, the form of his handsome father changed to that of someone more malevolent. The eyes sunk into the skull, and the dark, lustrous hair receded from the forehead and shoulders. Finally, the coat fell from him, overtaken by the ash to reveal a simple dark suit.

Deverell retched onto the dead earth. When he cleared his eyes of the vomit-induced tears, he saw he was no longer in the forest on Black Hill in front of the preacher, but in a great, dark hall. All he could discern of its structure were large archways that galloped yards overhead in exuberant display. The hall itself seemed an endless echo of the same arch, and the place smelled stale, the air of claustrophobic ages. All around the large, cold hall people stood still and pale. Deverell first assumed they were statues, but on further analysis, their humanity was unmistakable. Their faces were lit from below as if each held a candle. To Deverell's horror, he saw that their eyes had been picked out, and blood trickled down their hollow cheeks like flesh-eating tears.

In unison, the mass of sightless beings bowed in supplication as Dark Eyes appeared out of the shadows once more. Deverell tried vehemently to stand, unwilling to be a participant, even by accident, in the worship of such a harmful, heinous thing. Too weak, he fell back to the ground, vomiting once again. The vertigo imprisoned him there like heavy chains drawn over his shoulders.

Dark Eyes approached him, chanting syllables that made no earthly sense with the crowd. The words were half words, without any true meaning tied to them. They only gained their power from the belief of the blinded souls who sang them. Deverell refused to look away from the towering figure, defiantly focusing his eyes on the preacher, even as he shed tears of pain and clenched his jaw to ready himself for whatever was to come. Dark Eyes reached for Deverell. The crowd of supplicants chanted in jumbles of letters and highs and lows.

Yet as the Dark One's hand drew near, something snatched away the encroaching terror. The blind worshipers disappeared in a plume of smoke, their echoes fading instantly. Slowly a forest of green trees and lush vegetation began to reappear. As Deverell's eyes welcomed the light, a familiar object connected with Dark Eyes's approaching hand. A weathered blade with a peculiar curve cut through the Dark Preacher's wrist. A small quake shook the ground.

Deverell crumbled to the earth, but felt the nausea fading away and the vertigo diminishing. He lifted his head slightly, still woozy from his encounter, relieved to find Dark Eyes/Darcy gone. In his place, standing between two large guard-like conifers, was Minerva True wielding her scythe.

"Come, child," she said gently. "There is much to do. I have been foolish, and it has nearly cost me you."

As Deverell found his feet, ecstatic to once again see her, he noticed the dismembered hand sinking into the earth in a morbid adieu.

PART IV—
LINES DRAWN

THE BATTLE ON THE ROCKFACE

A TRUTH was revealed the night after Deverell and Minerva encountered Dark Eyes on the hillside in the phantom cathedral. As the stars and distant worlds glinted above, a vision was handed to Minerva True. She dreamt she was walking slowly, trudging along the rocks by the river, on a singularly familiar day, one she had seen before: that very design in the sky, that very shape of the water. Familiar faces from the valley's yesteryear watched her pass, those who had gone away from the river lest the darkness envelop them. Each one looked concerned, but bore the hint of surrender on their faces, as if their apprehension could not be helped. Minerva looked to her hands and feet and realized with slight alarm that she was not herself. In this vision she took the form of Clara Parma on her lonesome cursed stroll toward death.

She entered the chapel grounds with no hindrance or care, whispers and moans of fear and sorrow in the background from those on the beach who watched her go. "*Come back, Clara!*" they cried. Though the dark vines twisted at her feet like irritable snakes, they did nothing to impede her. She stepped over them easily, snagging her gown only twice on the thorns. The fog too parted so that she might find her way without interference to the chapel steps. As Clara/Minerva climbed the stairs to the large opened doors, she was finally privy to the hidden minions of the chapel, the crocodiles and hounds for the first time exposed.

She saw the perverted hierarchy of the place. Inside waited and moaned the ensnared ones, the souls taken against their will, each in their distinct misery. But there also were those who came willingly to the chapel grounds, those who had stood with Pastor Wade as he had flogged Angela Children. All seven of them who had given themselves to the chapel with all their hearts, having been promised their desires. Their souls were twisted, blighted things now.

Gazing about her, Clara/Minerva saw the seven hounds in horrific detail. The rumors of crocodiles, as the boys had called them—she'd imagined large, slithering silhouettes like dinosaurs in the mist—proved somewhat unfounded. They resembled a more common monster: naked humans whose skin had been stretched and whose bones had been plied and manipulated. They had no pigment or hair at all, their flesh blanched as white as corn. Their heads were but pale flesh lumps with mouths and nostrils, their eyes overgrown with pockets of flesh. For movement, they pulled themselves about using double-jointed arms, dragging their lifeless legs behind them like broken tails in spasmodic shuffles of stilted pain and rage. They seemed to hunger constantly. These were men and women not fully formed or, more aptly, in a state of devolving. They hissed and screamed, ushering the woman into the chapel.

As Clara entered the chapel doors, unaware that the family she sought to be with was held captive by the vines behind the chapel itself, she gave herself to the power of the preacher.

Minerva awoke.

IN THE following days, Minerva became stronger than ever in her determination to save the valley from falling into a prescribed order like the Ordinary Places of the world; a place sick with fumes, arbitrary laws, and the unobservant masses. She began teaching Deverell in earnest the ways of the River Dwellers. A young girl would have been best, a descendent of a River Dweller, but that was an impossibility. Branwenn had been the last hope, and there were no more young girls left in the valley to bring up in the old ways. Deverell, Minerva had decided, would do fine, the perfect constitution of masculine and feminine. Strength in every form.

The dark vines that had crept dangerously close to the trees on the bluff whilst Minerva was weighed down with grief were quickly and viciously seen to. If ever something could be termed a massacre, it was Minerva wielding her weapon on the creepers. The time-trusted scythe slashed through the distorted tendrils so fiercely they shrank to the base of the hill, revealing the last few bones of the men below. But the vines were not going to give up those so easily. They clung to them, wound tightly, threatening to crack them into flecks and chips.

"There's mischief here," Minerva said. "The black vines taunt us. Do you see?" She half grinned, almost relishing the job ahead.

Deverell stared angrily down into the deformed thickets of wrestling ivy. He crouched on the bluff, ready to leap on them and have at it.

"We will persevere," she assured him. "We have an epoch's worth of sleeping River Dwellers to assist us. The vines have but marred earth."

Far below, the vines' grip grew even tighter around the bones as if understanding her words. Deverell gave Minerva a quick glance.

"Scaling the rockface is too dangerous," Minerva answered. "That would not be wise. If one were to fall, it would not be the reach of the vines that one should fear, but what waits beneath them. You are very strong, but can you battle dragons?"

She had explained to him her vision of the crocodiles and exactly what and who they were. The crocs, she understood, were ready for meat. The vines had been allowed the kill off the Parmas, holding the family high above the ground to die slow deaths away from the crocodiles' jaws. Dark Eyes's seven pets were not keen to let the same thing occur again, and so were becoming more and more daring, even challenging the crawling vegetation for the unfortunate forest creatures caught wandering onto the chapel grounds.

Minerva had once again begun her vigils on the beach, watching the chapel. That very morning she had witnessed the true burgeoning strength of that cursed plot of land. As she stood, wrapped in her shawl, the early morning mist subduing the colors of the valley, a small patch of the chapel grounds seemed to move. It twitched and jolted out from the chapel itself, a crippled hand out of the fog. *A crocodile.* The chapel was at last reaching into the valley, ready to make its claim.

Minerva loosened her shawl and strode toward the creature. Though it had barely laid its bent paws from the chapel grounds, it was enough for her.

"No more!" she shouted at the large eyeless demon. "Return to where you crawled from!" She did not have her scythe with her, but she still struck a formidable figure.

The crocodile seemed shaken by her fearlessness. In the shape of its face, she recognized Pastor Wade. Minerva grabbed a stick from the ground and, wheeling it over her head, ran toward the creature, striking the air in warning. The creature hissed, the teeth of its oblong jaw pointed and yellow. It promptly turned and slid back into the wretched stink of the chapel's embrace where other creatures hissed on its return. The mist began to close again.

Though Minerva felt a certain victorious rush she had not felt in a very long time, she noticed the chapel had indeed lost its dreamy, hallucinogenic appearance and was now more fully present than it had been since Pastor Wade had first arrived in the valley on his foolish crusade. It had crossed the threshold between worlds. It stood a whole and complete structure, as if it had been worked on every night by a township of wheezing minions. The crocodiles congregated and curled on the chapel's steps, gasping their throaty curses at Minerva.

The valley reverberated with unease. Its fear was tangible; she could taste it. And as she turned back to the river, the morning mist that lay over the water parted, and she saw across easily, the distance seeming to shrink to but a few feet. The Othersiders watched her with interest. Some stood along the shore. Some watched from their treehouses with their lanterns; others manned small rafts and floated just a little from their own bank. They seemed to wait for something. She wanted to reach out for them, to ask or plead for their help. But would it matter? Would they even hear her? Perhaps it was already too late. Her mind was riddled with questions. First and foremost, why would they not let her cross over the river? Why had she not been ready so many years before?

The Three, floated a whisper across the water, *the Three shall vanquish him.*

Remembering those words from the early-morning hours, Minerva now bent and kissed Deverell gently on the forehead. He was still watching the vines. Daring them. Minerva turned for the circle wood, using her battered scythe as a walking stick. Deverell remained where he was.

Emerging from the wood and into the circular clearing of the cottage, Minerva caught a glimpse of something small, only a couple feet in height, scurrying behind a tree. She spotted its shiny pelt just as it disappeared, and knew for certain that it was not one of the Breed. They had disappeared altogether. Probably taken by the crocodiles and the crawlers, she thought shamefully. That broke her heart, but she would not dwell on it now.

Though she did not look for the creature, she was curious as to who had called it. She recognized the spirit and it brought her some relief. The Passions, as the animal spirits of the forest were called, did not show themselves often, and if she had caught a glimpse of one, it was certainly no accident. She had been meant to see it as a sign of hope. The calling of the animal spirits was reserved for times of dire need, usually decided upon by the spirits themselves. Minerva had only seen a Passion once before, as a child, and then it had been called forth by Mother True. So, she thought, it could only have been the Mother this time as well.

Or was she wrong about that? She felt so very uncertain these days.

DEVERELL FOUND the scythe where Minerva had left it, leaning against the side of the cottage. He carried it back to the cliff after he was certain Minerva had gone into the forest searching for spices and mushrooms. It dawned on him that in all his years living at the cottage, he had not once touched the scythe. It was heavier than he thought it would be. Minerva seemed to wield it with such ease that Deverell had reckoned it would be as light as air.

He knew Minerva would not be in favor of what he was preparing to do, but her warnings this time went unheeded. He intended to do this because he felt he truly had to. Just as Minerva had her role in the war, so had he, and here he would make his first deadly strike against the enemy. Retribution for all that had been done, for the mother he never knew, and the father whose image had been stolen, soiled, and garbled. The preacher hid behind Darcy Crocker's handsome visage to mask his own virulent depravity, and Deverell meant to rectify that or at least have a hand in its remedy.

Deverell pulled a winding trumpet vine, thick and rough, from the massive oak at the edge of the cliff and, holding tightly to the scythe, descended the rockface perhaps a little quicker than he had expected. As he lowered himself, he stared down the dark ivy, challenging it. His hands were already raw from the prickly old vine he clung to. The dark ivy began to rustle slightly, awakening. Sensing the challenge, it began to steal slowly up the rock. Deverell flipped the scythe in one hand as a show of dominance. A single vegetative tentacle dared reach for him, and he swung the weapon, cutting the ivy clean through. Others followed suit, an expected rush from the hydra. Deverell gave an emphatic grin, welcoming the advance, and swung again. Pieces of dark vegetation scattered wide to gasps and hisses. He used the strong vine from the oak to swing across the rockface, dispatching the creeping poison with ease. With every swipe he managed to descend closer to the remaining bones at the base of the cliff until he was almost within reach of them. One more clean cut and he could grab them.

As he swung heartily, a crack overhead startled him—the sound of breaking wood. Thinking quickly, he reached for the rockface, digging the scythe into it with astonishing force. The stone bowed to the blade. He positioned his feet and free hand like a mountaineer on the small geological imperfections and impressions of white stone. The trumpet vine he had held whipped past him, falling into the darkness of the ivy, which quickly devoured it.

He dislodged the scythe from the rock, swinging it just in time to thwart a dark tentacle's thorny grasp. But another reached for him at the same moment, strangling his hanging hand of feeling as he desperately clung with it to the rockface. Bestial hissing rose from below him, but he was uncertain whether it was the ivy or the hidden crocodiles. The dark ivy squeezed his wrist tighter, other tendrils reaching for him in an obscene frenzy bordering on lust.

Gritting his teeth in defiance, Deverell used the scythe once again, this time as a pick ax securing himself and releasing the rockface with his strangled hand. With all the power left in the wrist—summoning the strength his mighty father had passed on to him—he yanked the vine completely out of the earth. Its grip immediately loosened, and Deverell threw it as far as he could with a satisfying rage. Though another dark creeper managed to take hold of him, he was able to easily twist free, receiving only a light scratch on his bare back in the process.

Finally, he swung the fatal blow, tearing most of the ivy that accosted him from its sickly soil. Though a few smaller tentacles reached for him still, it was in vain. Deverell snatched up the remaining Parma bones just as he spied a hissing creature of intolerable visual turpitude charging at him. It scuttled in a seizured assault, the musky scent of the virile young man guiding it to where Deverell clung to the rockface. Ready for the battle to be finished, Deverell jabbed the scythe's hard oak handle into where the crocodile's eye should have been, then swung the blade about and hacked the creature's strong jaws clean off. The crocodile released a gurgling rasp of pain as dark blood gushed over the defeated and stricken ivy that quivered and shook at his feet. Deverell held tightly to the bones, breathing heavily. As he turned to ascend the cliff once more, the silhouette of a slender well-dressed man at the chapel's back door caught his eye. But that battle was for another time. He hadn't the strength for it now.

It took him a while to climb back up the bluff. There was no longer any concern from the ivy below, so he rested as he needed, though he felt certain seedlings lay ready to take the fallen vines' place. He was tired and hot and bruised, and the rockface was a treacherous, selfish thing, unwilling to provide a clear path up. The jutting rocks were spaced awkwardly, alternately taunting and battering him. The scythe's cutting beak aided him to a degree, but his strength had waned. He carried the bones in the crotch of his pants, and they stabbed at him uncomfortably with every pull upward.

With a triumphant sigh, he completed his ascent. The sun beat down on him, having chased away the rain clouds. Deverell looked victoriously out over the valley.

"You *are* your father's son," Minerva spoke from behind him. She stood near the oak, anxiety fleeing from her face. The twisted remnant of the trumpet vine hung from a broken tree branch. Deverell wondered if she had witnessed his triumph. "He never listened either. It's useless to tell you anything sometimes. You could have been taken, Deverell." She spoke with maternal concern.

Deverell reached into his pants and pulled from them the last bones of the Family Parma. Minerva approached, taking the bones from him. Tears of appreciation clouded her eyes. She gently touched the wounds on his shoulder.

"So, you have defeated them after all," she said. "You have won your battle. I knew you would. These bones will be set with the others, and the Parma men may find some peace at last."

Deverell bowed slightly in some courtly gesture as if he were a knight in an old tale. With the midday sky behind him, he turned for the circle wood and the earthen cottage, in need of rest. Minerva remained at the cliff, surveying the devastation below with pride.

As DEVERELL was yet descending the bluff, Leith took his daily leave of Calpurnia and walked the gravel road, sided by the goldenrods and hundreds of playful butterflies, on his way to the college campus. It had been quite a while since he and Aubrey had seen Albert Higgins, and he missed the learning experience. He could feel his mother's penetrating gaze on his back as she stared from the long window. He had never been more uncomfortable around her than that summer of fickle weather. She seemed stranger than anytime he could recall. Which is to say, she was acting *sane*. It was something very recent. She had started behaving thus, directly after she had given Garet's sword to Leith. *Sane*. As sane as any of the collegiate young men he passed on the way to his lessons. Her moods had not shifted at all since presenting him the sword, and this was indeed an oddity. Calpurnia had never trod on the narrow path of sanity as long as Leith had known her. The road she walked was broad and broadening all the time, little trails branching off here and there. Hers was a delirious path, easily distracted. He was sure there had been a time when she was a logical person, but that was surely long before he had entered the world. Her sudden sanity was the most ominous and frustrating bellwether of things to come that could possibly be imagined.

Entering the forest, Leith felt at last free of her—at least for a time. Whatever darkness lay in the recesses of Black Hill, be they trolls, goblins, or zealots, he would happily confront them in exchange for peace from Calpurnia's frightening, calm eyes. Even the rumored Dark Preacher could be no match for that woman!

The only thing that provided relief to Leith was the fact that Calpurnia had recently taken her first steps to leave her room. Why she did this, he did not know. *Sanity?* But he had watched her as she stood, violently shaking, in the doorway of her bedchamber, one freshly manicured bare foot poking tentatively beyond the threshold. He had been bringing her dinner when he witnessed the spectacle. If she succeeded in freeing herself from her isolation, he too would be freed of his unwarranted servitude. His heart raced at the prospect. He gripped the tray tightly. But she had clung to the doorframe like a drowning person desperately clutching a lonely piece of driftwood. Her eyes grew wide, as if she had never seen the hallway before. She stood there for over an hour taking in all that she hadn't seen in years, and then, to Leith's great disappointment, she withdrew. Still, every day she tried anew, each time remaining a little longer, and every day her son's hope grew. Perhaps soon he would be able to leave her altogether and make a safe and comfortable life somewhere with his Aubrey Avonmore, Prince of the Valley. Somewhere without Calpurnia. They could be the adventurers Tristan had claimed to be but never really was.

As he was thinking, a strange sound, alien to the valley, sang gently through the low-hanging branches and fluttering leaves. It was a faintly recognizable song, but familiar only because Leith had heard it sung from many a tree limb on the farther edges of Greenbriar campus. There, birds still gathered, if in wary and reduced numbers. There, they yet sang morning choruses. But this was the first birdsong Leith had ever heard in the valley or on its crowning hills.

He stopped and glanced around in wonder. Even the trees seemed to pause in their windy twittering and listen in astonishment. Though a little thing, it was as conspicuous a sound as a canon echoing down a canyon. The ground beneath him suddenly began to vibrate and rumble, moving with thousands of terrified insects and worms, all of them sent askitter by a solitary birdsong. The earth pulsed from their slithering, creeping panic, and muddy pustules formed in the overcrowded dirt, ready to explode.

Leith dropped his books to the ground immediately, eagerly darting into the forest. He swept around every tree and thicket, a young man obsessed, scouring the dense wood for the lone bird. The birdsong carried a queer note of urgency to it. The melody bounced off the trees and stones, confusing Leith all the more with its solitary brazenness, until he stood dizzy and breathless amidst unfamiliar arboreal giants.

He had run downhill, jumping streams and leaping over the forgotten barrows, and now found himself in the section of the forest where green began to give way to petrification and ash: Lower Black Hill Road. Leith stole himself behind a lifeless trunk, noticing Aubrey standing beneath the asphaltic arbor that bore his carved name, staring upward into the lifeless branches in some silent conversation with a garrulous rain crow. Though the bird's coat of feathers made it appear beaten, it piped on incessantly in zealous chirps, mixed intermittently with excited hops. It seemed at times to be scolding Aubrey, very much like a parent.

Aubrey held up his hand in a sign of calm whenever the bird became agitated, and the old crow became still. Leith could not make out what was passing between the two. There were no audible phrases. He knew, of course, that Aubrey had a special connection, a mingled destiny and oath, with the forest and the valley.

Finally, the aged bird leapt into the air with some effort and flew high and upriver. It whistled a melancholy farewell. Leith did not know birds, but he knew a good-bye when he heard one.

Aubrey stood for a moment, his head bowed, his face drained of color. Though certainly troubled, his expression betrayed nothing more than deep thought. "Come out of hiding, shy boy," he called suddenly. His skulk warmed into a smile. "I think you got lost on your way to school."

Leith was startled, but then wondered at his own surprise. Of course Aubrey had known he was watching the entire time. Leith stepped into the petrified woods. "Are you okay?" he inquired. "You look… concerned. Are the birds returning? That's the first I've seen a bird around here! Have you seen many others?"

"I'm fine, silly," Aubrey said, the color returning to his lovely face. "That was an old friend. I did him a favor once. He just came back to give me some news. He's gone off now. Pro'ly die somewhere on the other side of the river." His voice betrayed only a twinge of heartbreak. Aubrey knew things about the Other Side, so maybe, Leith concluded, death there wasn't as tragic an affair.

Still, Leith felt downhearted. "I was hoping maybe it would stay, that maybe all the other birds might come back. There would be birds in the trees again, whistling and singing to the sun. Then everything could be different."

What could be different? *Everything.*

"Everything *will* be different. You just wait and see, young'n. Things are gonna start changing real fast around here, so hold on to your britches." He put an arm around Leith, squeezing him tight. There was still something melancholy about his manner, as if the secrets he held were now somehow heavier and more burdensome.

"What do you say we go to the old barrows tonight?" Aubrey posited. "We need to spend some evening time in the forest. Summer'll be over soon."

"But the barrows are so close to the chapel," Leith objected.

"I know," Aubrey replied. "But it's something we have to do. Trust me, it will be a time you ain't ever likely to forget. We'll bring plenty of drink and wear the horns and antlers like they did in the old ceremonies Minerva tells us about."

"It's that important, huh?" Leith inquired.

"It is." Aubrey swallowed. "Let's find Deverell. This is his responsibility too. No school for us today, lover. Mr. Albert Higgins will understand."

Sweet Speckled Sparrow

Neko was a song.

Sadly, her name had been completely forgotten, and those who heard her at twilight making love to the beauty of the dense forest simply referred to her as Song. She was the melancholy voice Calpurnia had first heard at Autumnday when she chased after River Dwellers and phantoms. She was the Mysterious Gloaming Call the young men of Greenbriar College imagined as some lonesome songstress down in the valley. They would gather at dusk on the bluff under Mother True's tree and listen carefully to Song's faint melody as they puffed on their pipes. Never a word was spoken. Just the plaintive plea in the air of things not yet lost, because they had never been found in the first place.

She had never been an actual person, though that had been the Othersiders' intent. The body which Song was given to inhabit, the beautiful fiery-haired young River Dweller named Neko, was now buried deep in the barrows of Black Hill and had been for many years, long before even Minerva's birth.

Song was carried to the valley not by a majestic dove or an elegant swan, but by a tiny—some would say insignificant—and innocent sparrow. It took great pride in its task, and determinedly fought hurricane winds and feral hawks to bring the gift of Song to the young lady. *Even the smallest of birds can carry great souls*. It was said to be the most beautiful voice ever lifted into the world, and all the other birds were jealous that the tiny sparrow was chosen over them to relay this gift. The swans, the doves, the flamingos, the peacocks—*especially* the peacocks—ruffled their plumage in agitation.

But the young Neko died, brought to her death by a lustful valley phantom before the sparrow could sing out Song onto her. Neko's body was found one grievous dusk, floating up the river like a bathing water sprite. The craven phantom was shortly thereafter caught by the River

Dwellers, banished into rotten wood, then buried deep in the mud at the bottom of Black Hill.

The poor sparrow, its heart too small and fragile to contain such enormous grief, flew into the forest and died alone in the hollow of a tree. Without the sparrow to hold it any longer, eventually Song was freed into the trees. Though it did not have the lovely form of the lady Neko, it resided resolutely near her barrow for all time. Every evening Song sang, sometimes in wails, other times in happier tunes. Her song was most felicitous when a visitor would come across the barrows by accident— for the mounds had been lost to time, and only a few knew they were even there. Song loved an audience, and she would sing gratefully for them. But they often ran in utter terror at the sound of such magnificent beauty, such naked truth, piping from the wood and air. There were but a few who stayed long enough near the haunted barrows to give her the respect she was due.

Aubrey Avonmore, Deverell Crocker, and Leith Cather knew of her barrow. They knew of all of the barrows, having been told about them by Minerva and played amongst them as young boys. They had listened to Song's melodies all their lives. Song was beautiful to them. Now, on the eve of unprecedented change in the valley, the three sat against Neko's barrow with a small fire in front of them, drinking and wassailing into the night.

Song, delighted by the boys' presence, serenaded them with melodies more pristine and echoing than she had ever done. Her joy at not being so alone on this night, the anniversary of Neko's death long past, was mirrored through her syllables.

They were naked but for the small loincloths that hung by strings around their waists, rows of brass and wood bracelets jangled on the boys' strong arms, black liner graced their eyes, and ancient headdresses of deer, antelope and ram, worn with pride. Their moods glided swiftly from contentment to joy as the evening progressed. They danced about the barrows with wooden goblets of ale as Song caroled. It was a hint of the type of party the forest had not seen since the days the very headdresses they wore were used in true ritual.

And Song sang:

Sweet speckled sparrow
Don't trust the owl

Dance, but be wary
Of this late hour

And how Aubrey and Leith danced and swayed with one another as Song's voice haunted the moonlit woods!

Sweet speckled sparrow
Such sorrow comes to
Those who will dance
As joyous as you

And how marvelous was the third one, the large quiet one who lay atop the barrow kneading his sinewy, muscular thighs as he stared up at the sky with a sensual grin!

La-di-da-di-da-di-dum

The boys joined along with Song.

La-di-da-di-da-di-dum!

Sweet speckled sparrow
The words come too late
Sing and the sky
Shall mourn your fate

So the evening went. The grass sparkled with dew, and the air glimmered with night flies, and the boys pressed flushed flesh beneath the thick canopy.

As the night wore on, the shadows and moonlight made the trees seem all the more animated; the exhausted boys rested near the fire, drinking. Their heavy breaths of exertion were mingled with slight laughs and giggles, the signs of a party's settling. Song still sang, but it was a yielding melody now, almost a cradlesong that drifted around their ears.

The frivolity drew to a close with the arrival of new friends. Though Aubrey had drunk just as much, if not more, than either Leith or Deverell, he began at once to take on a more serious and altogether sober demeanor, peering into the high flames in deep thought. It was as if something within the flames spoke to him and demanded steadfast attention.

"What's the matter, Aubrey?" Leith asked, crawling toward him, his words slurred. He nuzzled up to his companion like a contented puppy.

Aubrey looked up and past the fire, into the darkness of the moon-bathed barrows and trees. Even farther his eyes seemed to search, across streams and sinkholes. He appeared to be watching something as it approached, something riding the dark like a chariot.

"They draw near," he said lowly and cryptically.

"Who?" Leith asked with some anxiety as he suddenly sat to attention. "Why do you stand up? What are you looking at?"

"Welcome," Aubrey said to the darkness behind the fire, offering a gentlemanly bow. His was the headdress of the ram.

Deverell, beneath the headdress of the antelope, stood as well and seemed to recognize another presence in the forest just beyond the fire. Even Song had quieted, retreating into the recesses of the barrow mound.

Leith fumbled to find his footing and squinted into the dark past the fire. At first he saw nothing, only the light of the moon glistening on the grass and brush of the barrows. But then, to his fright, he saw three short, hirsute figures approaching, stepping out of the night. They walked on strange, thin legs and were all of three feet tall, if that.

"Goblins? Gnomes?" Leith wondered aloud, questioning his drunken mind.

Aubrey hushed him with a touch on the shoulder. "Deverell and Leith, these are all that remain of the Passions, the animal spirits of the forest: Fox, Wolf, and Cougar."

And indeed, they were exactly that. Only there was a certain anthropomorphic quality to them. Firstly, they walked on their hind legs, and their eyes held a different kind of presence than one might expect to see in ordinary forest creatures'. Their front legs sprouted hairless pink fingers at the ends so that it looked as if a child were hiding in costume somewhere within.

"Shall we begin? There is much to do," said Wolf, the middle spirit. He spoke without menace or fairy-tale rasp. Wolf sounded, in fact, not dissimilar to an educated Greenbriar College professor. His muzzle opened and closed completely before and after each perfectly pronounced word.

The Passions arranged themselves opposite the three boys, their fierce features illuminated by the fire.

"Things to say, we have things to say," said Fox, quickly. "Deverell, very good!" he continued, running his words together so that they tangled with one another like wild strawberries. "Very good to fight on your own terms. I was there. *I saw it!* You are a great warrior. Silent, yet brave. Good, good, good!"

Leith was unsure of what they discussed. Perhaps the quantity of ale he had indulged in was impairing his memory.

"Oh, the young hero has not told you of his greatness?" Fox pondered, recognizing Leith's disoriented expression. "Such modesty he has! Good, good, good!"

"He slew the darrrk ivy and a vicious drrragon," Cougar commented. A feminine voice, steady and strong, her *R*s rolled from her tongue like rhubarb. "The Darrrk One sees we arrre not so weak afterrr all."

"The time has come to strike," Wolf concluded. "Never has the world been in such a precarious state, but the valley can be reclaimed if you can manage it."

"Of course we can manage it!" Aubrey answered assuredly, as if any implication to the contrary were absurd.

"You will need the sworrrd," Cougar said to Leith. Flames flickered in her yellow feline eyes.

Leith felt ill at ease with the sudden attention. He finally found courage to speak. "I do not want it," he said quietly. "The sword was my father's, and it did him no good. Why would I need such a thing when he was so much more a man?"

"That does not matterr," Cougar responded. The fire popped and sizzled, roasting tranced-out beetles and bugs. "Therrre arrre things one cannot escape. This path was laid beforrre you by yourrr fatherrrs," she said to both Deverell and Leith. "You must take it. You cannot rrrefuse."

"It's part of your soul's plan," Wolf said. "You know it deep inside. Your fathers"—he looked from Leith to Deverell with equal gravity—"should be remembered as far better men than they have been."

"Friends and enemies," Fox jumped in. "Garet and Darcy, lovers and foes."

Leith glanced to Deverell, who gazed back intently. Deverell looked every bit the warrior in his headdress. Leith doubted the same could be said for him.

Wolf turned again to Aubrey. "Tell Minerva True, the Breed is not gone from the earth. They live, but are deep in hiding in the forest and will remain so until they think it safe to reappear."

"She will be pleased," Aubrey responded.

"As for you," Wolf continued, speaking sternly to Aubrey. "Have you given thought to the message of Rain Crow?"

Leith flashed him a look of puzzlement.

"I have," Aubrey answered Wolf with some consternation.

"He was unwilling at firrrst to deliverrr ourrr message to you," Cougar said. "He sees you as kin, afterrr all."

"It is your decision," Wolf said.

Leith and Deverell looked to Aubrey. Aubrey simply stared ahead.

When Leith and Deverell returned their gazes to Wolf, Fox, and Cougar, they caught only three furry silhouettes vanishing into the trees. They had risen silently and stolen away without a word of farewell. It felt like a dream, an illusion ended before the mind could piece it all together. The fire was beginning to die.

Aubrey rose without a sound and walked over several of the barrows until he, too, was out of sight. Leith didn't call after him. There seemed no point to it. He would get no explanation of the strange conversation. The drink had become weighty, pulling Leith's thoughts into unfathomable pools of dismay. Once again, he wished he had never lived in the valley, that the valley and its dread hills had never existed. He cursed it where he sat.

Deverell lay against Neko's barrow, his eyes growing heavy. He still held a goblet of ale between his thick thighs. Again, Song began her serenades. Deverell once more climbed the barrow mound and lay atop it to sleep. Song poured all her attention on him, cradling him there like a lover. Her glory caressed his thighs, kissing them with musical notes.

Leith, still intoxicated and confused, fumbled and crawled over and between the mounds. Each time he fell, he cursed their obstruction, a direct assault on his being. He needed Aubrey at that moment to settle him. Leith needed to understand things. He wanted Aubrey to tell him everything. Why were there never any explanations on Black Hill? Why were there never any "tried-and-trues"? The outer world seemed to have them aplenty.

It was still dark when Leith found Aubrey. He lay in a shallow stream, his arms stretched out, the water gurgling past his naked flesh. The headdress had been abandoned under a nearby birch. Leith approached quietly, removing the stag's horns he was adorned with. He waded into the cool night stream and settled himself adjacent to Aubrey. The moon hung full over them. The small stream feeling like the sole waterway in all the world. Cicadas and crickets chirped along with the call of the water. Aubrey's eyes didn't flinch; they stared ceaselessly past the branches and leaves and into the night sky.

"What are you thinking about?" Leith finally asked. His voice hushed the night crickets.

"Things you shouldn't be concernin' yourself with," Aubrey said. "I don't want you worryin' about nothin'."

"Too late for that, Aubrey Avonmore," Leith confessed. Though chilled at first, Leith adapted quickly to the temperature of the stream.

"I suppose you're right, and I'm sorry for it. I cain't seem to hide my feelings from you."

"I just know you well, s'all. As well as a man can know a being of your nature."

A brief pause in conversation encouraged the night chorus to rise again.

"What did Wolf mean?" Leith asked, peering into Aubrey's moonlit face. The strength of the ale was making him tired, blurring his vision. "What decision do you have to make?"

"We make decisions every day," Aubrey responded casually. "Some are more important than others."

"And this one's important?" He wasn't going to let Aubrey avoid the question.

"It's very important, Leith. It's about the valley; it's about us, and how we live. It's about who's left after us to watch over things. We're all connected, and the watching-over is an awesome responsibility. It's for the good of every soul."

"I don't understand." Leith sat up in the creek bed. He ran a wet finger down the middle of Aubrey's chest.

Aubrey finally looked at him, seemingly on the cusp of disclosure. He wiped at his cheek and then studied the smear of eyeliner on his hand. "Remember," Aubrey said, "Remember how Minerva told you that memories are spirits and they live in trees?"

Leith nodded.

"Do me a favor, Leith." He took hold of Leith's hand where it remained on his chest and squeezed it gently.

"Anything, Aubrey! Anything at all."

"Never forget that. Always remember the trees. Do that for me." He sat up beside Leith and wiped his eyeliner away with his thumb. "Remember about spirits and trees."

"I'll always remember it. I promise."

"That's all you ever need to do for me, lover," Aubrey declared. "That's the only request I think I've ever made of another person, at least in this life."

"Well, I'm honored for it."

Their lips met under the moonlight as the stream flowed around them. The fireflies did their nightly summer dance, and the crickets sang their evening symphony. Far off in the woods, Song wandered. The moon shone gallantly down on the wet bodies of the two boys in love and at one with a stream. They lay down once again in the coolness of the water and made love, their hands discovering exciting new places under the moon, their breath as hot as the sun.

THE GENTLE melodies of water over rock and the morning breeze through the leaves invigorated Leith when he awoke naked beside the stream. The sun gently warmed him, having long since dried him off after he and Aubrey had crawled from the water the night before to continue making love on the forest grass, careful to avoid the poison ivy as they rolled about. It had been a strange, frightening, and wonderful night. There were surprises and mysteries now forever locked in its passing. Leith gazed into the clear blue sky, reminiscing on the hours past, his mind free of the haze of drink. While he certainly knew he loved Aubrey, he was still worried by the message from the Passions. What was the decision Aubrey had ahead of him, and why did it seem to frighten him so? Leith had never known Aubrey to be scared by anything. Not anything at all. But at the firelight convocation he had been unmistakably thrown. In turn, this newly discovered aspect of Aubrey brought a great deal of concern on Leith's own part.

He turned and watched Aubrey sleeping and pushed back a long strand of hair from his brow. Aubrey *was* the valley to Leith. It was that simple, and he respected that truth. Indeed, it was all the truth he needed or ever wanted to know. As Aubrey was a part of the valley, Leith was a part of Aubrey.

Aubrey stirred, and his eyes opened with an intoxicating flutter that caused Leith to momentarily lose his breath. "Mornin', Leithy," Aubrey greeted, a coy smile crossing his face.

Leith grinned. He knew he needed to fetch Calpurnia's breakfast, but he didn't want to leave this treasured moment. He didn't want his mother anywhere near this day.

"Come on, then," Aubrey said as he rose, lifting Leith by the hands along with him. They began walking along the stream, leaving their headdresses by the wayside.

"Where are we going?" Leith inquired.

Aubrey clasped his hand tightly. "I got something to show you; something you need to see."

They walked a bit downhill in silence; the ferns and tall grass brushed gently past them. Their private parts hung free, pleased from the night's rigorous lovemaking. The sunlight through the trees dappled their flesh, and they soon left the company of the stream.

"You're scared, aren't you?" Leith at last posed. He immediately regretted asking such a question, for it buffeted the serenity around them. So abrupt and unprovoked was the query, the words hung like icicles in the air.

"I am," Aubrey admitted after a lengthy pause. "But that's why there's courage. We all got courage and resilience, Leithy. It's the gift what gets us through the learnin' times."

"I'm not sure if I do," Leith admitted, low and hushed, avoiding eye contact. "Have courage, that is."

"Oh, I think you do. Courage is standin' up for what is right in the face of a gigantic wrong. Courage is doing something even when you're nearly scared to death to do it cause… well, you just gotta do it."

"But I don't know if I have that strength. Don't you see?" Leith's voice became pleading. "I don't think I could be a hero. Not like those knights in the old stories Mr. Higgins taught us. Not like the valley tales Minerva used to sing us to sleep with. Certainly not like you: Aubrey Avonmore, the Prince of the Valley. Maybe you could give me some?"

Aubrey glanced at him with a knowing look. "You have courage," he assured Leith. "It'll come to you at the right time. It'll raise up like a suit of armor, and you'll do anything 'cause you'll know there ain't no other way. You'll see, lover."

They had perambulated a long way, much farther than Leith had imagined. Now, they walked nude, holding hands, near the bottom of Black Hill. The sun shone resplendently on the river and whitened the rocks of the beach.

"Don't worry," Aubrey said. "There's no one in the valley, remember? They've all gone. And believe you me, those across the river spend quite a bit of their days naked too. It's a free-swingin' time. Here on this bank, though, it's just you and me and the forest things. And they're naturally naked anyway, ain't they?"

The road finally freed them onto the beach, and they walked in the direction of the chapel. The rocks were smooth and warm beneath their feet.

"What are we doing, Aubrey?" Leith asked.

"You're just full of questions lately," Aubrey said with a grin. They stood face-to-face now, the chapel grounds a few yards away. "I'm going to show you how easy it is to be courageous. You asked for courage; I'm gonna give it to you. You see, the key is to face the fear blindly; just go in without thinking about its outcome. It's all in the mind. You just need to keep your own idea of what *should* happen. See? What you believe *will* happen if you're true to heart."

"But that could be very dangerous." Leith's voice began to take an excitable tone. The idea sounded ridiculous. No amount of thinking could deter disaster. Not when it lurked so near.

"That's why it's called courage." Aubrey kissed him quickly on the cheek. "Wish me luck!" he yelled, running toward the chapel grounds, leaving Leith wide-eyed and disbelieving on the beach.

"*Aubrey! Wait! Come back!*" Leith screamed, though his feet were frozen to the rocks as if he were anchored there.

Aubrey slowed nearing the grounds, straightening his posture as he approached the gates.

Leith wanted to close his eyes, but he couldn't. His whole life stood in jeopardy there in front of him. *How could a man close his eyes to that?* Leith wasn't crying; he was past tears. The moment was too terrifying for them. He didn't even notice Deverell join him on the beach. They both watched, mesmerized and breathless.

Yet as Aubrey crossed the threshold of the chapel grounds, now clear of the mist, the horrors Leith had expected failed to transpire.

Aubrey strode assuredly toward the chapel itself. The crocodiles hissed and convulsed, now fully exposed by the sunlight and clearly disturbed by the presence of the young man, yet they did not strike. In fact, they seemed to recoil as though shocked by some unseen static emanating from Aubrey's form.

Aubrey surveyed his surroundings like a conqueror. He plucked a large stone from the rotten earth, slamming the rock down heavily on the brass handle of the chapel door. He hit it continuously, even as the crocodiles snapped, growing increasingly agitated, threatening like cornered dogs. Each hit thundered over the grounds. His face held an expression of perseverance and grit, and he hammered at the handle without pause until it fell to the landing with a defeated thud. Aubrey dropped the stone, stooped to pick up the brass handle, and calmly walked down the steps past the preacher's minions.

Leith's heart continued racing even as Aubrey stepped from the chapel grounds and the mist closed behind him like greedy hands. His feet finally unfrozen, Leith ran to his hero. Deverell was close behind.

"Why did you do that? *You could have been killed!*" Leith screamed. "You're stupid! That was so foolish."

Aubrey put a hand on Leith's shoulder. He palmed the brass handle like a ball. "You walked onto those chapel grounds with even less of a mindset when you was a baby. Minerva told me she found you there. See. You've got the courage."

"I don't understand you at all," Leith admitted, his eyes welling with tears. "I think I know you, but I'm a fool."

Aubrey kissed him and handed him the brass handle. It felt wrong for Leith to even touch the thing, though he couldn't say just why.

"This is for everything the chapel's taken from the valley… from you," Aubrey said. "This was *my* strike against it," he said, nodding to Deverell in acknowledgment of the latter's own battle on the rockface.

"From *me*, Aubrey?" Leith inquired. "You mean my father?"

"Yes. That, and your hope, your joy in everyday things, your curiosity, your freedom. Things you've never really possessed because it just wasn't allowed. But you see, there is hope, Leith." He was whispering now, his forehead pressed against Leith's. "There's always that bit of hope, like a seed just waitin' to sprout. It's like the air we breathe; it fills our lungs. What we believe… it becomes our reality. You got to believe in yourself and better things; you got to see yourself as the hero in your own tale. That's all you need to survive."

"But you're my hero," Leith explained. "You're what I need...."

"And I'm part of you, just like you're part of me. Be brave for me, Leith. Let's be brave for each other, eh?"

Leith nodded, feeling a single tear making its way down his cheek.

Deverell stepped past them, staring at the chapel. The mist had parted once again and on the landing stood a figure, at first silhouetted, gradually becoming clearer. The preacher leered at the trio from the steps. The crocodiles rasped at them from the grounds' threshold.

Aubrey and Leith stood beside Deverell, hands locked together. "He ain't your father, Dev," Aubrey assured him. "He never was. He just needed a disguise of strength, and Darcy Crocker was an attractive one; a man who struck fear and respect in people. On the chapel grounds, ol' Dark Eyes doesn't need a disguise. You can see him for what he is. But outside, he neither has the strength nor the *courage* to be himself."

"I don't think he's very pleased," Leith noted. He glanced quickly away from the preacher, fearing his gaze.

"War ain't a pleasing thing," Aubrey retorted. "Especially for the loser."

LEITH WALKED into Walterhouse Manor too close to noon. Calpurnia must be starving, he thought, though he hadn't seen her watching for his return from the long window as she usually did. He had borrowed some pants from one of the many abandoned homes for his journey back home. Many of the valley folk had left in a hurry and not packed all of their belongings. He was, at the moment, wearing Lucas Bowkindle's trousers. They hung a bit long, so he rolled them up at the bottom. Exposing himself to his mother by coming home in a loincloth or naked was the last thing he needed. He was still shaken by Aubrey's distressing actions at the chapel grounds. He fumbled about the kitchen as he over-fried the eggs.

The day, however, was not finished with its surprises. He nearly dropped the silver platter when, as he ascended the old stairs, he caught sight of Calpurnia outside of her room. She sat in an old rocking chair, which usually occupied an equally useless space at the end of the hall just beneath the window. She had somehow managed to go get it, bring it back, and position it just outside of her bedchamber door. She was dressed nicely in a once-lovely green gown she had purchased just before Garet had disappeared some years before. She was still barefoot, though; the particular idea of wearing shoes still eluding her scattered mind.

"Calpurnia?" Leith said, in a tone that questioned whether she was indeed the same woman.

"I'm not hungry," she answered. "You can take it back." She spoke in a rushed manner, as if out of breath from some physical exertion. She neither looked at him, nor made any attempt to rise.

"I'm sorry I didn't get it to you this morning. I fell asleep…."

"No matter, no matter," she hushed him irritably. This was more along the lines of the mother he knew. "I'm really not hungry, so don't go apologizing. No, I've been quite content this morning. I've done very well without you. See, I've been adventuring. Like Tristan. How did you find Tristan? I found him exquisite. Just exquisite!" She shot Leith a quick, stony glance. "Do you see that I've been adventuring just like him? Do you see?"

"I see that," Leith said, placing the platter on the floor beside her anyway.

"I've been out here all morning. Since before the sun was fully over the treeline. It was frightening at first. But I knew… I knew I needed to get this chair. And I did. It took some time, but I did it." She clutched the armrests tightly with pride and a tinge of malevolence. "You know what I'm thinking?" she asked, her eyes suddenly becoming as large as saucers.

Leith stood numb, unable to cope properly with this newest surprise. He barely shook his head in response.

"I was thinking I might go downstairs today!" She grinned hysterically. "Isn't that wonderful? I'm going to eat down there, make my own dinner. You don't have to do a thing. You can go play with Aubrey."

While the prospect of the end of his servitude excited him, he doubted it was an absolute possibility any time soon. "Calpurnia, I think…."

"*Hush, boy!*" she rumbled. "I will cook for myself, and that's that. Things will be different from here on out. You'll see. Yes, things are going to change quite drastically. Calpurnia Covington is getting her second wind, and by God it's not too late!"

Leith backed away slowly, not fully understanding what had happened to her, why and how she had changed so drastically so fast. Had his absence the night before been the cause of this most recent peculiarity?

"Your having been gone all the livelong day and night, I learned some things," she said, perhaps reading his thoughts. "At first, I was quite scared and I cursed you up a blue streak, I'll admit it. Oh, if you could have but seen the color of the air! But as time passed, I realized I had to learn to get things done for myself. I don't know why it never occurred to me before. I'll only get what I want if I go after her myself...." She quieted suddenly, not wanting to give away a secret. "You... you should do something tonight," she posited. "Since I'm going to take care of myself, you should go down to the river with Aubrey... and Elijah." She said the latter's name with a resounding crunch.

"Deverell," he corrected her absently. "At the river naming ceremony, Elijah became Deverell."

"Deverell," she repeated, overly politely. He knew it, she knew it. Screw it.

"I was going to head to the beach later. Minerva is having a ceremony for the Parmas, now that all their... bones have been recovered." He spoke lowly, afraid that any single word might shatter her current calm.

"Have they?" she asked, feigning interest. "Every one of them? That's very thoughtful of you and Minerva to have found all of those bones. Bones stick together like puzzles, don't they? Such a thoughtful son I have. And you say Eli—*Deverell* is going to be there as well?"

"Y-yes. Aubrey and him both."

"Funny you should mention Deverell"—disregarding the fact that it was she who mentioned him—"I was thinking how lovely it might be to have Lara's boy over for dinner some night. Wouldn't that be nice?" She didn't pause for a reply. "Yes. It would be lovely. Lovely, lovely, lovely," sang she. She maintained her death-clutch of the armrests of the rocker, neither rocking nor looking particularly at ease.

"Lovely," Leith agreed, more as a frightened echo than an answer.

"You know, you should ask him tonight! Yes, set up the particulars tonight. Ask him at this party you're going to."

"It's not a party, Calpurnia. It's—"

"I'll make something tasty! Mmm. Like I used to. Remember how I used to? Remind me. You know, I think...."

Leith stood exhausted as she went on and on about her future elegant dinner and a propensity for refinement which he could never remember witnessing. Not to mention, he had never before heard her say such decent things regarding Deverell. It puzzled him. When he realized she was no longer conversing directly at him, but instead up and around him, Leith slowly turned and walked down the stairs. He paused for the longest time in the center of the Great Hall. His mother's voice had dissolved into incoherent mumbles through the floorboards. He wanted to scream. Her madness was making him mad. Surely she was intent on just that result, he told himself. Mother and son, mad as rabid dogs, locked together for all time.

Calming himself, he glanced toward the hearth, above which he had once again fastened his father's sword.

EVENING SETTLED over Greenbriar College, and the someday-to-be-eminent Albert Higgins stood near the bluff overlooking the river, listening to the beautiful voice that floated up with the breeze from somewhere down below.

"Someone should find that woman and marry her," one of his fellow classmates remarked. *Tactless.*

Albert leaned against a strong, solid tree, smoking his pipe, a habit he had just recently acquired, and one that his fiancée had encouraged. "A sign of good breeding," she had written him.

It was nice to get away from the heart of the college for a bit. He had heard there were plans to extend the campus as far as the bluff, and that, he thought, would be a shame, for it would mean the lovely lawn and the few trees that stood around it would need to be sacrificed. Still, he supposed that was the price one paid for progress.

The moon peeked out from behind dark clouds. The strange rainy season seemed to have at last passed. Albert watched a bonfire far off on the beach in the valley with mild interest. Perhaps his young students, Aubrey and Leith, were having a late-night soiree, drinking and being merry as young men do. Where had they gotten to, he wondered. He had thought about going down into the valley himself, several times in fact, but it was a difficult descent and an even harder return trip. Or so he'd been told by some who claimed to have made the trek. He was glad the students of Greenbriar College were no longer forced to cross the

river by raft as they had years before. There were more civilized routes
now. There was a bridge, albeit a precarious one, and even a dirt road
that wound through the woods that surrounded the school. The river no
longer carried the import it once had.

Albert Higgins cocked his head in curiosity as the bonfire began
to move slowly. It seemed to be on the river and floating away, floating
upstream. He took a puff from the pipe and made an involved *hmmph*.
It could prove an interesting day's adventure, he thought to himself.
A trip to the valley to catch a glimpse of what inspired the fairy tales
Aubrey and Leith often spoke of. A good day's sociological research.
He decided then, caught up against his better judgment in the airs of
a mystery, that he would indeed make the treacherous descent into the
valley someday very soon. A little end-of-summer adventuring would do
him good. Maybe he'd even take his fiancée on a walk through the trails
of College Hill. They could find the boys and inquire as to whether they
ever intended to show up for their lessons again. If not, it would have
been polite to let him know.

Yes, she might enjoy that.

GIVEN TO PURPOSE

PARMA PLACE was situated at the base of one of the smaller hills in the valley between Black Hill and Poorman's Tower. Though a rocky parapet loomed over it, the homestead was never in any danger of a rockslide due to the angle at which it was built, stepped to the side, allowing any loose boulders to tumble into the river. Above and to the right of the large home wound a series of large stone steps. Now covered with moss and surrounded by tall grass due to years of infrequent use, the stones were still as strong and solid as when they had first been laid two hundred years before. They led up the side of the hill to a land shelf, a small, narrow plateau on top of which, at one time, had stood another, more elegant and lyrically designed, home. A home that seemed to spring from the very earth and which last housed a music man. Its latticework and railings, gutters and roof tiles, all had a remarkable line of beauty to them, so that when it showered, it was as if a chorus of chimes and cymbals were being lovingly conducted. No one really knew what the last occupant's given name had been, and he had never taken a river name, but everyone called him Trumpet—though, truth be told, that was the one instrument he did not possess.

When Trumpet finally left for the Other Side of the River, long before any of the recent horrors in the valley, his home was never again inhabited. The lovely, lyrical home fell into decrepitude and, reluctantly, the color drained from its singing walls.

One night during a particularly harsh summer storm that swept up the river in a fury, the house was struck by lightning even as it sang and burned to the ground in melancholic melody. The only thing to survive the fire was an old piano Trumpet had grudgingly left behind. It was nothing special to look at, just as simple as a minor key, but had played more luxuriantly than any piano before or since.

Years passed. The earth claimed the burnt floorboards and scarred foundation. The piano was laid claim to as well by morning glories, forget-me-nots, and honeysuckles. They embraced the large instrument, adopting it so that it too seemed part of the natural environment, a polished block of wood with a row of black and white teeth. A squatty cypress grew directly behind it, having found a path through the remaining floorboards. It stood over the piano as a watchman. The ivory keys still played when it rained hard enough, so that the plot of land which once possessed this most unique of homes had never been without music. The sound of the abandoned piano had lulled Deverell and Aubrey to sleep on many a stormy night at Parma Place.

Aubrey climbed the winding stone steps to Trumpet's old homestead. Seating himself, he played a gentle, out-of-tune melody on the piano. He and Deverell had decided to continue living at Parma Place, even after they had found Minerva again. They were young men, after all, and needed their own space. Every time one of Aubrey's fingers touched a key, it was a thought given song. Goose bumps rose in waves on his flesh as the morning chill brushed past him.

His morning had begun with the realization that this would be the day he would have to say good-bye. He left Leith, who had spent the night with him, still in the bed—Aubrey slept inside whenever Leith stayed over for the night—eyes closed to the chill of the world.

Leith, for all he had been through with Calpurnia, had not lost his childhood innocence. He still trusted vaguely; he still sought guidance. It was a reality that broke Aubrey's heart, for to live in the valley, to survive in it and fight for it, one had to be both a willow tree and of its branches. One had to be able to bend, but also know when to break free. The drizzling day brought with it many new things, chief among them the twin titans Life and Death—the End and the Beginning. Aubrey feared Leith might never bend, only break.

"It's broken. It needs tending to if you plan to keep playing," Leith spoke as he approached Aubrey from behind. He had a heavy quilt wrapped around his shoulders, and he unfolded it to share with the shirtless Aubrey whose skin glistened from the mistfall. "You'll catch cold out here like this. You didn't sleep much last night."

"How do you know?" Aubrey asked playfully, masking his inner turmoil.

"I just know. We were up most the night making love. I fell asleep while you sang to me."

"Maybe I fell asleep right after."

"No," Leith replied knowingly. "You didn't. You watched me. You always watch me. I see you watching me in my dreams. I would never have to worry about falling asleep in the forest of Black Hill because you would be there."

Aubrey stroked the keys lightly, each one a heartbreak.

"Why do I feel like the color of the sky today, Aubrey? Why does everything seem so gray? And why are you like the river, sliding out from under me so fast?"

Aubrey felt as if any small gust of whispering rain would break his very body—muscle and bone and guts all. He closed his eyes, feeling Leith's warmth surround him.

"*Would you look at that!*" Leith said excitedly. His embrace loosened as he watched two cardinals fly directly overhead and toward the other side of the river. They glided with ease, unconcerned, looping and playing, bright and red against the sad sky. "There are birds, Aubrey! Birds in the valley! I knew that rain crow couldn't be the only one."

Aubrey turned and smiled bittersweetly. "Yes, sir," he said. "I reckon there are, Leith. How about that." He kissed Leith on the cheek as they stood wrapped beneath the quilt.

MINERVA EMPLOYED a tiny pair of tree shears that had once belonged to Mother True and cut a few switches from the mightiest and oldest willow she could find. She rarely made it to the willow grove these days. It was a long walk over many steep inclines and across four swiftly flowing creeks. The grove had once been a favorite place for the young lovers of the valley. The wind blowing through the willow branches was romance in itself. Minerva had made love with Hamlin Marsh beneath the willows on many a younger day. She shed a final tear for him as she remembered this. Abandoned now, the grove hadn't seen visitors for quite a while, and had grown exponentially since last she had been there. Remnants of its past still lingered, though. An old wooden swing hung from a branch; the ground was still worn down beside the stream; a faint walkway still ambled through the orange tiger lilies.

An upset stomach had been causing Minerva great discomfort, and the leaves of a willow tree mixed into a warm herbal tea were a known remedy. She collected whole switches in a burlap satchel slung leisurely over her shoulder. The day had an uncomfortable, indecisive air about it. Would there be rain as the clouds suggested, or would they break, letting through the sun? They weren't dark and heavy clouds, after all. They seemed quite innocent as a matter of fact. If but a handful of people still dwelled in the valley, they could have taken a collective breath and blown the fragile wisps away.

As Minerva continued about her amassing of leaves, she perceived a faint melody, as if someone were whistling. Forgetting the task at hand momentarily, she walked among the trees, their lazy branches tickling her skin as she passed beneath them. Coming through the grove, in the opposite direction from where she had been, was a young woman. She wore the outfit of a man: brown pants, boots, and a plaid shirt. Over her shoulder she carried a sack of the same coarse material of Minerva's satchel. Her golden hair was curly and cut short. Her face shone with fortitude. Her skin bore a strange similarity to that of Aubrey. She spied Minerva and, after a moment's hesitation, nodded in greeting. She appeared to search for reaction from the old woman.

"She moves and dresses like a man," Minerva whispered to herself. A delighted grin overtook her face.

"Hi there!" the young woman said as she entered the grove. Her arms swung wild and free.

"Good day to you," Minerva greeted.

The woman walked toward her with wide steps, assured and proud. She extended her hand. "I'm Emmy Everplace," she said with a smile. She had measured Minerva up to be someone she could trust.

"Nice to meet you, Miss Everplace," Minerva said, taking her hand. "Minerva True."

"Might you be able to tell me where I am, Miss True? I'm looking for a river valley. My mother was there once and said it was the most magical place. There's a college what looks over it, I hear. If I'm right, it should be in view very soon."

"Oh, you're very near it indeed," Minerva answered, intrigued. "I am in fact from the valley. This grove and these hills are of that property. But I'm afraid there is hardly a soul left there anymore. Just empty homes." Minerva fought off her grievous thoughts. "Why do you seek the valley, dear?"

"I plan to live there," Emmy explained, putting her sack of belongings to the ground and sitting on them. She pulled a wild onion from the earth and began to twittle it with her teeth. "I plan to find a nice plot of land and move onto it as soon as humanly possible, Miss True."

Minerva was so startled by the statement, she stood dazed for a moment, then sat easily on the grass near Emmy, her old age not an obstacle. "You mean to move here?" she asked. "But there's no one… and there is danger. You mean to move *here*?"

Emmy pulled at a willow branch that hung over her shoulder. "There's danger everywhere, Miss True. I 'spect you know that. You look like you've seen troubled times. And as far as people go, the less the better, I say. I'm looking for quiet, ma'am. It'll just be me and my gal, Lucy. To be away from people… that wouldn't be such a bad thing at all. And you seem like a kindly neighbor. If you're all what's here… well, that's good enough for me and Lucy."

"I believe I would be a fine neighbor if, in fact, I lived *in* the valley. Though I am from it, I reside on one of its hills," Minerva spoke. "But you are quite welcome here all the same."

"I appreciate it. Of course, I want to get a look at what homes there are, if any. Even something in ill repair can be fixed up with determination and heart, and I have that. Yes, ma'am. I have that aplenty. If there were something I could get to working on, why that would save me some time and hard work, rather than needing to build from scratch. Then, I'll go back the way I came and get my Lucy. She's so excited to travel on."

"And from where is it that you came?" Minerva pried. She smoothed her gown out of habit.

Emmy seemed to think for a moment. "Too far away," she said, with a new quiet in her voice. "It's strange how far from home one must get sometimes to *feel* at home."

Minerva put her hand on Emmy's knee. "You're home," she said.

"I see that you're *at one with nature*," Emmy noted, gesturing to the grove around them. "Lucy is gonna love you. She'd mother the natural world if she could."

Emmy breathed in the air, damp and relaxing. "I best get on, then," she said, offering Minerva a hand as she rose. "Looks like the clouds may break at any moment, whether it be for wet or dry is hard to say." She tossed the wild onion to the ground and adjusted the sack over her shoulder.

"There's a path to the river just below that hill," Minerva said. "It will take you there without much trouble at all. You should arrive just below Poorman's Tower."

"I thank ya, Miss True," Emmy said, kissing Minerva's hand.

"Call me Minerva." Emmy pleased her. She made her giddy for some reason. But then a touch of discomfort settled on Minerva's face as she placed a hand on her upset stomach.

"Stomach ache, huh?" Emmy diagnosed. "These willow trees will cure that," she said as she turned to go with a bow. "See you soon, Minerva, Lucy and I both. We're gonna be the best of neighbors to you. You'll see."

"Stay clear of the chapel!" Minerva called out, suddenly remembering where it was the girl was headed. "Don't go near it."

"No need to tell *me* that," Emmy replied with a playful wink over her shoulder. "Haven't been to church in years. I'm not starting now."

Minerva felt a swell of relief; she saw some light through the darkness. She still had her battle to face with Dark Eyes, but now it seemed much more easily won. As if a cavalry were being assembled.

"People in the valley once again!" she exclaimed in wonder. "*Women* in the valley again. How marvelous!"

ALBERT HIGGINS was beginning to think that taking the path down College Hill with his lovely if slightly pretentious bride-to-be, Alice Mayfield, was a bad idea. At first the notion of a stroll down to the valley beach struck him as just the quaint sort of thing Alice would love on her visit with him at Greenbriar College. He had actually written her to come for just that reason. She had always enjoyed walks through the botanical gardens back home, after all. But then, he hadn't counted on the tricky weather or the steep descent down a muddy path strewn with fallen limbs and vegetative debris. The path clearly wasn't used very often. Two other realizations dawned on him as well: the botanical gardens in the city were a controlled environment and actually resembled very little the true chaos of nature, and Alice was not a quaint sort of woman. She did not like quaint sort of things. Albert soon wondered what had gotten into him.

When they began their adventure to the valley, Alice's yelps and sighs of struggle had been cute, very feminine and attractive. But the deeper they journeyed, the more tiresome she became. He found himself wondering if he even knew the woman he was engaged to wed. Had she always been so... helpless? She carried her umbrella with such prickly daintiness, Albert found himself quite literally grinding his teeth every time he glanced at her. He half desired to be alone so he might enjoy his surroundings, which proved surprisingly breathtaking. Of course, it wasn't Alice's fault. She had been raised by parents who abided by the strictest norms and codes of polite society. Only, society was never truly polite, was it? Society was a ravenous hound that ate you up and then shit you out. *Defecated is the proper term, Albert. Let's be tasteful.*

"Albert, my darling," Alice moaned. "Surely there are more pleasant things to show me. What are we doing down here? Seems as if we're sliding right into that disgusting river. I'd much rather just view it from above." Her high-pitched whine drilled into his ears as painfully as a screw.

"Two of my pupils live near the river," Albert answered, exasperated. "I've told you about them. I wanted to take a look at where they are from. They tell such tales. I thought you might enjoy the trek as well. You don't find it at all interesting? Not the least bit?"

"Not at all," she said shortly, flinching from leaves and ferns that touched her as if they were begging her for money. "And why are you associating with young men who wander about in trees and on rivers? Why not teach more civilized boys?"

"Oh, Alice, I do wish you'd be quiet!" He said this before he realized he was going to say it. He turned to her, his shocked eyes meeting hers.

Her dark hair was piled on top of her head perfectly, not a hair out of place. Her perfume offended the natural air of the forest. She frowned and whimpered like a wounded puppy. Her umbrella limped in repose.

"My dear, I'm sorry," he began. But just as he had spoken, the path beneath his feet gave way, and Albert fell down the steep hill in a gushing mudslide. Bushes and tree limbs smacked his face as he tumbled, rolled, and slid. Above him, he heard Alice screaming deliriously.

"*Help!*" she cried to unconcerned air. "*Help!*"

He heard her shrill voice still when he came to a sudden splash and grunt at the bottom of the hill. He collected his thoughts, shaking off the excitement. He sat, covered in mud and leaves, not wanting to answer his future wife's call, and wiped the funk of mire from his face. He had received a few lashes to his cheek, a cut to the lip, and an aching bum. At least the day wasn't boring.

The peculiar notion of being watched crept over him, even as he sat in momentary respite from Alice, and he searched the dense woods around him warily. It was the oddest sensation, more curious still because the woods surrounding him looked so uninhabitable: thick, unruly, and unmanaged. It didn't take Albert very long, though, to spot a small figure peering at him from behind an ancient tree. It was a little girl. She smiled with curious delight, and her giggle echoed enchantingly through the forest. It made him smile too, something he had rarely done since Alice arrived, something he had rarely done at all.

Strange that, he thought.

He tried to stand up in the muck, but slipped and landed again in the large puddle. His face was decorated with more mud, his moustache becoming a catch-all for the detritus. Alice still called to him frantically from above. The sound of her shaky voice was nearing as she struggled to descend the hill without falling herself. She would never give up her umbrella: the outfit would be incomplete. Albert was hoping she might give up and head back to campus. *Hope springs eternal, as they say.* When he returned his attention to the charming little girl, she turned and playfully ran off.

"Little girl!" he cried. "Come back!"

He finally succeeded in standing, though his legs still shook in caution. *"Little girl!"*

"I'm coming!" Alice cried. "I'm coming, my darling!"

Albert paid little attention to her, however. He made a few careful strides through the mud in the direction in which the girl had run. But she had vanished, and he knew he would not be able to find her in this clustering wood. Yet he swore he could still hear giggles gracing the air, like diaphanous butterflies flittering about him. To his own astonishment, he himself began to giggle as well.

"There you are," Alice cried upon finding him. She nearly tumbled into the very same puddle he had fallen into. The bottom of her gown was muddied and stained. *"Oh, Albert! You look dreadful!* Simply awful. Now, didn't I tell you this was a bad idea? Come. Let's get you cleaned up back at the college. Oh, you poor, poor thing!" She reached for his arm.

He hesitated, but realizing the air was silent and the girl was gone, he at last accepted the clean hand of Alice.

"There was a little girl. Did you hear her?" he asked as they made their way back up the hill. He continued to look up and around as if expecting the girl to reemerge from behind a tree or bush. "She was the most beguiling thing. And lost, I think. Maybe forgotten. There have been cases of children living in the forest, far from adult supervision. What an amazing thing to see!"

"No, I didn't see a young girl." Alice squinted her eyes with concern… and annoyance. She tried very hard not to get any more of her dress muddy against his clothing. "You must have hit your head on your fall. Next time you'll listen to me."

He studied her response, the way she was regarding him. *It's all about upbringing and how one looks, Albert.* Hers was a more logical explanation. Perhaps he had hit his head just as she had supposed.

"Of course," he replied softly. "I hit my head."

"Yes, that's all."

But the little girl had seemed so very real. Somehow, she was at once there and not there, like a mirror's reflection without one reflected. For a brief moment, Albert thought Aubrey and Leith were not such silly boys after all. Their tales of River Dwellers and snovelfarks didn't sound so ridiculous. Maybe his father and his father's colleagues were wrong. Maybe there were unknowns in the world that couldn't be explained straight away. Maybe they never would be. Was that such an awful thing?

As he and Alice climbed College Hill, his fantastic thoughts were replaced by more logical solutions. His education, his father, his fiancée, all centered on him. The higher they climbed, the farther away from the river and the valley floor they journeyed, the easier it became for Albert to categorize the little girl as nothing more than a figment of his imagination brought on by trauma. It was all fantasy and had no place in the real world. Even his irritation with Alice earlier was merely his own cold feet at their impending nuptials. Yes, everything could be easily explained if one thought about it. He took a deep breath and found solace in his explanations. He kissed Alice gently on the cheek.

"Albert! Not in public." She blushed and playfully pushed him off.

So Albert Higgins left the valley quite certain he was in love with Alice Mayfield and that the world was balanced on strict, defined, unbreakable regulations. He would never again journey down College Hill. There was absolutely no need to do so. He had all the answers he needed.

THE MORNING had bowed to midday. Leith and Aubrey still sat on the hill with the piano—all that remained of Trumpet the Music Man's lyrical house. They watched the river accept the tiny drops of rain and mist into its collective flow. The large quilt was wrapped tightly around them as they sat on the edge of the land shelf; the light mist kissed their faces. In their hands they held earthen mugs of hot tea brought to them by Deverell, who had promptly returned to the confines of Parma Place. Shortly, he would climb Black Hill for the day's teachings from Minerva. Few words passed between Leith and Aubrey, but those that did break the silence were tinged with love and melancholy.

"I think we can finally leave," Leith breathed at last, his voice almost as hushed as the sprinkle-fall. "Soon, anyhow. After the battle, I mean. Calpurnia's gotten better, and soon she won't be needing me at all. Then maybe...." He paused, as if afraid saying his wishes aloud would curse them to never be.

"Then what?" Aubrey encouraged him.

"Then maybe me and you can leave. Go someplace up river. Maybe we'll even leave the river behind altogether."

"That's impossible, Leith. You can try to leave the river, but you'll always come back. You're just as much a part of the river as I am, fella."

"You won't ever leave it, will you?"

"You know I won't. But you're free to go. It would break my heart, but I won't make you stay. Mark my words, though. You'll be back, lover."

Leith sighed. "What good's leaving if you're not with me? We can stay in the valley. There's plenty river up a ways for new adventuring."

Aubrey looked at him tenderly. "Nice dream," he said. "But there's no tellin' what will happen minute to minute, let alone days from now."

"What do you mean? What's going to happen?" Leith assumed he was speaking of the approaching battle, but now he wasn't so sure.

"Things," Aubrey replied. "Unfortunate things will happen. They always have. All I'm saying is, Leithy, I would love nothing more than to head up river with you, do some adventurin.' And maybe someday we will. But this life isn't mine, you see? I've got work to do. I've been given to purpose. That's why I woke up across the river all those years ago and swam over here."

As Leith readied himself for more confused ramblings and questions, a strong feminine voice called them from nearby. They turned, startled to see a woman in pants coming down the hill that had sided

Trumpet's house. They stood, their mugs set clumsily aside, and the quilt falling to the ground.

"No need to stand for me, boys," she said. "I don't require it. In fact, I avoid that type of formality. That's why I'm here, to get away from all those stuffy rules. My mother never abided by them, and neither do I."

The boys looked at one another in bewilderment.

"Just passing through," she said as she approached and stood before them with an expectant smile. "Thinking of settling here in the valley." She looked from Leith to Aubrey with the pleasantry of a soul freed of obligation and set to wandering.

"Truly?" Aubrey inquired with an astonished half grin.

"Assuredly," she replied with a twinkle. "It's stunning, just stunning 'round here." She approached the edge of the land shelf and surveyed the river and hills beyond. "This will do just fine," she stated quietly. Then, as if explaining a statement, she continued, "Have you ever felt you had a calling? That you were supposed to do something, and if you didn't, it would be some inexcusable offense, or you just might explode from all the bottled-up pressure?"

Leith said nothing. Aubrey nodded in complete comprehension. They shared a kinship with this woman, though they couldn't explain how.

"I had a calling to come here," she explained. "I saw this river as clear as I'm seeing it now. A waking dream maybe, like every breath provides a clue to my existence. To the whys and wherefores. As if I were Moses or someone in those old Bible tales. You know the ones they brand into your head to try and burn the Fear into you?"

"I don't think I'm familiar," said Aubrey.

"Don't matter. The point is, I heeded the call. I'm a dove in a thunderstorm," she said, drawing her gaze from the river. "Anyways, I best be gettin' on." She paused before turning to continue down the steps. "I just met a real nice old woman up on the hill. Know of her? She was very kind in pointing me the path to take down here. I guess that's Poorman's Tower?" She studied a natural rock formation that shot into the sky behind Trumpet's Place like a massive lighthouse. "Imagine," she continued, "A woman that age with child. Wonders!"

"A woman with child?" Leith asked, confused.

"Yeah. The name was Minerva." She laughed to herself at their thunderstruck expressions, a social laugh. The kind that folk bring to parties. "Guess I loosed a secret, huh? Boys, you keep your mouths hanging open like that, and you'll plumb drown from the rain. I'm sure she'll tell you herself when it's time." With a whisper, she added, "Don't let on you know."

A Purposeful Dinner

Soon after the night of Deverell's river naming ceremony, the night Hamlin Marsh passed, Calpurnia Covington had rediscovered the Book. It lay beneath the cushions of a tattered chaise, itself smothered by strewn gowns, slips, and unfinished quilts. Amidst a fit of wailing desperation—which Calpurnia was occasionally prone to, given her isolated existence—she'd begun circling the bedroom, furiously scattering the many crowding space-holders of her cell like a windstorm trapped in a box. Leith had not returned from his ridiculous ceremony and, though she had eaten, she was in desperate want of company, even if it be the stunted normalcy of her son. She wanted a hero, an adventurer.

As she flung the articles of clothing and disregarded blankets from the chaise, she snagged her hand on the sharp edge of something sticking from under the worn cushions. Immediately, her remembrance of a onetime power came flooding back to her. It had given her whatever she asked when she was younger. She took the large Bible in her hands, holding it from her in trepidation and respect. Suddenly, her want for companionship slipped away like melted wax. She would not open the Book; no, not right away. But its very presence proved enough to relax her. Her heart beat with exhilaration.

Calpurnia had been cooking, baking, and otherwise experimenting with food all day. It was an affirmation, in the end, that she still had life in her. She was afraid she might have forgotten how many eggs went in the cake or the exact amount of salt to sprinkle into other dishes, but, after a few moments, it all came back to her. She stirred the cake batter with frenzied zeal and glazed the ham to perfection. By means of Leith she had long ago made a deal with a farmer, a real-worlder, who bordered her northern property. He would bring her groceries and other needed items, and in return Calpurnia would allow him to use one of the farther fields for seeding. She had never actually seen the farmer; Leith took care of those things. She found the icebox filled with eggs, ham, and other perishables when she finally made her way down the stairs to the kitchen; Leith had looked after her well.

Dinner was ready by late afternoon, just as the morning clouds had dispersed and the sun shone down on the glistening landscape outside. The house, including the Great Hall, had been tidied and reorganized at last. After years of not seeing the other rooms of Walterhouse Manor, living high in her tower, they all now seemed to Calpurnia to need a bit of rearranging. The placement of the timeworn furnishings rekindled the old ghosts—Winifred perched on her big chair, adjusting her wig. Echoes of the living existed there too, as she recalled Minerva's conference with her aunt. She would move things later; there was no time for that now. She dusted what she could and did her best to make the place presentable. She did not tread near the hearth where the sword hung, however; she refused to even look in its direction.

In her childhood, servants would have done all the housework for her—her father would not have allowed her to do such menial tasks—but until things were held to account and she could hire new servants, she would cope with doing given labor. She didn't have to do it all at once, not the entire house anyway. There would be plenty of time in the days to come, for though she was out of her room, it would take some time before she dared venture out of her front door. She would spend that time rediscovering the old Walterhouse abode and working up her courage to leave it.

After arranging the food and place settings—what was left of Winifred's prized china pried from the dusty recesses of a straw-packed crate—she stepped back from the table to admire her work. She had made too much for just four people, even if three of them were ravenous young men, but it felt so good to be purposeful again, and this dinner was just the beginning of her ambitious new existence. The ham shone, glazed in honey; a bird lay sliced in thick slabs—*oh, how fun that had been!*—beside a large bowl of gravy; hot rolls, butter, jam, and vegetables crowded one another; pumpkin, blueberry, and apple pies added to the dinner's aroma. She had even found wine to be served, a large bottle placed nearest Deverell's seat. And above the old oak table, the large deer antler chandelier glowed, the lapzine replaced with candlelight. Her eyes ate the meal before her, and that was all the taste of it she was prepared to partake of. This was not a celebration by any means, though the boys might have thought it so. This was a declaration of intent. Physical nourishment would not placate her soul. Calpurnia hungered for only one thing, and that was the return of what had been taken from her. She wanted Lara. The dinner before her was, for all intents and purposes, a trap.

She took a satisfied breath and turned for the stairs. It was approaching five in the afternoon, and the boys would arrive soon. She needed to ready herself, to pull out her best dress and look her most pleasing. She was the hostess, after all, and soon to entertain in the Great Hall of Walterhouse Manor. The place had seen parties before, but never an occasion such as this.

WHEN THE boys arrived, they found the large table in the center of the Great Hall spread with the many beautiful dishes Calpurnia had created. The smell was at once intoxicating and surprising; how had she accomplished such a feat? They immediately began to salivate. They had never seen such a meal, and so lovingly laid out. This, from a woman whose life, up until recently, had been reserved to a single cube of floor, ceiling, and wall.

Though Calpurnia was still readying herself in her chamber, the boys were prompted to seat themselves at the table by delicately written name cards. Calpurnia had had plenty of time to perfect the most elegant penmanship. Aubrey and Deverell sat across from one another. They had dressed in their most presentable attire, sensing this was an important occasion to Calpurnia—and thereby important to Leith—though they were a bit unsure as to why Minerva had not been invited as well. Over their cleanest white shirts they sported twill blazers—blue for Deverell, light brown for Aubrey. Their hair was as tamed as they could manage and slicked to shine. Deverell had needed much persuasion to dress in this manner. He had become something of a wild man, shirtless and barefoot day and night. The touch of any sort of fabric, especially high-collared dress apparel, made him scratch as if combating an irritating rash. His neck was red from his clawing.

"Do it for Leith," Aubrey had finally said, and Deverell had relented, though his scowl never faded.

Leith sat at one end of the table, equally dressed in discomfort to match his friends. Garet's sword hung over the hearth behind him. At the opposing end of the table, across the dinnerset and lit candles, Calpurnia would be seated as their hostess. The wait weighed on Leith, and his stomach murmured with anxiety.

His mother finally entered the double doors of the Great Hall as if she were a duchess whose guests waited with bated breath for her arrival. Which, in fact, they did, but not in the way she would have guessed. Her face gleamed with victory, though her eyes held an excitable madness. Her hair was piled high, and around her neck hung the only jeweled necklace she owned, a shimmering affair of faux diamonds and obsidian. She had even tried to apply rouge and eye shadow, though, even before Garet had vanished, makeup was never much use to her, and living in the valley she had never had much instruction on it. The pastels seemed too thickly applied, almost comic.

It was the dress that sent shivers down Leith's spine. Whirling into the room to her own mind's symphony, Calpurnia was costumed in her commitment gown. The dress she had worn when she pledged herself to Garet. Leith had never seen it worn; it was as if a ghost had been loosed in the Great Hall. The simple satin design was brilliantly white, angrily so, and its excess trailed along the floor after her. The sleeves were lacy things, long and billowy. Though she had aged, the garment fit her well, and her bosom looked pert and young, bunched together for show in the low-cut neckline. She hummed in a full circle dance around the dinner table, touching each of the boys on the shoulder with playful fingers as she passed. She lingered a bit on the broad shoulders of Deverell.

"You look beautiful, Calpurnia," Aubrey spoke up. His voice startled Leith out of his momentary coma, and he glanced at his friend with slight annoyance.

"Thank you!" she cooed. "I haven't worn it since my commitment to Leith's father. I haven't really had need to. *And look!*" She twirled once more, just in case any at the table weren't convinced of her beauty. "It moves like clouds around me, don't you think?"

"Absolutely," Aubrey placated her. "A very beautiful cloud. Why, you should be in the sky yourself!"

"Aubrey Avonmore, you flirt!" she giggled, finally taking her seat at the table. "Of course, if you were gentlemen, you would have stood when I entered the room, and then pulled out my chair for me. But that sort of propriety doesn't come from being raised in the lesser places of the world or playing all day in the woods." She nearly lost her composure as she spoke, but regained control very admirably, Leith thought.

"Sorry, Calpurnia," Leith apologized lowly, disgust and embarrassment crowding his mind.

"No matter now," she replied. "It's done. Let's all eat, shall we? Or should we give thanks to some god or other? Which is it? Who's the most popular deity of the day?" Her glance moved from boy to boy. "Some mother goddess or a stern, vengeful masculine figure? They all vie for attention it seems, over the same food, over the same earth. I've never heard of a god eating, though. If they've never tasted what we eat, how do they know if we have anything to be thankful for at all?"

Leith rolled his eyes. "We should just eat, Calpurnia," he said without looking at his mother. He watched the candle flames dance around the minor disturbances in the air.

"Very well, then," she said. "I'll be the good hostess." She rose from her chair, again circling the table dramatically, placing heaping servings of all that would fit on each of the boys' plates, though her own she left bare. To Deverell's plate she paid the most attention, piling it higher than all the others.

"You're a big boy!" she exclaimed. "You need lots and lots of food to keep those marvelous muscles fed."

His face took on a dark pallor when she drowned everything on his plate with dark, thick gravy. She filled his wineglass till it nearly overflowed.

Aubrey took hold of Leith's hand across the table, smiling to quiet his apprehension concerning his mother's actions. Leith simply dropped his gaze to his plentiful plate, his eyes locking on to the serving of fowl.

Calpurnia seated herself opposite her son once again, though this time Deverell rose to clumsily pull out her chair for her.

"There's a gentleman," she said with an odd stare.

"How do you like living with Minerva?" she asked, once Deverell had returned to his seat. "Oh, that's right! Leith was telling me, you and Aubrey live in the old Parma house now. Poor Prichard, and then Clara going mad as a sacked cat afterward. But you're living there now. How's that going?"

Deverell sat bemused, unsure if she wanted an answer direct from him or if she were waiting for Aubrey or Leith to speak up.

"He doesn't talk, Calpurnia," Aubrey politely intervened. "Remember?"

Calpurnia glanced at Aubrey as if he were a bothersome gnat. "Silly me! How could I forget? But then, it's been so long since I've really seen you. Isn't that so, Leith?" She cast nary a glance in Leith's direction, clearly holding little expectation of an answer. It was all a pointed jibe to demonstrate her absolute solitude all these years. "All I've known of you is what I can see from my window in my bedchamber. Your comings and goings have always held great interest for me, but unfortunately...."

"We would've visited if we thought our visits were welcome," Aubrey replied.

Calpurnia again regarded him with slight vexation. The big room was a cold, cold place at that moment. Everything echoed pent-up anger. The only elements of warmth were the candle flames. "You were always welcome here at Walterhouse Manor, my dears."

Deverell fidgeted uncomfortably in his chair, pulling at his collar. No one had as of yet touched his food. Aubrey turned to Leith, his eyes seeking some assurance as to how to best handle Calpurnia's strange attempts at dinner conversation.

"Leith, what's the matter?" Aubrey whispered, still holding his hand on the table.

"The meat," Leith answered. A gnawing uneasiness began to eat at him. "Look at the meat. What kind of bird do you suppose...?"

"I'm sure she got it from somewhere else." Aubrey studied his own plate. "The farmer who borders you. You have a deal with the old man, after all."

"Aubrey. I think she... Oh, Aubrey. I'm so sorry."

"You look as white as a ghost. What's going on?"

"Where... where'd you get the bird?" Leith said loudly over the dishes and candles.

"What does it matter, dear?" she inquired pleasantly. Her face remained serene, though it offered a challenge only he recognized.

Deverell poked at the gravy-soaked fowl with his fork.

"It matters!" Leith assured her.

"It's just a bird," she said. "Just a jittery old rain crow I saw from my window, jumping about in the yard whilst I was reading from my Bible."

Aubrey loosened his grip on Leith's hand and became suddenly ill.

"Strangest thing," Calpurnia continued, watching carefully the reactions from around the table. "When I came downstairs, the very bird was at the door, tap, tap, tapping away. Well, normally I would shoo away such a nasty lice-ridden creature. Any decent woman would, wouldn't she? But no, I thought to myself, 'Calpurnia, my dear, such a bird as this would make a wonderful addition to the dinner. It's small, but I bet it's sweet.' So, I opened the door, and it hopped right into my arms. It didn't make so much as a peep when I broke its little neck. I would have felt guilty, but… it *was* just a bird."

"*Just a bird!*" Leith yelled, standing to his feet. The terror of the situation threatened to unravel his mind on the spot. "There haven't been birds around the valley all my life, and you go and kill those that return? And that one… he was a special rain crow! He was Aubrey's friend!"

"*Special?*" Calpurnia countered. "What on earth could be so special about such an odious, ragged-looking, disease-ridden thing? I'm afraid you're quite gone, my boy."

"It was a bird. A sign of better things to come. He was Hope!"

"Who said so?" Calpurnia challenged in mockery. "Who told you this? Do they teach you such superstition at that school? Wait… no, it was Minerva True, wasn't it? I know it was." She huffed in resentment. "There is nothing of any good that can come from the unreasonable ideas you have been raised with. They dog you down. I don't know *why* I let it go on. It's an embarrassment to have you believe such things!"

"You, Calpurnia, didn't *let* anything happen!" Leith fired.

Aubrey, who had recovered temporarily from the shock of the rain crow, grasped Leith's hand to calm him.

"Don't speak to me so! I'm your mother, boy!" She gripped the table's edge and it cracked under her pressure.

Leith let out a loud guffaw. "You are no one's mother," he exclaimed. "You cradle your own selfish regrets and disappointments and have for years, while it was *me* who took care of *you*! You're just a child who cares nothing for me, for the valley, or the world!"

She stood in outrage, hot tears welling in her eyes, though whether tears of pain or rage none could ascertain. "You brat! You're not too old for me to take you over my lap! I can still punish you. I still have that right, that power."

"You're nothing but a bitter, insane, wrinkling old harpy!"

"Leith," Aubrey tried to hush him, but he would not be quieted.

"I want nothing more to do with you. You were never my mother! My mother lives in a hidden cottage in the woods of Black Hill. She's the mother of my brothers here as well. You don't even measure up to her knees." He knew he had at last said what he had to say, the venom that had been building up for years in his gut and gullet, but it wasn't enough. Not by far. "You might have been something once if you'd had the courage to be the River Dweller she thought you were capable of being. But you were too scared. You're always too scared. You don't need a son. You need a rope so you can follow it along or hang yourself with it!" Leith sat again, nearly collapsing into the chair. "Go back to your room, *Calpurnia,*" he muttered dismissively.

Calpurnia backed away from the table, her eyes blazing like twin coal furnaces. "*You don't know!*" she cried, her voice rattling like windows in a thunderstorm. The candle flames flickered madly above all the rushed breath. "You don't know how it was then. You don't know your father. You don't know me at all!"

"Well, then," Leith mumbled, shaking. "We have something in common after all."

Calpurnia tore from the Great Hall, rushing noisily up the stairs to her room. The door slammed, and her wails of rage filled the house.

Deverell looked at Leith quizzically. He rose from his chair and left the room heading for the stairs.

"Deverell," Aubrey called after him as the young man headed for the stairs.

He looked back once with an expression of loss, but continued on.

"Let him go," Leith groaned. "Let him try to be the son I can't be."

"Where are *you* going now?" Aubrey inquired as Leith rose to his feet.

"Away, Aubrey. I need to get out of this house. I don't know if I'll ever come back to it." He exited the Great Hall and then the house itself.

CALPURNIA STOOD motionless at her long window. The sinking sun cast long shadows over the fields from the imposing forest. She watched Leith cross the gravel road into the goldenrods and Aubrey follow closely behind. This was for the best. She couldn't work her charms on Deverell if Leith remained in the house. He eyed her so queerly sometimes.

She heard the knock on the door, soft and sensitive. Deverell had been waiting outside her bedchamber until her wails had distilled into calmer sobs. She had played the part well and grinned at her evolving plans. Deverell had always been more sensitive than the other boys. Even a stranger could tell that. And Calpurnia intended to use this weakness to her advantage.

She sniffed as if surfacing from a pool of tears. She felt the young man approaching from behind. Even his footsteps were mute, but he had such a strong presence there was no denying him any attention. He touched her gently on the shoulder, and Calpurnia whirled around to face him. "*Oh, sweet Deverell!*" she cried. "What did I ever do to him? Am I such a horrible woman? Though, I'm sure he is right. I was never much of a mother. I once lost track of him. He should have been taken from me then." It pained her to say such things, but she knew the outcome of her plan would be worth any discomfort she now felt.

She buried her face in Deverell's deep, broad chest. His arms closed hesitantly, nervously around her.

"I should have done him better. Oh, Deverell. You comfort me so! Truly, it's as if it were you who was my true flesh and blood." She let her warmth, her femininity, sink into him, and acutely sensed his pulse quickening.

She slipped her hands down his chest and past his cord belt. "My, how you've grown," she exclaimed, as she wrapped her fingers around his stiffening sex.

He jumped, but she held to him tight. "Come with me, Deverell," she whispered. "Keep an abandoned woman company. Hold me. Be mine, if just for the evening. I've noticed you coming and going with Leith. All these years I've needed to touch you, to be with you, Deverell, son of my only friend Lara." She scattered kisses on his neck and felt him tense, then relax and quake. "You're mine now, aren't you? Mine to command."

Calpurnia led him by the hand to the bed. She collapsed onto the covers, pulling him down on top of her. He began kissing her with extraordinary tenderness, his true nature bent to Calpurnia's whim.

Calpurnia smiled at the ceiling as she saw everything coming together before her. Her reunion with Lara was so near she could smell her sweet scent. Calpurnia's seduction of Deverell was the sacrifice needed to assure his own mother's return; Calpurnia had convinced herself of this. He would be hers now. The Book would not let her down again.

For Deverell, this was a new experience. Though he had known sensual pleasures on the night of his river naming, that now seemed but a brilliant dream. This was real, completely tangible. And though he felt a surge of guilt and repulsion knotting in his stomach, he found himself powerless to disobey Calpurnia's orders to take her. So he kissed her and rocked inside of her even as his soul echoed for him to stop. But something had him. He felt it twist his will as surely as one feels their hair pulled from behind.

NEAR THE edge of the field, where the slender goldenrods and the thick forest converged, where the tiger lilies bathed in the last flecks of the sinking sun and the pungent scent of wild onions filled the air, Leith paused, warily searching his surroundings for shelter or temporary solace. Calpurnia exhausted him. Even freed of his cell-keeper duties, she still loomed large over his world, holding the keys, shaking them at him. She could vanquish hope as quickly as Aubrey could inspire it. She stood as the antithesis of what a mother should be. But then, honestly he had no other example to compare her to, not really. He had books and stories of mothers, but he couldn't ever remember meeting one. Maybe they were all like Calpurnia. Maybe they killed all the fathers of the world, these angry mothers. But that couldn't be. Minerva had been a mother, hadn't she? And wasn't she going to be one again according to the woman they had met at Trumpet's Place? There was no better soul in the world, he thought, than Minerva True.

"What are you thinkin' about, lover?" Aubrey asked, standing motionless behind Leith, concern etched across his features. His voice was calm, sympathetic.

"I'm thinking I want to get away from her," he replied, uncertainty in his tone. "I just want to run. I want to run fast and free. I want every step to be downhill so this damn limp won't interfere with my speed."

"So... why don't you?"

Leith bowed his head in defeat. "She keeps me here. When all's said and done, she is my mother. Even if I don't like Calpurnia, I still gotta look after her. I don't understand it, though. She's a monster, Aubrey. How is it that I can feel an attachment to someone like her?"

"You're a nurturer. There ain't nothin' wrong with that. Sometimes, though, you gotta pull away. Let your momma struggle on her own. She'll do just fine. Maybe she's not so bad when she's given space. I heard once that familiarity breeds contempt, and distance do make the heart grow fonder."

The scent of the flowers and grass in the gloaming combined with Aubrey's voice to soothe Leith. The night beetles began to chirp and the dusk-light sun touched everything around them with gold.

"So, you're saying I should take off?" Leith raised his head, as if permission to leave was about to be granted.

"Right now," Aubrey encouraged. He drew closer, standing beside Leith as they both stared into the wood. "I'm sayin' we both take off right now, lover."

"Hell, I want to. But I can't leave." Disappointment rang in his words. He swallowed his pain.

"Maybe you cain't leave the valley. Maybe not even Walterhouse Manor for the time being. But you can run, right? Just a race through the wood? Come on. It'll do you good." The gleam of mischief gemmed Aubrey's face. He nudged Leith playfully in the ribs with his elbow.

Leith needed little more encouragement than that. "I'll see you at the bottom of the hill!" he exclaimed as he tore off his jacket and bounded suddenly into the forest. Aubrey laughed, flinging his blazer to the ground and kicking off his shoes. Then he too was ripping through the woods with incredible speed.

Leith had never won against Aubrey in any competition of speed or swimming unless he was allowed to win, and he knew this would be no different. But the breath in his lungs, the pounding of his heart, the blood of life pumping through him, they were a victory in themselves. As the endorphins kicked in, he was mastering insurmountables.

In short order, Aubrey was running barefoot next to Leith, leaping over fallen logs and clearing brush with the grace of a fawn. Aubrey didn't take the lead, though he very easily could have. The boys ran alongside each other, soul mates eclipsing the sunset. Leith had that feeling he only rarely felt in the forest: of being at one with everything and wondering why he would ever want to leave at all. Aubrey was his connection, generously transmitting energy from one world to the next. They were a rare breed, young stags racing in the wilderness. The world evolved a millennium with each collective stride.

The forest changed as they raced along. Familiarity faded, and undiscovered paths were laid out before them. Trees and vines so tall they held up the sky. Such was the way of Black Hill. Once one grasped the connection, he or she realized the forest was always changing. In its heart, a multitude of tiny things were happening each and every second, though unseen by most eyes. Black Hill was remade with each of the boys' footfalls.

Leith was amorously absorbed in that connection when he heard a large splash to his side. His heart beat rapidly, his breath short and heavy. His body shook from the adrenaline. He slackened his pace to a brisk walk when he realized Aubrey was no longer running alongside him. He was in fact nowhere in sight. Leith backtracked along the route Aubrey had been taking, peering between the mammoth wooden ancients covered with thick, furry moss, until he came upon a small pond in the middle of the wood. There sat Aubrey, grinning ear to ear as he lounged soaking wet in the shallow end of the pond, surrounded by lily pads and lichen.

Leith began to laugh between his sharp intakes of air. "It hurts!" he hollered, referring to his choking chortles.

"Help a devil up," Aubrey said, joining in the laughter.

Leith pulled Aubrey to his feet and began drying him off with his sweat-stained shirt. "I won!" he exclaimed. "I finally won! I beat Aubrey Avonmore!"

"You never did! That doesn't count! We never reached the bottom of the hill."

"Doesn't matter a twig," Leith defended. He dried Aubrey's mop of hair with his shirt. "I'm the fastest! I'm—"

"I will always be the Prince of the Valley," Aubrey proclaimed. He paused, giving Leith a queer look. "What's the matter?" Aubrey asked. "You've turned ash gray." He turned around to see what had caught Leith's eye.

Floating toward them over the rippling water of the pond, as if carried by invisible strings, was Darcy/Dark Eyes. His handsome face shone with a menacing grin, and his thick coat and tousled hair flowed like liquid in the silent dusk-light air. The forest seemed to wilt and die around him, and the pond water turned black as midnight's grave. The night crickets put down their instruments; the glow flies dimmed their lanterns. Not a sound as Death's door creaked ever so slightly ajar.

"Leith, go," Aubrey whispered harshly. "*Go now!*"

"You come too!"

"I can't. Now you run this second!"

Closer. Closer. The water still now, not a ripple.

"*Leith!*"

"Aubrey, come on!" Leith gasped, pulling at Aubrey's arm. "I'm not leaving you!"

"Stubborn ass," Aubrey sighed. He turned to face Leith, and with a roar the likes of which Leith had never heard, Aubrey screamed, "*Leave!*" His teeth revealed blinding and white, spittle flew forth, spitting the rage of a river sprite.

Leith let go of Aubrey's arm and struggled backward, trying to remain standing.

"Remember… I love you," Aubrey stammered through tears. A cold shadow brought his attention back to Darcy/Dark Eyes and he assumed the stance of a warrior ready to strike with a sword, if only he had one.

Leith ran but could not pull himself too quickly away. He turned continuously, wanting desperately to go back for Aubrey, but there was nothing for it. Aubrey was as obstinate as Deverell. The best Leith could do was to go back for help. Find Minerva. Her battle had come.

As he looked back a final time, Darcy/Dark Eyes was bearing down upon Aubrey Avonmore, floating above the water over the Prince of the Valley in his warrior stance. In a flash, Dark Eyes's coat fell from him. Not just the pelt, but the visage of the man fell away. Before Aubrey stood the source of all malevolence—the preacher with those two eyeless caverns that sucked in all the life around him.

PART V— THINGS WORTH FIGHTING FOR

MIDNIGHT TRAVELERS
ON THE ASTRAL RIVER

THE ELF-PATHS opened much more easily for Leith than before. As if sensing the impending darkness, Minerva appeared before him, hurrying in his direction like a wraith through the woods. Through his frantic words, she gathered what had occurred and bade him to show her the way to the pond. Though this gave Leith some hope, Minerva's expression exposed a breaking heart.

Leith led her to where he thought he had just been, only to have his hopes stricken down. They searched tree, stream, and ether, but found not a sign of Aubrey. The entire wood had shifted. It seemed as if the pond Aubrey had fallen into had not existed at all. The forest drained of all life and color in that moment of horrific revelation. Leith could not cry anymore, nor howl in anger, instead becoming silent and stoic as stone. He hadn't even the strength to whisper a curse on the trees. Minerva cradled his shoulders as they walked slowly onward. She whispered gentle words of comfort. As they cleared the wood and happened once again into the goldenrods now enfolded by night, they came upon Aubrey's scattered jacket and shoes. Minerva gave them to Leith to hold, and he snatched them near his chest with life-smothering strength.

AS HAPPENS often when any great loss is thrust upon one so sensitive to the world, one so aware of the connections that bind all—as befell Minerva at the death of Hamlin Marsh—Leith took to his bed at Walterhouse Manor, unable to cope. He stared at the ceiling, his eyes sketching out a horror he had never in fact witnessed. Deverell imagined his friend's fragile mind guessing and gluing bits and pieces until the mystery of what actually happened was replaced by a forged memory of his Aubrey's terrifying death. Leith clutched to Aubrey's ragged jacket underneath the sheets. He did not speak nor rise, and only ate when he was forcibly fed by Deverell, who acted as nurse, mother, and guardian spirit.

Deverell was, of course, duty bound to this obligation, both as friend and brother, yet also out of his own sense, however unfounded, of personal shame and grief. Minerva had come upon he and Calpurnia, wrapped in an awkward embrace. Minerva's face—stricken with pain and sadness—had further constricted with the dawning shock at what lay before her. She delivered the news of what had occurred in the forest as one gives bad news to strangers, in a distanced tone of sorrowful formality.

Deverell had looked to Calpurnia in astonishment at the news of Aubrey, yet she did not move. She didn't seem concerned in the least, not even of her own son's struggling mental and emotional state as he rested in the bed downstairs. She glared at Minerva with naked hostility until the old woman left.

It was Calpurnia's lack of warmth that scared Deverell the most. And so he took up the role she should have filled, sending encouraging vibes of hope and perseverance through smiles and touch even as he wanted to break into tears of his own over Aubrey's demise. Calpurnia would only occasionally visit Leith. She roamed the house more freely now, her barriers stretching outward. Most of the time she would stand near the door of the downstairs chamber, peering in at him as if he were some strange animal in a cage who would at any minute rise to feed or stroll about.

"He will be fine," she whispered from the doorway on one of her trance-like visitations. "I have it on good authority that he will be fine. I have been promised that everything will be given back to me." She looked at Deverell as he stared at her from Leith's bedside. "Come. I need you now," she commanded. And he would do as he was told, always hesitantly leaving his dear friend alone in the large room of four high, bare walls and one large bed.

It began to seem to Deverell that Calpurnia was deliberately calling for him more often, and Leith was being neglected due to her power over his will. He knew something needed to be done. With sadness and tears, he realized he could not care for Leith while Calpurnia was awake, while she watched. She *required* him, she would say. Required Deverell's touch to give her strength. *Couldn't he see that? Didn't he still care for her?*

So, one night after Calpurnia had fallen fast asleep, Deverell carried Leith in his arms wrapped in sheets from the house, down Black Hill Road in search of the path to the circle wood. The knowledge of the elf-paths was fading from him, but he found them with some luck and determination. In time, the elf-paths would be closed to him altogether if he could not rend himself from Calpurnia's pull. When Minerva opened the door of her cottage with candle in hand, she said nothing. She only stared for a moment with compassion at the young man she had raised.

Minerva sighed with understanding and stepped aside to let him enter. He laid Leith on the hay bed, then kissed Minerva on the cheek and disappeared into the night.

"Stay strong," she had whispered after him as the darkness absorbed his silhouette. Returning her attention to Leith, she set the candle down and felt his forehead. "We're almost upon it," she murmured softly. And as the words had passed her lips, she'd realized the truth of the statement. The battle was very near. It hung over the valley like a savage drought ready to drink up the river.

In the days following Aubrey's disappearance, Minerva's journeys up College Hill to visit Mother True's tree on the bluff became less and less frequent. Leith needed tending to. Without Aubrey, he had fallen into bleak despair. And now that Calpurnia mysteriously controlled the affections of Deverell, Minerva was left alone to care for Leith.

The growing restlessness of the valley, and the river in particular, felt like a strong gust of wind coming at Minerva with full force. It threatened to suck the life from her at times, so frantic could it become. Things were floating to the surface of the deep river; it was like a boiling pot, loosening and stirring. Wood, debris, and remains drifted up from the hold of their ancient mud graves. The Othersiders watched with growing concern, at times peering out from the canopy of the trees. Minerva wished she could get to them, ask them for help, but that time had passed. The rafts had become waterlogged, bashed to pieces by the forces of nature long ago. Even the raft she and Deverell had used to travel to the sacred place was no more, the raft boy gone from the valley forever. Even if she had the means to travel across, who was to say if she would be allowed to step foot on the banks? Theirs was a holier place.

Most important was the child she carried. A biological impossibility to be sure, but the morning sickness was undeniable. She remembered it well from carrying Branwenn. Climbing College Hill was a task she would not risk. A fall on the steep, muddy incline could prove fatal. She smiled at the thought of what Leith's college tutor, Mr. Albert Higgins, would say. Could his scientific, logical, and learned mind wrap around a woman Minerva's age carrying a child, a woman who had seen more decades slide past her than the young men at the college could ever imagine? There was no lore of this type in her studies of the faiths of the river folk. It sounded like an excerpt from another belief's book, one that was becoming more clichéd, offensive, and oppressive as the years passed. How, indeed, would Mr. Higgins explain Minerva True?

Her meditations once solely experienced under the tree were instead practiced nearer the earthen cottage now. She never wandered too far from Leith. He was key to the battle to come, she was sure, and thus, she had to see to his recovery and his safety. As she walked among the untamed forest, she no longer needed to ask Mother True questions. Instead, answers floated into her, even as she began to formulate her inquiries. It became as simple as inhaling. She wondered why it had never been as easy before.

Minerva understood certain things as if she had known them all along. She realized the valley would indeed survive and grow. The world would always find a way. Procreation was not a matter of male and female. Things were born from desperate necessity. The valley was in the process of rebirth even now, in its very embryonic state. Everything was ephemeral. And as an echo touches those things and beings nearest it, so too rebirth had touched those like Minerva who remained in the valley. Minerva herself had been born anew after the struggle with Hamlin's death, just as Leith would be reborn from the ashes of his love for Aubrey. Deverell was now facing his own struggle as well, one that she could not interfere with no matter how much it caused her old heart to ache.

But what of Aubrey Avonmore, the young river sprite she had grown to love so dearly? The young boy she was now certain she had known in a life before.

"He will not return as he was known to us," she said quietly as tears filled her eyes. His rebirth, she knew, was yet to come. "It will be hard on Leith, but it is necessary. Things must be set right. Aubrey's sole purpose is yet in the process of fulfillment."

Like the river, things had their natural course, and Minerva saw a steady calm ahead. But before that, the waters would be stirred most ferociously, and she would be the one at the churn. Yet she was not completely alone there. It would require the others as well. Leith… Deverell… and even Calpurnia.

Would they be ready? *Would she?*

IN HIS dream, Leith walked through the thin mists that separate the worlds and trod upon the delicate layer of ether that caresses the earth. Below his bare feet, the river glittered under a strange bright moonlight. He had no fear of sinking into the water as his feet touched it. He walked upon it with ease and faith. Leith was both participant and witness to what he saw, as is the case with most dreams.

Ahead of him strode a lone familiar form making assured, emphatic steps. Leith smiled with delight and relief. He tried to call to Aubrey, but found he could not speak. His voice had flown out of him like a firefly; he had seen it scatter into the night. Aubrey looked over his shoulder, beaming a devastatingly glorious grin and beckoning Leith to follow him. They continued down the center of the astral river, midnight travelers on an ancient waterway road. Leith was mesmerized, as he always had been by the presence of Aubrey, not noticing much else but the swagger and swing of two beautiful naked mounds of flesh gleaming white in the moonlight.

In time—though dreams, like reality, are composed of a single point of no-time in which everything happens at the very same moment—Leith was led from the riverway to the banks. He suddenly stood facing the limestone columns of the ceremonial place where he had been given his river name, unbeknownst to his mother, when he was much younger. The moon hung with a blue glow that both lit and calmed the valley. Around him crowded many beings: ancient River Dwellers and unfamiliar spirits, familiars, bugaboos, Passions, and those of the valley who had lived and died there as watchers and guards. Song exhaled her rapturous peal through the valley air. And there were others as well. Faces of the Othersiders, those forever hidden behind the tree line. Leith could tell by their expressions, the hint of *more* in their eyes, they were from the far bank. They watched him expectantly, as if waiting for him to act or to follow through on a promise. Then all their attention was stolen away from him at once, as a rustle of wind introduced the arrival of another.

Between the two aged columns, joined in hands, the participant Leith and Aubrey Avonmore stared into each other's eyes. A garland of flowers lay on both of their heads. Each had become vigorously alert in their sex, reaching to one another as if in need. Mother True stood beside the two young men giving a blessing. It was a marriage, a covenant. Watcher Leith felt a tear of joy and love mixed with grief sliding down his cheek. The spirits around bowed to the figures as if in obeisance.

Another push of the winds, and the crowd dispersed, riding the breeze to a new destination on an endless, but rapturous, night's journey. Leith now watched himself standing alone with Aubrey at the river bank. They whispered to each other, but the Watcher could not hear the words being spoken. With the exasperated desire to be part of the dream, the two Leiths at once became a single character.

"I gotta go. You'll be okay," Aubrey was saying quietly. "I'll be just over there"—he nodded to the other side of the river—"and I'll be watching."

Leith was still unable to speak. But he *was* able to feel his heart shatter once again. Aubrey gently released himself from Leith's strong but useless hold. *Dreams deny physical strength; the subconscious alone knows when to let go and when to hold on.*

"Don't sleep too long, lover. You got stuff to do. We got promises to keep." Aubrey winked, and then he dove into the water. Leith watched as he swam clear to the Other Side without pause. He was allowed to see Aubrey climb up on the far shore and wave before the mists closed in and pulled him back into his own world.

DEVERELL SAT in a haggard velvet love seat in the Great Hall as the morning light eased through the window. He was slouched, his legs splayed, pulling uncomfortably at the collar of the shirt Calpurnia required him to wear. "It's not fitting for a man to walk around without a shirt," she had pronounced. She spoke to him now more on terms of master to servant than lover to lover. Strangely, however, he was more comfortable with the way she had started treating him. He no longer had to be the participant in transparent acts of love. She used him as a pillow in her bed chamber when she slept, that was all.

He had slid from her bed early in the morning and descended the stairs, trying to make as little sound as he could. He thought constantly of

Aubrey's disappearance, of Leith, and of the strange circumstances that caused the latter's necessary resettlement to the circle wood. Whenever he was afforded any solitude, he would use that time to mourn his sudden and numerous losses.

Behind all the grief, too, was the queer hold Calpurnia had over him. Why could he not refuse her? How was he drawn to her? There had never in all his life been any desire for another human being. And still, there was no real *desire* for Calpurnia as such, only an undeniable pull that threatened to tear him apart should it be ignored. He would curse his newfound situation if he had the tongue for it.

As he faced the hearth, the strength he had acquired from his victory over the dark vines all but forgotten, he heard Calpurnia saunter slowly down the stairs, a sleepwalker with eyes wide open. He had observed that even when she thought she was alone and not being seen by anyone, she was still ever on show with dramatic hand gestures and formidable if frightening facial expressions. Deverell had come to the conclusion that if there was such a thing as insanity, Calpurnia certainly suffered it; that she was in fact its very source. Either that or she was an extraordinary stage actress without a stage.

She walked sleepily to Leith's downstairs bedroom, taking chance to peer in on her forgotten son. She had seen Deverell in the chair, but apparently hadn't registered his presence. Soon, however, Deverell heard her panicked bare feet slapping along the hardwood floor racing toward him. She came breathlessly into the room in her nightgown, nearly pulling the love seat over as she grabbed the back of it. He did not flinch.

"*Where is he?*" she barked. "Where have you taken him? I demand you tell me!"

He sat staring into the hearth, grateful he could not speak and betray his friend and brother.

Calpurnia whirled around from the back of the chair to face him, falling to her knees in front of him and clasping his hands. "Please tell me, darling," she entreated. "I won't be angry. Just return him and all shall be forgotten. Forgiven even. You cannot keep a mother's son from her."

When he remained unyielding, Calpurnia grew impatient, maddened, slapping him all about the body with random, wild swings. "Tell me where you took him! I know you can speak! Leith is mine, do you hear? He belongs to me! You tell me this instant where he is."

The crazed and violent explosion from Calpurnia made Deverell jump to his feet, suddenly frightened. Her voice had reached a crescendo he had never thought possible, hitting a note almost too high for the air to carry. He moved back, but she lunged at him. She struck him forcefully on the cheek, and he nearly fell to the floor from shock. Deverell had never been touched so by another human being in his life. He held his face, staring at her, the pain a completely new sensation. He felt relieved that the elf-paths were closing on him, for even if she demanded that he retrieve Leith from Minerva, he could not, no matter how long he searched. Leith was safe.

Calpurnia simmered; her hands still trembled in tight fists. "Leave!" she exclaimed. "Leave here. I have no need for you today. Go nettle the trees of Black Hill with your contemptible silence and leave me be."

He hesitated before leaving the room, stumbling over his own feet, still jolted. Calpurnia looked on angrily from the window as he cast a glance back at Walterhouse Manor on his way down the gravel road to the forest. He held his cheek the whole way.

Rage staggered Calpurnia's thoughts, and she quaked like the earth's hot core at the thought of him, at what Deverell had taken from her, just like his father.

As she was yet pondering the Great Unfairness of Life, the kept air of the Great Hall was split by the presence of a new perspective. The walls and floor creaked and rumbled from the weight of it.

"You know he took the boy to Minerva True," hushed syllables coughed throughout the large room.

The sudden semblance did not startle Calpurnia. She continued staring out the window as if the low voice were her own angry thoughts. Yet she knew there was something there in the Great Hall with her, watching out the window alongside her in resentment. She knew it because she had invited it in. She wasn't sure how, but the hushed voice was of her doing. And in her way of thinking, one is never rude to invited guests.

"Yes, I know," Calpurnia responded inertly. "But I haven't the will to go into the forest yet. Even if I did, Deverell would lose me. He knows the bends of the trees, their voices, as Leith calls them. He knows the folds and the hollows. And without following Deverell, I could never find Minerva's place myself. The elf-paths are closed to most, especially those like me who have turned our backs on the ways of the River Dwellers."

As she spoke, she played with her necklace. "Ridiculousness," she said in a grasp for parenthetical conviction on this last statement.

She felt a hand, strong and heavy, placed on her shoulder. She spun around at the touch, but was somehow not as disturbed as perhaps she should have been at the sight of Darcy Crocker. Her mind fiddled with a paradox: it was him and it wasn't. He was more extraordinary-looking than he had been before, and he wore a thick coat of fur, the likes of which such a destitute man would have never possessed. She was dazzled with jealousy through her rage, causing a ripping vertigo between her hate for the man and sheer carnal desire for his flesh and what he had.

"Is my world going to explode?" she asked aloud as she steadied herself against the lightheadedness. "Am I to die?"

"Oh no," said Darcy without ever moving his mouth. The words projected from his eyes. "Your world will get better and better from here."

"Why?" She stared at him suspiciously. "Why will it get better? Is it because it cannot possibly get any worse?"

"Oh, my dear Calpurnia, we can *always* make things worse, now can't we? It's just a matter of reading the right verse." He clasped her hand, and she tensed as she felt tiny pins and needles numb her arm. "But, no. To make things better, you need only give me what you have already planned to give," he answered.

"*Let me go!*" she cried, squirming uncomfortably. He released her, and she rubbed her arm protectively.

"Give me Deverell," he said.

She stared at him, remembering at once her original plan. "Yes," she exhaled, a broadening and fanciful smile on her face. "That was my plan, wasn't it? Oh, I can be so smart! And you like it? You think it's a good plan, Darcy?"

"Absolutely, I do!" he assured her. His voice made her want to scratch her skin furiously. "You're a very clever woman. I've always thought so."

"Leith may never forgive me. He's lost Aubrey already, and now Deverell…." She nearly relented. "But he'll see. It's for the best."

"Of course, he will. Those boys need to be separated. It's time, don't you think? Boys must grow to men. They need guidance."

"Oh, yes. They've relied on each other too much." She was feeling better about her plan. "With Aubrey here"—She did not see Darcy flinch when she stated the name—"they were like some trinity, some childish trio of heroes. Even as children they referred to themselves as protectors and knights of the valley." She laughed almost wistfully. "Nothing could penetrate the world as long as those three were together. Can you imagine? As a child I was never caught up in such fantasies. I had a good head on my shoulders. My father had taught me the futility of flights of fancy. Still—" She paused in a moment of true maternal feeling. "—there was something sweet about it."

"Surely now, at this age, you're not beginning to believe such nonsense?" His pronunciation of the last word sounded like a hissing death knell.

"No, no…. Certainly not!" She walked to the red velvet love seat and collapsed onto it, her arms limp, the vertigo still distressing. "If I give you Deverell, I want Lara back. You can do that, right?"

He smiled. Or rather, he never stopped smiling.

"Those are my terms. I want Lara back… and Leith. I want nothing further to happen to Leith. He should live the rest of his days safe in the arms of his mother. Me. Safe in *my* arms. He can be our son, then. Lara's and mine. Is that fair, do you think?"

"I will give you your son, yes. That's fair," he offered with his dark, handsome eyes.

Satisfied that she would see both Lara and Leith again, she promised, "You shall have your own son, then. You shall have Deverell. I was wondering when you would show yourself to take him." She rose to her feet and strolled to the full-length mirror positioned in a corner of the Great Hall. She straightened her gown and fussed with her hair. Her eyes reflected appreciation back at her. "You'll tell Lara I look forward to seeing her again, won't you?"

There came no reply. Darcy's voice seemed to come from nowhere again, for as she looked past her own reflection, she could not find his image in the mirror. "Calpurnia, do you still have the Book? The one you found as a child? The temporary gift?" The voice brushed past her like a passerby in a crowded corridor.

She froze. "How did you know about that?" she asked. Had Darcy seen her find the Book at the chapel all those years ago? Had he followed her there?

"It was loaned to you. Please return it when you bring Deverell to the chapel."

"*The chapel?*" she cried as she turned around. "Why should I need to go there? Can't you…?" But she saw now she was speaking to an empty room. The presence was gone. She searched, but she came to the conclusion that Darcy had rudely found his way out without her escort.

The chapel was a more frightening prospect than she had counted on. It had never physically harmed her, but it had taken plenty. She was no longer able to claim ignorance to its power. Still, if it was what she had to do to get Lara back, she would. She wondered where Darcy kept her. Did they live in the chapel all these years? Calpurnia's mind began deconstructing and reconstructing her past so that things made sense for her. Unfavorable things were quickly forgotten or replaced with more pleasant renditions.

She returned her attention again to the mirror, but as she looked into it, her features shifted. She shook here head as if her sight were failing her. In the reflection, her face morphed into that of the little girl she had been, that little girl's face on an aging woman's form. Then, just as strangely, the face disappeared and was replaced by the one she had come to know in her middle age.

DEVERELL WASN'T certain he could find the circle wood. He had grown up there. It was his home; the elf-paths had always opened up, leading him to the earthen cottage before. But it had been difficult finding them when he had taken Leith to Minerva. And now, he was unnerved to find himself completely lost. The morning had aged into afternoon, and the trees with their hanging garlands and moss seemed to trick and tease him, holding back and uncertain of him. Had Minerva banished him from the circle wood for good now that he resided with Calpurnia Covington? Perhaps the events with Calpurnia that morning at Walterhouse Manor had just distracted him from the paths temporarily. Maybe he would get his bearings back. He tore his itchy shirt to threads in frustration, feeling a modicum of relief provided by the fresh air on his bare chest and abdomen. If he could find Minerva wandering the forest, he could at least learn of Leith's condition.

Hungry and exhausted, Deverell sat on a downy stone, his head in his hands. He could not return to Walterhouse Manor right now. He wanted to see Leith. Yet he knew as soon as Calpurnia wished him to return, he would have no choice but to oblige like some slave-boy djinni in a magic story of the desert places. Until then, until she called, he would continue searching, even if it were all pointless. It seemed he was always searching for the circle wood, and it was always just beyond him.

As he pondered his way through the useless map of the forest in his mind, he heard a rustle in a batch of mulberry bushes very near to him.

"Don't you worry! No need! No need!" came a quick, certain voice from within the bushes. "Help is here. Oh, yes it is!"

Deverell stood on guard against any disturbance on Black Hill, especially plants seemingly possessed of minds and voices of their own. He stood ready for combat, fists clenched, but he relaxed with relief as a familiar Passion leapt from the mulberry bush.

"Here you are again," said Fox. "And here I am again! And good thing, I think. Yes, very good. I think we're old friends by now. I bet you be looking for one of those trickster elf-paths. Tricky, tricky things!"

Deverell nodded desperately.

"I know the way!" Fox stated with characteristic enthusiasm. "Follow me, strong young man. Keep those arms bared. We'll be a-ripping through the trees. The forest is our friend, but it's mischievous. Oh yes!"

Fox turned, walking upright, his bushy tail waving like a separate entity, playfully teasing Deverell to follow. Deverell marveled at how small Fox was, something he had not noticed the night of the barrows. Why, the creature wasn't even to his knees!

"Minerva True is not there. No. I saw her leave. She's going to see the mad woman in the castle." Fox walked with an assured strut, with the manner of the most informed Passion in the forest.

"But you need to see your brother, and that be what I'm here for." The small animal walked briskly. Deverell had to almost skip to keep up the pace. And, as Fox had said, plenty of leaves and brush and limbs had to be cleared by Deverell's muscular arms as he followed through the trees. "There's only the two of you now," Fox said, sadness in his voice. "But there's still hope. You have to stay together. You understand? You are a powerful brotherhood, you are. Hope still breathes in the valley as long as there are at least two. The Third is not fully awake."

Hope of what? Deverell wondered. And who or what was the Third?

It wasn't too very long before they came upon a twisted but elegant mass of natural topiary. Fox halted. "Here we are," he exclaimed proudly. "Enter! Enter!"

Deverell stared blankly at the shrubs and vines that very clearly resembled giants frozen in the midst of waltzing. Why had he never seen this before? He had been searching in the vicinity all day. How had he missed it? He realized it was a question he had thought many times before, a redundant response to the ways of Black Hill.

"Look closer, silly, smart, strong boy!" Fox giggled. With a whip from his tail, the waltzing giants parted and a path evolved very rapidly through the dense undergrowth; brush and bramble rose or bowed so a cleared walkway formed. "Very tricky, these elf-paths," Fox said. "Now get you going!"

Deverell stepped onto the trail, peering down the green corridor to the small cottage hardly visible at the end in the circular clearing.

"Take care now," Fox said.

Deverell turned and gave the little critter a wave of appreciation as it scampered into the undergrowth. As he walked the path, he knew without looking that it was folding over again behind him, reclaimed by the forest of Black Hill. His heart settled with relief as he at last walked into the circle wood and saw once again the gardens and the lamps and torches and flowers and herbs. All that was missing was the Breed. He hadn't been gone too long at all, but it felt like epochs. He breathed contentedly for the first time in many a day and walked through the tall grass and flowers and into the cottage in search of Leith.

Deverell found him just as he had last seen him: clutching still at Aubrey's jacket and staring at the ceiling. He was pale and grieved to illness. Deverell felt his own heart breaking, as if he and Leith shared the same body, the same internal makings. Slowly, he climbed into the bed, under the covers with Leith. He wrapped a strong arm around the comatose prince and kissed him lovingly, mournfully, on the cheek. He would sleep, or at least lie with his brother, until Calpurnia called him back. His strength would become Leith's in their embrace.

CALPURNIA IMAGINED not too many things about people surprised Minerva True anymore. Which was why she was delighted to see the old woman so taken aback at seeing her standing on the roof of the old Walterhouse place like a weather vane. The River Dweller stared up from the gravel road at the mad woman whose white, sheer gown blew in the higher air, revealing the figure beneath.

For a long while, Calpurnia didn't let on that she had even noticed Minerva standing as tiny as a doll shrouded in black on the road. Calpurnia was casting her attention over the trees, trying to catch a glimmer of her own approaching dreams. Her hand was held above her eyes, blocking the sun, and her toes clutched at the roof tile like the claws of a cat. Finally, she looked at Minerva, her eyes narrowing in annoyance, though she wasn't even certain if her expression could be seen from so far below, especially by someone who was so very old.

"What do you want, old woman?" she yelled. "I'm enjoying my day. Say what you need and be on your way." She returned her attention to the horizon, looking ready to launch herself toward it.

Minerva smiled in her annoyingly polite manner and walked into the house. Heaven forbid she strain her voice from the road. Calpurnia sighed, taking a seat on the roof as she waited for Minerva to climb the creaky stairs to Winifred's old bedchamber.

Once in the bedroom, Calpurnia heard Minerva walk to the long window. The glass had been broken. Shards lay all around. The tool of the window's destruction, a heavy-heeled boot, lay thrown to the grass below.

"Calpurnia, my dear, you've broken your window," Minerva called as loudly as was needed.

"Obviously," Calpurnia answered under her breath. Then she answered more clearly. "But I wanted to be outside. And the window refused, I'm afraid, to open. It was stuck like a stubborn child, so I had no choice but to break it. I wish Deverell or Leith had been here to open it for me. Boys can be so useful at times."

"Might you come down so we can speak face-to-face?"

"I'm afraid not," Calpurnia replied after a long pause. "I rather like it up here. I am out of the house at long last."

"Yet you remain anchored to it."

Another pause. "Say what you came to say, then leave."

"Very well." Minerva sighed. "I shall say what I need to from here, though it will not be pleasant for either of us."

"Go on, then. Get it over with."

"Why do you not seem to care for your own son?"

"*How dare you!*" Calpurnia thundered, pounding her feet above Minerva's head. "I care for him deeply. It's the likes of you who offer him up to danger as if he were a fox in the hunt. Bring back my son,

Minerva, and I'll show you how I care for him. Though I don't need to prove myself to you, nor do I need your approval of my proof. I know you have him. I know De-ver-ell—" every syllable pronounced like a dictionary—"brought him to you. As soon as I find a way, as soon as I know the right passage to demand that Deverell bring him back…." She stopped, afraid she had given away a secret.

Minerva heard a scuffling of feet, as if Calpurnia had nearly fallen from her position, but had managed to steady herself.

Minerva had caught something in what she said. She was certain too, that she'd felt a slight push on her back as she leaned out the broken window. There was something unseen in the room intent on doing her harm. Minerva backed away from the window cautiously, glancing around her. Upon entering the house, she had sensed the chill of shadow. Walterhouse Manor had never felt like this before. Though it had been a while since Minerva had set foot in the structure, it was evident some mercurial act had been chipping away at any truth within. Calpurnia had been inviting mischief or even something much darker. Minerva heard groans and whispers from the corners of the old place. She had the sense of being watched by dark entities. In every creak of the floorboards she heard a threatening denouncement of her person.

Calpurnia's last statement stuck in Minerva's mind. She admitted she had the power to command Deverell to do as she wanted.

"You're dealing with darkness, dear," Minerva said, still eyeing the chamber. "I feel it here. This house is not well. Your boy is safer in the circle wood. I will not bring him here, no matter what you beg of me. I'm sorry. There is something here that intends harm and—"

"Minerva," Calpurnia shouted with pronounced clarity. "Know this: When I am able to walk on ground once again, you will have more than the chapel to fear. Now, if you will be of no service to me, then please leave!"

Nice of her to say "please" at least.

As Minerva turned to grant Calpurnia her wish, her gown snagged on a chaise. She bent to inspect what had torn at her and quite accidentally discovered the edge of a leather-bound book protruding from under the tan cushions of the chaise. Murmurs from the corners of the room rose as Minerva took firm hold of the edge of the ancient manuscript. She gasped when she pulled it fully from its cushy hold.

"*The Night Hammer!*" she whispered almost too loudly. She had never seen it, but had been told of its angry power by Mother True. Finally, all the pieces began to slide into place. This was how Calpurnia was controlling Deverell. But how long had she held the Book? Did she realize the true terror of what she possessed? To her it must have at first looked like just another Bible. When had she discovered its darker uses? Had any of the calamities in the valley been the result of her readings? A thousand and ten questions and semiaccusations flooded into Minerva's mind.

They mattered not right now. All would be rectified. For once in her life Minerva decided doing the right thing was to do the dishonest thing. She tucked the book beneath her gown, feeling the ice of shadows as it touched her skin. As she made her way out of Walterhouse Manor, Minerva realized with pleasure that she had spoiled some part of a dark plan. She had the advantage over the chapel at last.

THE INDESTRUCTIBLES

LEITH LAY in his coma. Minerva whispered comforting words as she washed his arms and torso with a warm, wet cloth. The cottage was quiet; the circle wood, still and expecting. The only sounds were the trickling of water continuously wrung from the washcloth and Minerva's own slight, barely audible sentences. An herbal tea filled the cottage with a sweet scent.

"Aubrey loved you so very much," Minerva said. "He would not want you to mourn him so, especially when there is much yet to do. But I do understand the desire to fade. I am not immune, as you have seen. Push on, Leith. There's hope to be found even in a world struggling in the absence of light. The Light, you see, it slips through cracks, and will not be denied even in the most oppressive of times. Search for that Light, Leith. Don't forget those who still depend on you here in this world."

She laid the damp rag on his forehead and kissed his cheek. "Push on," she whispered.

Restlessness had replaced fear. Minerva no longer trembled with apprehension at the thought of the confrontation to come. She could hardly wait for it. Her certainty in her own strengths was cautioned only by the youth and unpredictability of Leith and Deverell. She wrung her hands as she walked out into the light of her circle.

She had ventured near the stone gardens where the Parmas were laid, much in need of rest herself, when a sense of approaching cavalry, like a steady rumble through the breath of the forest, surrounded her. It warmed her with a sense of dutiful pride. The trees stood as soldiers, ready and strong.

A sound that had long been absent from the circle wood now drew Minerva farther from her earthen cottage and into the shallow beginnings of the forest. It at once filled her with fondness and wonder. She perceived the flapping of wings, and large wings at that. As if some storied bird or gryphon were landing nearby.

"*Minerva.*" The voice rustled on the breeze. Instead of a great Phoenix, there stood Mother True in a small clearing beyond a grove of cherry blossom trees. She was dressed as the River Dweller she had been in life, the plain white robe flowing down her form like the pureness of statuary. It had always been so striking against her pitch-black hair, the tresses tumbling down her narrow shoulders. But this was no vision of Mother True. She stood flesh and bone. Minerva gasped, and her tears blurred her vision.

"Minerva," Mother True whispered again in a motherly, more human voice full of affection.

Minerva hurried to her and fell into her arms at once, sobbing.

"I'm so very proud," Mother True said. "You've done so well." They shared a long moment of embrace. Minerva did what she could to convey every *I love you* never spoken in life.

"I miss you too much," Minerva said, collecting herself and staring into her mother's human eyes. She was so young and radiant. "How is this possible?"

"Because impossibilities are for fools and the weak-minded. And I am neither, young lady. My dear heart. My girl. But you must listen closely, for I can stay but a short time. I have something of importance to tell you."

Minerva straightened, still clasping Mother True's hands, feeling as though she were a child again, so proud of who and what her mother was and hoping to be just like her someday.

"Walk with me, my dear," Mother True asked of her daughter.

They strolled hand in hand past the cherry blossoms, through the cottonwood and pines. The breeze followed them. Mother True's palm was soft and delicate. "Do you remember the day the birds left, the day Branwenn was lost?" she inquired.

Minerva's eyes closed in pain. "You know I do, Mother. It is a daily torment I journey through. I can barely keep to my feet when I think of her soul in the chapel grounds, being corrupted of its purity." The trees moaned in the breeze as mother and daughter passed them, as if giving melancholy song to Minerva's sentiments.

Mother True squeezed her daughter's hand. "You were a good mother. But you needn't worry for Branwenn any longer, my girl. It would be wasted energy from here forward. It would be a silly waste of good energy."

"What do you mean?" Minerva asked, watching her mother obliquely.

"Branwenn's body may have entered the realm of the chapel, but her soul never touched its poisoned ground."

"I don't understand," Minerva said.

Mother True stopped walking as they stood under the oak on the cliff overlooking the chapel. They had taken an elf-path, which brought them in a half-meander around the circle wood. "There was a rain crow," she said. "Do you remember it?"

Minerva thought briefly. "Yes, I do. Faintly. It flew past just as she...." She stopped in a sudden realization. At the time, she had asked for the birds to help her, but did not think any had come to her aid. "It took her into itself?"

"For a very brief time," Mother True explained. "Branwenn has been with me for a while now, watching over the valley, and over you."

Minerva was silent, staring down the cliff. "Excuse me, Mother," she said finally. "But you have caused me so much grief by not telling me this sooner." Her voice strained with a mixture of anger and joy. "Why did you hide it from me?"

Mother True faced Minerva, holding both her hands. "It was necessary you think she was in the chapel grounds, my love. Your passion, your love for her, was needed to save the valley. I had to be certain you would do absolutely everything to destroy the chapel, to destroy the preacher Dark Eyes."

"I would have done," Minerva swore. "*Oh, Mother!* You've torn my heart out." She wrenched her hands away and turned her back on Mother True.

"Would you have done it? Would you have tried so very hard if Branwenn's spirit were not at stake?" Mother True approached her daughter and took her gently by the shoulders. "Yes, you would have certainly tried, but you would not have gotten this far, and then it would have all been for naught."

Minerva knew her mother was right. She loved the valley and would have done anything for its magic. Yet Minerva thought of the days of darkness after Hamlin had passed. Would she have pulled herself from that if Branwenn had not needed liberation from her imprisonment in the chapel? Or would she have let the valley fall, and herself along with it?

Would she have faded into the Nothing awaiting those phantoms who walk the world without questioning?

She met her mother's gaze again. "You are right, of course. But Mother... I just wish I could have saved her body as well. I just wish I could have seen her again."

Mother True drew Minerva close to her. "And so you shall," she whispered.

Even as she held her daughter's hands, Mother True seemed to grow to the height of the ancient oak that stood near. From behind her spread spokes of light, as if wings. "*The Battle begins!*" Her voice echoed through the valley with thunder to shame the skies.

Suddenly, in the midst of her awe, Minerva felt another genial presence emerging from behind her. She turned, knowing already who it was. Branwenn leaped up from behind the old oak to a low hung branch. She was giggling as she swung, carefree. "Hi, Mama!"

WITH A sense of conflict, Leith began to finally awaken. He perceived his hands pulling away dirt and darkness, his fingers stretched wide so he could handle large portions at once, as if he were buried alive in a deep grave. He felt nearly overcome and fought asphyxia until an infinitesimal speck of light pierced the filthy dark, kindling optimism. The light grew in abundance as more of the darkness was clawed away, until at last he lay free from constraint. He realized slowly, particle by particle, he was not in a grave at all, but in Minerva's small cottage on Black Hill. This gave him some respite, though Minerva was nowhere to be seen.

Just as he was adjusting to the comfort, he whiffed the scent of heartbreak that permeated the jacket he held to so tightly. He buried his face in Aubrey's personal aroma, long-stifled tears flowing freely at last. The twill jacket soaked them up generously, as if it were made for only that purpose. Leith choked on the air in the room. He thought of letting himself fall again into the grave, forgetting everything and surrendering anew, but that was not possible now. His heart ached so deeply, it would no longer allow him to ignore the grief. It had been silenced for too long.

When he opened his eyes again, knowing he would need to see through the pain if he were to see at all, a figure stood silhouetted by the daylight in the doorway. Leith sat up on his elbows as best he could. "Aubrey?" he whispered.

And however ominously, it was indeed the figure of Aubrey, but its soul seemed to have fled. What made Aubrey Avonmore the fearless knight he was had completely separated from his body. Now he stood in the doorway but a bogeyman. Aubrey's doppelganger didn't answer Leith's constricted call to him. Instead, he stood quiet with his shoulders hunched, his eyes vacant and his skin pale. His hair was matted with dirt and twigs, and his clothes and flesh were muddied and wet. The drops of water echoed as they hit the cold floor. Aubrey hung in the doorway, as if positioned there on invisible strings.

"Aubrey, what's wrong with you?" Leith cried. "I wanted to help you! Why'd you make me leave? It was supposed to be me and you, remember? Knights of the Valley. *But you made me leave!* I could have saved you!" His voice spread throughout the circle wood but found no listening ears.

Aubrey remained the same, his soulless eyes fixating on something in the past or something never real in the first place.

"*Say something!*" Leith demanded. "Say something to me. It's Leith. It's your Leith!"

Slowly, shadow fell over the doorway as if the sun were hidden by an eclipse. The figure of Aubrey seemed to retreat backward, but without moving. His shoulders still stooped, his head still fixed in a corpse's stare.

"*Don't leave! Come back! I'm sorry!*"

But Aubrey was gone, and sunlight returned in plentitude to the doorway. Leith fell back to his pillow, but his dark night was over, and he somehow knew his strange awakening had a purpose.

DEVERELL SWUNG the axe, chips of wood somersaulting through the air around him. Calpurnia had demanded that he start gathering wood for the coming fall. She had discovered the spells in the Book lasted for differing lengths of time, and the one that connected her to Deverell, the one that made him do whatever she wished of him, was, for the time being, still quite strong. He had been at it all morning without letup. He was to split the blocks of wood on the front lawn so she could watch him from the threshold. Though it was a struggle, with Deverell's sure hand to steady her, Calpurnia had finally made it out onto the old wooden porch. At last, she was out of the house and on level ground.

Deverell felt uneasy as he toiled away. Her eyes never left him, not for a moment. Soon, sweat had soaked clear through his clothing, making him all the more uncomfortable with the situation. When he took off his shirt, she didn't protest as she normally would have. Strangely, for once, he actually wanted to keep the shirt on, but the prodigious sweat from his exertions made it intolerable.

The sound of the blocks of wood splitting was his only comfort from Calpurnia's maddening gaze. He imagined as the axe fell on the wood, that it severed that powerful but invisible chord that bound him to her. This glimpse into Leith's world, what his friend had gone through all his life, proved terrifying and surreal.

Shaking, Calpurnia sat in the rocking chair that had been brought down from the upstairs hallway. She was dismayed to see the outside of the house in such a state. The once-gleaming home was paint-chipped and its porch rotted. Knowing she would not have Deverell to work for her much longer, Calpurnia decided she would have to hire someone to fix up Walterhouse Manor if she and Lara were to live there together. She began to look forward to things again.

Calpurnia watched Deverell with the fierceness of a mountain lion about to pounce. He was a prized find, a bartering tool, and a lovely one at that. Silent and beautiful, quite like his mother. As she examined his sweat-glistened skin, his bronzed muscles and strong arms and back, she felt a curious desire. Here before her was Lara's son; the closest thing to Lara in the world: the same facial expressions, appreciative manner, the same gentleness and desire to please. She perceived the same pure blood streaming through his veins, somehow untouched. Deverell was *of* Lara, a part of her left behind before she'd been locked away by Darcy in the chapel. In thinking this, as if the world had been laid over with a fresh coat of paint, Calpurnia no longer saw the strong figure of Deverell swinging the axe, but that of Lara. Mother and son became one for the moment.

Calpurnia rose shakily from the rocking chair, a new determination now raising her demeanor. She would be with Lara by way of Deverell. It seemed so simple now, she didn't understand why she hadn't thought of it as she and Deverell lay in bed together all those nights. She would bear his child, a girl. She and Lara would raise it as their own. Leith would not be needed after all. When Darcy gave Lara back to Calpurnia at last, she would surely be delighted by the news of their child. While it was true Deverell would ever be with Darcy, a boy should *want* to be with his father. Lara would understand that.

Calpurnia would use the Book to control the desires of Deverell once again. He would want to sleep with her. She would just need to find the right passage. She felt giddy with the formulation of her new plan.

Once inside the house, she felt safe again. She was no longer being attacked on all sides by invisible, ancient things, children of shadows and light; the indestructibles of the world made of wind and ether. The sky no longer stared at her.

She climbed the stairs to her room like a proud queen leading a procession. She lifted the cushion of the chaise where the Book was kept, anticipating the heaviness of it, the coarseness of its leather binding, the smell of wisdom and power. She salivated at the thought of what it was about to give to her, of what she was about to bring to herself.

To her horror, however, she felt no such hidden item, no immediate gratification whatsoever. Frantically, her hand slid farther beneath the cushion. When there was still nothing to be found, she ripped off the plushness with aggravated strength. *It was gone*. Calpurnia whirled around the room, an elegant cyclone of maddening intensity. She broke vases and the water basin. She threw books and clothes to the ground in reckless fury. The room became littered with her crumbling dreams. Finally, she hoisted her old writing chair over her head and pitched it with all of her might from the long glassless window frame. It landed very near Deverell with a splintering *crack*, and he jumped back.

She went to the bed, stripping it bare and ripping the covers and sheets in the process. All the while she muttered high-pitched sounds of horrific confusion and self-pity. In utter defeat, she fell to the floor beside the bed. Her mouth quivered and she shook violently. She had never intended to give Darcy the Book. It was hers and would remain so. But she would bring it with her to the chapel as asked so that she could be with Lara once again. A gesture. Nothing more. Once they were reunited, Calpurnia planned to run holding both her prized possessions. Now, that plan seemed ruined. Her grief convulsed inside of her, a retching serpent. She would not see Lara again unless the Book was found.

"Who would do this to me?" she mumbled, her voice pitiful and jerking. "Who would steal such a precious thing?"

And then her head snapped to attention, as if the answer were whispered to her from a descrying corner. Minerva. The old woman had been in the bedroom when Calpurnia was on the roof. The image of the River Dweller's face sent a bolt of rage shooting through Calpurnia's entire body.

"*You vicious, tricky old woman!*" she exclaimed. She hit the floor again and again, her knuckles cracking with the intensity of her balled fists. Her voice shook with crimson rage arriving in the skies on a chariot pulled by four bloodred stallions. As she shook, her hair came undone and fell over her face like a woman in the midst of seizure. "You knew it was here all the time," she hissed. "You just needed an excuse to come to my room. You whore! You witch! You thief of dreams!"

She calmed herself, still breathing heavily as she leaned against the bed. She would need her wits; she would need a clear head. *How to get it back?* That would prove most difficult against the likes of Minerva True. And the elf-paths were forever shut to her.

LEITH LOLLED in a half-sleep. He was rocked, it seemed, in the arms of a willow. And yet the willow was under the earth, in the cottage with him, and there was somehow plenty of room for it there. It didn't seem at all out of the ordinary. Roots and limbs resembled one another. Minerva's place always smelled of fragrant leaves, herbs and dewy grass anyway. As a lambent wind flirted through the branches of the willow, Aubrey reappeared in the doorway just past them. Leith was not afraid or stricken with grief as he had been before, for Aubrey now moved quite normally, his cocky strut intact as he lingered in the doorframe. He no longer echoed the image of a corpse; he was as fresh and bright as the night that they had spent in the creek bed past the barrows. He glowed with tenderness and joy, dressed in a clean white tunic and blue trousers and, as was his preference, no shoes.

He knocked graciously on the doorframe as he smiled and leaned in just a hair. "Wake up," Aubrey said quietly. "Can't you hear the trumpets calling?"

Leith did in fact hear faint trumpets. The clarion call of geese flying far overhead. He parted the willow branches to get a better look at Aubrey, but the sprite was gone. The open doorway was now crowded only by sunlight as it cascaded down the entrance steps.

When Leith awoke completely, he sat up forthwith. The willow tree was gone from around him. A sense of duty, of responsibility, coursed through him such as he had never known before. He rested his feet on the cold floor, a sensation of newness swept up from there to the top of his head. He felt refreshed. Though his legs were weak, he stood quickly and found the clothes Minerva had laid out for him, anticipating he would wake soon. He dressed promptly and left the cottage. Minerva's voice whispered behind him, somewhere near the cliff at the back of the cottage mound. A rumble of thunder echoed so near, it seemed it came from the circle wood itself. But he could not concern himself with that at the moment. Without giving any of it a second thought, the elf-paths unfolded, and Leith entered the forest of Black Hill.

He paid no heed to the trail or the road in the forest; he didn't see the gravel leading to Walterhouse Manor. His body simply took him where he needed to go. His mind became a sharpened tool, a pointed scope that sought and found.

LEITH'S DETERMINED stride and ferociously fixed stare were what startled Calpurnia and Deverell, both once again on the front porch of the old house.

Calpurnia had come downstairs finally, fit to be tied. She screamed obscenities and curses, pitching them into the air like cow dung and acid. Pacing back and forth on the porch now, she held her head in her hands. Her hair was a forgotten mess. Deverell had slowly walked up the steps. His hands went out instinctively.

It was Calpurnia who first saw Leith speeding toward the house. She stared in disbelief, still holding her head with shaking hands. "Leith?" she whispered.

Deverell turned quickly and a smile—his first in a long while—immediately adorned his face.

"I knew you'd return," Calpurnia said, not so much in the manner of a concerned parent as a pretentious teacher. She flashed her eyes at Deverell in warning as he stepped forward to run to his friend and brother. "He is not yours to hold," she chided. "You stay back, *Elijah*!"

Deverell folded back onto the porch like a poisoned flower, wishing she were but a dark vine. The axe lay by the halved wood and splintered chair.

As Leith approached, Calpurnia moved to the edge of the threshold as far as she could without stepping foot from it and held out her arms.

Leith seemed not to see her. He brushed her aside indifferently, nearly knocking her to the decayed porch floor. He entered the house, and the walls seemed to straighten in military respect at his vigorous strides. The darkness hidden in the corners crept into cracks or slid under floorboards. Calpurnia followed him hastily; Deverell remained farther back.

"What are you doing?" Calpurnia queried. "I'm here. I'm right here, darling! We'll never be parted again. Not ever!"

He entered the Great Hall and headed for the hearth, every step like a drum pounding out a battle hymn.

"I would have cared for you. I swear," she tried to explain. "I was caring for you in my own way." She was becoming desperate, grabbing at things that were half-truths even to her. "It was Minerva. She tricked this one"—she flung her hand out in wild gesture in the direction of Deverell—"into taking you from me."

Leith tore his father's sword from its position over the hearth. Knickknacks tumbled to the floor. Calpurnia flinched as he headed back in her direction. His eyes seemed to stare through her. She scurried out of the way before she was thrown off balance again.

"*Deverell, do something!*" she shouted, as Leith stalked out of the house.

Deverell tried to catch Leith's attention, but there was nothing. Calpurnia protested again, commanding her son be stopped. Deverell hesitantly grabbed Leith's shoulder, but Leith shrugged and was released. Deverell, perhaps fearing Leith would do something to harm himself, tackled him in the front yard amongst the chopped wood. Leith dropped the sword. And though Deverell's strength was incomparable with anyone for miles around, Leith managed to easily free himself and regain his feet. He snatched up the sword again. "I have something to do," he said with a voice of meditated calm, walking determinedly toward the forest.

"Stop him!" Calpurnia screamed. "Stop him, you fool! Do something right for once."

But Deverell lay on the ground watching his friend leave. There was nothing he could do. He no longer felt the urge to do as Calpurnia bid him. Her control was waning slightly, *just slightly*, but it was enough. Nor did Deverell actually want to stop Leith from whatever he was so intent upon. Leith possessed a much higher power than Calpurnia. He disappeared into the trees, the gravel of Black Hill Road his warrior's path.

"Get up!" Calpurnia urged Deverell resentfully. She clutched the porch railing. Deverell rose to his feet and looked back at her questioningly. What was his role in this confrontation that was now most certainly to take place? This battle.

Calpurnia ushered him impatiently toward her. "Help me. Hold my hand," she commanded.

He took hold of her quaking palm, not because he felt he had to, but because he needed to see this thing through, and Calpurnia was undoubtedly part of it. She held his hand with a vise grip and stepped warily forward, down the first step, still holding to the railing with one hand. The wood moaned as if in pain from her grip. Slowly, she brought her other foot to the first step. She stood there for a moment, raggedly breathing, looking to the sky. Finally, she released the railing with a jerk and proceeded down the remaining steps. Now both hands held tight to Deverell as Calpurnia focused on each step before her like it was a sworn enemy. On the final board, she wobbled hesitatingly, but then, with a great intake of air, forced herself to touch the worn earth below. She exhaled in relief. They stood together for a moment. Deverell studied her now bedraggled, pale features, made all the more abstract by the sunlight slowly receding behind a peculiar mass of dark clouds. A low rumble shook the sky. The stormy season had not ended after all.

Deverell was watching the dark clouds roll in, shrouding the valley in a kind of midday night. Calpurnia had relaxed a little, dropping one hand but tightening her grip on the other. "Come!" she said, dragging him forward. "This is what you were meant for."

Her steps were clumsy and halting, causing Deverell to run into her with each footfall. But as they walked down the gravel road to the forest, her gait became a bit more adept, if still distracted and deformed. She seemed in an impossible rush. He tried to imagine what could be so urgent down the gravel road.

Ahead waited the chapel grounds.

BRANWENN LEAPT brisk and light down the hill like the little girl Minerva remembered. Now, no longer the density of flesh and bone, she could fly easily, weightlessly, from boulder to tree top, waiting patiently for her mother to catch up. She was so quick Minerva had to listen for her giggles to locate her hanging from a cottonwood bow or skipping with dazzling speed across the narrow neck of a creek. Minerva was happy, indeed overjoyed, to follow wherever her daughter led her. She grinned with delight as she slid too quickly down the hillside, her long, black skirt ripped by brush and briar, and her hands getting scuffed and bruised. None of this bothered her. How could it?

"Follow her," Mother True had instructed before vanishing in a cacophonic chorus of lifting wings. "Leith will be fine. He has his own part to play. Go now."

Minerva did not need further instruction. She would have followed Branwenn happily into the deepest caves of the river if only to see her for a few minutes more.

Branwenn laughed at their game of catch. She played ring-around-the-rosey in a swirling kaleidoscope of colors. Minerva smiled briefly at the absurdity of the moment. Branwenn was leading her into battle, and yet Minerva found she didn't care. All she knew in that moment was that her daughter had not been in the chapel's hold all these long years; that she had been within the very trees Minerva walked among. She realized, too, that they were not headed directly for the chapel, but traveling in a straight descent down the hill, past the chapel grounds. For some reason, Branwenn was taking her elsewhere. They were headed to see the Othersiders. Branwenn began to run across the river as light as a feather in a spring breeze. Minerva found a weathered old raft waiting at the shore and soon followed.

PART VI—
THE OTHERSIDERS

BATTLEGROUND

THE SKY above the valley had become an angry, churning vortex. The menacing gray-black clouds looked ready to birth some new terrible thing into the world, ready to spit an odious bile, rank and poisonous. Fresh nightmares might rain from the clouds or be pitched to the earth by a raging, titanic cyclone. The ground, it seemed, would not withstand the assault.

Leith stood on the beach of rocks, sword at the ready, staring down the entrance to the chapel grounds as Minerva had done many mornings before this. The thick fog was rapidly decreasing, revealing the chapel in its new formidable and lustrous shell: gleaming an unworldly white and welcoming Leith to the arms of his destroyer. Slashing the wind with his father's sword, Leith kept his glare unblinking as he approached the challenge with steely fortitude. Once he set foot on the chapel grounds, the remaining mist scattered in ribbons, cut to shreds by the swordsman. Thunder growled from above and a foul wind blew.

The crocodiles focused on him from beside the steps as he strode to the chapel, but kept their distance. Aubrey had been right. Once these beasts had sensed true courage, true faith, they were paralyzed by indecision as to what to do. Leith was clad in armor as light as air. The seizing villains could not follow through on their own convictions, hysterically reaching out for him over the distance with their long nails, but nothing more.

Leith paused motionless at the chapel steps, his stance wide and threatening. He dared the chapel itself to rise and fight. If it did, he'd etch a pretty scar across its pretty façade. The wicked vines, which had repaired themselves from Deverell's bashing, curled out in loops and waves from beneath the foundation of the structure. The crocodiles surrounded Leith in a wide circle, six in total, the seventh having been destroyed by Deverell. They snapped at one another, guarding their claims to the spoils.

"Come and fight, Dark Eyes!" Leith growled. His ferocity made the minions flinch; his voice shook the valley. It was then he knew he had what Aubrey termed "courage." He had nothing else to lose. He felt more sure of himself than he ever had. Certainty filled him until *it* was all *he* was. The Being in the Moment. Looking at the door, he took pleasure at the sight of the hole where the brass handle should have been. The handle lay at the bottom of the river now.

The dark vines made sickly squishing sounds as they slithered over the ground and over the trees' petrified roots toward him. Leith sliced a tendril in twain with little concern as it tried to sneak up on him. The others quickly, if momentarily, retreated.

The doors of the chapel opened slowly, revealing only a quiet, desolate darkness inside. The dark interior was sizing Leith up, studying his possible weaknesses. Out of the shadows appeared an elongated torch, as if a stream of fire had seared itself onto the dark. Slowly, integrating with the light, the somber, stoic figure of the preacher Dark Eyes stepped out of the chapel onto the top step. In his pale hands he held not a torch but a sword laced in flame. Flickerings licked at his hand, yet his sickly flesh did not burn.

The crocodiles turned about in disappointed groans as Dark Eyes descended the steps. They would not be awarded the kill. Leith refused to move. He kept his eyes fixed on the only enemy he had ever known, the killer of Aubrey and Garet. This man formed of reckless hatred and power had nearly killed the valley itself. Nothing more would die by the hands of the Dark Preacher.

Dark Eyes stopped still for a moment on the steps as the flames of his sword shimmered in Leith's fierce eyes. Supposititious eye-pockets, the black pits like sunken sand holes, peered at the young man. Leith felt his stomach turn with disgust. The night shocked him into movement like muscles shocked to motion. It was he who began the Battle at last.

The first strike was laid as Leith raised his father's sword with a resolute grimace and brought it down on the flames of the preacher's blazing blade. Dark Eyes leapt from the steps, swinging in return. Leith caught the strike in the air, and as he held it there, he saw in the horrid eye pits of his foe the screaming souls of every being ever taken into the chapel grounds. They cried and grasped at him in a gurgling maelstrom of naked, pawing flesh.

Leith broke from the blade lock and leapt at Dark Eyes again with a ground-rending yell, a battle cry of release and redemption.

Down the hill, around the turns, and through the brush scrambled Calpurnia Covington. She had accelerated mightily since her first steps from the comfort of Walterhouse Manor; indeed, one would hardly know she had been a woman caged for so many years. She now moved and looked—her hair snagged by branches and a catch-all for leaves—like a wild child of the forest. Next to her, Deverell seemed the more cultured one. The bags and circles around her eyes gave validity to the notion that she was of an abnormal yet resolute mindset.

"We'll not be late, will we? Oh, you don't think we'll be late, do you?" she asked the darkening forest around her, her temperament from sentence to sentence as unpredictable as the weather. Continuously smacked in the face by wild ferns and tripped by crawling logs, Calpurnia remained undeterred. The abuses merely encouraged her as she short-cut through the woods.

"We'll come from behind, you see?" she explained to herself. "We won't be expected from behind. You must hurry!" she shouted at Deverell. "*Hurry you!* I shall not miss out on my chance to be with Lara once more on account of you, foolish boy!" Her words bounded into the air like phrases from a dead stage play.

The thick greenery soon passed into somber solid masses of wet gray and ashes. She stopped suddenly, lifting a cloud of ash at the edge of a hanging ledge just above the chapel grounds, part of the cursed concrete forest. The entire landscape shocked her, but most of all she was surprised to see an actual structure in place of the chapel ruins she had known as a child. Peering cautiously from behind a tree that in her eyes became a strangely placed stone sculpture, she watched with infantile fascination the swordfight occurring but yards away. Leith had never before handled a sword, and yet it seemed he was an expert, as though something other than he scripted his stealth.

Across the yards, Deverell could see the cliff he had fought upon, at its top the mighty oak anchored strong. The vines of the chapel had survived, but they were no longer concerned with the rockface and piercing the circle wood. He recognized at once that he and Calpurnia held a precarious position. He pulled at Calpurnia's hands, trying to draw her attention to the encroaching danger. Black, seeping tendrils crawled nearer to them, reaching for the sloped ground. Calpurnia paid no heed, however, shaking loose his hand in annoyance.

"What sort of mother am I?" she moaned as the unsettling tide came in. "Look! I've sent him to his death. My precious son!" A tardy realization, the knowledge that her reality had, in some way, separated from the realities of those around her.

"*What do I do? What do I do?*" She clenched her hands in anguish.

Deverell looked about for something with which they could defend themselves against the vines, but the concrete forest was unyielding. At last he grabbed Calpurnia by the shoulders, fingers forcing divots into her flesh.

"Get your hands off me!" she bellowed, hitting him full force with undiluted rancor. "That should be you on the chapel grounds, not my son! Not *my* son!"

Deverell backed away, astonished at her renewed violence.

"Your father wanted you. You *are* him! And both of you adulterated sweet Lara: each of you inside of her in your own festering way, polluting her of her purity. She sacrificed so much!" Calpurnia's hysterical demeanor was growing ever more. "*Come!*" she commanded, grabbing his hand like a mother rebuking a problem child. "It's your turn to make a sacrifice." The sky cracked, and she nodded to the corresponding theatrics from above.

As she spoke her angry words, the tendrils at last reached the slope upon which she and Deverell stood. Deverell held tightly to Calpurnia as she screamed, first in fury at his hands upon her again unbidden, and then at the horrific realization she was being dragged over the ledge. Deverell plunged down the hillside with her, unwilling to sacrifice Calpurnia. The dark vines released their grip and Calpurnia and Deverell fell helplessly onto the sallow, bedewed grounds.

Calpurnia scampered to her feet, her arms aflail as if she were afraid even to touch the air, her face taught with absolute terror and confusion. Her hair was a mop of mud.

Deverell remained on the ground. The vines swirled about them, mimicking the black clouds angrily besieging the sky. Many of the vines rose up like cobras ready to strike.

On the chapel path, Leith lay unconscious on the ground. Dark Eyes had thrown Leith with ferocious strength into the cold stone trunk of a tree, and the boy had been knocked unresponsive. His sword lay useless by his side. Dark Eyes peered indifferently over his shoulder in Calpurnia and Deverell's direction. Sword of flames in hand, he strode toward them over the vines and truly poisoned ivy.

Calpurnia stood balanced like a trapeze artist, the crawlers in striking distance.

"Where is he?" Calpurnia demanded, now addressing Dark Eyes as he watched her and Deverell cornered by the vines like animals caught in a whirling pool of thick, black water. "Tell him I'm here. I've kept my part of the deal." Her voice shook, and she kept her eyes averted from the preacher's chasmic eye sockets.

Deverell rose to his feet, surveying the situation for a means of escape, regarding her ignorance with astonishment. Had she thought it was Darcy the entire time? Was her madness too thick for her intuition to even peek through?

The preacher cocked his head. Then, as if to appease her, his features began to change. Only the slightest transformation initially, like tiny streams of water on a window, but gradually a new face grew over the other. New muscle, fresh blood, cartilage, and pink flesh overlapped and rose like waves until before them, in face only, was Darcy Crocker. The body remained that of the Dark Preacher wielding his bladed scepter of flames.

Deverell stared in disgust and horror. He didn't remember his father's face, but he felt certain this wendigo before him was nothing like his father, no matter how close others swore the likeness.

"Darcy," Calpurnia said, relieved. "Call off these horrors." She gestured to the twisting vines. "I've brought him, see? I've brought your son to you."

Deverell did not register the comment, his focus on discerning a way to get to Leith, still exposed and unconscious on the ground. The crocodiles crept and shook ever closer to his limp form.

The preacher kept his eyes—Darcy's eyes—on Calpurnia as she continued speaking. "We had a deal. You're an honest man. You wouldn't renege. I have kept my part of that deal. Now…." She gestured again awkwardly.

Dark Eyes's gaze betrayed no emotion as his black serpents began writhing in a more frenzied manner, rising and whipping the air around Calpurnia. She whimpered like a lost child in the woods. "The deal! We had a deal! You've had Lara for too long. Give her to me."

Deverell seized the moment to his advantage. Though he hated to see Calpurnia so cornered, the vines had temporarily lost interest in him. He slid toward Leith, still somehow unmolested near the chapel doors. It seemed almost too easy for him to find a break in the horde of vines, and he realized Dark Eyes was yet watching him.

Calpurnia yelled for Deverell to return as he raced to Leith, cracking a crocodile on the snout with a large rock when it headed for his friend and brother. As Calpurnia screamed, the vines shot up like dark flares and fireworks, arresting her in tight suffocating bindings. She was held still by their writhing tentacles as Dark Eyes grabbed the skin of his face—Darcy's face—and tore it, flesh and muscle, from his skull. Calpurnia's screams continued, her skin bleeding of any color. The preacher threw the now useless flesh to the ground and smiled at her with his own emaciated grimace. The detached face of Darcy was consumed by the undergrowth of the vines.

Dark Eyes returned to the matter of Deverell and Leith. Yet Leith was nowhere to be seen. Deverell faced Dark Eyes alone, ready to fight.

A groan of irritation rose from the very ground. Dark Eyes strode quickly toward Deverell, flashing the sword's flames, pointing at him with the blazing tip. Deverell fumbled back onto the chapel steps as the sword came ever closer. He crawled backward, a small animal threatened into a cage.

Regaining his footing, he stood in the open doorway of the chapel. Dark Eyes paused at the bottom of the steps and flaunted an ominous smile. Deverell knew then that he had fallen into a new snare. Before he could act further, the chapel doors slammed in on him, enclosing him in the eternal darkness of the structure.

He pulled and pounded on the massive wood doors, kicking them with a force that would have decimated a brick wall. But there was no give. He had no idea of what was happening outside the chapel walls; no sound penetrated the chapel's interior. He would not let Leith or the valley down; he would not be an accomplice to the death of a way of life that he had known since first breath.

As his eyes adjusted to the sparse light within the chapel, he began to see shapes like statues. They were eerily familiar. He soon realized he had stepped into his nightmare, the very one he thought he had imagined in the forest. Around him were silent parishioners, their eyes gauged out in forced supplication.

Leith had become conscious again as Deverell kneeled beside him. The crocodiles kept their distance, scared of either Deverell or himself; in his fog, he wasn't sure.

Ultimately, it was Calpurnia's scream that helped clear the clouds from Leith's pounding head. The black vines had become a glimmering gown of intense mourning around her. The Dark Preacher towered over her. Terrified, Leith picked up Garet's sword and ran to the back of the chapel. He would catch his breath, think, and then he would spring back into action. Hearing the echoes of scuffle, he realized Deverell was being closed into the chapel itself. Who to help first? Mother or brother?

Quietly, Leith crept along the side of the building. The crocodiles' attention once more menaced Calpurnia, much easier prey, as she fought with the ever-tightening grip of the shadow vines. Dark Eyes stood at the center of the grounds apparently searching for Leith, his sand pit eyes sucking in the world.

Knowing a silent attack would be useless on these unhallowed grounds, when the villain's back was to him, Leith charged the preacher with Garet's blade. Leith thought only of running Dark Eyes through, no other outcome. His vengeance was unclouded. Though the steel sank into the preacher's flesh with liquid ease, Dark Eyes did not fall. He did not stagger or gasp. He twisted about, throwing Leith, who still clutched the hilt, to the ground. Effortlessly, the preacher dislodged the sword from his back and tossed it to the earth.

Leith rose, weaving among the crocodiles as they returned their combined attention to him. He ran to the screams of his mother and began at once tearing the vines from the ground by their centipede-like roots. She lay immobile and almost completely suffocated by them. His palms grew bloody from their razor-sharp thorns, and it soon became apparent that his hope to free her had been a useless and anserine notion, for he too was swiftly overtaken by the horrendous barbs of the ivy.

As a dim light grew within the walls, the faces of those lost in the chapel came into focus. Some were familiar to Deverell, others had had their faces erased by time and were known to no one. All were assembled in varying degrees of Death, its long colorless aura stretching over their forms.

They moved toward Deverell with interconnected unease, one causing a chain reaction through to the next. Soon they were stumbling in nightmarish union, shuffling in twitches and shakes toward him, their hollow, torn eye pits resembling those of the Dark Preacher's. Deverell did not pause to think. He acted quickly, grabbing the first of the wasted souls with his strong arms and throwing the young woman—what remained of her, as her stomach was ripped open, exposing blackened muck—at the encroaching legion. They fell en masse, like a row of dominoes, silent and twitching for a moment, before rising and collecting again determinedly.

Deverell conceded he could not continue playing this sport. There was no time for such a tedious quandary; he had to get out. While the swarm of souls gathered themselves anew, he tore a wooden pew from the floor. The splintering of wood resembled the crack of thunder as it reverberated off the chapel walls. He had never appreciated his astounding strength more. All of the insults and teasing from his childhood now seemed worth the tears. He swung the long bench, flattening the parishioners and finally busting the chapel doors wide open. The pew fell down the steps as above the thunder and lightning from the swirling clouds worsened.

Turning his attention to his escape, Deverell failed to notice more of the eternal parishioners grouping behind him out of the impossible depths of the small chapel. They crowded him just as the grim light of the outside world shone in. Expecting an unglorious end, he raised his arms to his eyes. But the parishioners, unable to pass the threshold, vanished in an innocuous whiff of smoke and foul air. He espied Garet's sword lying in the muck near the steps of the chapel where it had been thrown by the preacher, and he armed himself with it as he ran, like his brother, Aubrey the Light Bringer, to the rescue of another.

A crocodile dared to stand in his way, raising its powerful jaws. Deverell made a running slash to its throat with the sword. Meeting the beast's determined struggle to have a final meal, Deverell took hold of the deformed animal and tore its upper jaw clean off. Its body twisted away in agony, its arms flailing about. The other five crocs, now even more wary of Deverell, fed mercilessly on their wounded kin instead, even as it gurgled and howled an almost human cry of torment.

Dark Eyes was now facing Deverell, displeasure darkening his features. Leith lay with Calpurnia in the tangled, dark heap of ferocious vines.

"Get out of here, Dev!" Leith screamed.

But Deverell had no intention of leaving him. Not ever again.

As Dark Eyes raised his fiery blade to strike down the son of Darcy Crocker, Deverell threw Garet's sword with great force and purpose. It whistled through the air and reached its target perfectly, slicing the preacher's sword-wielding hand off, the same hand severed in the forest vision. It fell to the ground, the blade lighting the vines, which hissed and popped in anguish.

Seemingly at command, however, more vines charged at Deverell. Even as he ripped at them, they climbed his legs and coiled around his arms, ripping his clothes from him until he stood completely exposed. These were thicker vines, evolving from their previous defeat at Deverell's hands. They hoisted him into the air and molested his helpless form, strangling and tearing at his loins. Try as he might, he could not wrest himself from their torment.

Dark Eyes grinned, apparently unfazed by the loss of his hand. "I'm afraid," he growled and gurgled, "your strenuous efforts have been in vain. If only you had entered without such resistance."

He approached Deverell. The vines whipped around him, their thorns biting into his flesh. "I am not Darcy," the preacher admitted. "Nor have I ever been. His was the fearsome guise with which I chose to step into the outside when I was still not strong enough." His mouth formed the words contemptuously. "I am strong now.

"Suffering is what I do. The power to bring suffering is what I am. I control the masses." He spread both arms wide, the handless appendage pouring dark blood to the vines, their chosen wine. "They look to me for guidance. Only the few, like yourselves, do not see the futility of your long fight. The end is here. The Battle is mine."

"Your words are puzzles!" Leith shouted with a sneer, struggling to free himself.

Dark Eyes ignored the accusation. "Would you like to know your parents, Lara and Darcy?" He leaned toward Deverell. "The people who called you Elijah?" His voice no longer contained its phantasmal quality. It was becoming stronger and more coherent. "I know nothing of them really, other than that they were weak, and in the end, bowed to me as you will. It's inevitable. The whole world will pay obeisance to the power of the chapel. What I do know of your parents is how they met their ends. After all, it was I who gave them *that* precious gift. They suffered exquisitely, seared to the bone."

"No!" Calpurnia screamed, waking from her whimpering daze at Lara's name. "We had a deal! I brought him to you. We made a deal! My Lara!" A vine tightened its grip around her tender throat, cutting off her words.

"And yes," Dark Eyes posited, turning his attention to Leith, "your father and your beloved Aubrey suffered as well. At the end, both saw the truth. There is only I, none other worthy of worship. Or at least, none that cares. The names will change—science, technology, religion—but it is all of me. Each in its purest, most unrelenting and intolerant form. I am the Monster of Humankind, you see. I am the world's rapist. I am the baby snatcher. I am the mind controller. *I* am the great apocalypse. I am the snovelfark. I wanted to be like your kind once. You were my god; but in the end, it is I who will control your visions. I will progress and march on until the valley, and then the world, lays cold and numb. The human mind is such a terribly easy thing to control, you see. It's so easy to convince a person love never existed if they cannot see it, if there is no definition for it."

"You will lose," Leith protested vehemently. "You don't know our strength."

The Dark Preacher grinned. "And who do you believe can stop me? Your trinity is broken. The Third cannot strike me because he has been obliterated. You made sure of that when you turned tail and ran away, leaving him by the pond. You marked your own destiny."

Leith felt a pang of guilt, as if the preacher's blade had already been driven into him and was turning his innards to liquids with its molten steel. Through his pain, though, he saw what looked like a figure of a winged man squat in the branches of one of the petrified trees. It could have been nothing more than limbs sculpted by the strange sky, but still, this gave him hope.

"We had a deal. You promised," Calpurnia pleaded again, her voice dying slowly, like a wildflower in a drought. "You said you would return her to me… if I brought you your son."

Leith viewed his mother now with a raging contempt, even as he met her howls of betrayal with pity.

Dark Eyes approached Calpurnia. She averted her eyes yet again. As he stood before her, Lara's voice echoed dreamily through the grounds, singing a sweet lullaby. It braved the air around them like a lost bird. Her voice issued forth from the chapel itself, its doors now broken and scattered by Deverell's strength.

"*Lara!*" Calpurnia cried in cautious excitement. Deverell shook in his aerial imprisonment.

"It's not her, Calpurnia," Leith decried. "It's a trick."

"It's no trick," Dark Eyes corrected him. "That is indeed Lara. But, I tell the truth when I say she has no reason to be singing so." As he said this, the gentle lullaby fell away like a dropped mask, and emerging from the chapel were sobs and then a curdling scream. Calpurnia tried relentlessly to free herself of the vines, but she was not to get to Lara.

"I don't believe you," Leith objected. "That isn't her. Don't you believe him, Deverell!"

"Do you know of the idea of Hell?" the preacher inquired condescendingly. "It's a notion from the faith of the chapel, and it serves me well." Turning back to Deverell he said, "Your mother has been burning in Hell for quite a while. Most of your life, in fact. You see, it is I, as the head of the chapel, who has the power to save or damn a soul. Humanity has given that power to me all too easily, and it is an awesome and satisfying thing to wield. But why would I save anyone?"

Calpurnia began to whisper and moan incoherently. She rocked in her bondage like a lazy weed.

"Where's my Book?" Dark Eyes inquired of her. He still bled as he stood over her. But there was no reaction to his demand. She merely continued with her bound and wriggling dance of grief.

The five remaining crocodiles, the blood staining their pale faces and hands from having consumed the sixth, began to swarm under and into the vines that held Deverell aloft. Their sickly white flesh, lacking any pigment, seemed to be caressed most strangely by the black whips of the ivy. The very image of creeping, nightmarish death transfixed Deverell as he watched the maniacal horde awaiting his fall to the ground. He could not survive a battle with both dark vine and putrid animal. Hisses, groans, rasps, and moans emanated from them, though it was unclear what noises emanated from which demon.

"Where is my Book?" the preacher repeated with increasing force.

But Calpurnia was already gone away, her soul frozen like the blood in her veins, leaving her body to mumble in futile, helpless oblivion.

Dark Eyes retrieved his severed hand from the ground; it still clutched the blazing sword, its fingers curled around the hilt like a grotesque adornment. With sickening indifference, he slipped his attached hand into the fallen one like a glove. The sword-wielding hand seemed to grow and accept the other into it. The wrist closed around it tightly, as would a shirt cuff. The skin from the hand remained splayed, the intrusion causing blood to stream from the nails and fingertips. The sword itself had fallen as the hand was being "fitted." The flames lit the ground and scorched vines, though most of the surrounding earth was already barren of grass or vegetation.

Grasping the sword again with his recycled hand, Dark Eyes approached the trapped hero, Leith. "Very well," he said coolly, addressing Calpurnia. "I shall find it in my own way. I will weed the *Night Hammer* from you perpetually if I must. Page by page. But first, you will watch your flesh and blood die." He slashed at Leith with the blade, the flames cutting a quickly cauterized scar on his cheek. "*Very*—" He slashed the other cheek; Leith winced in agony. "—*very, slowly.*" Dark Eyes branded Leith's leg with his sword, and Leith screamed in pain. The smell of burnt flesh filled the air.

Deverell fitfully wrestled the vines, managing to get an arm free and rip away a long, powerful rope of black. But no sooner had he accomplished this then another was there to subdue the Herculean boy again.

Calpurnia stopped her mumbling and rocking and looked at her son as if awakening from a coma. She could not comprehend who Leith was or what terrible thing was happening to him, but she knew it *was* terrible, and she knew the terribleness would not end. The sky would remain as menacing and unsteady for all time, and the preacher would stand like a tower above them, hacking them to pieces.

As the preacher lifted the flaming blade high, so that he might begin to render Leith in halves and quarters, something happened which gave the very wind, the gathering storm itself, pause. Dark Eyes seemed to feel it even before the rumbling began. A million scampering things underfoot. Worms large and small, beetles and bugs, gnats and spiders, all manner of tiny living organism crawled from shallow holes and from the shelter of small rocks and began frantically writhing, wriggling, and pulsing hysterically away from the grounds. They flipped and flopped and slid over Dark Eyes's feet, over the dark vines, over the roughened, moist skin of the crocodiles. They made such a noise that one would think a very small but great cavalry had come upon the valley. But this was not, evidently, a charge; this was a retreat. The entire chapel yard, every inch of ground, was now covered with millions of insects and organisms that had been allowed to flourish in free rein without the fear of birds.

The sky flashed and bellowed.

Dark Eyes lowered his sword slowly, head moving as though peering about himself in utter confusion. Though he possessed no eyes, his bewilderment could not be hidden. His cadaverous jaw had gone completely slack. He had failed to realize that while he might have the power to control minds, he had no control over the valley itself. Not yet.

The crawlers and wrigglers marched and jumped over Calpurnia and Leith. Calpurnia became fitful. Her blood finally thawed and her mind became unalterably scrambled. She fell irreparably, gracelessly into the grips of a stronger, darker madness. She reeled under the blackened cords and thorns that were now crowded with roadways of earthworms and vulgar silver flies; she began spitting nonsense, screaming curses, coining obscenities, and spewing forth her mashed brain matter like poisoned air expelled from her lungs.

Dark Eyes turned and faced the forgotten entrance that led into the chapel grounds from the beach. His gaze lifted at once to the sky between the stone trees. At first, Leith wasn't certain of what the Dark Preacher saw; he wasn't even sure what he himself was seeing. But then, a wisp of darker cloud on the threatening sky became something more formed and fearless. Soon, the sky was a sea of birds, their cries reverberating a chant or song. The feathered creatures of all blessed sizes approached with ferocious speed. The insects and pests tried to take what cover they could, many hiding themselves in the mouths and nasal passages of the crocodiles as well as those of Leith and Calpurnia as they crawled over them.

Though disgusted by the insects, Leith smiled brilliantly, spitting and sneezing spiders and bugs from his nose and mouth, for he thought he caught sight of something quite spectacular and battle-defining yet on the horizon. Just for a chill-inducing moment, there was a white flash in the heavens and Aubrey Avonmore stood upon the wind draft of the birds, riding the gale like a charioteer leading his army of rain crows to a charge. When the vision faded, Leith's anger lessened, and his strength and hope were replenished.

What happened next was in such unison and quick succession that neither Dark Eyes nor his minions had time to react. The vines stiffened and loosened their grasp on their three victims as the tremendous flock of birds dove into the chapel grounds in a blinding flurry. The tendrils were retreating back to the chapel foundation. The birds pecked and tore at the vines, ripping them to shreds as they gobbled up the worms and maggots that crawled upon them.

Deverell, rending the remnants of the masticated vines from his body, stood where the vicious vegetation had dropped him and quickly surveyed his surroundings. At once, he leapt to the preoccupied crocodiles, ripping them apart with his bare hands as they hissed and howled, caught in confusion as the birds aided Deverell in his attack. The cracking of the crocodiles' bones rose even above the onslaught from the skies. Deverell decimated the beasts, and their reeking corpses and strewn parts littered the spoiled ground.

Leith had managed to climb out of the relaxed and trembling vines. He watched in a disassociated stare as Calpurnia jerked and wailed at the bugs, the birds, the vines, the memories, the lost chances, the betrayal of destiny. There was nothing more he could do for her; he was through being her servant. Now, she owned the role of stranger. He lost sight of her behind the curtain of feathers and wings.

Once free of the vines, Calpurnia jumped to her feet, running past Dark Eyes to the steps of the chapel, all the while defending herself from imagined enemies. She collapsed on the steps, looking to the broken, splintered doorway. Peering into the darkness, she saw blank figures approaching, but hesitating just beyond the threshold.

"Lara," Calpurnia cried to the silhouettes. Her face lifted in a joyous, glassy grin. "I'm coming Lara!" she said to the central figure in the doorway and raced into the arms of the fading silhouette, into the steep ascent of the dark half-life within the chapel itself.

A proud, expecting hush lay down in layers over the chapel grounds as the cavalry of aerial warriors took to the frozen branches, fed and satisfied. The thick curtain of feathers lifted as if in lieu of greatness to come.

Deverell, his body stained with crocodile blood and entrails, aided Leith to his feet, and they watched the entrance to the chapel grounds in wonder as a mystic parade marched toward the looming figure of the preacher. Minerva True with a new gleaming scythe in hand, walking upright and radiating self-reliance, led an army of faces Leith could never remember seeing in the valley.

"The Othersiders!" Leith gasped as the truth fell on him like rain. "She's brought them over." Deverell stared, seemingly awestruck, holding tightly to his brother as a fierce wind began to blow.

Far from the mythical beauties Leith had imagined from Aubrey's tales, the Othersiders seemed quite ordinary, even a little antique in their dress. Yet there was something… something that gathered about them like aura; a presence of truth and acceptance that had long since disappeared on their own side of the river.

Minerva stood at the center of the grounds, facing the demon preacher. The Othersiders encircled them all, locking hands as if ready to begin some children's game. Two figures approached and gently guided Leith and Deverell out of the circle's enclosure and then returned to their place in the band of hands. The birds remained silent on the branches; the storm howled and twisted above like a constipated cyclone not permitted to touch the earth. Lightning fractured the sky in fury. The dirt and mud spasmed with the remains of the black vines and bugs.

"This ends here and now, preacher," Minerva spoke, cracking the silence like a whip of thunder. Garet's sword lay at her feet, flung there in the chaos of the birds' assault.

"Minerva True," the preacher growled, clenching his sword of flames. "I remember you well. It was on this very spot where you were nearly taken under some years ago."

Minerva did not react to his angling.

"You have no power. Even if you were to thwart me again, I would rise anew. One River Dweller has not the strength to take on the chapel. Your entire coven barely achieved it before. Your trinity is broken; the Book is vanished. You can but send me into a temporary abyss without the Third to strike me. I will rise again, and sooner than before. And then I will succeed. Every time I rise, I grow stronger. And you and your line will writhe in torment for all time. Your own mother couldn't destroy me. Why would you be able to? You're so much weaker than she."

Minerva remained unmoved.

"Are you to stare me down as you have the chapel?" he hissed, circling her like a predator. "So useless! A woman afraid to act for years. You cannot kill me, Child of True. I am an indestructible."

At once, he swung his sword at her. But, just as quickly, she snatched the blade from the ground and, with both sword and scythe, held the fiery steel in a lock above her head.

A whisper, which began from one Othersider and spread like a wildfire, encircled the grounds. Leith listened, but the words could not be understood. A blessing came upon the spoiled earth, wave upon wave. With each voice that joined in, the earth became more cleansed.

"Hack me to pieces." Dark Eyes challenged as his sword sizzled and sparked against Minerva's strength. "Chant and pray all you want. This ground can never be yours. Not without the Third; not without the Book. As long as the pages still turn somewhere, the world will be mine."

Minerva grinned. As if waiting for this very statement, a fireball in the shape of a bird, or an opened book, was hurled from the midst of the Othersiders circle. *The Night Hammer* lay, newly alight, on the ground before Dark Eyes, its pages curling in flame and then carried away by the wind. The preacher struggled with Minerva, trying desperately to free his blade from her snare. He growled in rage, but his angry fit was of no use. As the pages and the leather burned to nothing, the remnants of the vines littered about the grounds shrank into blackened tendrils, writhing like lit fuses to the chapel foundation. Upon the spark reaching the chapel, the structure whooshed into a magnificent bolide, the flames carried upward into the storm funnel that hovered contemptuously over the grounds. All who were inside—every lost and tortured soul—were released to the world; escaped banshees on the wind. Dark Eyes watched his work plundered while Leith noted the outline of a winged man rising into the air. The angel Azrael had found all his lost souls.

With a last great effort—a thing generally unfamiliar to Dark Eyes—the preacher extricated the now-simmering blade from Minerva's interlock. Yet as he prepared to strike, she reeled about with the agility of a child, slicing his midsection with the scythe then running him through with Garet's sword. It was only then that he realized, as his flesh curled and fell from him like that of a leper, that the Third was very much alive.

"How foolish of you not to see it before," Minerva whispered as the body crumbled and fell piece by piece to the ground. He was not even allowed a satisfactory final yell of defeat.

The surfeit of remaining maggots and bugs scampered to the rapidly vanishing debris, even as it sank into the mud. The birds then swooped to eat of the wriggling masticators until there was nothing of life moving within the blessed circle but Minerva herself.

She moved to be with the boys outside the ring of Othersiders. The chanting had grown so low as to be nearly inaudible. Leith and Deverell had hardly noticed her approach at their side. "It's time for us to leave here," she said to them. She handed the sword back to Leith. "Good of you to remember to bring that." She smiled, somewhat out of breath. "Do not worry about your mothers and fathers now, boys. They have been met by a guide, one who will take them across the river."

"But what are *they* doing?" Leith asked, staring at the Othersiders as he limped away after her, leaning heavily on Deverell's strong shoulder.

"They have work. Work that we are too few in number right now to do," Minerva replied, leading them from the chapel grounds. "They're cleansing the earth."

The whispers of the Othersiders faded as the trio journeyed farther away, much like the sound of a swift water stream left behind. Once a good distance away, they stopped and watched from the river where the water churned in discord. The stagnant funnel cloud finally descended onto the chapel grounds and seemed to gather all the mud and ashen coat from the trees and earth, pulling it up and away with godlike vehemence. The earth and fire and chapel vanished into the sky without explanation, as if creation were removing a bothersome wart from its being without the assistance of mankind.

What Albert Higgins Saw

AND SO, an age passed in the valley, as ages had done for epoch upon epoch without much notice from a self-concerned humanity. As a funnel cloud howled above, the brave young men of Greenbriar College gathered near the bluff to watch in wonder. The grass and grounds of the college were spotted with students in suits and the fashionable clothing of the day, gawking in varying degrees of bravado and daring.

"Should we be seeking shelter?"

"Why does it stay aloft so? I've never seen a twister act in such a manner."

"Are we safe?"

"The weather here is so very queer!"

Nearest the old tree at the edge of the bluff, where the young men would often see the strange woman sit for hours, stood Albert Higgins, his curiosity having won over his common sense, courting danger. He could hear the questions of his classmates clearly because they were the same inquiries skittering about in his own mind, bumping off one another in a frenzy. The cyclone above the trees pounded the ground at last, ripping up the world yet still refusing to travel up or down river. Very unscientific. It was clear to Albert, though, that something had been destroyed. The peculiar desire to investigate seized him for a moment. In the time span of a breath Albert wanted to see the valley again, to hear the giggling he had convinced himself was only concussion-induced delirium. But was it truly that? Could there be more? More to the world than water, land, and air? Were there mysteries, after all?

Then, quite suddenly, the funnel cloud vanished, and the skies became less menacing, if still a little angry. Albert easily shrugged his questions away as the fantastic yearnings of a grown man remembering childhood tall tales.

"There's the valley for you," he said aloud with pretentious knowing.

Of course, it was just the valley, the location. Miracles are easily explained by science, he assured himself, and that thought gave him great relief. It was so wonderful, he thought, to live in an enlightened age, to be attending a school with such enlightened, like-minded men, each one having a woman to marry and greet him every day after work, and to happily raise their children.

An adventure in the valley? He snickered at the idea. No, he was going to be quite happy, content at least, with his books, with his teachings, with his practicality and explanations. And with his future bride.

What more could he possibly want?

EPILOGUE

WALTERHOUSE MANOR had seen its last days, however unfulfilled. Winifred would have wept at its misuse. Once standing like a majestic castle at the end of the long climb up Black Hill Road, it now seemed a rotting corpse impeding further journeys.

For Leith it held the suffocating stink of a prison, and with nothing left to keep him there, he left the house for good. Within its walls, placed above the hearth, he left Garet's sword and then walked away forever with nary a look back over his shoulder. It was as if the entire structure had collapsed in his mind already, time deciding the old place had dodged the sickle for far too long.

In the coming years, it would be looted and robbed of anything of real worth, the precious little that was. Most of its furnishings and art would simply fade away into dust. Only ramblers and schoolboys on dares would occasionally occupy its creaky innards, and then for but a night. For shadows devoid of their demon commander still resided in its corners and closets.

The sword would see more of the world, however. Taken by a passing vagrant and lost in a gambling bet to an ornery river captain, the river captain would then parade about with it hung proudly from his hip like a war trophy until the day he died, drowning with his ship on a night when he had imbibed a bit too much. The sword would eventually loosen itself from the moldering belt strap that held it in the captain's watery grave, pitched to the surface during a storm. Found by a curious little girl collecting rocks by the river, the sword would have many new adventures in more peaceful and respectable hands. Eventually, it would return once more to find rest in a small community across the river from the modest liberal arts college that looked out over the valley. There it would stay.

As Leith walked down the gravel road of Walterhouse Manor one last time, the sun shone brightly overhead. He imagined Calpurnia running along ahead of him with her childhood friends Lara, Garet, and Darcy. He imagined them happy and unbound, wanting to remain as innocent and carefree as that forever. He smiled as one would smile watching a stranger's child, for truth be told, that was what they were to him: other people's children, other people's kin. His biological parents, Garet Cather and Calpurnia Covington, were not truly family; only outward perception made them so. No, they were nothing more than distant acquaintances or, more aptly, Leith's catapults into the world. Yet he never had to search too far for his real family: Minerva True, Deverell, and Aubrey Avonmore. Leith thought Garet, Lara, Darcy, and Calpurnia were most likely happiest the way he perceived them now: infant spirits playing beneath the sun, residing in memory.

So Leith came to live with Deverell at Parma Place as autumn approached. But as the trees began to yawn, he began to yearn. Every night he and Deverell curled into one another's arms, listening to the valley. Every night they became better acquainted with the ghosts.

"Do you hear that?" Leith would whisper gently into his brother's ear. "That's the River saying she waits for us, but not just yet. And that? Those are the rain crows singing your victory song. And, what do you know! I hear Neko as well. She's come from the barrows. She's free to wander the valley again with Song."

Deverell would smile and sigh, and then they would fall asleep. It was a way to placate and pray, a way to pacify their yearning with poetry until they found the courage to journey on.

THE VALLEY was awakening again as if from some long, debilitating illness. Yet as with any illness, things could never be the same afterward. Truth would have to evolve its scope to survive a new reality, a world controlled after all by man. The rafts were no longer used to glide up and down the river or from one bank to the other. The Othersiders were again rarely seen, and when they were it was in quick glimpses, like will-o'-the-wisps, an uncertain trick of the mind by the eye.

Roads and bridges were built to make the deeper regions of the valley more accessible and more acclimated to progress. The college was expanding. Farther down the river, the valley was at last being developed by industry. It was only a matter of time now until that industrial madness crept its way upriver.

One morning touching the colored edges of spring, Emmy Everplace arrived with her gal Lucy, a dark-skinned woman of gentle grace. Though clearly poor, there was never a more content couple. Of some wealth once, they had come upon tough times in the city. The fortune they'd had was all but lost. Emmy and Lucy entered the valley on foot in a long-awaited homecoming. They brought very little with them. Minerva, the child growing strong inside her, was there to greet them as they came down the narrow pass between the hills that found their commencement up by the willow grove.

"You've arrived," Minerva spoke cheerfully. She stood with her back to the river. It was a gray day, but serene. The water was calm. Trumpet's Place afforded Lucy her first breathtaking image of the mighty waterway.

"I promised you we would come, Miss Minerva," Emmy replied with a tip of her straw hat. "I never renege on a promise. I've been waitin' for this day on pins and needles, ma'am." She introduced Lucy, a petite woman with big, blooming eyes, and Minerva bowed gracefully in response.

"See?" Emmy said to her gal, looking around them. "Didn't I tell you this here was the perfect place to be?"

She was answered with a kiss. The three of them headed down the stone steps toward the riverside, Emmy and Lucy to either side of Minerva.

"Is the trouble gone? That which you spoke of last I was here?" Emmy inquired of Minerva.

"Quite." the older woman nodded thankfully. She held her stomach with tenderness. A sparrow flitted on the rocks nearby. "So, you've chosen Lone Place to make as your own?" Minerva queried as they continued to walk along the pebbled beach.

"Yes, ma'am. It'll take some work, but it's in better shape than most homes here. There's flood damage, but it ain't that bad. It's in a perfect place with a nice forest of trees right below it and a big ol' courtyard. And we can watch the river flowing, keep an eye on the coming storm of industry. We'll try and stop that big ol' steel monster if we can."

The river made riversong, birds flitted in the gray sky, a pleasant breeze met the three women at the river.

"It's a fine home," Minerva replied. "I have many wonderful memories of that home from when I was a child. There was sadness there once, but now the halls echo with the friendliest of spirits to anyone who will listen."

SOME COME into the world in booms of fret and fright, immediately needing protection. Others find their souls anchored on to an angry temperament. Beatha True was a child born completely expecting of the world, ready to charm its hidden fortresses and bastioned castles. Her eyes were wide from the very beginning, taking the newness on with the heart of a gentle warrior, a Boadicea. Her birth sounds were not cries of terror, but awes of wonder. And when she was placed in Minerva's loving arms by Emmy Everplace, she locked eyes with her mother at once and two old souls were reunited.

"I am yours, you are mine, we are… *We are*," glinted the tiny black pearls of the infant child. "We spread the light into the world. It may dim, but it will never die."

"Will she be a River Dweller?" asked Leith as he and Deverell stood admiring the child at Minerva's bedside in the earthen cottage. It was very early spring, not long after Emmy and Lucy had come to the valley.

"Oh, I don't think so," Minerva replied to his surprise. She continued staring transfixed into her child's eyes. "The time of the River Dwellers is over. Humanity in this age has no place for the guards of old. From here forth it will be the battle of the individual, I believe."

Leith contemplated for a moment and then said, "I knew that. I knew it the end of last summer at the Battle of the Chapel Grounds."

The Battle of the Chapel Grounds. Such would be the name of the tale if there were any left to tell it. Only the birds would remember it, though, the birds and the trees.

Not long after, Deverell and Leith decided at last to take their leave of the valley. It could hold them no longer, and they realized they were keen to spill out into the world, to venture on to new truths.

Minerva held a small banquet for them in the circle wood to commemorate their departure. She was quiet throughout, watching as they interacted with the old world around them, a wispy echo chiming through her soul. They danced in the dusk light with the trees of the wood and the great oak at the cliff. There was wine and ale, and fresh breads and sweet meats from Minerva's kitchen. Memories and ghosts, one and the same, visited, draping from the trees, waltzing from the branches like shimmering, transparent moss. Bugaboos and familiars, River Dwellers and rain crows. Music chirped from the night bugs; there was Song. Fox, Wolf, and Cougar played about the gardens as Emmy and Lucy watched the scene in wonderment. And more recognizable visitors came as well in the less corporeal forms of Mother True, Branwenn, Hamlin, the Parmas, and even Trumpet. It was a reunion of family and the fantastic, the family the boys had known and come to accept as such regardless of blood or social appellation. Sadly, Aubrey Avonmore was nowhere to be seen.

Minerva shed a tear in happiness at what the circle wood embraced that night. It was a gathering that would never happen again in the more modern world. The great warmth of love from her spread through the wood and a melancholy hush descended on the party. Even Beatha did not stir in her tiny cradle perched outside so she could appreciate the Last Great Party of Black Hill. Minerva approached the boys, kissing them both gently as twilight embraced the world. "Go now," she whispered, "and do great things."

Behind them, the elf-paths opened, lit by a galaxy of fireflies.

"The elf-paths will always be open to you," she said.

The boys smiled and bowed. Turning to leave, they waved to their valley family—the living and the ascended. They were met with an encouraging farewell. Minerva, Beatha, Mother True, Hamlin, Emmy and Lucy, Fox, Wolf, and Cougar, and all the others gathered together and bid them good travels.

The elf-paths closed behind them as they journeyed silently in joy and sadness until they came out on Black Hill Road. The sound of the gathering was hushed by the thick foliage as they stepped farther off. There, waiting for them with ears twitching and eyes as warm as molasses, was a young stag, a stag of the Breed. It was the first seen since the summer before. Leith and Deverell clasped hands and followed the young deer down the hill.

Birds dabbed the tree limbs, lifting the valley with new music as the stag led the boys to the foot of Black Hill. The wood was healing. The ashen landscape of the chapel's fiery annex had been pulled away like a crusted outer casing, under which was yet delicate life. Though grown to fullness, the trees exhibited a greenish tint to their bark, like that of a sprout in its first year having survived a bitter season. The leaves and brush were the greenest in all the valley, even at the height of spring, and did not fade of their color as the other trees did during the fall. This place would not surrender its youth.

From the sloped road, Leith and Deverell could see where once the chapel had stood. The land was now a lively swamp abuzz with toads, dragonflies, and plump cattails. A small stream trickled into it from the river. Not a splinter or fleck of paint remained of the chapel itself.

As they followed the stag down the slope, the boys were surprised to see the figure of a naked young man standing to the side of the road under a familiar tree. He was soaking wet, as if he had just come from a swim, and now looked at his surroundings with the curiosity of a child. His hair was a mess of thick black rings, and his skin the color of ivory under the brightest sunlight. There was a fey quality to him. He watched with wide-eyed alarm as Leith and Deverell approached.

"Hello," Leith said, standing a few feet from the stranger. "Are you lost?"

The young man seemed to examine the query for hidden meaning, and then said, "No. I don't so. I think I'm right where I should be."

Leith's heart burst in warmth at the familiar-sounding voice, at the assuredness and stubbornness in it. Deverell gripped his friend's hand tighter, his own pulse quickening as well.

"You…," Leith muttered, then, collecting himself, "This is Black Hill. Up yonder is Greenbriar College, and thataway is Lone Hill."

"I know," said the young man. "Where are you goin', then?" he asked, studying them acutely. He approached, reaching out as if to touch the clothing Minerva had made them as gifts for their journeys. "You're lookin' all prettied up."

"We're going away," Leith answered, swallowing hard. "There's adventure waiting on down the river."

The boy surveyed their surroundings again. "Isn't there adventure here?"

"Yes. But… well… one adventure here is very much like another."

"I suppose that's the way pretty much everywhere, huh? Only different."

"I imagine so." Leith grinned. The young man returned the grin.

A tear rolled gently down Deverell's cheek.

"What're your names?" the boy asked, reaching forward and wiping the tear from Deverell's face with his thumb.

"I'm Leith. This is our... this is my brother, Deverell." And then in a delightedly frightened whisper he asked, "What's your name?"

The young man was taken back. He didn't seem prepared for the question and cocked his head, giving it some thought. Staring at first with uncertainty at Leith and then Deverell, he looked around, as if his name was perhaps written in the air or could be whispered to him by a passing dragonfly or hummingbird. Then his eyes rested on the green-barked tree under which he stood. Jagged lines of script caught his attention, deep graffiti from another age that had survived the battle.

"My name?" he said, and then he read it aloud. "Aubrey Avonmore. My name is Aubrey Avonmore."

And the angel Azrael smiled as he watched from the treetop.

AGE HAD finally caught up with Minerva True. Yet she wasn't distressed by this. She received it as one would welcome a forgotten sibling whose worth was only just now appreciated, whose wisdom could split open ages of ignorance. She climbed College Hill, holding tight to Beatha, who snuggled and sighed at Minerva's bosom. Old Age was walking alongside her now, not Mother True. Minerva had heard no whisper of her mother in the woods of late, except for echoes in deeper gullies and from dark, unfathomable caves. The world Minerva loved was learning to conceal itself, a preservation for the good of further generations. The magic of the world, the clear-cutting truth and honest beauty, now took to hiding from an ever-threatening humanity, from a reliance on industry and a disregard for spirit, from an invading and controlling ideology, from the books of an angry god and the bookies of religion.

Yet the hope—and Minerva could smile at last with this—lay in the generations to come; the ones after her, and those after them, and then after those. There would always be a small group of people to fight and resist the powers of this new world. Science, so demonized by some, so taken to by others, was to be the answer after all. In science, Minerva finally understood, there was to be found spirituality's salvation from religion. They would balance one another out.

As Minerva stood beneath Mother True's tree, Beatha now giggling in her arms, she watched across the river valley like the Mother of Creation: concerned, yet proud and ever hopeful. Young collegiates made daring treks down the muddy paths of College Hill now, unaware of the magic that had until very recently held sway throughout the valley wood. Even if the magic were still there, they would never see it. Their eyes would glaze over it, always on the watch for more important discoveries, intellectual truths, and proven dynamics. Giddy whispers and sweet echoes of memory did not interest them. They had found science, but it had taken them over, much as religion had claimed others. In-betweens were the stuff of children's stories.

"It is you and I, my darling girl," Minerva whispered to Beatha. "The Othersiders have gone for good now, and it is you and I and our friend Time." She kissed the child lightly on her soft forehead. "I was a River Dweller, and there shall be no more after me."

High in Mother True's tree sat a great bird on a strong branch. It ruffled its feathers and took to flight, soaring aloft, above the trees, above the river, above the valley. The world was vast and fascinating below, an extensive garden if viewed from the right height. The world belonged to the great bird, so round and full of light. And into it every beautiful thing danced and flew, ran and swam, burst with light, wept in darkness. Everything that was and had ever been was caught in the twin currents of the air and the river in an entanglement of strength, epiphany, and compassion. This history and future erupted into the world, exploding upon it as an enveloping tsunami of grace. And the great bird saw with interest that this entanglement of truth and poetry was thus carried even farther upriver by three courageous young men, saviors unaware of the beauty of the knowledge they would feed the world.

ERIC ARVIN resided in the same sleepy Indiana river town where he grew up. He graduated from Hanover College with a bachelor's degree in history and has lived, for brief periods, in Italy and Australia. He survived brain surgery and his own loud-mouthed personal demons.

Facebook: www.facebook.com/eric.arvin.5

galley proof

ERIC ARVIN

Fiction writer Logan Brandish is perfectly happy in his peaceful small-town routine with his best friend, his cat, and his boyfriend—until he meets the editor of his next book, the handsome Brock Kimble, and the lazy quiet of everyday living goes flying out the window. Faced with real passion for the first time, Logan becomes restless and agitated, and soon his life and his new manuscript—a work in progress he'd always thought would be completed—are in a shambles.

But as Logan is learning, you can't always get what you want… at least not right away. To take his mind off the mess, he takes a trip, but even the beautiful Italian, um, scenery can't keep his thoughts from his erstwhile editor for long. Logan just might have to admit there are some things you can't run from.

www.dreamspinnerpress.com

WOKE UP
in a
STRANGE
PLACE

Eric Arvin

Joe wakes up in a barley field with no clothes, no memories, and no idea how he got there. Before he knows it, he's off on the last great journey of his life. With his soul guide Baker and a charge to have courage from a mysterious, alluring, and somehow familiar Stranger, Joe sets off through a fantastical changing landscape to confront his past.

The quest is not without challenges. Joe's past is not always an easy thing to relive, but if he wants to find peace—and reunite with the Stranger he is so strongly drawn to—he must continue on until the end, no matter how tempted he is to stop along the way.

www.dreamspinnerpress.com

ANOTHER *enchanted* APRIL

ERIC ARVIN

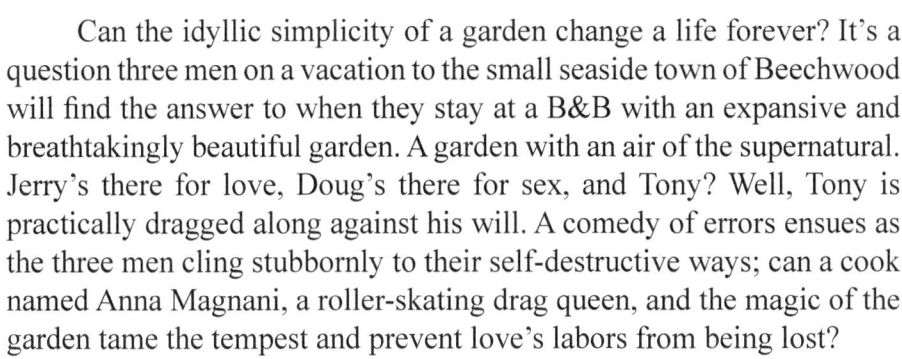

Can the idyllic simplicity of a garden change a life forever? It's a question three men on a vacation to the small seaside town of Beechwood will find the answer to when they stay at a B&B with an expansive and breathtakingly beautiful garden. A garden with an air of the supernatural. Jerry's there for love, Doug's there for sex, and Tony? Well, Tony is practically dragged along against his will. A comedy of errors ensues as the three men cling stubbornly to their self-destructive ways; can a cook named Anna Magnani, a roller-skating drag queen, and the magic of the garden tame the tempest and prevent love's labors from being lost?

www.dreamspinnerpress.com

Simple Men
Eric Arvin

Chip Arnold is a well-liked football coach at a small liberal arts college, but his personal life is in a bit of a rut. He goes out drinking with his colleagues, gets along well with his players, and dates all the prettiest women in town—he has the life most straight men dream of. But lately none of the women he dates seem to be igniting any passion in him. Then he meets the new school chaplain, Foster Lewis.

Romantic attraction to another man is new and terrifying, and Chip just can't put his finger on why he's drawn to Foster, but it's stronger than anything he's felt for anyone in his life. Never one to back down from a challenge, Chip decides to go for it. But love is never simple, and sometimes it's a downright mess!

www.dreamspinnerpress.com